PRAISE FOR AJ WHITTIER'S WORK

ALWAYS NEVER MEANT TO BE

"Whittier deftly creates moral ambiguity in the characters' actions... This engrossing, plot-driven novel will keep readers glued to the pages. Similarly, as the duo scouts movie locations, traveling from popular tourist haunts like Pike's Place Market to lesser-known scenic parks, the author creates a love letter to Seattle, such that readers might find themselves planning a trip... The ultimate outcome is neither predictable nor trite. An engaging, thought-provoking love story."

— *Kirkus Reviews*

ALSO BY AJ WHITTIER

Magical Seattle Book 1
Always Never Meant To Be: A Love Story
(published Summer 2025)

More coming in 2026!
Sign up for my newsletter for news, updates, and a special,
same-universe bonus story at AJWhittier.com

MAGICAL SEATTLE SERIES

THE GOD IN 3B

AJ WHITTIER

To Stephen
For reading my stuff, cheering me on, and always putting up with me. I love you.

CONTENT NOTES

I ALWAYS LIKE TO say that Magical Seattle is a place where anything can happen and love is always on the menu. Seattle is also a city replete with sights full of wonder and beauty, bolstered by countless unique neighborhoods that fashion its whole.

Kirkland, Washington is a real suburb of Seattle, sitting just across Lake Washington and left a bit. It's a warm, lovely spot full of beautiful homes and a charming, waterfront downtown. The Kirkland represented in this book is both real and not real. It's very true to the spirit of Kirkland, but embellished a bit from the past and a bit from my imagination. I'd say it's a third new Kirkland, a third old Kirkland, and a third imaginary Kirkland. But if you visit, you will definitely recognize the version in my book. Like Seattle and all its surrounds, it's a magical place.

The God in 3B is about what happens when a sexy girl and a hot god move into the same otherwise empty building, and it's so much fun! I hope you love it as much as I do. That said, there are a few things you might want to be aware of before you begin.

Clarey is a beautiful, plus-sized woman who mostly feels good about herself, except when she steps into her bathing suit. That's when all her worst anxieties and negative self-talk come to play. While this book isn't primarily about internalized fatphobia, she does wrestle with it a bit. Does she overcome it? Perhaps with the help of a handsome god? You'll have to keep reading to find out.

Also note that this book includes on-page sex, on-page drinking, and the off-page death of a major character. But I promise it will be fun! Still, if any of those things are concerns for you, please read with care.

CHAPTER ONE

MOVING DAY

IT SHOULD BE STITCHED on a pillow somewhere. Sharing a house with your ex-husband is a bad idea. And never *ever* share a house with your ex-husband and his girlfriend.

Clarey contemplates these eternal truths as she sponges out her mug and sets it gingerly in the dish drainer, fighting every instinct to slam it into pieces instead. She returns her gaze to the mug now tipped to Derek's mouth, the mug with a photo of her beloved bulldog Roxy printed on it, which she distinctly remembers rolling in bubble wrap and sealing into her kitchen wares box last night. Her Roxy mug, now in Derek's hand, now tainted with his backwash and bitter, over-brewed coffee.

It probably took her too long to reach this conclusion, in retrospect. And far too long to do something about it. But now, as he casually places the mug on the table like the most ordinary thing in the world and offers his usual carefree smile at her, the urgency of the realization booms like a foghorn. "All set?" he says.

"What is that?" Clarey instantly berates herself for not being more direct. As if they don't both know what that is. "Why are you using my Roxy mug?"

"Oh, this? There weren't any other clean mugs handy."

"There was a whole dishwasher full. I just used one."

"I was in the middle of making breakfast and didn't have time to unload the dishwasher in the moment."

Clarey eyes his empty cereal bowl, quietly fuming. "But you had time to rip open my carefully packed and sealed box?"

Derek shrugs. "The scissors were right there."

One of the movers, a beefy, red-faced guy with a shaved head – Jake? Jack? Jasper? – lumbers into the kitchen. "About done with the boxes out there. Anything in here? This going?" He points at the freshly reopened box no longer containing the mug.

Clarey swallows her frustration, determined not to take it out on Jake/Jack/Jasper. "Yes, but I need to reseal it."

Before she reaches the packing tape, he grabs the box. "I got it." He folds the four sides into themselves and foists the box onto his shoulder as he whistles his way out of the room. Clarey draws her eyes back to Derek. His shabby robe and shaggy hair projecting every inch the affable good guy.

"It's my mug."

"I didn't think you'd want it." The words roll out in his usual casual tone. How does he make everything sound so reasonable? Yet, his fingers snake around the mug again, asserting his possession.

"Why wouldn't I want it? It's mine."

"Your mug? My mug? Who can tell anymore? That's like saying Roxy is yours."

Clarey stares at the face of her sweet bulldog clenched in Derek's hand. "Roxy *is* mine. And you gave me that mug as a gift. So, it's mine too."

"I've always used it more than you. You don't even really drink hot beverages."

Clarey seethes. She's gladly left behind most of the trinkets and gifts he gave her over the years. He could keep the hot sauce multi-pack, the beer-of-the-month club subscription, and the ducks he'd somehow decided she liked. (She didn't.) Any sentimental attachment she's ever felt to any of his gifts has faded since she moved into the small bedroom and surrendered the main suite to Derek and his new girlfriend Lydia. Lydia is nice enough, sweet even, but five months of listening to their grunts and moans through the far too thin walls has effectively erased any lingering nostalgia Clarey felt for better times with Derek.

But she's taking the books. That's the one thing he got right, the one thing she actually loves. The books and her Roxy mug. Yet, there sits Derek, clinging to her mug like the Hope Diamond. After all, *she doesn't even really drink hot beverages.*

Clarey fancifully imagines snatching the mug from his hand, splashing the dregs of his coffee in his face, and parading her trophy out the door. But that's not Clarey. Besides, maybe he's right. She doesn't use it *that* much. She inhales deeply and pastes on a weak smile. "I guess you do use it more...."

"Exactly. I knew we'd be on the same page. Always get there in the end. Huh, Clare?" And despite the fact that they were very much not on the same page, and hadn't been in years or they'd probably still be married, Clarey sags and slouches into the living room.

Jake/Jack/Jasper lifts what Clarey would have thought an impossibly heavy armchair and marches it out the door. Nearly done. She climbs the stairs to the primary suite where she'd kept Roxy safely contained while the movers did their work, but when she glides open the door, she finds only an empty room. No happy grunts of an impatient English bulldog desperate for a long overdue reunion after ten whole minutes apart.

"Roxy," Clarey calls out, listening for the scamper of the dog's nails clicking on the floor. Nothing. She peeks into her now nearly empty bedroom, then runs down the stairs screaming. "Roxy!"

Jake/Jack/Jasper steps back in the door and announces, "We're ready to go, ma'am."

Clarey runs around the lower level, then shoves the guy aside to look out the open front door. Roxy has never been a bolter before. She always stays close to home, glued to Clarey's side whenever possible, but she yells out the door anyway. "Roxy! Come!" Terror runs cold through her. "Oh my God, oh my God. Derek!" Clarey rushes into the kitchen where Derek still sits, scrolling on his phone. "Roxy's gone."

Derek's eyes fix on his screen a moment longer before he lifts a languid gaze up to Clarey. "Sorry, what was that?"

"Roxy's gone. I think she got out."

Jake/Jack/Jasper calls from the front room. "Ma'am, we really need to head out."

"Oh... no," he says. "I think Lydia took her for a walk."

"What?"

Derek nods like a murder witness faking a new recollection he was intentionally holding back until now. "Yeah. She mentioned she might take Roxy for a walk. Get her away from all the hubbub, so she didn't get anxious."

"Right when I'm about to leave?"

Jake/Jack/Jasper chimes in from the other room. "Only, we have another job after this so..."

"Why didn't she tell me?"

"You were probably busy with something."

Probably busy with something seems like a damn poor excuse for making off with someone's dog without saying a word when they're about to leave. Clarey pulls her phone out and hits Lydia's number. Lydia's Taylor Swift ringtone blares from the front room.

Derek shrugs. "Looks like she forgot her phone."

"What's going on, Derek?"

Jake/Jack/Jasper tiptoes toward Clarey as gently as his heavy frame will allow. "Sorry to interrupt. But we do have another pick-up scheduled after this, so we need to get moving. You'll meet us there?"

Clarey nods, her eyes still fixed on Derek's far-too-relaxed expression.

"See you at the new place then?" When Clarey says nothing, the mover adds for emphasis, "In about half-an-hour. Should take about half-an-hour, right?"

Clarey huffs out her exasperation. "Yeah. Half-an-hour. Got it." Then to Derek, "Whose idea was this walk?"

CHAPTER TWO

STROOPWAFEL

IN THE HEAT OF the midday sun, hot tea is the last thing Zack wants. Then again, in the heat of the midday sun, he doesn't need it. He tears open the stroopwafel package and slides the Dutch delicacy out, discovering the caramel already molten within – without the aid of a steaming cuppa – despite having just walked out of Goldfarb's air conditioning. This sun is no joke.

He eases himself onto the edge of the gurgling, abstract fountain that's part organic, riverside boulder, part sharp-edged, futuristic spaceship and takes his first bite. The gentle crisp of the waffle exterior melts into a gooey, buttery caramel symphony that reminds him why he keeps going.

Or perhaps not why. His purpose is his why and his purpose is as clear as it was on day one. But it *is* part of the how. The sweet indulgences and simple pleasures have helped him ride out a seemingly interminable lifetime of slings and arrows. Of course, he's spent most of his life ducking the worst of that outrageous fortune, but that can be as exhausting as standing and fighting sometimes, and twice as demoralizing. Stroopwafels help.

Zack was delighted to discover when he returned that Herb was stocking them in the store. His delight over the stroopwafel only eclipsed by his joy at seeing the old man's face again. He shouldn't have been surprised. Herb has probably been stocking them all along, just waiting for Zack's return. But it's been an awfully long time this time. He's been away too long.

The sun reemerges from behind a cloud and Zack is briefly blinded by his own reflection in the store window. His wild blond locks almost precisely the shade of the sun, his white shirt, and tan slacks all merge into singular blast of light reflecting off the window. When at last the glare breaks, a woman has appeared from nowhere, running toward the shop door. Her curly, red-orange bob catches his eye first, but her generous curves hold it, despite his best efforts. He's no lech. If anything, he's the opposite. Practically a monk these days. But there's something about the way her bright curls shine, and – okay, fine – the way her sensual softness jiggles as she rushes in that keeps him glued to her until she disappears through the door.

Simple pleasures indeed. But there's nothing simple about where those thoughts lead. So back to the stroopwafel.

Barely sixty seconds later, the woman shoves out the door with three water bottles cradled in her arms, but she seems to jolt as she catches sight of Zack. She stumbles from the momentary distraction, sending her water bottles rolling in three different directions. She's adorable with her flushed cheeks and mild panic spreading across her face. Zack jumps to help her, but he's too far away and gets waylaid by passing traffic. By the time the cars have passed, she's collected her bottles and dashed.

He watches her dart around the corner and breathes a sigh of relief.

Chapter Three

They're All the Same

CLAREY THRUSTS THE COLD water into each of the mover's hands by way of apology for keeping them waiting. Back at the house, she gave Lydia fifteen minutes she couldn't afford to return with Roxy, but eventually had to surrender and leave with Derek's shallow apologies and promises of a swift return of her pup.

Her guilt assuaged, Clarey plops onto the wooden dining room chair that's currently the only piece of furniture in the whole condo. With the receding sound of the grumbling men and the quiet, mechanical hum of the service elevator doors closing at the end of the hall, the room stills. Clarey studies each wall, each corner, each beam and fixture with swelling pride. This place is hers – all hers. The hardwood floors. The industrial feeling brick wall. The large south and west facing windows filling her space with warm Seattle sun. The wraparound balcony granting her unimaginable views of Lake Washington. And perhaps best of all, the enormous wall of built-in bookshelves. It's everything she's dreamed of and more.

Admittedly, being the sole occupant of the still under construction building was not part of the dream. Nor was spending quite as much money as she ended up paying. But with only one unit completed and granted a certificate of occupancy before the builders ran out of money and shut down construction, she's likely to be all alone for quite some time to come. Perfect. Given her most recent living situation, she craves nothing more than alone time.

When the two men return, they're carrying her live edge dining room table. She shuffles out of her chair to make space for them to place it where she wants it. A wedding gift from her parents, it's one of the few things she's brought with her from her old life. It'll take time to fill the place with new things, with the new Clarey, but a new sofa will be delivered this afternoon, along with a new bed. She probably could have brought the double she was sleeping in back at the house, but she wants a proper bed. A bed that says she's ready for sex, thank you very much. At least, she's open to the possibility.

The movers work quickly. She watches the men shuffle in and out, regretting she didn't have the foresight to buy extra water bottles for them, but at least she has A/C making the work tolerable. She does her best to direct items where she thinks she wants them. Her reading chair to what seems like a cozy spot. Her antique dresser against the brick wall in her bedroom. The few kitchen wares she's brought to the kitchen.

The books were the first thing to be loaded on the truck, so the last to be unloaded. Dolly after dolly of stacked boxes, each the weight of a small Kia, rolled up and nudged onto the floor in stacks by the built-ins, a series of stalagmites in a quickly forming book cave. As Jake/Jack/Jasper pulls his hand truck out from beneath the last stack, he knocks the neighboring stack and the top box Clarey had just opened crashes to the floor. He mumbles an apology and tries to restore the contents, but the structural integrity of the box is destroyed and the books spill out into a heap of bent covers and broken spines.

Clarey winces at the wreckage, but smiles grimly. "Don't worry about it. I'll get them."

"They wouldn't have spilled like that if the box weren't open," he grumbles. "You could have waited 'til we were finished."

Valid point. She could have waited. She's just so eager to settle in and make it home. Still, she probably should have waited. On the other hand, should he really be so sharp when he's the one who knocked it over? She is the customer, after all, and he's at fault. Then again, she did keep them waiting when they got here. One bottle of water each was definitely not enough.

As her brain seesaws between guilt and blame, her mouth skips ahead to the apology. "You're right." She glances at the pile, then back to Jake/Jack/Jasper. "Sorry. I got carried away."

He shrugs. "That's okay, I guess." And now, somehow, he's forgiving her for spilling her books? He reaches for his clipboard atop the last stack he wheeled in. "So that's everything. The office will charge your card for three— no, four hours." The quote was three hours or less, but that was before she made them wait. Apparently every portion of an hour counts as an hour. "Sign here, please."

Clarey signs and hands the clipboard back to him. He tears off a copy for her records, then remains in place. He's waiting for a tip. With the nearby book carnage still haunting her peripheral vision, she reaches for her wallet and pulls out a few crisp twenty-dollar bills she took from the ATM for this purpose. She'd debated how much to tip when she pulled the money. It was a small move and would be a short and sweet job. So, she reasoned, a good, but modest tip was in order, though she might up it if they were exemplary. Did spilling her most prized possessions all over the floor count as exemplary? "Here you go," she says handing him the whole stack.

Closing the door on the movers, Clarey revels in the renewed silence of her own space. A space blissfully devoid of a too charming, quietly manipulative ex-husband, the constant chatter of his perky girlfriend turned housemate, and the almost nightly torment of bumps, thumps, and moans that made Clarey realize she and Derek hadn't been nearly careful enough when they shared the main suite and Carlo lived in the second bedroom. The only noises she did miss were the smooshed-snout wheezes and grunts of Roxy. But she'd have her again soon. She may as well use the dog-free time to get the place in order.

Kneeling by her book graveyard, she attempts a gentle resurrection of each book, flattening bent covers, caressing cracked spines, and placing them carefully on a shelf. She lifts the last one to the shelf, and something flutters out of it and flaps to the floor. When she realizes what it is, she's flooded with a memory.

She and Derek had been in the process of switching bedrooms. When they'd first split, he'd graciously moved into Carlo's newly vacated smaller room and allowed her to keep the larger main bedroom. There was definitely something to be said for such an amicable split – especially since neither of them could afford to break the lease and move out yet. This was his showy attempt at chivalry, which she gladly accepted since it was the room with the bookshelves. But when Lydia moved in five months later, Clarey had reluctantly agreed to switch as long as her books could stay in the main until she found another solution. Since neither Derek nor Lydia had many books to house, they agreed.

A couple months later, over wine and spaghetti, Clarey was talking about a great book she was reading when Derek made a cryptic comment that sent Lydia into peals of laughter. "Those book shelves have certainly fueled a lot of good nights."

Clarey's antennae flew up. Derek was not a reader. "What does that mean?"

"What do you think it means?" he said with a sordid grin.

"I have no idea, though I take it you don't mean literary pursuits."

"Come on, Clare, you know." He gave her a shit-eating smile so wide her skin crawled. No good could lie behind that smile.

"I don't know. Why don't you tell me?"

"You know, the condoms." Derek gave her a look that suggested she was unusually slow on the uptake, and Lydia burst into a new fit of laughter that seemed disproportionate to this decidedly unfunny revelation.

Clarey nearly dropped her red sauce covered fork into her lap. "I beg your pardon?"

"That's where I stash my back-ups." Said like it was the most obvious thing in the world.

"In my books?"

"Yeah. You knew that!" He managed to look as confused as Clarey felt, but Clarey wasn't buying it.

"I assure you I didn't."

"I did it back when we were together too," he explained. "That way, even when I run out, I have a buffer supply until I get to the store."

"We didn't use condoms when we were married." She side-eyed Lydia. "Sorry, Lydia." Lydia shrugged.

"But we did when we first started dating. And I, you know, refreshed after we split."

Clarey cringed at the notion of her books providing prophylactic storage for Derek and his conquests. "Derek, I don't want to hear this. Please remove your condoms from my books."

"What harm are they doing?"

"They're my books. That's the harm."

Derek sighed hard and rolled his eyes. "Fine. No problem. I'll take them out."

"You'll take them out?"

"Sure. Of course. No problem."

Now she looks at the condom in her hand. She flips it over to examine the date. Still good. She briefly considers keeping it, but she won't need it in the foreseeable future, maybe ever if her current annoyance with the male species persists. So she shoots it across the room and fist pumps the air when she lands a rim shot into the trash. "Fucking Derek."

***

Clarey drops into her reading chair and gazes at her now fully organized bookshelves with pride. She may not have touched her kitchen stuff or bothered to rescue her clothes from the worst of their wrinkling in overstuffed boxes, but her wall of books looks magnificent. An accomplishment indeed! If this doesn't warrant a well-earned reading break, nothing does.

Her phone pings with a text.

Jessa: *how's it going?*

Clarey: *Amazing. Look at this!*

Clarey snaps a photo of her bookshelves and sends it.

Jessa: *only you would go giddy over a bookshelf*

Clarey's phone pings again, only it's not Jessa this time. It's Hope. How has she managed to go all day without updating her sisters? And why must they always bombard her at the same time?

Hope: *Are you all moved in? Are you okay?*

Clarey to Hope: *I'm fine. Define "all."*

Clarey to Jessa: *Book lovers love bookshelves. It's a whole thing on the internets.*

Hope: *Do you have all your things in one place?*

Clarey to Hope: *Does this answer your question?*

She sends the bookshelf photo to Hope.

Hope: *Ooooooohhhhh, I LOVE IT.*

Clarey to Jessa: *See.*

Jessa: *see what?*

These two are going to be the death of her. They're probably rooms apart and you'd think they're on different planets. Clarey exits out of both threads and goes to her group message to them both.

Clarey to Hope and Jessa: *STOP TEXTING ME. You guys are like a human cyclone. I can't keep up.*

Hope: *We just want to know you're okay.*

Jessa: *speak for yourself. i'm just bored*

Clarey: *Touching.*

Jessa: *can't help it. i'm so tired of being cooped up in this room with nowhere to go*

Hope: *You could come clean up the kitchen. Or help with the kids.*

Jessa: *maybe i'll go watch porn*

Hope: *NOT IN MY HOUSE YOU WON'T*

As the two are busily bickering, Clarey is overtaken by a sneezing fit. A tingle in her nose builds and builds until the first blast. But one is never enough for Clarey. If she's lucky, there will only be one more, but no such luck this time as her body is thrown around by two, three, four, no, five sneezes in a row. When at last the sneezing stops, she goes in search of a tissue box, eventually settling for toilet paper when the sad reality of her situation sinks in. Mental note: add tissues to the shopping list. When she eventually returns to the phone, her sisters have carried on without her.

Clarey: *Did you even notice I was gone?*

Jessa: *gone*

Hope: *Gone where?*

Clarey: *Sneezing fit.*

Hope: *Oh, honey, are you okay?*

Ever since Clarey's dodgy lungs had taken her to the hospital for a week as a teenager, Hope had been borderline pathological about them. And even Jessa, who took virtually nothing seriously, got a little panicked at mentions of Clarey's lungs. But this was just some messy, stupid sneezing. Her lungs were fine. More vulnerable than the average lungs maybe, but she'd been fine for years. A little moving dust wouldn't hurt her. Not that you'd know that from her sister's reaction.

Hope: *Do you have your inhaler?*

Jessa: *do you need anything?*

Clarey: *I'm fine. It was just dust. But you two clearly have things to work out. I'll let you go...*

Before Clarey can drop her phone and pick a book, it rings. The caller name says Annika's. Oh shit! She's lost all track of time, but it's five-thirty and her furniture isn't here yet. Wasn't the delivery window three to five o'clock?

A husky male voice responds to her answer. "This is Annika's Furniture delivery. We're supposed to be delivering a couch and a bed to your premises today."

A pit grows in Clarey's stomach. "Yes?"

"Well, I'm so sorry, but we've had a breakdown on 520, which has obviously put us behind schedule." Okay, behind schedule isn't so bad. She can work with behind schedule. The guy continues, "Looks like the truck needs to go into the shop, so we have to get another truck out here in order to make the delivery."

"Okay," she says, worry drawing out the syllables as her back straightens with tension. "I can wait."

"Yeah, about that. See, it being five-thirty already, and Saturday, there aren't a lot of guys still working. And to get your pieces to you tonight, we'd have to wait for another truck, transfer it..." When Clarey says nothing, he continues. "And with all this traffic out here, that might take a while."

"That's fine," she says, praying this isn't headed where she thinks it is.

"Which would push the guys into overtime."

Clarey pinches the bridge of her nose. "I get it, but..."

"It also might not be too safe," he adds. He's laying it on thick.

"I see." Neither of them says anything for a moment, waiting to see who will crack first. "The thing is," Clarey finally says. The writing's on the wall, but she has to try. "I need that couch and bed. I have almost no furniture here. Where am I supposed to sleep?"

"Where you slept last night maybe?" Wow, this guy has balls.

"That's not really an option." Is it? Ugh, no.

"Sorry, ma'am. We can get it out there first thing in the morning."

"But what about—"

"Look, if you really want it tonight, we can try to make it happen."

Clarey flops back into her chair. "That would be great."

"Only, it's Spitzer's birthday and the guys are going out for drinks."

"Spitzer's birthday?"

"Poor guy, his wife left him. So he needs this. But don't tell him I told you."

Clarey drops her face into her hand. "Wouldn't dream of it."

"But I mean, if you really can't wait..."

This guy should sell used cars for a living. "Well, since it's Spitzer's birthday."

"Thank you, ma'am. We'll give you a call in the morning when we're on our way."

Clarey shuffles into her almost empty bedroom and stares at the gaping hole where she expected a new bed to be by now. She has her new king-size sheets ready and everything. Somewhere. In one of these boxes. But they'd have to wait one more day.

Despite the joy of being in her new place, this day isn't turning out how she hoped. She wanted to think her new independent life would lead to a new, self-assured Clarey who could handle anything. Yet, she keeps letting people walk all over her. Especially men. Derek. Jake/Jack/Jasper. Mr. Annika's Furniture. Of course, Derek was no surprise. There's a reason she divorced him. But the others? Men weren't looking good on the scoreboard tonight. She might be a pushover, but why are men always so eager to push? It was enough to beg the question, are there any good ones left?

CHAPTER FOUR

OLD MEN

ZACK WATCHES HERB WANDER the aisles of the small shop, straightening here, tidying there, groaning as he picks candies up from the floor. The flickering of one dying fluorescent bulb overhead is more noticeable now that the sun has gone down. "I thought you were closing," Zack says.

Herb's half gray, half bald head keeps disappearing as he dips down to straighten things. "This is how I close," he croaks. "The store doesn't tidy itself, you know."

"Then how can I help?"

"Turn the cooler lights off. The switches are—"

"I remember," Zack says as he reaches for the first switch. "What else?"

"There's a broom in the back. You know how to use it?"

Zack chuckles. "You're getting salty in your old age."

"I've always been salty. I just never let you see it."

"I can handle it, Herb. Trust me."

"Oh yes, you can handle anything." Herb straightens a row of Mexican Cokes. "Anything but coming to see me, that is."

"I'm here now," Zack says, pushing the broom past the front register.

"It's been a long time," Herb opines. He's laying the guilt on thick.

Zack catches him at the end of an aisle, wraps his hand tenderly around the old man's bald head, and kisses his forehead. "I'm sorry. I was away too long. But I'm never that far away, I promise."

"I know, Zachary. You're very good to me."

Together they finish the closing routine, switch off the lights, and make their way out. Before locking up, Herb doubles back to the cooler and pulls out a bottle of limoncello he'd stashed at the back. He switches the open sign to closed, arms the alarm, and locks the door behind him. Outside the air is crisp with the late-night cool that so often sets in after warm Seattle days. He hands the bottle to Zack and gestures at the bench conveniently placed right outside his store. Zack holds up the bottle. "Is this for me?"

"I thought you might like a little taste of home."

"Italy's not home, Herb."

"I know, but you like Italy. And I like to think of you in the Mediterranean sun, overlooking the sea, drinking a limoncello. Feels like it's where you belong."

"That's an incredibly specific vision."

"But it's a nice one, isn't it?"

Zack nods. "Very nice."

"I want you to be happy, Zachary. If you can't go home, you deserve to be somewhere that makes you truly happy."

"I'm happy here. Seattle's great. There's sun here. At least in the summertime. And there's sea. And most importantly, you're here." The streets are mostly quiet, though a few folks stroll or walk to their cars after late dinners and drinks. Zack checks the clock on his phone. "You should start closing earlier, Herb. You need your rest."

"But the neighborhood needs me."

"Two people came in all night."

"And if I weren't here, those two people—"

"Would have had to get in their cars and drive to another store," Zack interrupts. "Which is what everyone does these days. It's not a hardship."

"Not everyone, fortunately. Because if everyone did it, then I would be out of business." Zack frowns at Herb's logic while Herb continues. "Sometimes filling a demand is how you ensure the demand remains. Besides, you can't get all this," he gestures back at the store, "at the big grocery stores."

Herb's right about that. There's nowhere else in the Pacific Northwest quite like Goldfarb's. And Zack should know since he's traveled every inch of it. Local foot traffic may be Herb's bread and butter, but people come from all over the greater Seattle area to shop his unique collection of international treats and delicacies. Hell, Zack himself would make the trip now and then, even if he weren't keeping an eye on Herb.

"Alright, Herb, you're right. As usual."

Herb smiles triumphantly, a hint of boyish glee lighting his face. "I know."

"Come on, let's go up," Zack says with an upturned nod. "It's getting late."

***

Herb shuffles out from the back of the apartment with sheets and pillows in his arms.

"The place looks good," Zack says, scanning the room. The last time he was here, Herb was just moving in. The place had been used for extra inventory, so it was still packed with cartons of all sizes, with only a small daybed and a TV table in the bedroom where Herb was both sleeping and eating at the time. Now it's furnished and dressed with curtains, pictures on the walls, and even a couple throw pillows.

"Yes, it's small, but it suits me. Makes me not miss Mimi so much. There's no room in here for her ghost," he laughs.

"You're lucky to have a space like this, right above the store. There aren't many old-school mixed-use buildings like this around anymore."

"I *was* lucky. I couldn't afford it today. Oh, I still have your boxes in the back."

"Thank you."

"I'm only sorry I don't have a bed for you," Herb says dropping the sheets and pillows on the sofa. "You know you're welcome to stay as long as you want. Family takes care of family."

Zack warms with the words. "Always."

"But wouldn't you be more comfortable somewhere with a bed? You deserve a bed."

Zack plops onto a chair next to the couch and pulls off his shoes. "Actually, I've got a lead on a place around the corner. With any luck, I'll be out of your hair in a couple of days."

Herbs stretches the fitted sheet over the cushions of the couch, "Out of my hair. Such a funny expression." He turns and runs his hand through Zack's messy hair. "Remember when I had hair? Those were the days!"

"Seems like only yesterday."

"Seems like a hundred years ago!" Herb laughs. "You can't imagine what it's like to get old."

"Can't I? I may not have an aching back or creaking joints..."

Herb jumps in. "Or the tragedy of watching your body grow more wrinkled, saggy, and bald by the day."

"But where it counts..." Zack pauses to tap his temple twice. "I'm as old as the hills."

"That's as may be. But talk to me when it takes you five full minutes to go from lying down to standing up in the morning."

"Come on, Herb..."

"No, you think you know. But you can't possibly really know. Look at you! A gleaming young man, all muscles and teeth and shine, an old soul perhaps, but in the body of an Olympian."

"An Olympian?" Zack's voice rises in mock displeasure.

"Oh, you know what I mean," Herb tuts back. "It's just, getting old is hard."

"I know, old man." Zack rolls the comment around in his head, feeling for the hard truth of it. "I know."

CHAPTER FIVE

FIRE IN HER BELLY

CLAREY WAKES TO A Twilight Zone of sensations. Even before she opens her eyes, the half-dead arm she can barely feel under her body issues a final cry for help before it goes full zombie. Curled on her side, she opens her eyes to the sight of the floor? And baseboards? And the faux-fur trim around her winter coat hood, so close it's nearly pushing into her eyeball? Her hip shrieks with pain as she attempts to roll onto her back, which protests by locking into a rigid steel beam.

But the large, black metal framed window shining bright sun into the room warms her. And the twelve foot ceilings, which look even higher from this perspective, remind her exactly where she is and why she's suffering this indignation. A quiet glee rushes in. Her first morning in her place. This should be exciting – if only her body hadn't cemented to the floor in the night-time.

At thirty-six, she's far too young to hurt this much. Then again, at thirty-six, she's also far too old to be sleeping on a pile of clothes on the floor. Roxy's the one who should be sleeping on a pile of Clarey's clothes. And getting yelled at for it. But still... Roxy.

With considerable effort, Clarey manages to peel herself off the ground and stand up. Everything hurts. A woman with her substantial curves should definitely not be sleeping on a mattress of hardwood. She needs a soft bed that gives in all the right places. And with any luck, she'll have one soon.

When Mr. Annika's Furniture calls, she's just hopping out of the shower. She's got barely enough time to dress and run down to the store around the corner to grab something for breakfast. She towels off, pulls a wrinkled tee and some shorts from her pile of bedding, and runs for the door.

Renewed by her shower and the bright sunshine, Clarey practically bounds across the street and down to the corner. She couldn't have asked for a better location for her building, located right on the edge of downtown Kirkland, a literal stone's throw from all the charming shops and restaurants that give the town so much character and life. With the lake a couple blocks away one way and the library couple blocks the other way, it's a dream come true.

But as she rounds the corner, she's halted by the sight of someone emerging from a doorway not far from the entrance to the shop. The guy she saw by the fountain yesterday saunters toward the other end of the block. He's glorious. That seems a singularly unhelpful thing to think in this moment. She's in a rush and certainly doesn't need to cloud her mind with thoughts of random dudes on the street when she has furniture to receive and boxes to unpack and a doggy to collect. But his broad shoulders tapering to a perfect... no, there is no time for this nonsense.

At the corner, he crosses the street and walks out of sight. Phew. Clarey unfreezes and looks up at the sign before she enters. Goldfarb's. She didn't have time to look around properly yesterday, but now she spares a moment to run her eyes across the shelves. Her realtor Dana had mentioned this place was a draw when she was looking at the condo. Apparently their carefully curated collection of international goodies brings the world to Kirkland, and the single wall of convenience store essentials brings the neighborhood to their door. Now she can see why. From British HobNobs to Icelandic skyr to Japanese matcha candies, this place has everything.

She can already tell she's going to spend a lot of time exploring these shelves, but for now, she just needs a quick bite. On the back wall, she spots a stand full of fresh fruit and something akin to a Hudson News collection of standard snacks and drinks, with an assortment of cereal and bread at the bottom. She grabs a box of Cheerios, a couple apples, and some milk.

The old man at the counter greets her with a big smile that lights up his eyes. "Good morning. How are you today?"

"Very well, thank you. This is a great store you have here."

"Thank you so much. Are you new to the neighborhood?"

"How do you know that?"

"You came in yesterday, didn't you? I remember you rushing. Now you're back first thing this morning. You must live close to come twice in two days. And I've never seen you before, so..."

"Impressive! Do you remember all your customers?"

"Well, the pretty ones anyway," he says as he rings her last item.

Clarey laughs and hands him her credit card. "Now I'm coming back for sure."

"So, are we neighbors?"

"Just moved in around the corner."

"Wonderful! Then I look forward to seeing you again very soon."

As Clarey pushes open the door, she spots him. The blond guy's at the fountain again, this time lying along the ledge, soaking up the sun. Like yesterday, he's all in white and tan and he catches the light like a crystal, beaming it right back out and drawing her eye as if by magic. He looks like he should be sailing a boat in a men's cologne ad. He's mesmerizing. Clarey shakes herself back to sense. Who is this guy anyway? Doesn't he have anything else to do? Seriously, he's beautiful, but get a life, buddy. If he doesn't have anything more to do with his time than sit around a fountain all day, there's clearly something off. Besides, she's sworn off men.

He looks up from his phone and catches her staring. Oh crap, is she staring? Yes, she's still staring. He smiles at her and she feels the heat rising to her cheeks. She clenches her bag tighter in her hand, gives him the closest thing to a disinterested sneer she can manage in her current state of mortification, and takes off.

***

Once the sofa is in place and the bed is fully assembled, it's finally time to get Roxy. Clarey texts Derek. When he doesn't reply right away, she digs out her new sheets and dresses the bed. With the fitted sheet in place, she flops onto the mattress and runs her hands over the surface. The silky softness of her splurge bedding reminds her this is her new life, one where she can choose romantic printed sheets in deep navy saturated with sensual purple and white flowers if she wants them, and there's not a damn thing anyone else can do about it. No more passively giving in to a man who somehow always convinces her it's better his way. Derek doesn't get to ruin this.

Speaking of which, where is he? She texts him again. Then calls. Voicemail. "Derek, where are you? I want to pick up Roxy. Call me back." Then, for good measure, she calls Lydia, but she doesn't pick up either. Something's going on. She grabs her keys and heads for the garage.

When she pulls up to the house, only Lydia's car is in the drive, but when she knocks, no one answers. Not even Roxy with her excited, gruff bark. Clarey hesitates to let herself in. It's only been a day, but somehow the house already feels like foreign terrain, and increasingly it's feeling like enemy territory as well. But her name's still on the lease, so she slides in the key and steps in. She calls for Roxy, but there's no sign of her. She walks around the house to be sure, then calls Derek again. "Dammit, where are you? I need to get Roxy today. Call me as soon as you get this."

Something's definitely going on.

***

Clarey grabs for her phone the moment it pings. She's texted Derek ten times, and Lydia about half that, but it's neither of them. It's Jessa planning a dinnertime Zoom.

chinese? Jessa suggests.

How about Italian? Clarey counters.

how about chinese? Jessa replies.

Fine, Clarey relents.

Ninety minutes later when the buzzer rings, Clarey heads for the lobby. It's stranger than she expects to walk through the empty building knowing there's absolutely no one else there. Part lap of luxury, part isolation cell. Like a lonely queen of her own empty castle. Or perhaps an impoverished queen who's begun selling off her riches to survive. It matters little that her castle is headed the other direction eventually, from bare to lavish – the effect is the same. Skillful millwork details walls that are strangely devoid of artwork. Bare cement floors awaiting carpet. Functional overhead lighting, but wall sconces missing their bulbs and shades. A gleaming elevator accented with a strangely lifeless glass mural on the back wall because the light behind it either hasn't been installed or hasn't been switched on. And when the doors open, a large, polished lobby that would surely welcome guests in style, if only it had a single piece of furniture to fill the palatial space.

The gym to the left of the entrance does have most of its equipment, one of the early perks installed to entice the first buyers, but the electrical hasn't been completed yet, so the treadmills and ellipticals can't be used. And Clarey isn't a weights girl. But the pool was also filled, literally a day before construction shut down according to the realtor. So maybe she can give that a try. Since there's no one around to see her in a swimsuit for once.

She opens the lobby door to the delivery guy. He thrusts the bag toward her. "Moo shu pork and spring rolls."

"No, I ordered vegetable fried rice," she insists. But even as she says it, she takes one look at the delivery guy's face and knows she's going to end up accepting the moo shu pork.

Minutes later, she's signing on to Zoom and unwrapping her stupid-ass moo shu pork. Squeezed in shoulder to shoulder with their food on the table in front of them, her sisters are not best impressed by the tale. "Moo shu pork? That's a fourth-tier choice, at best," Hope says.

Clarey frowns. "Tell me about it."

"You should have sent the dumbass back," Jessa insists, slurping lo mein into her mouth.

"Jessa, please," Hope responds with a heavy eye roll toward her sister.

"What? She should have!"

"Of course, she should, but do you have to be so crass?" Living together is clearly getting to the two of them. It's only been a couple weeks, but without middle sister Clarey there to bridge the gap, the two seem more like fire and ice than ever before. And Hope's two antsy kids on summer break, a husband loudly talking through virtual meetings all day, every day, and Hope's own home office therapy practice becoming ever more demanding probably aren't helping.

"So, living together's working out nicely for you, I see," Clarey says with a pointed smirk.

"Oh, you know, she's as big sister-y controlling as ever," Jessa shrugs.

"And she's still the rebellious child raging against every rule," Hope counters. "And it's not controlling to ask you to control yourself around my family."

"That's literally the definition of controlling," Jessa snipes.

"Nobody made you move in, you know."

"Fine, I'll find another place to live. I might have to find a job first, but—"

"Don't you dare!" Hope says, grabbing her sister's head and smothering her with kisses. "I can't be apart from both of my gorgeous sisters."

Jessa giggles and pushes her off. "You see what I have to deal with."

When they've finished, Clarey reports on the events of the past two days. The mug, broken books, the condom, the furniture, and most importantly, Roxy.

"That bastard," Jessa says.

Hope swallows her chicken. "There we agree."

"Oh, he's not so bad. He's just... Derek."

Jessa groans with disgust. "Why do you always defend him?"

Hope places a calming hand on Jessa's arm, then turns to Clarey. "Sweetie, it's perfectly natural for you to harbor unresolved feelings for your ex-husband."

"I don't harbor any unresolved feelings for him. Believe me. Fully resolved."

"Your identity has been wrapped up in him for a lot of years," Hope continues. "First as a girlfriend, then a wife, then as a disgruntled ex."

"Amicable! We're totally amicable. Remember?" Until this Roxy thing, anyway. She's feeling less amicable by the minute.

"But it's important for you to sever that connection. To assert yourself in order to reclaim your sense of self."

Clarey drizzles some sauce onto a cold spring roll and bites into it. The lightly sweet, greasiness assaults her already battered taste buds, but she keeps going, comfort eating her way through the conversation. "Well, I have severed the connection. I've moved out. Can't get much more severed than that."

"It's not about physical separation. You have to stand up for yourself with him."

"Not just him," Jessa chimes in. "You let everyone under the sun push you around."

"Including you?" Clarey asks.

"I'm different. Obviously."

Hope intercedes with a soft, motherly cadence – or is it her therapist's voice? – "All we're saying is you need to—"

"Stop taking everyone's shit," Jessa says.

"Yes," Hope nods. "That."

"Maybe," Clarey concedes. "But I think what I really need is a long break from men."

***

Clarey can't identify the source of her discomfort at first. Is it an actual digestive issue or sheer, unadulterated rage? Derek still hasn't responded to any of her texts or calls and there was still no one home when she swung by after dinner. Surely that was enough to give anyone a stomachache. But her doubts evaporate when the first cramps strike. After a frantic dash to the toilet and a painful evacuation process, she drags herself to a nearby pile of boxes. One by one, she tears each open, rooting around desperately for the Imodium. She's forced to abandon her search when a second wave hits. Sitting on the toilet, doubled over in pain, she groans, "Moo shu pork." When she finally emerges from the bathroom, she skips the boxes, grabs her wallet and dashes out. With any luck, Goldfarb's will still be open.

She heaves gratefully as she rounds the corner and spots the light still on. She runs in and up to the counter. The shopkeeper behind the register greets her with his smiling eyes and voice. "Hello again, young lady. How can I help you?"

Relief washes over Clarey. Help is on the way. "I'm so glad you're still open."

But before she can ask where to find the Imodium, a deep, amber voice – do voices have colors? Because this one does – rumbles in from a back corner. "He shouldn't be."

Clarey turns slowly to find the source of the voice and breaks into a cold sweat when she sees the blond, four-alarm fire from earlier leaning against a cooler sipping a La Croix and scrolling his phone. But the moment her eyes land on his flawlessly sculpted face, he looks up and locks eyes on her. She startles back to the old man as he says, "Nobody asked you, thank you very much." Then back to Clarey, "Now, how can I help you, dear?"

This can't be happening. She can't have her first, possibly only encounter with this perfect man while she's bang in the middle of a category-five gastrointestinal storm. She's had nightmares like this. She mumbles her request, keeping her voice as low as humanly possible. "I, uh... need some, um..." Another cramp hits, warning of impending danger. Clarey clutches her stomach and winces.

"Cramps?" he asks kindly.

"In a manner of speaking." She glimpses over her shoulder, but keeps her eyes down. Why won't this guy leave? Doesn't he have a fountain to drape himself over or something? Before she can speak, another cramp rips through her lower abdomen and she grips the counter to steady herself.

"Maybe this will help," the man says pulling a box of Midol from the wall behind him.

Clarey pants through her cramp before whispering, "No, I have, uhh...diii..." The old fellow leans his bald head in and places a finger lightly to his ear, straining to hear.

"Diarrhea," the guy calls out from behind her, sounding exasperated. "She has diarrhea." Clarey feels her eyes pop open so wide she fears they might freeze that way as yet another cramp strangles her gut. "Just give her something and let the poor thing go home."

"Oh, God," she says, her body caving in on itself as much from the shame as from the pain.

The man at the counter pats her hand then turns sternly to her devastatingly handsome source of mortification. "Why don't you get out of here and go bother someone else? You're disturbing the customers."

"The customers? Plural?" The younger man smirks and glides off the cooler like a slow-motion flame, a sensual wave of movement that's both hypnotic and sizzling hot. It's a wonder he hasn't melted everything in the case behind him.

Clarey realizes that this is her one and only chance to reassert herself in this scenario. She might just shit herself in place, but she'll do it with her head held high. She stands up straight and thrusts her jaw forward toward the old man, ignoring the liquid flame sending heatwaves across her back as he approaches. "I'll take something for diarrhea, please." She forces her chin even a millimeter higher, determined to own this interaction. It may be catastrophically embarrassing, but it will be hers.

"Atta girl," the walking firestorm of a man says as he reaches the front counter. He moves in a languid, intentional way that sends non-digestion related shivers down Clarey's spine. "See you later, old man." He pushes open the door and smirks again. "See you later, Red."

Clarey's body ignites from his trailing sparks as he goes. Her face must be as crimson as the ringlets that surround it. The man behind the counter rolls his eyes and shakes his head. "Don't mind him."

"Is he around here a lot?" she asks, unsure whether she's asking on the shopkeeper's behalf or her own.

"Lately, yes. But never mind. Let's get you what you need."

***

Lying in bed an hour and three anti-diarrheal tablets later, Clarey's stomach has finally calmed, but her head roils. Where the hell are Derek, Lydia, and Roxy? Are they okay? They better be okay. God, what if they're not okay? She's mad, but she'd never want anything bad to happen to them. And what about Roxy? If anything happens to her droopy-faced, snoring, grunting, adorable under-bite puppy love while she's with Derek, Clarey will have to kill him. And assuming Roxy is okay, she'll have to kill him anyway because where the hell are they?

Eventually her brain runs out of steam from circling the same track endlessly, and she begins to drift off. But in her gentle fade to sleep, her brain trips onto a new thread to pull, and that thread leads directly to him. His words echo in her head. *Let the poor thing go home.* How humiliating. She prays she never crosses paths with him again and recommits herself to sleep. But as slumber takes her, she hears his voice again. *See you later, Red.*

She bolts awake, now hyper-alert in both her mind and her body. Certain parts feeling very alert indeed. This can't possibly be good.

Chapter Six

I'll Take It

Zack watches Herb pull the whistling silver teapot off the burner and pour it into two mugs on the table. Herb drops a spoon in each mug and by the time he reaches Zack, the air has filled with the scent of herbal lemon tea. "You see, that young woman needed me tonight."

"That young woman needed meds."

"And I was there for her. She wouldn't have made it to the big grocery store. What would she have done if I hadn't been there?"

"Stayed on the toilet, I imagine."

"And you would want that for her?"

Zack thinks of the voluptuous redhead with her cheeks flaming from pain and embarrassment. He nurses a pang of empathy. And guilt. He shouldn't have embarrassed her. Or flirted with her like that. Both were unkind. But for some reason, he couldn't resist. "Of course not."

***

Zack crosses the empty room, his sneakers making muted thumps on the hardwood floor. He casts his eyes up to the high ceiling. The beams are a nice touch.

His green-haired realtor Dana follows his gaze. "Aren't the beams fabulous?"

Zack nods and wanders into the kitchen scanning the large space. The cabinets and island are installed, but no countertops. No knobs. Zack wedges one of the smoky gray cabinets open with his finger.

"Like I said, the certificate of occupancy was issued right before they shut down," Dana says. "Plumbing, electrical, HVAC, all done. But as you can see, there are still some finishes to complete. The builders weren't planning to put it on the market until it was ready, but if you're willing to take it as is..." Zack swings open the large, glass doors leading to the small balcony. "It's a cute balcony, isn't it?" Dana calls out. "Just enough space for a table and two chairs. Cozy!" Zack looks down the street and spots the lake. "And you've got a great view," she continues.

He looks up and down the street to his left and his right, then straight down to the ground. To his surprise, the front door pops open and none other than the redhead from the shop struts out. "Great view," he mumbles. She bounds down the street toward the lake, vivid curls gleaming in the sun, clearly feeling better. He smiles.

"I should warn you, only one other unit is completed. And these are the only two with occupancy, so it might be a while before the building is finished and others move in."

He watches the woman walk, drawn to her every move, until she turns out of sight. "I'll take it."

***

Zack expects to see her while he's unloading, but three trips from his car and he's completely unpacked with nary a glimpse of the cute redhead. But if she's his only neighbor, it's got to be a matter of time before they meet again. Next time, he'll be polite and respectful. He'll hold a door for her or compliment her... something. He'll find a way to let he know that he's not such a bad guy. That as sole neighbors in this half-finished building go, she could do a lot worse.

He slings his last load of stuff onto the floor of his new condo and looks around. It's a nice place. A place he could stay awhile should it come to that. At least until Herb... well, that's something to reflect on another day. With any luck, it's still a long way off, at least for Herb. For Zack, it will be no time at all. But it's not today. Today, he's got to unpack.

He tugs out his single air mattress, attaches the pump, and presses the button to inflate. He's never needed more than this. A few clothes, some kitchen essentials, bathroom basics. And since he's staying put, he's collected the handful of old knickknacks he's been keeping in boxes at Herb's. They weren't really remnants of a life. With a life as long and shapeless as his, that was impossible. But they were souvenirs of special places and times. Small things that carved their nook in his heart such that the actual objects became mere representations of their imprints. The imprints almost more real than the objects themselves. A vase, a bottle of wine, an old tapestry... so many miscellaneous things that meant nothing. And everything. Besides Herb, they were all he had to show for his time wandering this crazy planet. It wasn't much.

His mind wanders back to the redhead. Why he should want to please her, he's not sure. He hasn't cared about anyone but Herb and his family in, well, forever. It's been basically an eternity of looking after one family and no one else. Not so much as a smidgeon of real concern for anyone else. Sure, there have been brief spells as this noble person or that wealthy tradesman, or in more recent times, as this earnest student or that software programmer or yet another banker or lawyer or firefighter – each with its share of brief, meaningless entanglements. There wasn't much he hadn't been after thousands of years. Except in love.

That was a new one. One he wasn't about to start now.

CHAPTER SEVEN

INTERLOPER

CLAREY SQUINTS DOWN THE street to the bit of lake peeking out from this angle between the buildings and cars and smiles. Things are definitely looking up. The call from Derek this morning put her mind at ease. Everyone, including Roxy, is fine. Well, not fine exactly. Waiting for her lunch, she slides into a chair at a table outside the restaurant and dials Hope.

Hope picks up. "I have four minutes before my next appointment. What happened?"

"Apparently they went hiking with no signal and Lydia sprained her ankle on the way down. They spent all night in the emergency room."

"Is she okay?"

"She's in a boot on crutches. Has to stay off it for at least a week."

"Ouch. Poor Lydia. She's a sweet girl."

"She is," Clarey agrees. Lydia's never done anything worse to Clarey than having sex with Derek in the next room. Admittedly, it's not a great point in her favor, but it's no great detriment either, given they were divorced at the time. And Lydia's likely as clueless about how those noises carry as Clarey was until she switched rooms. Carlo had always stayed over at his girlfriend's, and Clarey certainly never got any during the months she and Lydia were both there. "She deserves better than Derek. But that's a different story."

"And you let them keep Roxy?"

"Just for the week. Until Saturday. For Lydia, not him. She can be Lydia's emotional support dog while I work and get the house set up."

A voice shouts from inside the restaurant, "Clarey!"

Clarey stands as Hope continues, "Well, you're a better person than I am."

"You'd have done the same," Clarey says as she steps through the threshold. "But Jessa would have ripped him a new one."

***

By the time Clarey finishes her first afternoon call, word has spread to Jessa, whose indignant text reads, *she's YOUR DOG!!!!!* Jessa so rarely uses capital letters that when she does, she means it.

But it would break Lydia's heart after I promised. She's injured. I feel bad for her.

Jessa wastes no time in shooting back, *what about your heart????*

Clarey frowns, thinking of Roxy's little clip-clops on the floor and her sweet snuggles. *It's only a week. I do miss her tho.*

of course you do, Jessa writes. *that's why you need to get a spine and go get her*

Clarey looks at the clock. *Have you abused me enough yet? Because I have another client meeting in a little while and I need to prepare.*

you still have clients?

So far. And I'm trying like hell to hold onto them if you don't mind. Clarey wakes up her computer and pulls up a project planning timeline she's been mapping. She's got to get ready, but then she needs to work on a proposal for another prospective client. She really needs to get some momentum going or McGill Consulting is going to be over before it starts. And new condos don't pay for themselves.

Jessa's little dots bubble for an uncomfortably long time. Jessa's usually a shoot-from-the-hip girl. She says whatever pops into her head with little filter. If she's actually thinking about her response, or writing something longer than a quick-fire snark attack, it's likely to be lethal.

Finally, the message pops in. *fine, leave your dog with that jackass for the week. but if you're not gonna get your dog, then you sure as shit better start channeling her. you need to toughen up and start fighting for yourself. next time someone tries to sweet talk you into something, you need to growl and bare your teeth like a bulldog. BE ROXY.*

Jessa forgets Roxy is also the sweetest, most loving, silly Velcro dog ever. But when she wants something, or doesn't want something, she's as obstinate as they come. She'll grab onto her toy, or lock her ass on the ground, and there's not a thing in the world that can move her until she's good and ready. No one's more stubborn than Roxy.

Jessa may have a point.

***

The next day, Clarey drops the few books that don't fit on her shelves into the box and folds in the top flaps. The bookstore around the corner only takes used books by appointment now, and she's got 10 minutes to get there. She foists the box into her arms and heads down, but by the time she reaches the lobby, it's clear she's chosen her box poorly. It's not crazy heavy, but the size is too large and awkward for her. As she struggles to push her way out with her box in the lead, someone grabs the door and pulls it open.

The dude in white.

Today it's a bright white T-shirt instead of a button-down, and instead of chinos, he's wearing jeans. And oh boy, is he wearing them! But why is he lying in wait? By her building? She blocks the door. "Can I help you?"

"No, but let me help you," he says with a smile as he pulls the door wider.

"Sorry, what do you need?"

"Oh, I see. It's okay. I live here."

Clarey imagines Roxy growling her stranger danger warning. Time to be her own bulldog. "No, you don't."

"I do though?"

"That's not possible."

"I think it is." He flashes a beaming grin that reveals two annoyingly irresistible dimples.

But Clarey's not falling for it. She can be as tough and stubborn as Roxy. Grrr. "I got the only finished unit, so no. It's not."

"I'm Zack."

"I didn't ask."

"In 3B. And you are?"

This man who calls himself Zack is very charming. And she might possibly have peed herself a little when she heard his voice from this almost intimate distance. But this is her personal safety in question. She can't let some random man into her building no matter how godlike he may be. Channel Roxy. A low rumble escapes her throat. Was that an actual growl? His brow quirks in stunned confusion.

"Not interested. And I'm not going to be charmed into letting some random layabout or interloper, or whatever you are, into this building."

"Layabout and interloper? You do know this is the twenty-first century, right?" He barely holds back a chuckle and adds, "Are you going to call me a rapscallion next and accuse me of besmirching your virtue by speaking to you unchaperoned?"

He thinks he's funny. Guys who think they're funny never really are. Clarey gives him an unamused sneer, while a choked half laugh accidentally slips out. Maybe he's a little funny.

He brings his free hand to his face and absently runs a finger over his perfect mouth, veins notably popping over his biceps as he does. Not that she noticed.

"I'm still not letting you in," she says.

"I really do live here."

"Please let go of the door and step back," Clarey says. Zack shrugs and steps away, holding his hands up like he's got a gun pointed at him. "Now excuse me."

As she squeezes out between him and the door, waiting for it to slowly close, he points to the lock. "I do have a key, you know."

"Sure, you do," she says as she walks away. Jessa would be proud. Gloating, Clarey glances back over her shoulder one last time as she reaches the curb. He's still standing there watching her, smiling. Ha! He knows he's been bested. "Nice try, buddy."

***

On her way back from the bookstore, Clarey swings by Gold-farb's, intent on finally taking a proper look around the little shop. The old man stuffs sodas into a cooler as Clarey enters. "One moment," he says at the entry bell. He places one last bottle, thumps the door closed, and turns to greet his customer. "Ah, hello there. How are you feeling today? Better, I trust."

"Much, thank you." Clarey watches the man collapse the empty carton and toss it onto a pile just beyond the doorway to the backroom.

"You're always here," she observes.

"Always here."

"Don't you have any help?"

"Not at the moment, I'm afraid." He pauses to lean back with his hands on his waist and cracks his back before returning to the register. "I had a part-time fellow, but he had health problems, so it's just me for the moment."

"So, are you Mr. Goldfarb? Of Goldfarb's fame?"

He extends his hand across the counter. "Herb Goldfarb. Nice to meet you."

"Clarey McGill," she says, shaking his hand. She turns her eyes to the shelves and steps toward them.

"McGill sounds like a good Irish name. Or is it Scottish?"

"Irish in my case." She picks up a crunchy foil wrapper with bright colors and Spanish writing. It's clearly a snack, but she can't tell if it's savory or sweet, though she sees a word she thinks might mean banana.

"And Clarey?"

"Family name. My grandmother's maiden name was about to die out in our family. Until I swooped in and saved the day by being born." She rounds the corner of one aisle and heads back along the next.

"Ah, I know a thing or two about carrying on the family line as well."

Clarey pauses, a box with French writing in her hands. "Oh?"

"Far too long a story to tell."

She runs her eyes over the vast assortment of international candies filling the endcaps of each aisle. "You have a great store here."

"Thank you. It was my late wife Mimi's concept, but we built it together. It's her legacy now. And mine, I suppose."

"I can already tell I'm going to have a lot of fun exploring."

"That's the idea. Take adventurous locals around the world while bringing the homesick from afar a little taste of home."

Clarey drops the foil Spanish package on the countertop. "I'll take this."

Herb lights up with an appreciative smile. "Bold pick. Do you know what it is?"

"Not a clue. But I'm feeling adventurous," she replies, gazing out at the unoccupied fountain across the street.

***

Clarey bathes in the red glow of the setting sun through her window as the descending shadows inch her direction. She hits the save button on the proposal she's been working on. The Renton Foodbank is preparing to begin strategic planning for a service expansion and she's promised the director Gabi a revised proposal by tomorrow morning. Gabi has decided to roll together planning for two locations at once, which means going virtual. Adapting her highly inclusive, collective planning model to an entirely virtual format has proven more challenging than she expected. It's taken her all day to research the tools and conceptualize the process. It will take her most of rest of the evening to write it up. But she needs a break.

She stands to stretch her legs, then circles the large, open concept space to get both her brain and her blood moving. When she reaches the center of the living room area, she stops and stands there, listening. With the windows and balcony doors closed, there's no street noise. There's no noise at all. No neighboring conversations. No blaring TVs. No creaking footsteps. No elevators. No sweet puppy snores or tappity-tap of Roxy's nails on the floor. Nothing.

Clarey kneels to the floor and drums her nails on the wood in a pitter pat rhythm as if Roxy were running to her. She plops on the floor exactly where she is and texts Hope. *I'm lonely.*

Hope takes only a moment to respond. *Aww, honey, I'll get Jessa and we can Facetime. Give me ten minutes.*

When Hope appears on Clarey's phone, Jessa isn't yet onscreen, but she screams from a distance, "Tell her I'll be right there. I just have to finish peeing."

Hope calls back, "Please close the door!"

"It's closed!"

Hope rolls her eyes at Clarey. "Then how am I talking to you?"

"I only cracked it to talk to you," comes the reply.

"Then stop talking and close it all the way!" She finally focuses on Clarey. "It's like having a third child, I swear."

Clarey laughs. "You're the one who invited her to stay."

"I didn't think she'd take me up on it."

"Well, living with family isn't for the faint of heart. At least you get to see her." Clarey makes a sad puppy-dog face.

"You can see her too," Hope says. "Here she comes at last."

Jessa slams into the seat next to Hope. "What are we talking about?"

Hope elbows Jessa into submission, then turns to Clarey. "I think Clarey's lonely."

Clarey considers before she answers. "I'm fine, really. It's just so quiet. I'm glad to have my own space, and I do like the quiet most of the time. But it's a little creepy being all alone here at night. And I guess sometimes I wish I had someone around to talk to."

Hope smiles sympathetically. "You can talk to me anytime. Except when I'm with clients. Or the kids. Or Mark. But anytime, really." She leans over and nudges Jessa.

"You can talk to me anytime," Jessa says. "I've got nothing."

"If only you weren't an hour away," Clarey rasps. The move from West Seattle to Kirkland had seemed reasonable in most regards, but getting even further from her sisters had been the down side.

Hope goes on, "Another thing that can help is finding activities that nourish you. Besides work, I mean. And reading. Engaging in new activities, especially with movement, can release endorphins that are very beneficial for mood stabilization."

Clarey considers a moment. "I did want to try the pool, I guess."

"That's a great idea," Hope says. "Just be careful since there's no one else there if anything happens."

Jessa's face lights up. "You could go skinny dipping!"

"I'm not skinny dipping."

"You have to!" Jessa insists. "You'd never do it in nature. This is your one, best chance."

Hope sighs. "Jessa..."

"Do it! Live a little! Why not?"

"What if there are cameras?" Clarey fires back.

"Is anyone watching those cameras?" Jessa raises her brows emphatically.

"I don't intend to find out the hard way, thanks."

"Fine, if there are cameras, don't do it," Jessa relents. "But if not, it is a moral imperative that you get naked."

***

Clarey pads carefully into the pool room, emboldened at least a little by the liberating feeling of walking down in nothing but her suit, her swim tee, and flip flops. It's like vacationing at a luxury resort, except she's the only guest. The bad news, no cabana boy to bring her cocktails with paper umbrellas. The good news, no one has to see her in her bathing suit.

Normally, Clarey eschews her internalized fatphobia. She's well aware how harmful it is, and most of the time, she's got it beat. She feels good in her clothes, stays healthy and active, and doesn't worry about what others think. Getting naked with someone new is always a little scary, or at least it was back when she did things like that.

But doesn't everyone feel that way? And if they get as far as getting naked, he's clearly interested, so she just goes for it. Yep, mostly she's fat-positive and feeling fine.

Until she puts on a bathing suit. Something about sliding that piece of clingy spandex and nylon over her hips and stomach, seeing every dimple and crevice as they bulge through the fabric, and lifting her breasts into place with arms that suddenly look so much bigger than in daily life that shatters her confidence. No doubt a triggered response from childhood when other kids at the pool used fat as a slur, and that was only the tip of a very ugly iceberg. But knowing the source of the pain doesn't make it hurt any less.

No one's here to call her anything tonight, however. The pool is all hers. She makes a careful study of the ceiling, then every corner, searching for security cameras. Finding none, she sets down her phone, slips off her flip flops, and slowly lifts her swim shirt over her head. She's worn that protective layer, or one like it, for nearly 25 years. She never swims without it. She revels in the transgressiveness of removing it. But who does she have to hide from now?

Clarey walks to the edge of the pool and dips a toe in. It's warm. They must be spending a fortune to keep this thing heated. Some-one really should use it. She steps in and walks down to the bottom, luxuriating in the combination of warmth and weightlessness. She takes a couple steps, then dives under and swims across to the other side. When she emerges, she hooks her arm to the lip and looks over her very own private pool.

She swims back across and when she emerges this time, she's in front of the pool chair with her towel and phone. She stares at the phone. It mocks her in return. The phone echoes Jessa's words. The phone says, "it is a moral imperative that you get naked." She looks around the walls and ceiling once again. No cameras. She looks back at the phone. "This is your one, best chance."

Clarey takes a deep breath and holds it as she reaches for the shoulder straps of her suit. Slowly she pulls them off her arms, but pauses holding the bra over her breasts before regaining her courage. She resumes the careful peeling of her second skin, curling her legs up against her as she finally tugs the suit off her feet. She clutches it to her chest and giggles, before her giggle grows into a full-blown cackle. She's really doing it. She sets her suit on the side of the pool and dives under again, naked as the day she was born.

The sensation is unbelievably freeing. Hope was right. She'll be living off these endorphins for days. When she returns to the shallow end, she dives under and does a handstand, kicking her legs in the air while she counts. When she comes out, she pops above the water and giggles again. She's a carefree mermaid celebrating the simple joy of playing and being one with the water. She does another handstand. Then another.

When she tires of handstands, she tries a somersault. Then two, tucking in her head and legs, diving under, and popping her ass out as she rolls. All the silliness she loved as a kid. She's positively giddy. After the double, she goes for a series to see how many she can do. Round and round she goes, only on her third pass her eye catches something and she falls out of the roll in a floppy panic. She bounces up from below the surface, sputtering the water she took in, and squints the droplets out of her eyes. And when at last she can see straight, she ducks immediately back into the water.

Standing halfway between the door and the pool is the blond god himself. The guy who swore he had a key. The guy who assured her he lived here. The guy she refused to believe. Zack. And he's frozen like a Medusa victim. Ten seconds ago, her ass was sticking out of the water. Eight seconds ago, her boobs were. Her ass and boobs have turned him to stone.

Oh. My. God.

Clarey stares at the beautiful statue wordlessly. Stooping beneath the water, she does her best to cover herself, but what can she say? Oops, sorry about my ass and boobs? Sorry I just gave you an eyeful of something that's probably best seen in half-light after a bottle of pinot noir. And even then, only by someone who is definitely not you.

"I, um...," he stutters as if he might possibly wrangle a thought from his head, but nothing more comes out. He doesn't seem capable of speech, and it's her fault.

How does one begin to apologize for this humiliation? And why is it she's the naked one, yet she feels the need to apologize? "I thought I was the only one here," she finally sputters by way of explanation.

Zack offers a polite half-smile, then turns and walks out.

CHAPTER EIGHT

SEEING RED

ZACK STARES AT THE empty wall in front of him. The wall is as blank as his mind in the moment. "What the hell was that?" he chuckles to himself. The image of that voluptuous redhead rolling through the water, naked, runs through his head in a loop. And then when she popped out. Damn.

Her panicked voice leaks through the pool door. "Oh my God, oh my God, oh my God," on repeat. She must be dressing. She'll come running out any minute. He needs to move.

Back in his apartment, he pours himself a glass of the limoncello Herb gave him and steps out onto his balcony. He would do well to forget this ever happened. Nothing's changed. No matter how long it's been or how horny he might get now and then. Getting involved isn't an option. Despite those rather spectacular... oof! Gotta shut this thing down.

Above him to his right, balcony doors open. He looks up, hoping to catch a glimpse of her, but she doesn't come out. Still, she's up there. So close. His pulse rises, and not just in his chest. His cock stirs and he forces out a slow, easy breath. This can't possibly be good.

***

The next day, Zack opts for a run rather than a swim. Just in case. Better to give his new neighbor, and himself, some space. He runs past Goldfarb's, pauses to tap on the window and wave, then keeps going toward the water. He reaches Marina Park on the shores of Lake Washington and slows his pace. The park's crowded with families and individuals taking in the sun, playing on the beach, and dipping their toes into the still cold water. He walks out to the end of the pier where the lake tour cruises depart and looks to downtown Seattle across the way.

Funny to think how far away Seattle seems since he came back. Kirkland's well within the Seattle metro area, and he could be downtown in twenty minutes. Yet, somehow this charming lakefront suburb feels like its own little world. Maybe that's always life in the suburbs. He's usually opted for the anonymity of city life or the unobserved remoteness of rural living. He's never considered suburbia until now. Of course, living in downtown Kirkland isn't all that suburban. This place feels special. Like a small seaside community with all the quaintness and picturesque scenery of a vacation getaway, but also all the amenities needed for real life.

The added bonus is being this close to Herb for once. For years he's kept his eye on Herb, from both near and far, but he's never managed to get a place quite so nearby before. With Herb getting up there in years, being close seems more important than ever.

Break over, he jogs through the park, then picks up his pace once he escapes the crowds. He heads over to 85th and shoots up the road, past the Cow and Coyote sculpture, past Peter Kirk Park and the empty baseball diamond, then cuts through the parking lot for the grocery store to circle back. And there she is. Red. He ducks behind a column as he watches her walk from her car to the grocery entrance.

Zack exhales a breath of relief. How does she do this to him every time? He's usually so good at shutting it down, but somehow she always manages to permeate his defenses without even trying.

He shakes it off and stretches his quads, but before he can start running again, Red walks back out. It's only been a few seconds. Something must have changed her mind because she hasn't had time to shop, yet she climbs into her car and pulls out.

Once her car clears the lot, Zack starts running again, following his same planned route. Even if she's driving straight home, she'll easily be parked and back in her condo by the time he gets back on foot. So he makes his way over to Kirkland Avenue and heads back toward the lake, planning to detour to Herb's for fruit and a check-in. But as he approaches Herb's block, damn if she isn't right there again. Walking into Goldfarb's. Much as he loves Herb, Goldfarb's isn't usually the place folks go for their primary shopping. It's smaller, and inevitably, more expensive. It's the place you go for speed and convenience, or fun discoveries from around the world, not the household necessities. Yet, there she is. Interesting.

***

Back in his condo, Zack sets the paint down against the wall. His once empty space now bulges with lumber, tools, and painting paraphernalia. Cabinet doors lie flat across a worktable where he's been sanding and a large paint sprayer blocks the hallway to the bedroom he never uses. He walks into the kitchen and tugs the refrigerator out from its nook. He unplugs it and disconnects the water line before he drags it across the Ram Board floor covering he's installed to join the stove and dishwasher in the living room. He lightly sands the side of the cabinets where the fridge was to scuff the surface, then wipes it down with a damp cloth. Almost ready to paint.

He steps back and looks at the cabinets with their insides masked off. It's a lot of work to repaint brand new cabinets that already look good. The gray isn't bad. He'd probably like it with a stone countertop, but it won't work with the butcher block he's going to make. He holds the paint sample up again. The warm forest green will be perfect.

A thought dances through his mind. Will Red like this color?

This has got to stop.

***

The gleaming rooftop grill opens with a loud, grinding metallic clang. Zack wonders if it's hooked up, but a quick look underneath reveals it's not. He could fix that. They probably wouldn't like it, but by the time things reopen, would they even remember it wasn't connected before? The rest of the outdoor kitchen is polished and sleek as well. Still needs some tables and chairs, but this roof deck will be a great space when it's finished.

Scratch that. It already is a great space – all the better because he doesn't have to share it. The 360° view beats his balcony by a lot, and he can breathe better up here. Closer to the sky, closer to the gods. Not really, of course. That's not how it works. But it does sometimes feel like that. Like somehow, if he could climb high enough, he could escape the earth's gravity and fly free at last. It's a silly fantasy, but one he clings to when he feels too alone. Although a fifth floor rooftop is nowhere near high enough, at least it's above the fray. If the cozy streets of Kirkland can be called a fray.

He approaches the edge and gazes out to Lake Washington in the distance. On an impulse, he hops up onto the wall and stands on the ledge. He makes a slow, careful spin, checking the view in every direction. He turns back to the lake, smiles, then looks down. It's not that high really. Then again, it's not that low. A person could do some damage falling from this height.

Behind him, the roof door clicks open. There's only one person it can be. "Oh my God," she cries. "What are you doing?"

Zack quickly spins around. A hair too quickly as his balance wavers and he tips a little. She shrieks, but he steadies himself and hops down immediately. "I'm okay. Everything's fine."

Her whole body is vibrating. "What..."

"I'm fine. Really. I was just taking a look around." Zack winces at the fear on her face, a current of guilt tearing through him.

Her mouth hangs open a moment before she seems to remember herself, and perhaps, her lingering humiliation. She closes her mouth, lifts her chin, turns around, and walks back inside.

***

The bright lights of the building's gym, off to the side of the lobby, ensure maximum visibility for the gym's users. Like in any paid gym, those working out are put on display for the world to see, both to flatter their vanity and to attract the interest of passersby. For a new block of luxury condos looking to attract buyers, a great gym full of fit people would certainly be a selling point if they were actually in a position to sell.

However, Zack's the only user at the moment and he has no interest in putting on a show. Despite his appearance, he generally does his best to fly under the radar. He neither craves nor chases the adoration of others. He may catch eyes, and his looks certainly smooth the way for him from time to time, but whenever possible, he deflects unwanted attention and keeps to himself. It's easier that way. So, working out in front of the world isn't something that particularly appeals to him.

But he does like a good workout. He likes the focus and Zen of the process, zeroing in on one single activity, turning off his head and simply feeling his body in motion. Again and again. The repetition driving out all other thoughts. Running. Swimming. Lifting. The physicality of workouts bring a kind of intense presence followed by deep calm that can only be matched by one other activity he knows. And he doesn't do that anymore. Besides, working out is what people expect guys like him to do.

Zack lifts the 100 pound dumbbell in his hand and bounces it lightly to get the feel of it. He lifts both hands over his head and begins a set of tricep extensions, checking his form in the mirror. His range of motion is good, but he can do more. After the first set, he switches to the 125. He bounces it again, shrugs, and does his next set, squeezing his abs and glutes. He's not breaking a sweat yet, but he's warm enough to strip off his shirt, which also allows him to better monitor his form. With the third set, he watches himself more carefully in the mirror, to ensure he's engaging where he should and not leaning back too far.

With his last rep, he lowers the dumbbell to the rack and looks up. In the lobby outside the window stands Red, watching him. He raises a slow handed wave and smiles, but when he catches her eye, she jumps. Her eyes flicker to his chest, then dart away as alarm flushes her face. She tears out the front door and away from him.

***

She dodges him again in the parking garage, and bashes the Doors Close button on the elevator when he walks up to the mailboxes seconds after she steps away. She refuses to make eye contact with him, but he gives it a shot anyway. "Hey, can we talk?" he calls out to the closing doors. He doesn't blame her. Her intense embarrassment radiates in an emotional blast that his sensitivities are too finely tuned to miss. Then again, a mossy rock probably couldn't miss her embarrassment. If he could take it back – having walked in on her in that moment – he would. But he won't be performing any miracles today. He needs to find another way to break this tension.

Friday afternoon, he goes into the shop to give Herb a break and do some stocking. Herb may insist on keeping his store open too late, but heavy lifting is at least something Zack can take off his plate. He kneels at the end of an aisle and unpacks a carton of canned tamales from Mexico. The entry bell rings and a voice calls out. "Hello?" Her voice races through him electrifying every nerve ending. He feels her voice like a touch.

He closes his eyes a moment, takes a beat, then glides out from the aisle offering his warmest smile. "Hi."

She freezes in the middle of the floor. "What are you... I was looking for Mr. Goldfarb."

"He stepped out for a minute," he says. "Can I help with something?"

Her eyes dart around the store avoiding his. "I'll come back," she says with a quick turn for the door.

"Wait. Please," he calls out. Then again as she's about to release the door and walk away. "Please?"

She takes a deep breath and takes a single step back toward the entry, still leaning on the open door. She crosses her arms and looks at the floor. She won't even come all the way into the store with him?

"I'm sorry about the other day. I didn't mean to walk in on you like that." Her cheeks flush brighter than her hair, but she stays put. "I barely saw anything, I swear." Actually, he saw everything, but this is no time for semantics.

"Okay, I..." She scratches her head nervously and turns again to leave.

"But are you really going to keep avoiding me forever? We're neighbors, you know. We're literally our only neighbors, in case you didn't notice." She purses her lips, but says nothing, so he continues, "I'd like it if we could be friends." When his words are met with a hostile huff of disbelief, he adds, "Or at least friendly?"

She stands in the doorway an uncomfortably long time, saying nothing. His time's running out and this might be his last chance to smooth things over. It would probably be best if he left it alone – that's what he would normally do – but for some reason he can't. Zack reaches his hand out in a tentative gesture. "I'm Zack. From 3B." She pouts, but slowly steps forward and shakes his hand, saying nothing. He'll take it. He pivots. "Maybe we should exchange phone numbers, since we're the only ones in the building. In case of emergency. Or in case we want to borrow a cup of sugar."

Finally, she speaks. "Do a lot of baking, do you?" She raises her brows skeptically.

He shrugs. "I dabble."

She shakes her head and moves back to the door. "Have a nice day."

CHAPTER NINE

BAKING AND BUBBLING UP

CLAREY POUNDS ON HER keyboard in a fury that has nothing to do with her work and everything to do with that impossible, beautiful man haunting her goddamn life. Zack. Humph. She doesn't even like blonds.

Why is he always everywhere she goes? And why does he have to look like that? Nobody looks like that. At least, nobody should. Not when she's sworn off men for the time being. And not when she wouldn't want to anyway because he was witness – nay, cause – of the single most humiliating moment of her life, short of the time when she was seven and peed her pants on the swing ride at an amusement park never to be named again, and well, we don't want to relive that.

An odd noise distracts her from her musings. A very faint shuffle and tap somewhere nearby. She scans the room for something, anything, that could have made the noise in her mostly empty condo. There's nothing on her dining room table but her laptop and notepad. The sofa and chair sit empty, nothing on them to slip to the floor. And sadly, no Roxy to roam around making noises, though at least that finally changes tomorrow.

She looks to the balcony for a bird perhaps. No birds, but on the ground lies an unexpected intruder. A paper airplane lies with its pointed nose butted up against the door. Dread and intrigue mix in her mind as she crosses to the door and pulls it open. She stares at it as if it might be an explosive too dangerous to touch, but after a few seconds of consideration, she picks it up. She flips it around, but sees nothing unusual about it. Just an ordinary paper airplane. Ordinary other than the fact that it somehow landed on her balcony, anyway.

She heads for the recycle bin, but pauses before dropping it in. She unfolds it and finds a message written inside. "I stocked up on sugar. In case you need any."

***

Gabi is easily Clarey's favorite client. Clarey only has three clients at the moment, but even if she had a dozen, Gabi would be tops for fun. Meeting with her on this grumpy Friday afternoon is precisely the tonic she needs. Plus, her partner Dana found Clarey this incredible condo, so bonus points there.

"So, how is it? Tell me everything. Give me a tour." Gabi says it all in a single breath, eager for the scoop.

"It's amazing. I love it," Clarey says. She lifts the laptop and gives a short, slow turn around the room, showing the kitchen, the balcony, the living room and bookshelves, before finally tipping it up to show off the beams.

"Ooh, Dana told me about the beams. Those are nice! I'm officially jealous," Gabi declares. "Tell me again how you afforded this place," she says as Clarey lowers the laptop back to the table in front of her. "Sorry, I know that's a nosy-ass question, but the people need to know."

With another client, Clarey would probably balk at the presumptuousness of the question, but Gabi's become a friend. "When my grandma died, she left some money to me and each of my sisters. A little nest egg each to make our dreams come true."

"Wow, where do I get a rich grandma? Got any extras lying around?"

Clarey laughs. "If only."

"Oh, I hear you have a new neighbor. Have you met him yet? Apparently, he had basically no stuff so he was moving right in."

Clarey cringes. "That would have been really helpful to know a week ago."

"Something wrong?"

"Never mind."

Gabi twists one of her tiny braids in her hand and leans in toward the camera. "I'm probably not supposed to tell you this."

Clarey looks to her left and right as if someone might hear. "Tell me what?"

Gabi lowers her voice. "Apparently, he paid all cash. That day. And somehow, he got the paperwork done overnight. Like, that's literally not possible. There are too many players, too many steps. But Dana put in the offer one day, and somehow by the end of the next, they'd closed. It was like magic."

Clarey's own closing took ages. She wasn't even supposed to have this unit. She originally offered on a smaller unit on the second floor that was expected to be finished in about two months. But when the builders ran into money problems, all construction halted with only one condo finished, the premium top floor corner unit. It had just been permitted for occupancy, but the original buyer pulled out for reasons of his own. Meanwhile, Clarey's original unit was on indefinite delay, which meant so was her getaway from the untenable roommate situation with Derek and Lydia. Suddenly, the higher price tag didn't seem so unreasonable, and when the builders said they'd cut her a deal – better some income than indefinite carrying costs – Clarey jumped at the most glamorous escape plan she could have imagined. It meant she'd have to work even harder to make McGill Consulting a success, but so worth it for this place.

Still, all of that took, what, 45 days? How'd he do it overnight? Clarey frowns. "Can we change the subject?"

***

When Clarey steps on her balcony, her eyes instantly lock onto the figure on the balcony below her to the left. He sits sipping something yellow – lemonade maybe? – with his legs stretched out on the railing. Shirtless, because why not? Her first instinct to run away loses out to her second, much stronger instinct to stare at his shredded chest and perfectly defined arms. The bright, late day sun casts a golden glow on him that makes him look like the sun god himself. She can easily imagine him in gleaming armor driving a chariot across the sky. Or stripping off that armor and—

"Hi!" he calls out.

With a gazelle-like leap, Clarey bolts out of sight and hides behind the door. Did he actually see her? Of course, he saw her. Why would he say hello if he didn't see her? She holds her breath, waiting for the danger to pass.

The danger calls out again. "Want to come have a neighborly drink?"

Clarey flattens herself further against the wall, sweating. She fights the urge to cry and finally shouts from the safety of her barricade, "No, thank you."

***

The next morning, Clarey rolls up to her now former house grinning ear to ear. Roxy's finally coming home with her. The place won't feel so lonely with her sweet girl lying at her feet, tugging on her favorite rope toy, or snoozing on her beloved squeaky dinosaur. With Roxy by her side, all these other distractions and annoyances will simply disappear. Okay, maybe there's really only one distraction, but he's annoying enough for a whole platoon.

Lydia's car isn't in the drive, which is too bad because Clarey was hoping to check in on her. But at least that means Lydia's able to get out and about now, which is perfect timing. She won't need Roxy's company anymore. Roxy wouldn't be staying either way, but now Clarey doesn't have to feel bad about it.

Clarey knocks on the door, but no one answers. Including Roxy. She knocks again. "Hello," she calls out. When no one answers, she unlocks the door and steps in. "Anyone home?" She takes a couple steps and looks around. No Roxy.

Her phone pings with a text. Derek writes, *Hey, sorry, we had an emergency. Lydia's dad had a heart attack. We're on our way to Bend.*

Clarey clutches her own heart before texting back. *Oh my God! Is he okay?*

We'll find out more when we get there. I'm not sure if we'll be able to see him, but at least we'll be there for her mom.

Poor Lydia. What an awful week. Clarey types back, *Tell Lydia I'm thinking of her and hoping for the best.*

Will do.

So where's Roxy?

With us.

Clarey types her response even as she processes the words on her screen. *You took her?* To Bend. They took her dog to Bend, six freaking hours away.

What else was I supposed to do?

Leave her here!!!!! You knew I was coming to get her today.

Clarey watches the dots of his stupid, selfish, dog-stealing, little thought bubble. *Sorry, Clare Bear.* How dare he call her that! *With everything going on, I completely forgot.*

Yeah, right. He always makes it sound so reasonable, as if Clarey's the one being unreasonable by expecting him to actually return her dog to her. But Roxy is her dog. She adopted her. She bought all Roxy's toys. She feeds her. Or did until this week. She pays the vet bills. Maybe they've helped out with occasional walks, but Roxy is still her dog.

***

Clarey startles at the knock at her door. Hasn't her day been bad enough already? Roxy should be barking and scrambling over to the door right now. But she's not. And while that might not be Zack's fault, if he's got the gall to show up at her door today, he might have to pay the price anyway. Clarey marches to the door and swings it open in a furious rush. "What do you want?"

He holds up a plate covered in a napkin. "I baked."

"What?" she says, not properly processing.

"Peace offering," he says. She has neither the time nor the energy for whatever this is. She stares at him blankly, unsure how to interpret this gesture as he continues, "Also, I saw you walking earlier, and you looked upset. So, I baked you scones."

This is either the sweetest thing anyone has ever done for her, or the creepiest. Possibly both. Do stalkers bake? Stalkers probably bake. That's how they get you. Those sexy, soft-spoken charmers lure you with their scones laced with sweetness and lies, and next thing you know, you're their prisoner. If Mark Wahlberg had baked in that movie, it would have been over for Reese Witherspoon. "You saw me walking and baked scones?"

"Please take them. They weren't easy to make without countertops."

"You don't have countertops?" she asks. He answers with a shake of his head. "Yet, somehow you had what you needed to bake scones?"

"I went out and bought what I needed."

"For me?" When his only answer is a shrug, she adds, "You know that's weird, right?"

"I like to think of it as neighborly."

"How do I know it's not poisoned?"

"Why would I poison it?"

"You could be a psychopath."

"I *could be* a lot of things" he says with a sexy drawl and a suggestive smile. "But statistically, it's unlikely I'm a serial killer.

Besides, how many serial killers have you heard of who kill with cranberry-orange scones?" He holds up another container with sub compartments.

"And that is?"

"Clotted cream and jam," he says. "For the scones."

This guy doesn't mess around. "Clotted cream?"

"I didn't make that. I got it from Goldfarb's."

Clarey eyes the food again and looks up at Zack. If he weren't so wildly out of her league, she wouldn't even consider taking it. It would feel too fraught with intention, flirtation, or expectation or... something that wouldn't be fulfilled, even if she wanted to. Which she clearly does not, since she's not a believer in lost causes. But what could this guy really want from Clarey? Except maybe, like he said, to be friends. Or at least friendly neighbors.

"Please take it. I'm beginning to feel a little silly here."

Clarey cautiously takes the food from him. "Thank you. This is kind."

Zack nods graciously, like a regency era bow. "Well, mystery neighbor, I will leave you to it. I hope your evening is better than your day was."

As he walks down the hall, he hits the crash bar on the door to the stairwell. She calls out, "Clarey." He stops and turns around as she says, "My name is Clarey."

"Hi, Clarey. I'm Zack." He flashes a blinding smile, and she barely manages to hold her own back as she closes the door.

***

Once Clarey finally tells her sisters about Zack and the pool, the evening's Facetime call goes completely off the rails.

"Oh my God," Hope says. "I would have died."

"How could you not tell us this, Clare?" Jessa says, hanging her head. "A sacred trust has been broken." She turns her head dramatically to the side.

"And then he made you scones," Hope swoons with a romantic sigh. "How were they by the way?"

"So good," Clarey says. "Like it's not fair how good they were. And he's so freaking gorgeous, it's actually uncomfortable to be around him. He's like this perfect, tan, blond god."

Jessa looks at Clarey and sneers, "Blond?"

"No, I know," Clarey says, "but it works on him. It's like he sprouted from a clamshell, naked and spectacular, and was dressed by angels. He's what it would look like if Ryan Gosling, Chris Hemsworth, and Austin Butler all got together and had a baby."

"Is that what Three Men and a Baby was about?" Jessa quips.

"I don't think that's how biology works," Hope says sensibly.

Jessa grins. "Oh, but wouldn't it be fun to watch them try?" Clarey bounces her brows at Jessa with a mischievous smile and laughs.

Hope chokes back a chuckle as she looks back and forth between Jessa at her side and Clarey onscreen. "You're both ridiculous."

Jessa nudges her. "Come on, you can't pretend you wouldn't enjoy that show."

"I'm not into porn."

"Who's talking about porn?" Clarey says. "I'm talking about being in the room with a front row seat!" Clarey might be getting a little overheated. She blames Zack.

"Speak for yourself," Jessa counters. "I'm no benchwarmer. Put me in, coach!"

Hope shakes her head. "I can't believe I'm related to you two."

They all burst into the giddy cackles that only they can bring out in each other. When they finally catch their breath, Jessa nods at Clarey. "Meanwhile, Clarey's got the real thing right downstairs and won't even talk to him."

"I've talked to him," Clarey replies indignantly. She's said at least three or four sentences. Granted, if she added up everything she's ever said to him it might not tally a hundred words. But you can say a lot in hundred words or less.

"You wouldn't even tell him your name."

"Well, he could be a wacko."

Hope interjects with a professional admonishment as she stands up. "Don't say wacko. That's not okay," she says as she walks away with her empty glass.

Clarey rolls her eyes. "Sorry, he could be *dangerous*."

Hope's gone offscreen, yelling toward the next room about homework and TikTok, but Jessa doesn't miss a beat. "Based on what?!"

"Based on he's too good looking."

"Oh, well. As long as this is evidence based assessment, then fine."

"Why would somebody that good looking want to bother with me? Seems sus."

Hope sits back down with a fresh glass of wine. "Maybe he just wants a friend in the neighborhood. Which you want too, by the way."

"Yes!" Jessa agrees. "Or he has eyes and sees how smoking hot you are and would be a fool not to want to get to know you."

"Either way you should talk to him," Hope says.

Jessa leers comically as she adds, "And by talk, we mean bang."

***

Clarey and Gabi reconvene on Monday morning since their Friday session ended up being mostly an unproductive gabfest. "How was your weekend?" Gabi asks.

"Fine," Clarey mumbles through a mouthful of scone, with sloppy clotted cream and jam sticky on her lips.

"That looks good," Gabi says as Clarey wipes her mouth. Clarey grumbles and shoves the plate away. "You doing okay?"

Clarey reflects a moment, then responds, "I'm fine. I don't know. I thought living alone would feel so good. And it *is* such a relief to be out of my old house and situation." Gabi's well-versed with Clarey's prior accommodations. No need to go there. "But I thought I'd have Roxy with me. And when I first made my offer, I assumed I'd be around other people. Now..."

"You need a buddy," Gabi says definitively. "Someone to pal around with, at least until you get settled in."

"My sisters are in Tacoma and my parents are in Lake Chelan." Clarey stares out the open balcony door as a siren zooms by on the street below. "All too far to grab coffee."

"Any other prospects?"

Clarey lifts her laptop from the table and moves to the chair by the balcony, curling into a comfy criss-cross applesauce. She might be getting a little too comfy with Gabi, but she's past worrying about it. "I wouldn't know where to start."

"There must be someone you'd like to spend time with besides your sisters and your ex."

Zack flashes through Clarey's mind. But how can she want to spend time with him when she doesn't even know him? Maybe it's just his muscles and deep blue eyes and tousled golden curls extending like rays of sunlight from his perfect –

"That's a hell of a look on your face," Gabi says. "Apparently, you have someone in mind."

Clarey shakes herself back to reality. She shouldn't be objectifying him. Is she really that shallow? She might be, yeah. Then again, he did bake her scones. "What if you think you might want to spend time with someone, but you're not sure?"

***

Clarey hits Save on a website update as Jessa's text pings in. *peach gin fizzes tonight*

What's in a peach gin fizz?

no idea, but i want one. That is such a Jessa answer. *see you at 8!*

That girl really does get everything she wants, doesn't she? Clarey clicks away from her text and checks the clock. Time enough to grab lunch. She grabs her wallet, but before she can head out, there's a knock at her door. She calls out, "Who is it?"

"It's Zack... Your neighbor?" he says, voice tinged with mirth. Of course, he's amused. Who else could it be in their locked building? She's an idiot.

"What do you need?" she asks through the door.

"I was hoping I could talk to you a minute. I wanted to run something by you." When Clarey says nothing, he adds, "Would you mind opening the door? Or I could meet you downstairs if you prefer."

"Stand back," she says suspiciously.

"Already am," he reassures her. She opens the door cautiously and finds him standing a very respectful ten feet away. "Hi," he says with a tentative smile.

"Hello," she replies non-committally. "What can I do for you?"

"Well, I had a thought. And this may sound crazy since we don't really know each other."

"We don't know each other at all," she corrects.

"Right. The thing is, I thought maybe we could change that."

"Meaning?"

"Since you and I are, let's face it, the only people in this building, which isn't changing anytime soon, we're kind of on a desert island here. So, I wondered if you might want to try being friends."

"Friends?"

"Yeah, it's where–"

"I know what friends are." In fact, she was just discussing it with Gabi. She looks over at her balcony door, now closed. Could he have heard her?

"Maybe it's out of left field, I don't know. But we're in each other's lives whether we like it or not." He pauses, letting her process the idea before adding, "And I personally wouldn't mind having a friend in the building."

Clarey's head plays the Law and Order dun-dun and lays out two separate, but equally important thoughts. On one hand, she's lonely, he's hot, and he actually seems kind of sweet. Wouldn't she be crazy to turn down an opportunity like this? On the other hand, he's been witness to two deeply humiliating moments in her life, the diarrhea and the pool. A one-two punch she'd prefer to forget. She'd be much more comfortable never seeing him again for that reason alone.

And most importantly, she doesn't know him. But when she points that out to him again, he replies, "Would you like to?"

An unexpected heat pools between her legs. This guy doesn't play fair. "I, uh…"

"Look, it's just practical. We're the only two in this whole building. We should look out for each other."

"You don't look like someone who needs someone looking out for them."

"I'll look out for you then. Does that sound so terrible?" he says, and something about the way he says it rolls through her. The heat returns. "Look, I'm between jobs right now, so I'm around a lot. I do help Herb out at the store, but other than that—"

"Herb?"

"Herb Goldfarb." Helping Mr. Goldfarb? When this guy was no more than a loitering barnacle, that was one thing. But this puts a whole new spin on things. He sounds sincere, but something about this isn't adding up.

She looks him up, then down, then back up again, sizing up the threat. "I'll think about it," she finally says before giving him a small wave and gently closing the door in his face.

***

Clarey didn't bring much from the kitchen at the house, but she did bring her SodaStream machine, thank goodness. And hopefully, Goldfarb's will come through with the peaches and gin. She could run to the grocery where she'd definitely find what she needs. She's got enough time. But she prefers supporting Mr. Goldfarb. Besides, he's right there. And he might be a source of premium intel.

The door jingles announcing her entry. "Hello, Mr. Goldfarb."

"Clarey, hello! Call me Herb. Please."

"I couldn't do that. I was taught to respect my elders."

"But Mr. Goldfarb is so formal. Are we not friends, young lady?"

"Okay, how about Mr. G then?" she says, crossing to the small produce section.

"Mr. G. I like that. Now, what can I help you with today?"

Clarey steps up to the register with two large peaches. "Got any gin back there?"

"Indeed I do." He walks to the back room and returns with a step stool. He places it in front of his alcohol section behind the register. For the first time, she notices how frail he seems as he sets the stool in place.

As he mounts the steps slowly and cautiously, Clarey dares a query. "So, you know Zack?"

"Do I know him?" Mr. G says, scanning the bottles. "Goodness me, I've known Zachary my whole life!"

Clarey chuckles at the slip of his tongue. "*His* whole life, you mean."

Mr. G clamps the bottle in his hand and descends as carefully as he went up. "What, dear?"

"Never mind," she says with a smile. No use embarrassing an old man.

He places the bottle on the counter and scans it. "I'll tell you what, you could do a lot worse for a neighbor. Zachary is an absolute angel. A guardian angel."

"Is that so?"

"There aren't a lot like him walking around, I can tell you that." He weighs the peaches and taps on the register. "$32.94."

***

Clarey watches Hope, who appears to have overdone it slightly, hold her drink in one hand and raise her other in a thumbs-up. "Two thumbs up for peach gin fizz."

"That's only one thumb," Clarey says. Hope uses her free hand to lift Jessa's free hand in the air and mold it into a thumbs-up, then puts her own thumb up again and grins.

"Never mind that," Jessa says. "Did he really call him a guardian angel?"

"Swear to God."

"That's laying it on a bit thick."

Hope is giggly and bleary-eyed, but she straightens up and attempts earnestness. "All that matters is he was sincere," she says. "Clarey, do you trust Mr. Goldfarb's?"

Clarey holds back a giggle at Hope. "Yes, I trust Mr. *Goldfarb's*."

Hope takes a sip and nods thoughtfully as if she's listening to a lecture on nuclear physics before freezing as if someone pressed pause on her brain. Then she looks at Clarey again and leans in close to computer. "And do you trust this guy? Zack?"

CHAPTER TEN

WHAT HAVE I DONE?

Zack has made a catastrophic mistake. He paces his living room concocting ways to take it back. Because he has to take it back before it's too late. Being buddies, or whatever he'd called it, with this woman is not an option. Who comes up with this stuff?

Only one buddy option exists, the same one it's always been. Herb needs him. And even if he doesn't, Zack needs Herb. Nothing's changed. That's his family, that's his focus. The only thing that matters. After all this time, more time than he ever could have imagined when he made that first decision to step in, an eternity of recommitting day after day, year after year, to one family. And now, one frail, old man. A lifetime of immeasurable sacrifice and singular purpose. Herb's the reason he's here. No one else matters. There's no room for anyone else.

There has never been room for anyone else.

There have been plenty of others along the way, of course, to meet certain kinds of needs. Living the life he's lived, in the body he's lived it in, has presented more than his fair share of opportunities. Fleeting encounters to take the edge off, to stave off the loneliness for a night or day. But Zack always made sure either he or they were gone by the time the sun came up. No one ever got close. No one but Herb and his family and every generation before, for all this time. That's been enough. No one has even been *close* to close in as long as he can remember, and he remembers a pretty damn long time. And for good reason. Doing this is unprecedented stupidity.

What if she says yes? That can't happen. The plane of existence does not exist where he can get close to this woman. This mesmerizing woman with the fiery curls, the adorable blush, and the killer curves he would love nothing more than to sink into, in more ways than one. This Clarey. What has she done to him?

Zack stares out the window, imagining her marching out the front door like he's watched her do so many times already. Always with so much intention. Clarey's not a stroller. Unlike him. He's spent most of his life quietly strolling in and out of places and situations, always observing, always alert, but seldom engaging and never attracting any more attention than he wanted. Drawing focus when needed, but mostly content to watch.

That's exactly how he strolled into the pool that night a week ago. And he could have watched *that* show forever, if she hadn't been so embarrassed. She was a feast for his eyes after a long, self-imposed famine. It was, in fact, only a few seconds, but the way her cheeks reddened captivated him even more than the delicious naked breasts that burst out of the water like a breaching mermaid, glistening with a million tiny droplets he would have gladly licked from her body. Her fleshy softness triggered his most hedonistic impulses, but the sweetness of her expression as her unadulterated joy melted into abject humiliation touched something much deeper in him. His humanity – such as it was.

Suddenly, he wanted to see more. Of her body, not that there was much more to see, and of her heart. When he saw her choose to shop at Goldfarb's over the grocery store, he recognized it for what it was. An act of kindness. And when she saw him on the rooftop ledge, the genuine panic on her face, and the concern behind it, sliced through him. Probably anyone would react the same way in such a moment, misunderstanding or not, but he'd never let anyone close enough to feel the remorse that followed the worry he'd caused. He'd never let anyone else close enough to care. Until Clarey. He wants to touch her, yes. But more than that, he wants to know her.

Zack teeters on a slope so slippery he should be wearing skis. A light flirtation. An embarrassing mishap. A few scones and a casual invitation. The next thing he knows, they'll be drinking wine and Netflix and chilling – or whatever the kids do now – then going for long walks in the park and picking out rings and what the actual fuck? Is this woman really as special as she seems? More likely she's just the right person at the right time, catching him in a moment of weakness. Everything else – everyone else – has always come so easily to Zack. But not Clarey. Maybe that's why she's so damned irresistible that he keeps making these wildly unhinged decisions. Maybe something in him needs the challenge. Or maybe he's finally willing to engage. Except he can't, remember?

In any case, something has broken, and he better fix it fast. And the place to start is by rescinding that ridiculous invitation, which she probably won't accept anyway because she detests him, but better safe than sorry. He'll go down there now and apologize. He'll say he was drunk and lonely, and that he's prone to making bad decisions when he drinks. In reality, he hadn't had a drop, but he'll convince her. For her own good. Let her think the worst of him. Let her think he's a mess, too much trouble, and she's better off staying away from him. All true.

"Dammit," he mutters. In an unfettered moment of frustration, he kicks a carefully stacked pile of lumber and the boards explode through the room like a bomb. The beams spread into a perfect arch in every direction, moving in what almost seems like slow motion. Beams crash against the ceiling and wall with monstrous impact. The ones kicked into the floor embed themselves into the floor in a way that will definitely mean new flooring. Great. When the last of the wood finally settles, splintering into almost every surface, the boards have scattered into a sprawling mountain of wooden refuse across his dining room, now more pulp than lumber.

He surveys the damage of his fleeting loss of temper. What a mess. Money and time he's got. What else is he going to do with himself? But he hates the waste. Then he hears the real problem.

"What was that?" Clarey says behind him.

Oh. Fuck.

Zack closes his eyes a moment and tries to recenter himself, quickly rushing through a laundry list of excuses. He turns and puts on a smile. "Clarey, hi."

"What did I just see?"

Can he laugh it off? Or play dumb? Maybe she didn't see anything really. "I don't know, what did you see?"

Clarey looks slowly around the room, at the scattered shards that only moments ago were actual pieces of usable lumber. "You kicked that lumber and it exploded like a sandcastle."

Right. She saw everything. This is a problem. He could make her forget, but the resulting use of his active powers would trigger the alarms yon high, so that's out. He could get his secret god bestie Xara to do it, but he'd have to get her here first, and Clarey isn't going to sit still long enough for him to summon her. Besides, he's not entirely sure he wants her to forget. Weird.

He tries the indirect approach. "It's not really what you think. It probably looked like—"

"No, I know what I saw. How did you do that?"

"I, um...." This is not going how he would have liked. Change of tack is called for. How about deflection? "How did you get in here?"

"I knocked and the door pushed open."

This is working. He keeps going. "So you just walked in?"

"I didn't so much walk in as, like I said, I simply knocked, and the door pushed open. But—"

If he didn't close his door properly, that's a problem, too. But that's a problem for tomorrow's Zack. Today's Zack has got a very large fish of his own to fry at the moment. "You know, this isn't a public space. You can't just waltz in here like it's your living room."

She pauses with a stunned look on her face, then shifts into attack mode. "I didn't waltz in anywhere. The door was open. I can't help it if you didn't bother closing the damn thing!"

She's falling for it. With any luck, he can derail this whole thing and shuffle her out the door without another word about what actually happened. And she'll be mad and they'll be finished before they even began and he can go back to his recluse ways. The only way. "Well, if you don't mind, I have things to do that don't involve random interlopers in my house."

"So now I'm the interloper! Ha, that's rich!" He marches her toward the door as she speaks and he nearly manages to close the door on her. "Fine, I'll go," she says as she shuffles out, but at the last possible second, she puts on the break and spins around. "But first tell me, what are you?"

Zack feels himself slam into the words like a brick wall. This close. He was this close to getting out of this clean. If he had managed to close that door on her, she would have left confused and frustrated, sure she saw something impossible, but incapable of explaining it. Then, by morning, that certainty would have faded in brightness a tad, as it would each day until it was just some weird thing that happened that she can't quite remember. And as long as he dodged her for a few days, by the next time they crossed paths, she'd have decided she was better off without him and would have left the mystery where it belonged, in the unsolved case file. Now, instead, he is face-to-face once again with a choice he'd really rather not make.

"I saw you," she says. "Kick that wood. I saw what happened." She pauses and he allows himself a split second of reflection, desperately seeking a solution that involves anything but the truth. Until she says, "And I saw you lifting weights, and you were lifting twice what a normal guy can do. Without breaking a sweat." Oh boy, she noticed that, did she? Okay, harder to explain two things than one. "And those scones were like something from heaven. No normal guy can make scones like that."

Well, the scones were just his mad baking skills, so she was wrong there. But the other two were fair enough. "Clarey..."

Clarey searches his face for an answer. "Are you a circus strong man? Except no, that doesn't explain the baking?" She pauses and thinks a moment. "Maybe like a super spy with a super formula that makes you—" A super spy? Well, this woman certainly has quite an imagination. But is it big enough for the truth?

"Clarey, I'm a god," Zack finally blurts out. It wasn't what he had intended. The truth has a way of breaking most people, which is why he's only told it a handful of times outside Herb's family in all these thousands of years. And every other time, he got Xara to take it away within a day. But right now, in this moment, he wants Clarey to know the truth, even if she hates it. Even if she doesn't believe it, which is more likely.

She parses the words carefully before repeating them. "A god?"

"Yes," Zack says matter-of-factly.

"As in eternal, superpowered being sort of thing?" She says the words as if she's amused, but Zack senses something darker behind them.

"Something like that," he replies evenly.

Clarey stares at Zack for a long, excruciating minute of absolute silence, then turns and walks away. Well, that's one way to put an end to this.

***

Zack watches Xara, the dark-haired beauty that haunts his life like the perfect angel she most assuredly is not, as she peers out the window from his barely assembled living room. "She was never going to believe you. You knew that," she says, her boredom hyped up to maximum power for effect.

Xara's right. It was the only response possible. The only thing Clarey was ever going to say was nothing. Well, she could have screamed and called him a liar and thrown things. This was better than that option, all things considered. Silent disbelief is as good a variant as he could hope for, really. But it was always going to be disbelief of some kind. Still, Zack never likes admitting Xara's right about anything. "Will you please get away from the window?" Zack replies. "And close the balcony doors. I don't want her hearing you. She's upset enough."

Xara tosses her long, raven hair over her shoulder in an unnecessarily dramatic gesture, the only kind she ever makes, before rolling her eyes and closing the doors. "Why are you so concerned with that little mouse anyway?"

"That's my business."

She looks at him for a long moment, giving him time to make up his mind. "So, do you want me to make her forget? Or not?"

***

"What have I done?" Zack plops onto Herb's couch and drops his face to his hands.

"You've told the truth for once. Is that so terrible?" Herb says, easing himself back in his seat. Slowly, he lifts first one leg, then the other, onto the ottoman.

"I don't know," Zack replies without looking up.

"Have you called your friend in? To make her forget?"

"Not yet." Zack rethinks and rephrases his answer. "I mean, I did, but I didn't have her do it in the end. I don't want to for some reason."

"Well, then, maybe you should try talking to Clarey. Maybe you can make a friend." Herb pats his lap and grunts with approval. "Like I have."

Zack's too distracted to process what Herb's said. "A friend? Is that what we're calling it?" He rubs his temple and stairs at the ground. "Not a huge fucking mistake?"

"Why, hello there," Herb coos gently as an unexpected vibrating sound permeates Zack's thick fog of regret. He lifts his eyes to find Herb holding a tiny black cat with one white tuft at its chest.

"What is that?"

"It rather looks like a cat, don't you think?"

"Why is it on your lap? Where did it come from?"

"He's been hanging around the back a couple of days now. I gave him some water, but no food at first. I wanted him to find his way home." The cat curls into a loud, purring ball and begins the lengthy process of making biscuits on Herb's leg. "But it seems he might have done that already."

"You can't keep him."

"Can't I? I'll see if he's chipped and put up signs around town, but if no one claims him...." Herb scratches the soft fur ridges of the cat's head, and the cat responds by head butting his hand and turning up the volume on his purrs. Zack watches the old man dote on the furry creature and smiles despite himself. Herb looks up at him. "Everyone needs a friend, Zachary."

"You're my friend."

"After all this time, don't you deserve something more than a crotchety septuagenarian with arthritis and a bad back to keep you company?"

"I've got Xara."

"So, you are going back to that life then?" Herb waits patiently for Zack to offer a response, but none comes. "Well, maybe while you're evaluating, you could try to make Clarey understand."

"It's not fair to her."

"What will you do when I'm gone?"

Zack looks from the cat to Herb in shock. "Don't say that."

"But you need to think about it. Because it's coming. Ever since we lost David, you've refused to acknowledge how things have changed. How things will change for you." Zack wanders to the small kitchen and puts away some dishes in the drainer. Anything to avoid this conversation, but Herb persists. "What will you do?"

Zack slumps and finally looks back at Herb. "I don't know. But it can't be this. It can't be Clarey."

"Why not?"

"You know why not."

"Things change."

"It will hurt her too much. I don't want to hurt her."

"Of course you don't." When Zack comes over to pet the cat in Herb's lap, Herb clenches his wrist. "But maybe she's not the only one you're worried about." Zack pulls away, searching for another distraction. "You've looked after me, after all of us, for so long. You don't know anything else. Maybe it's time to consider what looking after yourself might look like."

Zack brings a dirty teacup to the sink. "I do. I watch out for myself."

"Watch out, yes. But when was the last time you *took care* of yourself?" Herb says, running his hand around the furry loop of the purring cat's curled body.

"I don't need—"

Herb cuts him off. "When was the last time you allowed yourself to really live?"

CHAPTER ELEVEN

FACT FINDING

HOPE'S BURIED WITH WORK and kids all day and Jessa's roaming around on some sort of geo-scavenger hunt thing, so Clarey reluctantly settles for a group chat.

Jessa: *maybe he's telling the truth you did say he looks like thor*

Hope: *Not helpful.*

Hope: *Honey, does he seem mentally ill?*

Clarey: *Think I'm qualified to assess that?*

Hope: *Okay, do you think he's a danger to himself or others?*

Clarey: *No, I think he's a liar.*

Jessa: *but he gets points for creativity*

Hope: *Jessa, can you stop for one minute and try to help?*

Jessa: *i'm lightening the mood. that's helping*

Hope: *Who is it helping exactly?*

Jessa: *you may find this genuinely hard to believe but not everyone has that giant stick up their asses*

Jessa: *some people actually like to laugh*

Hope: *Is that so? And do those people pay bills? Or help around the house? Or, I don't know, help their goddamn sisters get through the day with two kids bouncing off the walls while they're talking patients off depression ledges all freaking day long????????*

Clarey: *Um, guys, maybe I should let you both go.*

They both object and insist they're there to help, but it's clear that whatever answers Clarey finds won't come from her sisters. They might be divine inspiration, but they're hardly diviners of the truth. After a little more back and forth, she cuts them off and promises to touch base later. She needs some time to think.

Meanwhile, all this Zack stuff has nearly made her forget about Roxy. When is she coming home? Clarey pulls out her phone and reviews her text thread. Derek's last missive said Lydia's father was stable, so hopefully that means they'll be home soon. She taps out a message, forcing herself to politely ask about Bob, Lydia's dad, before forging on to the only thing she really cares about at this point.

He's better. They might release him tomorrow, fingers crossed.

Getting out of the hospital sounds promising. Getting out of the hospital sounds like a good sign it's time to go home. *Great to hear,* she types. *And how's Roxy?*

Derek responds with the cutest photo ever of her sweet, chunky girl. She's looking up at the camera with her droopy eyes and a tennis ball fully lodged in her jowl, her little underbite on proud display. God, she misses that dog. It's time to bite the bullet and be direct. *So when will you be home?*

Not sure. Judith may need help when Bob comes home.

These shenanigans are hammering on Clarey's last nerve.

Good thing we're all working remotely these days, Derek continues. *We can stay as long as we need to.*

The unmitigated gall of this mofo. This mofo who has her dog. She needs to put her foot down right freaking now. Roxy is her dog and it's time to stop putting up with this crap.

Thanks for being so understanding, Clarey.

Thanking her? He's thanking her? After stealing her dog. So typical. Screw him! *Of course,* she types with a deep sigh.

***

Clarey finishes her only meeting of the day, with the women and family care facility, and closes her laptop. The meeting went well, with her clients borderline rhapsodizing about the results of their work together. With the help of McGill Consulting, they've taken their failing organization on the verge of closure a year ago and turned it around to a financially sound operation poised to end their fiscal year in the black, with only a tiny, hopefully brief reduction in services. A remarkable success, which will look great in a testimonial on her website, and make for an excellent case study. The only downside, her work with them is nearly done. She really needs to find more clients. When that contract ends this month, she'll only have two left. Grandma's money will sustain her a while, but not forever.

In the meantime, she could use a distraction to keep her busy. Something beside the six-foot-two, walking, talking, scone-baking distraction downstairs. Perhaps a visit to Goldfarb's. Some spicy Korean chips or Russian candies might be the inspiration she needs.

The door jingles as she enters, and Clarey's delighted to spot two others in the shop combing through the Asian foods. While Mr. G's business is officially none of hers, his apparent lack of customers has nonetheless rankled Clarey's propensity for worry. Mr. G wheels out a hand truck stacked with boxes, but catches his foot on a protruding push broom and stumbles. Clarey jumps to steady him and catch the boxes. She manages to keep him upright, but the top box tumbles to the ground, spilling open. "I'll get it," she offers as the couple approaches the counter with an armful of Indian fare, ready to check out.

"Thank you, my dear," he says once they're gone. "You're very kind."

"Glad I could help."

"You're a good girl. But do me a favor, will you? Don't tell Zachary about this." Mr. G grabs the hand truck and pushes it towards the back wall to unload. "He's always after me to slow down, and he would make far too big a deal of a little stumble."

"You don't want to slow down?"

"And what would I do with myself then? It's important to stay busy. Bring that cutter, will you?"

Clarey walks over with the box cutter and slices open the box for Mr. G. "I agree, it is important to stay busy," she says, following his cue and unloading cans onto the shelf. "But you need rest as well."

"What's the expression? I'll sleep when I'm dead?"

Clarey laughs. "That's a terrible expression." She pulls the now empty box off the stack and flattens it. She slices open the next box. "Mr. G, what if you had some help? So you could take at least little more time off."

"I can't really afford to hire anyone new at the moment. Zachary helps me. He comes every day for a couple hours. But I don't want him spending all his time with an old man in a tiny shop, bathed in the pallor of fluorescent lighting." As Clarey recalls, he didn't look so bad in that lighting. But never mind.

"How about another helper? One you don't have to pay?"

***

Gabi is unusually listless when they hop on their call the next day. "Fair warning. I'm grumpy today," she announces.

"Honestly, same," Clarey says, adjusting her camera and screen. "Why? What's going on?"

"Well, I still don't have my dog for one thing."

"Still?"

"He swears they'll be back by next week," Clarey grumbles.

"You need to black ops this thing for real." Gabi has long advocated for a superspy-style rescue mission, but Clarey hasn't been able to bring herself to be the bad guy.

"If they were nearby, maybe. But I can't shake the feeling that driving the twelve-hour roundtrip to claim my dog would make me the petty villain in this scenario. She's perfectly safe, after all, with people who love her." Besides, she reminds herself, Roxy is providing much needed comfort to the family in their time of need. "I can wait a little longer." Clarey sags with the weight of the lonely dog moms everywhere before adding, "I guess."

Gabi gives a sympathetic frown. "Well, what about your mystery buddy prospect? Do you have someone fun around to distract you?"

Someone like the guy who claimed he was a god? Is that fun? There was definitely something strange about him. No one should be that strong. Or bake that well – though she's beginning to think the baking is unrelated. But a god? That's pushing the bounds of even Clarey's very liberal imagination. "Ugh, let's not go there. What's up with you?"

Gabi's eyes puddle with barely restrained emotion and she grabs a tissue she's kept at hand. The glimmer of vulnerability unsettles Clarey. Gabi is always the light one, full of mirth. She reminds her of Jessa in that respect. But she also takes zero bull-shit. Nothing shakes her. "My wedding's canceled," she sobs.

"No! You and Dana?"

"Not the marriage. Just the wedding. My venue had a water-line break overnight and it flooded everything. They're canceling all their events for the next two months while they clean out and rebuild."

"So you reschedule. It will mean even more when the time comes."

"I don't want to reschedule for a year from now," Gabi pouts. "I want to marry her now. I don't need the whole big shindig, but I want to stand up in front of my favorite people in the world and declare my love and make it freaking official. Is that too much to ask?" She wipes at a sudden streak of tears.

"Absolutely not," Clarey says. This is not how this meeting was supposed to go. They were supposed to be planning the final details on the upcoming full-team work session, not com-miserating about the impossibilities of love and other monsters. Focus. "Another venue?"

"Every outdoor venue is booked solid for months. I even researched every park in the city. All booked."

"Backyard?"

"Unfortunately, my real estate guru love Dana, in her infinite wisdom, sold her house and moved into my tiny apartment while we look for a place together. So we could go in with an all-cash offer. And my bestie Sarah, the only other person I could ask, is in the middle of redoing her backyard. She's basically living in a construction zone for at least six weeks. Maybe longer."

That sounds familiar. "Well, don't lose hope. Something will work out. You'll see. There's always hope." She gives Gabi a reassuring smile, but a rattle of disbelief rumbles through her.

Clarey moved here to start a new, independent life, after all. She's been split from Derek for ages, but she hasn't really been alone. She wants that. She's been craving that. Time to be herself, find herself. Yes, that's what she wants. The last thing she needs is some dude coming into her life and messing her up again. Especially a liar. No matter how strong and anatomically perfect. Or dangerously charming. Or disarmingly sweet. Not to mention those dimples. Damn him.

***

Goldfarb's is busier than Clarey expected during her first afternoon shift. The customers don't come in droves, but they do dribble in and out one and two at a time keeping her sufficiently busy. It had always seemed so empty when she stopped in before, she'd worried how Mr. G was going to make it, but she's beginning to see what a special place he holds in the community. Mr. G shows her the register, then accepts her help restocking the drinks cooler while he stands at the counter sorting receipts.

A small, soft body hurls itself against Clarey's leg when she stoops to fill the lowest shelf. A tiny black cat mews as she scratches him behind the ear before scooping the bundle of fur into her arms.

"Noisy little thing, isn't he?"

"Who is this sweet boy?"

"Haven't decided yet. I'm leaning toward something literary."

Clarey glides her finger under the cat's chin and he begins to purr. "Shakespeare? Dickens? Chandler?"

"Dickens! Now that's an idea. I was thinking about Homer, as a tribute to Zack."

"How would that be a tribute to Zack?"

"Just a little joke," he chuckles, not looking up from his work.

Clarey releases the cat and returns to her stocking. "So, you've known Zack a long time, huh?" Clarey asks, hungry for any kernel of info about her too hot for comfort neighbor and his bs story.

"I'm not sure anyone will ever fully know Zachary. But I go back with him farther than anyone else certainly." It's an elliptical response, but Clarey senses truth behind it.

"You must have missed him when he was gone."

"I always miss him when he goes. But he has to keep moving, I understand."

There's a whole chunk of this story missing. "Why? Is he in the military?"

"He was once, briefly. I suppose Zachary's done just about everything once. But not anymore."

"So how long has it been since you last saw him?"

"You know, I can't remember. Time gets fuzzy in my old brain. Yesterday could be a year and fifty years ago seems like yesterday. A year? Five years? Ten? But he never forgets. He always comes back to check on me."

The timeline doesn't add up. Zack can't be much older than she is. In his thirties probably? Maybe she needs to take another tack. "How old was he when you met him?"

"Now, that's a good question," he says. "I don't really know, come to think of it. I was just a lad myself. But Mama was so in love with him. Well, you can see why."

A lad? Mr. G is in his seventies at least. His definition of a lad and hers must be very different. The entry door jingles and Mr. G turns to greet his customers, leaving Clarey to wrestle with a math problem even Good Will Hunting couldn't solve.

When Mr. G finally returns to their conversation, it's nearly time for her to leave. She drops her last flattened box on the stack and reaches for the sweater she placed on the stool. He takes her by the arm and looks her square in the eye. It's as if he's turned a corner and entered a new neighborhood entirely. He's not vague or distant. He's not reminiscing or absentmindedly wandering through memories while putting out boxes of chili from Chile. "May I say one thing?" Clarey looks at him seriously and waits for him to assemble his courage for whatever this is. "Zachary isn't a liar," he finally says. "He obscures things sometimes to make his way in this world. But what he's told you is true."

Wait, does he actually know what Zack told her? Would Zack have told him? Or has he fed Mr. G some kind of crazy lie as well? Surely, Mr. G is too smart to believe that madness. Unless Mr. G is losing touch with reality. She doesn't want to think such a thing, but isn't it more probable than the story Zack's peddling? Fear jabs at her insides. "What do you think he told me?" she says cautiously.

Mr. G gives a compassionate smile and says, "About himself. About who he really is. What he really is."

Mr. G keeps saying things that make no sense. It's a terrible thought, but if he's failing, maybe Zack's been taking advantage of him, manipulating him to believe all kinds of crazy things. That doesn't ring true – about either of them – but the alternative is literally impossible.

"Mr. G, I'm sorry. I don't mean any disrespect, but all this, I mean, it can't be true."

Mr. G clasps Clarey's hand in his own worn, but warm hands. "If there's one thing I've learned in all these years, the only thing that can't be true is the thing you refuse to accept."

***

After another day of radio silence, the paper airplane glides as smoothly onto her balcony as a figure skater taking to the ice. Clarey spots it immediately because she's been staring out the balcony doors like a hypnotized zombie for-approximately-ever. She leaves it where it lies, shooting mental fireballs in its direction, wondering if the telekinetic powers she always dreamed of as a kid might kick in with enough determination. She tried extensively as a child to bend spoons and float her stuffed animals with her mind, to no avail, but maybe she didn't have the right motivation then. Maybe all she really needed was a sufficient well of hard-earned bitterness and rage to trigger the on-switch. She glares as fiercely as she can at the plane, but it stubbornly refuses to ignite.

Fine. She crawls off the floor where she'd flopped herself hours earlier and collects the intruder from its magically aimed spot pointing directly at the center floorplate where the two doors meet when closed. How does he do that? For a fleeting second, Clarey considers opening it, indulging the tiny glimmer in her that still wants to believe he was real and not some pathetic fever dream borne of loneliness. But then the 99.9874% sensible portion retakes control. She drops it from a foot away and watches it fly itself straight into the recycling bin where it belongs.

Honestly, he wasn't even worth that much effort. The fact that he made her climb all the way up from her admittedly very uncomfortable, but still emotionally satisfying slouch on the floor to throw out his litter seemed the ultimate indignity. If only she could get her telekinesis up and running. A nice, destructive superpower would be just the thing to cheer her up no end.

Wait, superpowers. Gods must have powers, right? Like, what's the point of being a god if you can't do stuff mere mortals can't? If *he* – she loathes even thinking his name anymore – is a so-called god or whatever, shouldn't he have powers? Maybe she should call him on it. Then, when he can't produce, he'll have no choice but to confess to his lies. Exactly what good that will actually do escapes her, but at the very least, seeing him exposed... or no, that's not the right word. But seeing him squirm under the weight of his own humiliation should be satisfying. Turnabout is fair play, after all, and he's certainly seen her in enough compromising positions.

***

Clarey pounds on the door like the FBI with a warrant, intent on knocking it down next. Zack quickly yanks the door open with a hopeful glint in his eye. His hope seems unwarranted given the distinctively aggressive "I'm not screwing around here" nature of her knock. If he had any decency, he'd be answering the door with his head hung in shame, or at least have the courtesy to act blasé like nothing happened. This needy, hopeful vibe is throwing Clarey off. That's probably his plan. Tricky bastard.

"You got my message," he says in a half statement, half question.

"No, but my trash did. It says hi, by the way."

Zack hangs his head. That's better. "Do you want to come in?" he asks.

"Absolutely not. But I do have a question."

"Okay..."

"Do you have powers? Like, god powers?"

Zack takes a long, slow breath that sends his pectoral muscles pushing through his T-shirt in way that can't possibly be within the rules. Finally, he says, "Yes, I do."

"Like what?"

"It's complicated." He pauses dramatically, no doubt conjuring up a nice, juicy ad lib in case he has to go through with this. But if he thinks Clarey's letting him off the hook without hearing it, he's very much mistaken. He continues, "I have what you could think about as passive powers and active powers. Passive powers are the kinds of things that make my life possible here. They make things go the way I want, give me a sort of ease in the physical world. To be seen or not seen, as I choose. To accumulate the resources and knowledge I need to live and enjoy life. To be successful in my endeavors."

She's not impressed. "So basically, you're lucky?" Even as she asks, Clarey feels her body tightening. What was previously just a weird, upsetting lie in her mind grows with each word Zack says. If he had admitted the truth, maybe she could have gotten over it. But the further he digs in, the more she wants to dig in as well. Maybe other girls have bought into this baloney, but she's not falling for his gorgeous, muscly, dimply, sweet as pie act. Not today, Mister!

"I suppose that's one way to look at it," he says. "But on a sort of cosmic scale. And, of course, immortality."

"Oh, right. Of course," Clarey snarks with as much venom as her vocal cords can vibrate. Immortality. This guy's really going all in, huh? "Unfortunately, those are all awfully hard to demonstrate, aren't they?"

Zack pulls his door open wider. "Clarey, please come in. We can talk about this."

Clarey steps backward and crosses her arms. "What about your so-called active powers?"

Zack sighs deeply. She's got him. She's indulged him too long, but there's no way he can keep up this charade. "My greatest strengths are health and prosperity. I can heal and I can bless. But I can also, I guess you'd call it transport, and transmogrify. Among other things."

"Transmogrify? Did you pull that crap out of your hat? Or have you been planning this awhile?"

"I'm telling you the truth, Red."

"Don't you dare call me Red! You don't know me!" Clarey's whole body overheats, and not in the fun, sexy way. Her fury is reaching its boiling point and it's so much higher than she ever imagined it could be. The nerve of this dude. "Okay, transmogrify something. Turn that chair into a banana. Or a goat."

"I can change myself, not objects."

"Then turn yourself into a goat."

"I can't."

"Ooh, shocker!" she says. "What's the problem? Is your superpower battery pack recharging?"

"I'm not allowed to use my active powers."

This is quite a story he's concocted. Not allowed by whom? She's tempted to ask just for the fun of it, but she ain't buying what he's selling, and it's time to close this deal on her terms. "Well, that's convenient, isn't it?" Clarey sneers.

"Actually, it's pretty damned inconvenient at the moment."

It's unnerving how sincere he sounds at every turn. Maybe he actually believes this stuff like Hope said? More likely he's a sociopath, which is pretty much what Clarey herself said when he first brought her those damn cranberry-orange scones. And clotted cream? Only a very smooth sociopath would think of the clotted cream. She should have listened to her instincts then. But she refuses to be taken in now. "Goodbye, Zack."

CHAPTER TWELVE

TESTING, TESTING... 1, 2, 3

ZACK INSERTS THE PIN at 1,000 pounds, the highest weight setting on the machine, then positions himself into the seat and places his legs against the plate. He completes his first set of ten reps, pauses only a moment, then goes on. And on. And on. Working out feels pretty pointless at the moment. It's certainly not providing the meditative escape he usually counts on, but he's got to keep himself busy somehow. Herb kicked him out after a couple of hours morosely sitting around the shop scaring off customers. He's replaced the lumber for the countertops and fixed the floor where he damaged it, but he needs a break from all that.

When Clarey emerges from the elevator, he freezes, his legs still extended in a full press. He holds his breath, hoping against hope that she'll wave or even nod, or better yet, open the door and announce that she believes him and all is forgiven. After thousands of years among humans, he knows their nature too well to think she'll come around that easily. He's told her what amounts to an impossible story. But wishes come cheap, so he crosses his fingers and waits.

She catches sight of him and stops. Her jaw drops as if to say something – yes, say something! Anything! But she closes her mouth and marches out the front door. Zack slowly relaxes his legs and lowers the press to resting position, watching her walk past the outside window. But before she reaches the end of the building, she stops, reverses direction, and heads back to the entrance. Zack holds his breath as she enters and pauses outside the glass door to the gym. She looks at him. He looks at her. Then she yanks the door open.

"Hi," he says hopefully, a tiny balloon inflating in his chest.

Clarey cuts to the chase. "Why do you work out?" As he processes her question, she appears to do the same, adding, "I mean, you're a god, right? Presumably you're naturally buff or whatever?"

Zack swings his legs off the machine and shrugs his answer. It does pretty much come with the territory.

She rolls her eyes and repeats the question. "So why bother working out?"

Zack stands and Clarey flinches, stepping backward. He studies the floor a moment, listening to the quiet hum of the overhead lights. The car passing outside. The plane overhead. The couple chatting at the corner, waiting for the light. The way Clarey's throat clicks with tension as she awaits his response. All the things he normally tries to turn down. "It helps me drown out the noise. This world is a very noisy place for someone like me. There's a lot of stimulation. Exercise helps me quiet it. Gives me a stillness that makes it easier."

Something passes over Clarey's face. A glimmer of what looks like empathy, which for one glorious second he dares hope is a precursor to something even more precious – belief. But the next second, it's gone. Her jaw tightens. "Stillness," she says, apparently mulling over the word.

"Also, it's what people expect someone like me to do," he adds. "Reinforces the illusion."

"The illusion. Yeah," Clarey says before sighing and turning to go.

***

Zack slides on his goggles and dives gracefully into the water before emerging and beginning his laps. He pushes himself hard, viciously slicing through the water with every stroke, determined to find the stillness that comes only when everything else in the world ceases. The deeply physical acts that engage his body so entirely he must, of necessity, disengage his brain. Running. Lifting. Swimming. Sex. The last of these is the most fun, but the least indulged, because it's also the most dangerous. The one that comes with the greatest risk of a connection he's never dared sustain beyond a night. A connection that's never been worth either the logistical complications or the emotional labor.

In any case, water is the best place to find the stillness. Water makes him feel closest to home. Water feels eternal. And so he pushes through, allowing the vastness to reveal itself in each stroke as he blots out not only the noise, but the pain of his monumental mistakes. Like telling Clarey the truth. The fact that she doesn't seem to believe him does almost nothing to soothe the catastrophic ache of knowing she's out there somewhere right now thinking of him as a creep. Why this should irk him so much, he doesn't know. He's been a creep hundreds of times, thousands maybe, over the course of his very long lifetime. Why should this particular woman bother him so?

When he finally tires, he slows his paces, but as he eases up to the end of the pool, it's not the answer that appears. He stands in the shallow end and pulls off his goggles rubbing his eyes, and only when he finally cracks them open does he see her feet. His gaze travels up her body to her face, and bewitching as she is, her expression – along with her tightly crossed arms – make it clear she did not come to play. Or swim, for that matter.

"Clarey," he says, still blinking.

"How do you pay for stuff?"

Zack tilts his ear sideways, tapping out water. "Sorry, what?"

"Where do you get your money? Did you really do all those jobs?"

"I work. I invest. And yes."

"You're not working now."

"Things have a way of going the way I want them to. My work tends to be lucrative when I need it to be. And I made some very good investments a long time ago."

"When?"

"About a hundred years ago."

Clarey chokes out an annoyed chuckle. "You really are sticking with this, huh?" She rolls her pursed lips around, wrestling with her words. Finally, she resumes her line of questioning. "So, what? You're rich?"

"As you said, I'm very lucky." Zack climbs out of the pool and grabs his towel.

"Then why work at all?" she asks before averting her eyes, apparently uncomfortable being near him in this relative state of undress.

"Another word for work is occupation. I have a lot of time on my hands. Learning things, doing things, is a good way to fill it." He brushes the last of the water off his sides and yanks his T-shirt over his head. Hopefully she'll look at him now. Somehow it hurts when she looks away.

"And you move around so much because...?"

"It's safer to keep moving. To keep to myself. Building real relationships isn't something I get to do most of the time." Zack regrets his words as soon as they're out. They're true enough, and maybe even what she needs to hear in the moment. To understand. But he wishes he'd said the other thing anyway. The thing about how eventually people start to notice that they're getting older and he's not. That's true too – at least when he lingers in a life or job too long – and it wouldn't hurt her nearly as much. She'd be sure he was lying, but at least it wouldn't imply he was lying about the single most true thing he's ever told anyone. Now she'll just think he said it to get rid of her.

Somehow, he's managed to choose the most honest and most hurtful option at his disposal. Zack could pour the whole pool in his ear and it wouldn't be enough water to block out the pain in her voice when she almost whimpers, "Yeah..." She moves slowly toward the door, saying nothing.

"Clarey," he calls out. She doesn't look up, but she pauses at the door while he approaches her. "Why are you giving me so many chances?"

She doesn't turn around, but she also doesn't move. He waits, and finally she says, "What?"

As lovely as her bright red curls are in the overhead light from the street, he chances it to walk around and face her. Her face is up, but her eyes are down, avoiding his. Avoiding whatever insight he's about to offer, though she could have just walked out. She's willing to listen, which is more than he could have hoped for mere minutes ago. When he speaks, he does so with care. "You keep coming back. You keep giving me a chance. Why?"

She forces herself to look him in the eye. "I'm giving you a chance to come clean."

There's about a 99% chance what he's about to say is going to go terribly wrong and he'll be calling Xara to make her forget by tonight. But with that 1% chance hanging there, just out of reach, he goes for it. "If you want to believe..." He pauses, unsure what to say. What words will bring her around? What words will open the heart of this beautiful woman he's barely met, yet somehow desperately wants to know? "I can make you believe. Give me a chance."

She stares at him, and for a brief, brilliant moment, he sees her flicker. He sees her flirt with the notion of believing him. But even before he can name the light in her eyes as hope, it's gone. She huffs out a quiet puff of disbelief, pushes past him, and walks out the door.

***

Zack is poised atop his ladder screwing in the last bulb in his newly installed light fixture when Xara's telltale shimmer sounds. The air currents shift such that he knows without looking that she's right in front of the balcony doors. "Not so close to the balcony, please, Xara," he says as he tightens the bulb.

"No one's out there this time of night."

"Why do you do this to me?" he says as he climbs down.

"Because it's so much fun, darling. Besides, you wouldn't want your little mouse to see me coming and going, would you?" She steps onto the balcony. "Oh, speak of the rodent," she says under her breath. And then, a little louder, "Lovely evening, isn't it?" She steps back inside, looks at him sheepishly, or as sheepishly as her wicked glee will allow, and says with a pout, "Oops."

"Dammit, Xara!" Zack rushes behind her and closes the doors. "She saw you?"

"And she looked none too pleased, I must say."

"You did that on purpose."

"Believe it or not, I didn't. Just a lucky happenstance."

If there were ever any chance of Clarey forgiving him, it's over now. She already thinks he's a liar and a creep. Now she can add womanizer to the list. If Clarey assumes the worst about Xara, he's lost. And why wouldn't she? In a normal world where normal things happen, it would be completely reasonable to assume Zack and Xara were sleeping together. And for better or worse, Clarey lives in the normal world where normal things happen.

Zack flops back onto his lonely air mattress in defeat and rubs his temples. "So did you come here for any particular reason? Or were you just in the mood to fuck up my life?"

"Your life? That's a rich one." Xara hops up onto the kitchen island, her spine as straight and tall as the column beside her. She rubs her hands over the rough surface of Zack's temporary plywood countertop before making a theatrical event of crossing her legs. "You've been here too long. You've forgotten who you really are."

"I haven't forgotten anything. I've evolved. I know that's not something we usually do."

"Evolution is something humans do to move closer to a state of perfection. We're already there. At least I am." She gives him a stern look. "And you used to be, before all this." She waves a hand dismissively across the room and all it represents.

Xara could never understand. She's popped in and out of this world for thousands of years, like all the others of their kind. Tasting of the world, dabbling in its pleasures and fineries, then popping back out when they're bored. Now and then they might help someone, do a kind turn, even grow to love a human. But it never lasted long, and in what amounted to a blink of an eye in their time – though it might be years here – they would return to their own plane no wiser, no kinder, no more loving or compassionate, no bigger from their growth because there *was* no growth. Ever. This world is the equivalent of a weekend getaway for most of them.

Only Zack has experienced it through something akin to human eyes. Physically, his eyes are no different from the others like him, but the lens of time has shifted both what and how he's seen through them. And with it, what he's felt. Only Zack has stuck around when the heartache began, again and again and again. Only Zack remained when the grief took hold and walked through the loss with generation after generation. Only Zack saw the ravages of time and the cruelty of humanity through wars, crusades, plagues, environmental degradation, and reigns of terror. And only Zack stood witness to the joys of first steps, first loves, first homes, bumper crops, safe returns from travels and wars, graduations, marriages, babies, jobs, promotions, and retirements. Only Zack knew what it was to be human. Almost.

"The ability to change is a good thing," he says. "You should try it."

Xara looks over Zack, drooping on his mattress like a thirsty houseplant. "Yes, I see what wonders your recent changes have done for you." She flits her hand again, this time directly at Zack. "If this is the result of living in and amongst them, I'll pass."

Of course, Zack's very status as a resident alien is the one thing that's kept him from the most human experience of all. Falling in love. Because while the others could simply drop in, take a lover, and move on when the novelty wore off, Zack could not. Zack's permanence made such entanglements impossible. He couldn't simply disappear when the relationship grew stale or went awry. He was obliged to stay. And before the modern era, he'd had to stay quite close. Modern transportation – trains, then cars, then planes – has certainly made it easier for him to travel further afield, but that's very recent in the scheme of things. And the principle has remained the same.

Having a relationship with another person simply wasn't fair to them. It could never last, he could never be honest about himself, and they would never understand. So many nevers, why even try? For a night and some blissful release, yes. But there were far too many nevers to attempt a forever. And there could be no such thing as forever anyway since humans live such a brief spark of a life. Why allow himself to feel something that could only ever end in heartbreak? Watching over his charges was enough. Enough heartbreak, not to mention joy, anxiety, trauma, and love to sustain one tired, lonely god through the eons. Adding desire and longing to the mix would only complicate things. Clouding lust with love would only ruin both and leave countless casualties over time, including himself.

And that had all been fine and dandy for a long, long time. Until those fiery curls and bodacious curves walked into his life and turned it upside down, which was before he'd even glimpsed her heart the size of Mount Rainier. Now it seems like he might have managed to crush that mountain into dust without so much as a single date. Well done, Zack.

A rapid pounding at the door stirs Zack from his thoughts. Xara's face lights up in giddy glee as she sucks in a delighted puff of air. "Ooh, who could it be?"

Zack's first instinct is to run for the door, but he forces himself to take a measured breath and address Xara first. "I'm going to let her in. Please, I'm begging you, behave. If not for me, then for her. She hasn't done anything wrong."

"I'll be the judge of that."

Zack gives her one last pleading look before opening the door. "Clarey, hi. Come in."

"Oh, look! Come for some cheese, did you, little mouse?"

"Xara, you're not helping." He studies Clarey, and the irritation on her face shoots through him like a javelin to the gut. "Clarey, let me explain. Please."

"I came down here to say..." Clarey stops short and looks Xara up and down before continuing. "I came to say that I don't know what your deal is, but I'm out. I don't care why you're so strong or what other *powers* you have or if you have a third arm tucked away somewhere."

"That could be fun!" Xara smiles with sudden delight. "Imagine the possibilities."

Clarey shoots Xara a nasty look. "I'm out. Do you hear me? Out. So, you and your lady friend enjoy your evening. Have a nice life. I'm out."

Xara chimes in as Zack is about to speak. "She really doesn't know anything, does she, Elnossys?"

Clarey looks from Xara to Zack. "Elnossys?"

"Elnos, for short," Xara says with a cheeky nose twitch.

Zack shrugs. "I'm still Zack. And this is Xara. Xara's like me."

"Like you?" Clarey says, processing the meaning of the words.

"Yes, don't you see, little mouse? We're infinite beings beyond your ken, and you're a teeny, tiny, adorable little rodent. This whole life of his is just a disguise."

"Xara," Zack says with a ferocity he hasn't shown in millennia, "this life is more real than that one after all this time, so please... Shut. Up." For one heavy moment, all three stand in silent contemplation, as if each is measuring their next move. Suddenly, a light goes off. Xara can prove it. Zack can't use his active powers because of the rules, but if they're careful, Xara can prove the truth of all of this to Clarey without tripping the wires. "Clarey, I can't prove to you what I'm saying is true, but Xara can."

"What?" Clarey says with a surprising note of alarm.

"I beg your pardon," Xara gasps. "I'm not in the habit of doing party tricks."

"All you have to do is disappear. You'd go eventually anyway."

"But I come and go as I please." Xara returns to the island, leans firmly against it, and crosses her arms. "Not on your command."

Clarey turns, suddenly panicked. "This is all too much."

Zack clutches her hand. "Give me one more minute. Xara, please!"

"And what's in it for me?" Xara says. "Why do I care what the little mouse believes?"

Clarey bolts for the door. "I can't do this. I'm gonna go."

Maybe he's pushed her too far, but he can't bear to let her go now. Not when she's so close to seeing the truth. To believing it. "Don't go."

Clarey looks mournfully at Zack before stepping out the door. "I'll see you later, Zack."

Xara raises one hand and waggles her fingers in a wave. "So nice to meet you."

Clarey glares at Xara. "I don't like you," she says before closing the door and walking back out of Zack's life.

Xara frowns as she refolds her arms. "And I was so fond of her."

Zack hangs his head. "Why did you do that?"

"That girl is clouding your judgment. Your penance on this plane is nearly up. You're acting as if you're going to stay. But you don't belong here, Elnossys."

Zack considers her words. If there's a way out of what's coming, he hasn't found it yet. "Even if that's true, I'm not sure there's a place where I do belong anymore."

Chapter Thirteen

Embracing the Impossible

Clarey walks into Goldfarb's precisely at noon to relieve Mr. G for his bank run and lunch. She didn't work in the shop all weekend and hasn't seen him since the last time they discussed Zack. She's not sure what she wants to hear Mr. G. say about him today. A Texas sized swath of her wants desperately to believe the obvious lie is true. Not because she wants to be involved with a supernatural being – in fact, that sounds terrifying and confusing and destined to end badly. But because she doesn't want to believe Zack's a liar. Or that Mr. G's non compos mentis, as far as that goes.

"Ah, Clarey! I'm glad to see you," he says as he comes out from the back. "How was your weekend?"

"You mean Zack hasn't told you?" Given that Clarey spent most of the weekend riddling Zack with question after question, and that Mr. G obviously knows what Zack says, she assumes Zack will have spilled the whole ugly tale to him. Or at least some part of it.

"I'm asking you," he says.

"Well, not great, to be honest," she sighs, leaning on the counter.

"I was afraid of that. But I have something that might cheer you up. Or at least open a door." He walks to the back and returns with a small box covered in a faded flower pattern, the edges worn from years of opening and closing and being shuffled from place to place. He lifts the lid to reveal a treasure trove of old photos, the top three of which are clustered neatly together awaiting him. Black and white images with yellowed edges. "I dug these out to show you." He lifts the three photos, but hesitates before handing them over. "Now, please keep an open mind, dear." Clarey takes the photos and looks at the first one. Mr. G points to a little boy, probably about five years of age. "There I am. Little Herbie."

"Oh, you were adorable!"

"And there's my mama, and my papa. And there..."

Clarey stares at the photo in disbelief. In it, a proud family of three stands in front of their obviously new Oldsmobile, mother and father each with a hand on a shoulder of little Herbie. And at the front end of the car, leaning one-handed on the hood and gleaming brighter than the new automobile, a dazzling blond man with deep dimples who looks suspiciously familiar. But no, that's not possible. It must be a coincidence. She flips to the next photo. "And this one is even older. You see, I was just a newborn here."

His father's not in this picture. Perhaps he's taking the photo. Mr. G's mother is there, however, gazing lovingly at her new baby, but she's not the one holding him in the photo. That honor belongs to... "It can't be," Clarey says.

Finally, she turns to the last photo. This one looks like it's from the late sixties. It's in color, though faded to a washed-out memory of itself, and it features two handsome young men, one in his early twenties and the other perhaps a little older. They stand stiffly side by side smiling. One is wearing a graduation cap and gown, probably college from the looks of it. Mr. G's young and unlined in this one, standing tall and full of life – and hair – but it's definitely him. He's unmistakable. And so is the other man. Zack. Clarey tells herself again and again that it's not true, but it's undeniable. Different haircuts, different clothes, but otherwise identical to the Zack she knows. She flips the photo. On the back in smeared pen, it reads "Herbie and Z, 1968."

"Oh my God," she says.

"Exactly," Mr. G says with a nod.

"It can't be." Clarey holds the picture up to her face, then pulls it away, then close again.

"Look as closely as you want. It will still be Zachary."

"This must be some kind of trick. Photoshop. Or AI."

"You've seen me at work. I can barely manage the new register. Do you really imagine I'm using Photoshop to fool you? Or AI?"

"I don't understand."

"I'm only alive today because he got my mama and her whole family, my family, out of Germany in 1935. He saw the evil coming and he got them out. Brought them first to Britain and then here, to America, and set them up. They couldn't bring much, but somehow he always made sure they had what they needed, more than they needed. Zachary looked after them, even once they were established and settled. They never wanted for anything. Of course, my mama was just a girl then, a teenager. But when she got older, got married, had me, he looked after us."

Clarey's still trying to process. "But..."

"My whole life, you see, he's been looking after me."

Clarey's mind whirls with the Technicolor impossibilities doing the cha-cha through her head. None of this is real. Dick Van Dyke dancing with penguins. Dorothy killing a witch with her house. And Zack rescuing Mr. G's family and watching him grow up. Each more impossible than the last. "This isn't possible. It can't be," she finally says.

"No, it cannot." Mr. G shakes his head. "And yet, it is."

"But how?"

"That, my dear, is a question for Zachary."

***

Clarey stands outside Zack's door, staring. She lifts her hand to knock several times, but drops it repeatedly, not yet ready to face what awaits her when the door opens. She replays her conversation with Mr. G, then all her conversations with Zack since he first told her the truth. The truth. What a strange word. Instead of knocking, she steps backward until her back bumps the wall and she slides downward, folding her knees to her as she lands. She thinks a moment longer before the latch releases and the door arcs smoothly across the floor as Zack's feet appear. He leans against the doorframe and looks down at her with a gentle smile.

She feels pathetic and lost, notes the wobble of uncertainty when she finally speaks. "How?"

Zack steps forward and reaches out his hand. "Come in. I'll tell you everything."

Minutes later, Clarey curls into the balcony chair as best she can as Zack hands her a cup of tea. He drags the other chair over to sit in front of her and leans in. He reaches for her hand again and asks, "Are you okay?" And she knows what he's really asking is, *Are you ready to hear it all?* She's not entirely sure of the answer to this question, but she nods. He releases her hand and leans onto his arm, deep in thought. Finally, he begins.

"The Ancients, my people, usually come and go here like an amusement park. We like it here. We like the people. Most of them, anyway. But this isn't our home. And we usually keep a low profile. We take a form to fit in, enjoy our time here, then go.

"Occasionally, someone gets involved with a human in one way or another, and they use their powers. Either to help or simply to dazzle the humans and fuel their own egos. So, back in the day, some of the most egotistical among us gathered followers, and followers built temples. That's when we became known as gods or goddesses."

"Like the Greek gods?" Clarey imagines Zack rocking a gold laurel crown and white, one-shoulder toga, one perfect pectoral poking out. If anyone could make that look work, it's Zack. Actually, he was born for that look.

"That's one version, yes. But their idea of us is no more accurate than any other. It's just one that caught on. Anyway, one day, a very long time ago—"

"How long exactly?" Clarey asks, terrified to hear the answer.

"Almost three thousand years, which is a long time even by our standards. There was a woman, a mother. She had two children and her husband had been killed. They were starving and had nowhere to go. So, she went into a temple to pray. She prayed, then looked up for guidance and noticed an altar with food on it. The food was an offering to one of us, you would call her a goddess. She's known by many names here, but the closest translation of what we call her is Ixia."

"Like the flower?" Clarey says. Her mother was an avid gardener growing up, and while her mom's green thumb didn't stick, all the pretty flowers in her books did.

"Mm-hm. It was her temple. But the woman, in her desperation, dared believe the appearance of the food was the literal answer to her prayers. So she took it and ran to feed her children. And Ixia was infuriated."

"What would have happened to it otherwise? Would Ixia have eaten it?"

"No, it would have been left to rot and cleared away by a priest."

"So, what happened?"

Zack hesitates, as if reliving the moment it all happened. "She raged at the affront. It was nothing but pride, bluster, and grotesque ego. Over a minor slight, one that could save lives. But she'd become accustomed to being worshipped and felt entitled."

"You knew her?"

Zack nods grimly. "She wanted them punished. She was prepared to wipe them out as retribution."

"Wow, that's... extreme." Clarey sips her tea to quell the rising panic within. She reels at the story he's unfurling before her. At the notion that ancient gods taking retribution is not only real, but something that's somehow relevant to Zack's life today.

"When she got to them, the smallest boy had already died. The food had come too late. But the mother and daughter, still alive, cowered in terror. I was with Ixia when she went to them. I saw what she was about to do, and I couldn't let it happen. So I stopped her."

"Stopped her how?"

"I stepped in front of her and took her blast."

She takes a nervous sip of tea. "You can blast?"

"*She* can blast. She could kill me if she wanted – with the consent of the others, that is – but that blast wasn't intended for a god. And at the time, she had some affection for me, so she didn't want to kill me. Yet. Then I put them under my protection, which meant she was forbidden from hurting them. That's when her fury redirected to me."

Clarey's breathless. Her pulse races as if she's there, awaiting her own fate as she awaits Zack's words. "What happened?"

"Others interceded before it could escalate. The Ancients don't often fight. We're pleasure seekers by nature, and generally benevolent both with each other and with humans. It's an aberration when conflict arises, but it does happen. And when it does, we decide collectively how to respond."

"And?"

"It was ugly and heated. She was furious with the woman. And with me. Felt I'd betrayed her. She demanded justice, but her idea of justice was so twisted at that time. I argued the woman had suffered enough for such a minor offense. She'd already lost her son and been terrorized by what happened when we appeared." Zack takes a beat, shaking his head at the folly of it all. "In the end, Ixia was granted a modified retribution against the woman. They wouldn't be killed because they had my protection. But since the woman had already lost a child, Ixia cursed her and her line to only ever a single heir, no chance to grow and propagate. Always one child, and only one child so long as that child lived. And it was agreed that a hundred generations would be the length of the sentence."

"Sheesh, ancient Law and Order was no joke. A hundred generations?"

Zack cracks an ambivalent smile, both amused by Clarey and distraught as he recounts the tale. "There's a reason it's called a curse. But the sentencing didn't stop there. I had to pay a price as well, for my interference. Ixia said since I cared *so much* about this woman and child, I could have a choice. Withdraw my protection, walk away, and let Ixia do what she wanted to them, or stay indefinitely on this plane and give them my protection. She knew either option would hurt me."

"She really took this stuff personally, huh?"

"You have no idea," he says with a roll of his eyes. "At first I thought she meant stay to protect just them, but..."

Clarey sees where this is heading. "She meant all of them, didn't she?"

"All one hundred generations," he says heavily. "So, I agreed. What else could I do?"

"And Mr. G?"

"Herb's the last. He's the one hundredth generation. But he and Mimi had a son, David. I had already decided I would stay. Continue protecting them. I've been here so long, you see. And that family has been my life. I've wandered the world as well. As long as I remained here on this plane, my protection covered them, even when I traveled. But they became my touchstone and my home, so I always came back. I couldn't imagine simply walking away from David because he happened to be generation 101. I'd watched him grow up, like Herb and every generation before him. But..."

Clarey watches Zack's face sag with his posture, his story taking its toll. She'd gathered David had died long ago. Now she knows Zack must have suffered much as Mr. G and his wife Mimi did.

David was Mr. G's son, but they were all Zack's children. "I haven't had the heart to ask Mr. G what happened to his son."

"Suicide. A couple years after he came home from Afghanistan. The only thing I couldn't protect him from. I could keep him safe in the war, but not from himself."

"Oh, Zack. I'm so sorry." Setting down her tea, she reaches for his hand and squeezes it. "You couldn't save him?"

"I wasn't here when it happened. And I can heal, not resurrect. But I'm not supposed to use my powers anyway. It was one of the terms of our agreement. Passive powers, yes. Active powers, no."

Clarey silently ponders all the impossible wonders that have been unfolded for her and lands at last on a very practical, real-world question. "So, what happens when Mr. G is gone?"

Zack looks first at Clarey, then away, casting his eyes instead into some vague mid-distance that could be anywhere at all. "That is a question for another day."

CHAPTER FOURTEEN

STARTING OVER

SAWDUST BLASTS ACROSS ZACK'S face as he slides the wood past the sawblade. Slow and steady, he eases the wood forward until he completes the cut and switches off the saw. Once the shrill, high-pitched grinding noise dissipates, another, much lower sound emerges from beneath it. Knocking. He removes his protective earmuffs and discovers it's actually pounding. On his door. Here we go.

Zack tugs off his safety goggles and pulls open the door. Although he knew it was Clarey – who else could it be? – seeing her makes his pulse jagged. He savors his first up-close look since they agreed to try again at her full, pink lips as she speaks.

"Hi," she says.

"Hi." Clarey points at Zack's mouth and Zack remembers the mask on his face. He yanks it off with an apologetic, "Sawdust."

Clarey nods silently, then finally speaks. "I brought you a piece of cake." She thrusts the large white box taped shut toward him. "I don't bake like you do. Scones or anything else. But there's this great restaurant up the road. They're famous for the best cake you've ever tasted."

"I've tasted some pretty good cake in my time."

"Taste this," she says with an open, completely innocent smile that nonetheless sends Zack's brain down a very dark, very wet passageway.

This is why he doesn't let people in. Thoughts like this, on the rare occasions when he allows them, normally lead to unbridled, unrepentant nights of debauchery followed by swift exits and complete radio silence. But he can't do that this time. He slides his finger under the tape and unhooks the cardboard flap. Inside sits an enormous slice of delectable-looking carrot cake. "This is huge." Clarey nods proudly. "Want to share?" He opens the door wider and holds out his arm.

She pauses a split second, sucks in a breath, and walks in. She looks around the work zone that is his living space, which she hadn't really done during her previous visits. Nothing but tools, wood, paint, and a twin-size air mattress on the far living room wall. "Like what you've done with the place, by the way," she says with a chuckle. "Furniture's overrated."

"Good point," he says with a nod. "This isn't how normal human beings live. I'll get some furniture."

"Not on my account."

"I'll get some furniture," he repeats.

She really looks for the first time, taking the space in bit by bit, as if she's absorbing every detail and storing it. Nothing about her manner suggests judgment. She's observing, not assessing. Yet Zack holds his breath awaiting her approbation. "I can't believe you meant it about not having countertops."

"Not yet."

"Well, that sucks! But I love the color of your cabinets." She loves the color. He knew it! Well, he hoped. "Mine are gray. It's pretty, but this green is so much warmer."

"These were gray too. I painted them." Zack looks around, suddenly painfully aware how poorly equipped he is to host Clarey or anyone else. "Want to go out to the balcony?" Zack rifles through a plastic bag in the cabinet under the sink and produces two forks, along with two paper towels before they take their seats on the balcony at his only real table.

He hands her a fork, then quickly digs in before he can be distracted by the sight of Clarey eating. He assembles the ideal bite with just enough cake, cream cheese frosting, and chopped walnuts. Clarey does the same and they pause to clink their forks before tasting. "Cheers" they say in unison. Zack fixes his eyes on the lake in the distance as his bite melts into his mouth. She's right. It might not be actual ambrosia, but it's not far off. He allows the indulgence to rest on his tongue a moment longer before swallowing, feeling the rapturous smile glide onto his lips with the perfect lingering sweetness. "Not bad at all," he says, still smiling.

"So, tell me how you landed here."

Zack goes back for a second, much larger bite as he answers. "In this building? Or in Seattle?"

"Both," she says, digging in for another bite herself.

Normally, this would be where Zack would offer the official version of a very complicated story. How he left a tech job a while back and went traveling, before coming back for Herb, who needs more help these days. How he chose this building for proximity. It's only part of the story, of course, but it's also true, so he tells Clarey anyway, though he leaves out the part about the red-headed added attraction of the building that sealed the deal. He waits to see how much more she'll want, how much of the story she's really ready for, but she seems content to stop there for now. Finally, he says, "I guess I just want to spend as much time with him as I can right now."

Clarey gives him a sympathetic look. "I lost my grandma about a year ago. That's where the money came from for my place. But I'd give it all back to get a little more time with her. I know it was her time..." She trails off, her eyes watering. She picks at a smear of frosting with her fork while she gathers herself. "But loss is still hard. She was the first close family I've lost besides my grandpa who died when I was little. But you've..."

Zack nods curtly. "I've lost a lot of people. You get numb to it after a while."

"I don't believe that," she says.

It's true though, isn't it? After investing so much of himself again and again, hasn't he numbed himself? There's a reason he keeps his distance from everyone but Herb. To turn it all off, to silence the onslaught of feelings that this messy, bloody, sweaty, pulsing, heartbreaking, horrifying human existence would pump into him like a pipeline if he let it? Maybe he's too sensitive for this world. Maybe his receptors are too finely tuned to stew for so long in this sea of humanity. But keeping his distance helps. So, why can't he seem to do that with Clarey?

Zack turns his eyes from her to the lake in a clear sign he's ready to move on. She shifts topics. "So tech, huh? Why'd you leave?"

"Too much talking."

Clarey bursts into laughter until she clocks Zack's perplexed expression. She sobers. "Sorry. I thought that was a joke. Isn't tech supposed to be full of anti-social introverts? At least that's the stereotype."

"I liked coding. It came easily. Someone offered me the chance to get in on a start-up. We were small to start, and I was mostly left alone as long as I delivered. But we grew quickly, and the more we grew, the more we collaborated. Then collaboration turned into all-hands and all-hands led to morale events and suddenly there was this whole culture built around being a team that had 'fun together' to foster creativity and innovation." He feels the wound again like it's new. It was years ago now, but for him, it may as well have been yesterday.

"Is that so bad?" Clarey asks. "I thought that's what most people wanted these days. Even in tech."

"Most people maybe. I just wanted to sit in my room and figure stuff out. I've never really been much of a team player." He takes a final bite of the cake.

"So will you go back to it?"

"Mm, I've kind of moved on. Want something to drink?" he says, heading for the kitchen. "I have LaCroix or iced tea. Or something harder if you want."

"I'm good," she says, twisting to watch him move.

He laces his movements with an easy, almost lazy sensuality. He's magnetic when he wants to be and he knows it. He likes knowing she can't take her eyes off of him. He's letting her see him, something he's barely ever done, and never for more than a night before. Yet, her gaze on him feels good. It feels real. Maybe it's not, and tomorrow this will turn out to be just another passing fancy like a thousand before, but it feels different. It feels like something that, in another life, could last.

"So what are you going to do instead?" she says as he heads back toward her.

Zack returns to the patio with a glass of iced tea in hand. He eases into his chair, extends his long legs to rest on the railing, and takes a sip of his drink. "I'm doing it."

Chapter Fifteen

Paper Airplanes

When Clarey gets home from Goldfarb's the next night, she pushes open the balcony door. It's cooling down outside and the fresh air feels good. With the long summer days, sunset's still a couple hours away, but chilling on the balcony with the latest Kristin Hannah book and a glass of wine while she waits sounds about perfect.

She grabs a bottle from the half-full wine rack on her kitchen counter, but before she can find the corkscrew, she hears it hit. She looks out at the balcony and there sits another paper airplane. Her stomach flutters as she reaches for the missive. Inside, it reads, "Meet me on the roof? Ten minutes." The balcony, the book, the sunset – maybe a little dinner in there somewhere – really sounded good. On the other hand, it would be rude to say no.

She walks onto the roof ten minutes later carrying the bottle of wine, the corkscrew, and two glasses. The still mostly empty roof now has a makeshift table set-up with two sawhorses and a large piece of plywood. Zack has thrown a rich looking tapestry over it as a tablecloth and dressed it with two place settings and a drinking glass with three gerbera daisies. He's brought his two balcony chairs up to complete the tableau.

Clarey smiles at the scene. "What's this?"

"I felt bad that my place was such a mess and I didn't have any furniture to host you properly."

"You didn't have to go to all this trouble. We could have met at my place."

"Well, I didn't want to invite myself over."

She hesitates only a moment before speaking. "Of course, you're invited." This feels both incidental and monumental. The casual assumption that some guy she barely knows will get access to her personal space blows right past all good sense in a normal world. But this is not a normal world. And Zack isn't just some guy, much as she tries to pretend otherwise. "But this is great. Thank you." She gestures at the outdoor kitchen where Zack stands. "Does this mean you're cooking?"

Zack offers a sheepish half-smile. "It means I thought about it. But I don't have any cooking supplies to speak of yet. Unless you want more baked goods. That stuff I've got."

There's something distinctly elusive about him. Like somehow, for all his undeniable beauty, he almost disappears unless he lets you in. As if he's in complete control, choosing whether to draw your attention or deflect it. Would she even have seen him if he hadn't put her in *his* sights first? Glimpsed him, yes, but truly *seen* him? Her instincts tell her he allowed that to happen. He's allowing it even now. But as long as he's allowing it, she may as well take advantage. Clarey holds up her bottle. "So we're just drinking then?"

***

Half eaten tins of lasagna, spinach ravioli, and garlic bread litter the table as Zack pops a fresh cork and refills Clarey's glass. "I'm glad you got out of there. You should never settle for less than you deserve," he says.

"I didn't think I was settling at the time. Derek's incredibly good looking in an annoyingly shaggy, boyish way. Charming, smart, and the sex was great—"

Zack's back goes straight as an odd tension crosses his face. "I get the picture."

Clarey might feel bad saying all this to another guy, but she and Zack are just friends. Wouldn't make sense to attempt anything else under the circumstances – even if he were interested. Besides, there's no way a literal god could be insecure about anything, right? Let alone jealous. "And he treated me like a queen," she goes on. "Or at least that's how it felt. He made me feel beautiful and sexy and smart."

"Well, you are."

Record scratch. "And, he, um..." Clarey trails off, Zack's last words sticking like peanut butter in her brain. Do men say things like that to women in platonic friendships? Is that a thing a guy can just say to a woman? Even a god guy? Do god guys have different rules?

"So what went wrong?" he asks after a sip of wine.

"Thing is, don't most queens get their way at least occasionally?"

"Meaning?"

"Everything was *always* his way. I didn't notice it at first because I didn't usually care that much. If I wanted seafood and he wanted burgers, we had burgers. I wanted the romcom, he wanted the action movie, action won. I wanted a mountain getaway, he wanted the beach, we went to the beach. Even though the last thing I wanted was to be seen in a bathing suit."

Clarey regrets the example – which summons the incident at the pool – as soon as it's out of her mouth. She'd been doing her level best to pretend that never happened since it was literally the only way she could actually look Zack in the eyes, the same eyes that now flicker to Clarey's chest and back up. It happens so fast she would never have noticed if his every movement weren't broadcasting to her brain like a jumbotron at the moment. "But he obviously liked what he saw," he says.

"Except I started to realize he never really saw me. And never heard me. He only listened when he was trying to charm me by making me feel interesting, which is entirely different than actually *finding* me interesting, by the way. But somehow, when it came to priorities, his always won. Even when it really mattered to me."

"Like what?"

Unlike Derek, Zack is proving to be a very good listener, but she should probably stop talking about her ex, which is universally accepted as the worst possible dinner topic. Especially when the speaker can't shut up about it.

"Like when he talked me out of going to my childhood best friend's wedding in Nashville because that weekend wasn't convenient for him and he didn't want me to go without him," she says anyway. "I wanted to go. I wanted to be there for her. And I've always wanted to visit Nashville. But I let him talk me out of it. She was so hurt. Justifiably so."

Zack winces. "Ouch."

Yeah, ouch. Accurate. Definitive. A very apt button on the story. This is a good place to stop. Verbal diarrhea isn't a cute look.

"Or when he bailed on my sister's all-gender shower to go to a Mariners game. There are like 7,000 games a season. He couldn't miss *one* for me and my family? But he argued they didn't really want him there anyway, that the 'all gender thing' was just them being polite. And I knew that wasn't true, but instead of standing up to him and telling him how important it was that he come, I let him go to his dumb game."

"I'm sorry."

Zack appears to have the patience of a saint. But there are limits, and she needs to stop rambling before this tenuous little bubble pops wide open. "And that's another thing!" She can't stop now. "It was fine for him to spend the price of a small car on Seahawks season tickets, but when I suggested a 3-pack of inexpensive balcony seats to the symphony to try it out, he somehow convinced me it was an extravagance for something *we* wouldn't really enjoy anyway. And I actually accepted that answer."

Zack looks at her with an expression so soft she can almost feel it brushing across her skin like a cat's fluffy tail. "I'm sorry he never chose you over himself."

That's it, isn't it? It's not that they usually did what he wanted. That was no big deal. It made it easier if someone just decided most of the time. Someone had to choose, and it was better than spending all night every night in an endless "I don't know, what do you want?" loop. She didn't have strong preferences and was game for anything most of the time. It was just that when it really counted, he wasn't there.

"Not even once," she says. "Not even when it was important to me." She takes an outsized gulp of wine. "And I kept accepting it, again and again, like a dummy."

"You're not a dummy."

"I can't blame him entirely though. I let him get away with it. I've always been a pushover. But one day, I realized I didn't want to be married to a man who would take advantage of that fact."

"Cheers to that," Zack says, holding up his glass.

They fall quiet and look out at the lake. The sun is finally setting and the orange pink light is glorious over the water and distant shore. The breeze blows gently past them, picking up the scent of wine and roasted garlic. Clarey looks back to the table top where some tomato sauce is smeared on the elaborately embroidered, velvet tapestry covering the plywood that peeks out at the corner. "Oh, I'm sorry, I spilled on this incredible... I'm not sure what this is actually."

"Just something I picked up in my travels. Don't worry about it."

Clarey is horrified to have possibly stained something so exquisite. And it seems old, too. A rare and precious thing. "I'm such a mess. I'll get it dry cleaned for you."

"Honestly, it couldn't matter less," he says. He stills her hand where she's frantically dabbing at the spot. "Hey, did you enjoy your dinner?"

"Very much."

"Then that's all that matters," he says, his dimples doing a decidedly unfair sneak attack on her anxiety. She looks down again at the remnants of their feast, then back at Zack with a grin. "Why are you smiling?" he asks.

"We had Italian," she answers, so quietly it might only have been for herself.

Zack puzzles at her response. "Isn't that what you wanted?"

"But you wanted tacos."

If he notices the connection to their previous conversation, he doesn't show it. He shrugs. "I can have tacos another time."

A tiny, perfect firework explodes inside Clarey's heart.

***

The glamorous, flawlessly attired woman striding away from the closing lobby door is not what Clarey expects to see when she pokes her head out the window the next day. She was checking to see if the coming rainstorm was going to hold off long enough for her to get to Goldfarb's, but the sight of the tall, thin, dark-haired beauty walking away as if she owns the place triggers a different storm in Clarey. Clarey watches her glide down the street on her giraffe legs and disappear around the corner.

It was that woman from Zack's apartment. Clarey had tried not to think about her. If they're just friends, then it's none of her business who he spends his non-Clarey time with. But she's too beautiful. Exactly the type of woman a guy like Zack would choose. The type of woman any straight man and a not insignificant number of women would choose if the option were presented. And apparently, she's a goddess, which is even harder to compete with. It was too far to see her clearly this time, but as she had when Clarey saw her up close, she bore the magnetic aura of someone who knew all eyes would be on her and welcomed it.

Pretty much the exact opposite of Clarey. Clarey has to work damn hard to feel good about herself and her body in a world that would prefer her many sizes smaller. It doesn't always come naturally, but she tries. And she's attracted enough interest in her years to mostly believe her own hype. But a woman like *that* doesn't need to try. A woman like that simply knows. Men know it, too.

She's late for Mr. G, but she detours to Zack's doorstep anyway. "Hey, you," he says with bright, open smile so disarming it nearly stops her question before she's opened her mouth. "Good timing. I just got back from the gym." He pulls his shirt up to wipe his face, exposing his chest in the process. If the smile wasn't enough to stop the bullet train in Clarey's head, dear lord, the abs might be. Each carefully carved line and curve in high, freshly pumped definition. Is he doing this on purpose? Because if he were trying to distract her, this would be a brilliant way to do it. "Sorry I'm so sweaty," he says, dropping his shirt again. "I pushed myself pretty hard today. Come in."

He swings the door wider and turns to lead her into the room, but Clarey remains in the hallway parsing mental images of what she's just seen. She can't seem to say anything, so he continues while reaching for his water. "I hope you don't think too badly of me," he says. *Badly* isn't the word she'd use. "It's like I said before, I like the hyper focus of it. It helps me stay clear, block out all of the noise." When she still says nothing, he finally turns back to her. "You okay?"

He ducks his head to look her in the eyes and the connection finally snaps her out of her lust haze. "Yes. Fine. Thanks." She looks quickly around to steady herself, then speaks. "I can't stay. I'm on my way to Goldfarb's. But I wanted to say, if you want to hang out with your friend—"

"What friend?" he says, turning from her and walking toward the kitchen. He keeps his eyes on his bottle as he refills it.

"The ridiculously stunning brunette who walks like a slow-motion runway model? I saw her leaving the lobby. Xara?"

Zack takes a long, slow drink from his bottle. "Oh, her. Clarey, she's a friend. Literally. A friend. That's all."

"I guess I wanted you to know that it's okay. I don't mind. Your private life is your own." Why is she saying this? She doesn't mean it. She doesn't mean a single word of what she's saying, yet the words come flowing out like a waterfall. "I mean, we're just friends, right?"

"Clarey, *she's* just a friend. She stopped by while she was in the area, but I was working out. I talked to her for all of three minutes."

She hears him, but she can't seem to stop. Like she's determined to give him away to another woman. "It's just, I wouldn't want you to feel like—"

"Great, thanks," he says, as much to shut her up as anything. He takes another swig, then shines his dimples at her. "Want to hang out tonight?"

***

The paper airplane swoops in right before she opens the patio door. How does he do that? When she unfolds it, the message reads, "Want to walk to the lake?"

Clarey pulls a piece of paper from her printer and folds it into a plane shape. She gives it a toss across the room and it nosedives for the ground. She tries again with equally terrible results. She searches her phone for instructions and finds a short YouTube video, which she diligently follows. When her YouTube plane sails across the room in moderate style, catching at least a little air before its inevitable descent, she decides to give it a go. She scribbles a short message, then marches out to the balcony. She says a little prayer, takes a deep breath, holds it, and sends it sailing.

CHAPTER SIXTEEN

THE DANGER OF WALKS

ZACK CAN'T CONTAIN HIS grin when her cheers reach him. He doesn't even know why she's cheering, but the sound of her happiness triggers a Pavlovian joy in him as well. He'd like to think it was his invitation that prompted her response, but that much excitement over a walk seems unlikely. Whatever the reason, he wants to witness it firsthand.

He runs to the balcony and gazes up at her literally jumping up and down for joy. And oh, the way she bounces. He beams up at her. "What's going on?" Their balconies are close enough that he only has to raise his voice slightly to be heard. She does a little victory dance and points to his feet where a paper airplane of his own awaits him. She really is one-of-a-kind.

He opens it and laughs. "Okay," it says. All that effort for one word. One-of-a-kind.

They agree to meet in fifteen minutes so he can hop in the shower first. Intrusive thoughts of Clarey creep in as he showers, his stiffening cock reminding him he's getting far too attached to this woman. But what's even more alarming is the pattern he's noticing. As much as her flesh tempts him, he could cope with that. He's enjoyed the delicious bodies of so many lovers in his time, and simply moved on afterward. If he could do that with Clarey, it would be one thing. Maybe he'd be fine. But he can't do that with her. He can't do that *to* her.

And what's worse, he doesn't even want to. Now they're going for a walk in the park, just like he predicted. And it was his fucking idea. Because as tempting as her curves are, it's her vulnerability and heart that keep pulling him back. He's beginning to think it will take an act of divine intervention to pull him away from her. And that's the last thing he wants.

***

They stroll down the tree-lined Kirkland strip of eateries, galleries, and charming little shops. This is classic old Kirkland. To the east is all the recent development, like their own building, bringing new life and vitality to the growing suburb. But here, on this little street a stone's throw from the waterfront, it could be the Kirkland of fifty years ago. Inside, the spaces are as fresh as the new builds, as shining and hip as any in downtown Seattle, but from here, on the street itself, the quaint sense of cozy community abides.

When they come upon a bronze sculpture of two giant rabbits hugging, Clarey hops in next to them and commands Zack to take her photo as she wraps her arm around one of them. "I want to send it to my sisters." Zack dutifully accommodates her request. As she stands, her eyes fall on the storefront across the street. "Mmm, gelato."

"There must be a rule somewhere that every waterfront town must have an ice cream shop," Zack says.

"And naturally, Kirkland's gotta make it fancy," Clarey laughs.

Zack takes Clarey's hand and leads her across the street. "Let's get some."

She stops on the other side. "Oh, I shouldn't."

"Doesn't agree with you?"

"More like it agrees with me too much." She scrunches her face and flicks a quick gesture at her body.

It's an invitation she didn't mean to issue, but Zack takes it anyway. His hungry eyes look slowly down her body and back up, and when he lands on her face, he can see his gaze has heated her as much as him. He shouldn't say it. It's a genuinely terrible idea to say the words, but he says them anyway. "Trust me, that's not a thing you should worry about." He pauses, allowing himself the pleasure of watching her mouth tick up in a shy smile. "Have the ice cream."

Five minutes later, they're meandering through Marina Park, sampling each other's gelato, and debating which flavor is best, coconut or stracciatella. It's nearly dinner time, but the sun is still high and a couple of kiddos are still wading in the lake and playing on the beach, under the close supervision of their ever watchful mom. Zack and Clarey grab a bench near the gazebo and watch a boat puttering in toward the pier.

"How'd it go with Herb today?" Zack asks.

"Good. It was a bit busier than I expected, but I had fun."

"Glad to hear it."

"Mr. G is a force of nature," she says. "Hell, on sheer will alone, he'll probably outlive us all." Zack smiles, but says nothing, and after a moment, Clarey amends her statement. "Well, most of us."

Zack huffs a gentle laugh, then watches her face unexpectedly contort. Her mouth opens to a strange pucker and her eyes squint.

Her face hangs there a moment, like a twisted circus mask, and then bam! Six furious sneezes pour out of her like a waterfall gushing snot. She quickly reaches for a tissue tucked in her pocket and wipes her nose before apologizing.

"That was impressive," he says.

"Ugh! Allergies. Can't take me anywhere. At least, not without tissues," she replies, wiping again for good measure.

"You okay?"

"I'm fine." She sticks the tissue back in her pocket. "But if you asked my sisters, they'd tell you I'm dying. I had a sinus infection in high school that ended up moving into my lungs. I got bronchitis and pneumonia. I was in the hospital for a week. I almost died."

"Wow, scary."

"It wasn't great. But it was almost twenty years ago and they still act like it's coming back for me every time I so much as reach for a tissue." She pulls out her tissue and wipes her nose yet again, turning her back to Zack for a moment of privacy. Then she balls up the tissue, tosses it in her empty gelato cup, and tosses the whole thing in the trash can by the bench. "To be fair, my lungs are still kind of iffy. I'm prone to bronchitis and such. And I did have pneumonia one other time. But I'm really fine."

"I see that," Zack says with a soft smile that belies his own moment of panic at the idea of a hospitalized Clarey. He is really starting to care about this woman way too much. Meanwhile, the family on the beach packs up at last and puts their clothes on over their suits before heading out. Zack changes the subject. "This beach gets used a lot, huh?"

"Yup, they all do," she says, referring to the half a dozen little beach parks all up and down the Kirkland shoreline.

"We should try them out sometime."

"The beach? Pass."

"No?"

Clarey cringes. "Bathing suits, public places, and me, not my favorite combination. That's part of what I liked about our building, the private pool."

Zack watches Clarey's face as her words catch up with her and the memory hits them both like a ton of naked bricks. Zack tries as hard as he possibly can to keep the smile off his face, but he feels it sneaking onto his lips despite his best efforts. She catches his eye and freezes briefly, a moment of absolute mortification, but as his lips slip ever upward, she finally breaks and they both burst out laughing. Her peals of laughter blast across the park and Zack's body fills with a kind of warmth that, for once, has absolutely nothing to do with the blood flow between his legs. When Clarey's final giggles fade, she covers her face. "Oh, God! I was trying to wipe that from my memory. Now it's all refreshed and shiny and horrifying again."

"For what it's worth," he says, "I wasn't horrified." When her face colors with a royal flush, Zack immediately regrets his words. He looks at her plaintively and says, "How about we put it to rest for once and for all?"

Clarey catches her breath silently and asks, "How?"

"Overwrite it with a new memory. Let's go swimming. You and me."

Chapter Seventeen

Weightlessness

Clarey pulls her swim shirt over her suit and stares herself down in the mirror. All her efforts to love herself and embrace her curves fall by the wayside each time she slips on that suit. Why? What is it about that damn piece of spandex that brings out every anxiety she's ever felt about her body? Both of her sisters are curvy and they're so beautiful. She steadfastly refuses to believe the bull that the diet and beauty industries try to spoon feed her in lieu of actual food, choosing instead to love her strong, capable body that houses her sharp brain and giant heart. The same body that attracts appreciative stares from men when she puts herself out there, and enjoys the intense pleasure of their touch when she allows it. And yet all of that, every bit of that certainty, somehow dissipates like steam the moment the suit comes out.

The bitter irony is that swimming has always been one of her favorite activities because it's the one time she gets to experience something akin to weightlessness. The one time she feels as light as everyone else. How cruel then that the only physical activity she's ever really enjoyed – well, the only physical activity she can do in public – is also the only one she can't engage in without feeling bad about herself. How does that make sense?

She stares at her thighs, tugs her shirt down further, then wraps a towel around her waist. Here goes nothing.

***

Zack's already swimming laps when Clarey arrives. He stops at the opposite end of the pool and hooks his arm on the edge. "There you are," he says with a smile.

She's grateful he's already in the water, which partially obscures the chest she found so distracting earlier today. Let alone those two devilish lines of his Adonis belt, which – while they couldn't possibly be more aptly named in this case – are probably not something she should ever see again if she plans to maintain any level of cool whatsoever with this god-man fella. There's no missing his broad shoulders and rippling back muscles, however, as he swims across the pool to invite her in. She walks to the edge of the pool where the steps are, but hesitates before dropping her towel. "Will you turn around for a minute?"

"Seriously?" He shakes his head in disbelief, but turns his back as she steps gingerly into the pool. Once she's up to her waist, she lets him turn around again. "Okay, then," he says. "Demons exorcised, yeah?" She gives a reluctant nod until he extends his right hand above the water. "Pax?"

She looks at his pruney hand, then up at his wide eyes and ridiculous dimples. How can she hold a grudge against a guy who uses Latin, by far the nerdiest language, on her? She takes his hand and shakes. "Pax," she says, and at last, she means it.

They linger in the pool awhile, swimming, floating, and chatting about everything and nothing, until Zack finally asks something real. "So why don't you like to swim in public? You obviously love the water."

"Come on, isn't it obvious?"

"Not to me," he shakes his head.

"I mean, I don't exactly have a traditional beach body."

"All kinds of bodies are beautiful, Clarey." Despite the fact that these words are coming from this absurdly fit model of male perfection, he sounds oddly sincere.

"I know," she says, thinking of her sisters and all the gorgeous plus-size models she follows online who are always showing off their tummies and cellulite on the beach. "I do believe that. But maybe my conditioning is just too deep to embrace it for myself. Like, when I was a teenager, I always envied the girls at the pool in their bikinis, who flirted with the boys and got chased around before the boys would scoop them up like they weighed nothing and toss them into the pool. I always wanted to be those girls." She shrugs, then swims across the pool, suddenly needing to distance herself from Zack. She'd never be the skinny girl they tossed in the pool, but as long as she stayed in the water, at least she could feel weightless like them. And safely hidden.

As if on cue, Zack announces he's pruning and better take a break. Clarey averts her eyes as he climbs out and towels off, determined to stop her ogling before someone gets hurt. "How about you?" he calls. "You coming?"

Clarey makes her way to the ladder at the side of the pool so she's not right next to him as she emerges. Still, as she climbs out, she feels his eyes on her. She glances at him and knows he can see every curve and roll on her full body under the tight cling of her soaking shirt, so she quickly wrings it out in the front and shakes out the back to once again obscure her body. Once her shirt is sufficiently wrung out, her red one-piece with the ruching, low-cut back, and deep scooped front almost disappears beneath the now baggy shirt. She liked the idea of the sexy suit in theory, and on the stunning plus-size model, but the reality of anyone, especially Zack, actually seeing her in it hits different.

Fortunately, Zack's not looking closely. He's turned to scrolling through his phone. He summons her with his phone in his hand. "Come here, I want to show you something." He scrolls and taps as she approaches with a curious grin. When she reaches him, however, he throws down his phone, scoops her off her feet, and runs to the poolside where he promptly tosses her back into the water.

She yelps with glee as she falls. When she emerges from the water, she's laughing hysterically. "I can't believe you did that!" He laughs with her, dives in, and swims her direction. He pops up near her, and she laughs again. "That was ridiculous!"

He bounces his brows proudly. "Now you can check that off your bucket list. I did you a favor." She rolls her eyes, but there's no disguising her delight. She dips her head backwards to fix her hair and continues to giggle until she spots a new look in Zack's eyes. He walks toward her slowly, his wide smile fading to something more serious, laden, almost sultry. "Now can I ask you a favor?"

Clarey freezes in place, keenly aware of the water sloshing around her as he closes the distance between them. He stops in front of her, so close a gentle wave would cause their bodies to collide. She stiffens as the water around her rocks her body, and the humid air suddenly grows hot. Despite the warmth of the water, and the air, and her body, she trembles. "What kind of favor?" she finally says.

She watches Zack's hands slowly descend beneath the surface and move toward her sides. Her breath catches as his fingertips brush her hips, then hook beneath the edge of her swim shirt. He clasps the hem and pulls it up toward her head. The suction of the shirt tugs at her skin as it rises above water and peels away from her chest, and she instinctively raises her arms as Zack removes it, leaving her too exposed in just her bathing suit. He balls up the heavy, soaked shirt and hurls it like the god he is all the way across the length of the pool until it thwacks hard against the wall at the other end of the room. He looks her dead in the eye and says in a low, salt-water voice, "Don't ever hide yourself, Clarey. From me, from anyone." He looks down at her body below the water, and at her breasts floating above the water, now on rather splendid display in the red halter of her suit. He looks a hair too long, then says, "You deserve to be seen."

Clarey's jaw drops and her throat clenches. "I... um..." She's speechless. She's actually speechless. Hyper-verbal Clarey has been rendered wordless.

He smiles indulgently. "Just say okay."

Clarey nods, her mouth still hanging open, and finally the word squeaks out. "Okay."

He's still staring at her as the temperature climbs. Is that actual steam rising from the surface? He gazes down her body again, then at her lips. He's going to kiss her. This is it. This freaking god of a neighbor is going to kiss her. And it's probably a mistake that will complicate and ruin everything, but as the heat of his breath warms her face, it feels like the best mistake she could possibly make. Her mouth finally eases closed as her lips approach a pucker in anticipation. He looks in her eyes, then back to her lips, and she prepares herself for bliss. But after another beat, he seems to catch himself and think better of it. She has no idea what's happened, or why, but the spell has broken.

"Good," he says with a definitive nod and a friendly smile. The air cools noticeably as he swims to the edge and hops out. "You know, I just remembered I need to pick-up some baseboards before the store closes. I better run. I'll see you later?" he says as he pulls on his shoes and picks up his towel.

"Yeah," Clarey mumbles. Despite her engine revving like a Formula One racecar, she summons a polite smile. "Of course." Then he's gone, and Clarey is still swaying in his wake.

Chapter Eighteen

Accidents Will Happen

That was too fucking close. That was a code-red-def-con-one-action-stations-danger-zone he just swam into like a happy, little goldfish – and swam out of with about three seconds left on the detonation clock. This situation is raging out of control and he's the dumbass who's let it happen. Hell, who's he kidding? He's the dumbass who made it happen. Who keeps making it happen again and again. What is it about this woman that keeps him so off-balance and mesmerized?

There's only one thing for it. He's got to stop this cold turkey before it's too late. Chop off the limb to stop the infection from spreading. That's the idea anyway, though he suspects it may already be running in his veins and pulsing through his chest. That every inch of his body might already be fully afflicted with an incurable case of Clarey.

Then again, nothing's incurable for Zack. He's never met a bullet he couldn't dodge, and this is no different. It won't be easy. But better to hurt her a little now than a lot later. It's the only thing to do. He's got to pop this bubble.

***

It occurs to Zack as he rounds the corner that he should probably go the long way around. This is about the time Clarey goes in to help at Goldfarb's and the last thing he wants is to accidentally run into—

And shit. There she is.

He can't very well turn around and walk the other way now. He had thought about doing a gutless slow fade until she'd given up on him and decided he was just another creep undeserving of her time. Which would be more or less accurate and totally fair. But he can't do an abrupt U-turn right in front of her and march away like she did something wrong. Beautiful Clarey, with all her sweetness and squishy bits of vulnerability, deserves to walk away from this feeling like the priceless treasure she is, not to be cast aside like a worthless counterfeit when the party's over.

The best way to deal with this would obviously be head on. Talk to her face-to-face and tell her. Be honest. Tell her that he needs to focus on Herb, that he's very sorry and he shouldn't have started it in the first place and he's an idiot. At least that would be true. But he's too much of a coward to do that. All these many years, all he's done and all he's been through, he never thought he was a coward before. But recently he's learned that he is indeed just that. When it comes to Clarey McGill, he is one-hundred percent pure, USDA Grade A chicken.

But there she is striding down the street at the other end of the block. And now he's frozen to his spot and everything's happening in a kind of Clarey-induced slow-motion. And now she's spotted him. And now she's stopped in her tracks. And now she's staring at him. And now he's raising his hand in a pathetic, little wave. And now a customer is leaving Goldfarb's. And now a small black cat is darting out the door. And now the cat's dashing across the street.

And now Herb is running after him. And now there's a car. And now the car is slamming its brakes. And... Herb!

Herb shouldn't have been in front of that car. Normally, he couldn't move fast enough to surprise a car going 25 mph, but he somehow summoned the speed of Hermes to chase after that damn cat. Well, not quite. Hermes probably would have cleared the street. Now he lies bleeding in the road and the panicked driver is hyperventilating behind the wheel as Zack runs lightning speed to Herb's side.

"Herb, you're gonna be okay. I'm here."

Blood is everywhere, pouring from Herb's head, probably from the fall. And his leg lies at an unnatural angle. Zack surveys his surroundings, assessing the scene. The woman driving the car has climbed out and stands above them ranting, "Oh, God," on a loop. Clarey runs up.

"Oh my God, Mr. G!" Her mouth gapes.

Zack looks up at her. "Clarey."

"There's so much blood," she cries, kneeling to Herb's side.

"Call 911," Zack says.

"Mr. G," Clarey says.

"Clarey, listen to me. I need you to do this for me. Go over to the sidewalk where you're safe and call 911. Now!"

Clarey shakes with every breath, but she stands slowly. Zack glances at the "Oh, God" woman who has now shifted to "I... I... he... he..."

"Take her with you," he says to Clarey. Clarey pulls out her phone and presses buttons frantically as she somehow simultaneously takes the stranger's arm gently and ushers her toward the sidewalk. Once they turn to walk away, Zack returns his focus to the old man on the ground. "Herb, hold on. Trust me." He gently straightens Herb's leg and smiles at him. "You know I'm not ready to let you go."

"No, Zachary, no. It's okay..." Herb's voice is barely there. His eyes barely open, and when they do, they're glassy and unfocused.

"No, it's not. But it will be," Zack says with conviction.

"You can't. You mustn't. Just let me go."

"Not a chance, old man." Zack looks up again at the women on the sidewalk. Clarey holds her phone to her ear, staring down the street for the ambulance while the driver has curled into a ball against the wall and buried her face in her knees, sobbing. He looks back at Herb. "It's not that bad," he says as he gently places a hand on Herb's forehead and another on his heart. "You'll see."

"No," Herb repeats.

"You're going to be fine." Zack says before giving him a smile warmer than the sun overhead. "Trust me."

And then, as if on cue, the sun climbs even higher in the sky and the world is engulfed in a blinding white light. Only, it's not the sun. It's Zack. A warm bath of peace and well-being washes over Herb as his whole body nearly levitates back to itself, some perfect, whole, and complete version of himself. Maybe even a few shades better and a few years younger. It's whatever magical, impossible, glorious gift of healing Zack is, and Zack simply shimmers.

***

Zack glances toward Clarey who's standing with the paramedics driver, talking to a police officer. He walks Herb inside and to the back room where he sits him in the chair at his desk and kneels in front of him.

Herb hooks his hand around Zack's head. "You shouldn't have done that. You put yourself in too much danger."

"Shhh, don't worry about me. I've managed all this time, haven't I?"

"You've managed by being careful. Not taking chances like that."

"I can handle myself, Herb. And you know I'll always look out for you." Zack stands and kisses the old man's forehead like he's an exasperating, naughty child, then crosses the room with a sigh. Herb watches him thoughtfully as Zack looks out to check on Clarey's progress with the police. "She's a good girl. You can trust her."

"I do. I have. But there are degrees. And lines I can't cross."

"Can't cross? Or won't?"

A quiet jostling from the front of the store, something knocked or nudged, silences them. Shit. Did the bell ring? They didn't hear the bell. They hold their breath and wait.

"Mr. G," Clarey calls from not far away before walking back. "Look who I found." Clarey walks through the door with the small black fur baby nestled in her arms.

Zack takes one look and bellows, "Get that cat out of here!"

But Herb reaches out his hands and replies just as quickly, "Under no circumstances. Give him here." He pulls the cat into his arms and murmurs, "Did you cause all this trouble, Homer Dickens?"

"Homer Dickens?" Zack sneers as Homer Dickens answers with a loud meow.

Clarey giggles at the name, then sobers. "Mr. G, are you sure you're okay?"

"I'm fine, fine. So much fuss."

"Well, all the same, I'm going to help you all day tomorrow, okay? I don't want you to overdo it." She pulls out her phone to add the shift to her calendar.

"That's not necessary."

"It absolutely is and I won't take no for an answer. I don't have any meetings tomorrow, so it's no problem. I'll be here at 9:00?" She hits save and tucks her phone away, smiling expectantly about the plan.

"Very well," he concedes. "What a sweet girl," he adds, eyeing Zack meaningfully.

Chapter Nineteen

Warming Up and Cooling Down

DEREK TAKES OVER SIX hours to answer Clarey's latest text about Roxy and their return date. So when Derek texts, *Good news,* she's skeptical. This better be followed with the words "Roxy is coming home," or she might hurt someone.

Bob's doing much better. We plan to come home by this weekend. Maybe even Friday.

She responds immediately. *That's great. And Roxy?*

Silence. What kind of game is he playing? She has really allowed this thing to drag on way too long. It's been weeks. But what could she do? Drive all the way to Bend like an asshole? Where do Lydia's parents even live? Plus, Lydia had laid it on pretty thick about what a godsend Roxy had been through all the hard stuff.

To be fair, Zack *is* proving a very enjoyable distraction. Between him and all the time she's been spending with Mr. G, she's been managing well enough. Still, there's not a single thing, good or bad, in this life that won't be made better with Roxy by her side.

Finally, Derek's message pops in. *Yes, of course. Roxy too.*

Thank God! Only a few more days until her sweet, goofy girl comes home at last. Plus, Zack is due in just a few minutes. Things are definitely looking up.

Clarey runs a pick lightly through her curls and touches up her make-up, trying for all she's worth to achieve an "easy, effortless beauty." Zack has never seemed to need any of that before. He has always seemed to like her exactly as she was, however she was at any given moment. Then again, that was when she was determined not to care about him or what he thought. Being liked "just the way she is" as a neighbor is a pretty low bar to clear. But much as she's tried to resist the pull of that perfectly symmetrical, straight-nosed, cut-glass jawline of a man, she has finally, reluctantly, come to terms with the fact that she would very much like to clear a slightly higher bar with him. And she'd like to clear that bar tonight if possible.

As Jessa would say, it's time to get bubbling. Maybe not a full boil. Not tonight. But at least a simmer? She could definitely do with a nice, low-heat simmer. Then again, she probably wouldn't say no to a hard boil either.

Five minutes before Zack is due, a text pops in from Jessa. *i got a job!*

Doing what?

barista one of those drive thru dealies

Clarey's pretty sure there's supposed to be a comma or a period in there somewhere. And maybe a hyphen. What does Jessa have against punctuation anyway? And has she turned off autocorrect on her phone? How does she manage never to use capital letters? *The one with the bumblebee or the one with the mountain?* Clarey replies.

the one with the happy moose

Clarey's doorbell rings. She types a quick *Nice* and runs for the door. When she opens it, it takes her too long to invite Zack in because she's momentarily paralyzed by the look in his eyes. Like what's in the oven is entirely incidental because she is the main course tonight. Oh, how she would like to be the main course, thank you.

The swimming pool weirdness seems to have been forgotten in the aftermath of Mr. G's accident and things are starting to bubble deliciously again. At least, she thinks they are, though the whole god-thing complicates everything. In a normal relationship, she'd have some idea where she stands. Maybe it wouldn't be crystal clear, but it wouldn't be a big foggy mess of mixed signals. But this thing is like a crapshoot where she never knows for sure if she's about to shoot a seven or crap out. When she's feeling herself – like *really* feeling herself – Clarey knows she's hot. But hot enough for a god? How does a person decide they're hot enough for that? That's like elite level hotness, and way, way, out of Clarey's league, she'd have thought. And yet, there's that look in Zack's eyes.

The timer sounds, indicating it's time to lower the temperature. She waves Zack in and dashes off to the kitchen, humming to herself.

"You're in a good mood," he says.

"I am!"

"Any particular reason?"

As if Zack standing in her home holding a bottle of wine weren't reason enough? "Actually, yes! Roxy's coming home by this weekend."

"That's great!"

Clarey pulls out plates and wine glasses. "Yes, and more good news. My sister Jessa got a job."

"Doing what?"

"Well, she's a super gifted artist by vocation, but that's not exactly paying the bills these days. So she got a barista gig, which will at least get her out of the house a bit before she and Hope kill each other. Sounds silly, but I kind of like both of them and would prefer they don't come to blows."

Zack grins. "Sounds like we have a lot to celebrate. Hope red's okay."

"Perfect." Clarey grabs the corkscrew and meets him at the table. As Zack works the cork out, Clarey glimpses the label. "That looks old. How old is it?"

"It's a 1928 Bordeaux," he says without looking.

Clarey grabs Zack's hand before he pulls the cork. "Excuse me? You better be kidding."

"Why would I kid?"

"Why would you have a bottle that old? And why would you waste it on me?"

"Would I be opening it if I thought it was a waste?" He pops the cork and hands it to her. "Souvenir." Clarey holds it to her nose and inhales a surprisingly pleasant bouquet, as if she actually knows anything about wine bouquets.

"Not that I'm not flattered, but seriously, you should be saving this for something more special."

He pours a glass and hands it to her, then another for himself. "I don't want to save it anymore."

"How long have you had it?" He looks at the bottle and shrugs. "1928?"

Clarey laughs as she sips. Both the alcohol and the laughter warm her through and through. She's not knowledgeable enough about wine to differentiate flavors like apricot or smoke, let alone determine if it's earthy or flabby or balanced. But the way it washes over her tongue igniting pleasure centers she didn't know she had tells her the wine is working on her. Or something is. "Delicious."

Zack gives her a heavy-lidded smile that she feels all the way to the bedroom and his dimples make her want to lay him flat and drink wine from them. That would be a good start anyway. Zack raises his glass. "To fine wine, employed sisters, prodigal dogs, and great company."

"Cheers," Clarey says with a clink.

After dinner, more wine, and an excess of praise for Clarey's cooking, Zack wanders over to her bookshelves. "Quite a collection you've got here." If he's trying to seal the deal by admiring her books, it's unnecessary. He's got this thing locked down. But the way he runs his fingertips over the spines suggests genuine appreciation. "You've got a lot of great books. I love these old mysteries." He reaches her shelf of special, old leather-bound collectibles. "Classics, too, huh? I admire your versatility."

She walks up behind him with their glasses in hand, the final drops of the bottle within.

"The complete Dickens. Excellent," he says, pulling out a copy of *The Pickwick Papers*. "He was a great guy. So funny!"

She hands him his glass as he turns to her. "You knew him?" she laughs.

Zack swallows the remains of his glass in one gulp, then smiles. "He spent some time in Paris while I was living there."

Clarey leans in a little closer. "You've lived a crazy life. It's hard to even imagine it."

"It's mostly just like yours," he says with a gentle lilt. "But a little longer."

"Quite a bit longer," she says in a quiet, sultry voice. When he shrugs, she takes the book from his hand and lays it on the shelf.

"Ever read any romance?" she asks while intentionally leaning her body across him to pull out an Emily Henry book.

"Not really," he shakes his head slowly. "Not yet, anyway."

"I love them." Clarey blinks her eyes slowly at him, hoping the wine's working on him as well as it's working on her. She slides her body next to him and leans against the bookshelf.

"Yeah?" he says without moving. "What do you love about them?"

She flips through the pages as she says, "The sweet moments, the humor, the impossible situations." She pauses to look up at him. "The steam."

She holds his gaze a moment longer, extending the invitation. The air molecules dance around them as Clarey's temperature rises, and maybe the room's too, while she awaits his response. Her breath stills in a moment of terror that he's going to pull away, but Zack does not disappoint. He leans in and raises a finger to her chin to tilt her face toward him. They stay like that for a blissfully slow minute, taking each other in, considering what each of them is about to become to the other. What the next moments will hold for them, and then the moments after that. They feel every heavenly beat as they gaze longingly at each other. Then he leans in.

Their mouths sink into each other and it's magical. Long and lingering, all soft flesh and heat, then the tiniest flicker of tongue, a fleeting taste of what's to come. Wet with the sweetness of the wine, his full lips are warm and welcoming and feel like forever.

Their lips part, but only inches separate them still. "That was nice," she whispers.

"Yeah," he agrees, his breathing ragged and hot against her. He stares at her lips, then raises his gaze to her eyes. She watches his

Adam's apple bulge as he swallows. Then his back stiffens and he pulls away, clearing his throat. "I should go," he announces.

"What?" she says as he heads for the door too quickly.

"It's getting late. I promised I'd help Herb in the morning." Zack pauses to look at the remnants of the dinner, then back at Clarey standing in shock in the middle of the room. "Dinner was wonderful," he says. "Thank you for... a really lovely evening."

"What?" she says again.

"Good night, Clarey."

And then he's gone. Again. And now, Zack has been present for – no, *responsible* for three of Clarey's most humiliating moments ever. Clarey looks slowly around the now empty room and says aloud the three words that keep looping through her brain. "What. The. Fuck."

Chapter Twenty

It's Complicated

There isn't a shower cold enough to subdue the raging hard-on in Zack's pants as he walks back into his place. The water in Seattle in July is nowhere near cold enough. Hell, an arctic waterfall wouldn't be cold enough to still the disproportionate amount of blood rushing directly to his nether regions at the moment. But walking onto his balcony does the trick in ten seconds flat when he hears one of Clarey's sisters say, "But 3B would have to be an idiot, and a blind man, not to see how hot you are." Clarey must be Facetiming with them.

"Fine. Whatever," Clarey balks. "But I'm not 3B hot."

Zack winces. How can she think such things when that girl is as hot as the sun?

"Admittedly, I haven't seen 3B," says the other sister, "but you're the total package!"

The first sister agrees. "She's not wrong there."

"If I'm the total package, then why was I left unopened on my own doorstep?" Clarey wails miserably. "He ran out of here so fast, he may as well have stamped 'Return to Sender' on my forehead."

Zack steps back into his condo and silently shuts the door before he can hear another word. He feels like an absolute shit. No, forget *feels like.* There's no room for interpretation in this scenario. He *is* an absolute shit. He shouldn't have kissed her. This is all so wildly unfair to her and she deserves better. He knew better than to let it go this far, and now he's hurt her. Worse, he's broken her – because he's made her doubt herself.

If she blamed him, that would be one thing. He didn't want to hurt her, but blaming him is as it should be. After all, this is entirely about him and the impossible life he leads, the life she can't lead with him. No matter how much he would like her to. And he would really fucking like her to. But his reality hasn't changed since day one. Can't change. Won't change. A god is a god is a god, no matter how cute the girl is. So this thing with Clarey remains as impossible as it was the first day he laid eyes on her dropping those water bottles outside Herb's. But it's his fault, not hers.

And now she thinks it's because he's not into her? Because she's not attractive enough? When she literally plagues his dreams and stars in daily shower fantasies with her luscious fleshy curves that he would give anything to lift, stretch, and shape like sourdough. Yet, she thinks she's not good enough for him. And he's the shit who made her think that.

***

Zack's returning from a run when they cross paths at the mailboxes. He hoped he'd have something worked out to say by the time he saw her, but any ideas he'd started to develop instantly achieve escape velocity and flee his brain when he sees her. So he goes with the old classic, "Good morning."

"Hi, Zack, hi," she answers, looking everywhere but at him.

"Thanks again for dinner." Sweat drips down his face. Logically, it must be from the run, so why does it feel directly tied to Clarey?

"Of course. My pleasure." She's still avoiding his eyes.

"Listen, about last night..."

"You don't have to."

"It's just complicated," he says. Clearly, he's going to fully bungle this, whatever this is. "The god thing, you know?"

"Yeah," she says, pursing her juicy pink lips that he'd give anything to sample again.

"I mean, you're great, Clarey. Really."

"Sure, yeah... you... too." She manages a flash of a smile before looking away again. "I have to get to Mr. G's."

Zack should let her go. In more ways than one. There's no use belaboring this. The horse is dead, flogging not required, but he can't let her walk out thinking this has anything to do with her. That she's anything less than perfect. "We've got a good thing going here, yeah? I don't want to ruin it by muddying the waters."

"No, totally." Clarey checks the time on her phone and looks toward the exit.

"Good, right," he says.

"Yes, right, good. I was thinking the same, exact thing. It was just that ancient wine talking. Hundred-year-old booze does it to me every time. Chalk it up to the Chateau la coo-coo!"

"Great. Glad we're on the same page." They are absolutely *not* on the same page. "So we're good then?" He's asking too much of her. He should have given her time. And a proper apology. But here he is, screwing things up once again. There really is a reason he doesn't do this. Ever.

"Never better," Clarey says as she rushes out the door and away from Zack.

***

Zack hefts the large carton onto the countertop as Herb walks in declaring, "Okay, Mr. Homer Dickens is fed and watered, and so am I. You can officially go."

"What kind of name is that for a cat?"

"I didn't ask for your opinions, thank you. I think I said you could go."

"Alright, old man. I'll finish unloading this carton and head out." He removes several cans of what, if his rusty Thai serves, is Thai coconut soup, which he carries to the Asian foods section to stock.

"Yes, by all means, go find Clarey and fix whatever it is you did."

"What do you mean?" Zack asks as he flattens the box and tosses it onto the pile.

"That girl was sad today," Herb says.

"Sad?" Zack could handle mad. He deserves mad. Mad means she blames him. But sad is a knife to the gut. "Why do you assume I did anything?"

"She wouldn't say what was wrong, but she spent the day talking about her work, her sisters, her dog. And there was only one topic that was entirely off limits."

Zack flops onto the stool behind the counter. "Damn. I really screwed this up. I should have kept my distance. Like always. I knew it was a mistake and I did it anyway. I never should have listened to you."

"No, you should listen to me more! You might actually learn something about the human heart." Herb pulls out his phone and opens a favorite picture of his wife, then hands it to Zack. "I had fifty-five wonderful years with Mimi. Losing her was devastating. But it didn't end when she died. That's the thing you can't seem to understand. The love doesn't end."

Zack stares at the photo of Mimi. They were a great couple. Herb and Mimi were made for each other. They laughed together, they listened to each other, they fought like fiends, and they loved fiercely. They were affectionate to the end. Even when they lost David, through all the pain and grief, the knowledge that their line would end with them, they clung to each other. They navigated their sorrow as a unit, and they found joy again as partners in life.

Bearing witness to Herb and Mimi through their loss had given Zack strength as well. David's death, while only one in a boundless sea of losses, held so much more weight than the others. Because it was truly the end of the line. Mimi was too old to have another. Herb loved her too much to ever consider finding someone new after she passed, let alone someone young enough to bear children. People die every day. And family trees simply run out of branches. It happens. But it hadn't happened in Herb's line in 100 generations. When at last it did happen, they grieved like any other parents would mourn their children. They didn't carry the burden of history – of the 100 generations in an unbroken line, of the single heir in each of those generations who, when lost, was always replaced, until now. Nor did they feel the significance of its end beyond their own deeply personal anguish. The searing heartache of the loss was more than enough weight to carry.

But Zack carried that knowledge. And while Herb and Mimi helped him navigate the grief as he helped them at the time, he still hasn't come to terms with the ramifications. Zack stirs from his reverie when the entry bell rings. Clarey stands in the doorway. He lights up. "Clarey, hi!"

"Hey," she says, still reluctant to make eye contact.

"You're back!" Herb says with a smile before returning to his sweeping.

"Just for a sec," Clarey replies before turning back to Zack. "Saw you in here. I'm on my way to pick up dinner."

"You don't want to hang out?"

"I have a lot of work to do tonight. A proposal for a prospective client. Figure I better hunker down for a while." She says it with the cautious hesitation of someone who wants to be alone more than she wants to work. "I really need some more clients," she adds, emphasizing the absolute, work-based legitimacy of her need to stay the fuck away from Zack.

"Sure," he says. She needs time. He didn't give her enough this morning, but he owes her that at the very least.

"Just thought I'd give you some good news. We had a visitor today."

"A visitor?"

"Yeah, an electrician came by to finish wiring the gym."

Zack walks slowly around the counter and toward Clarey. "I didn't know they were restarting work. Wouldn't they have told us?"

"It was just him. He got a call because he was supposed to do it a while ago and didn't. I figured you'd be happy."

Herb's sweeping slows as Zack asks, "Did you let him in or did he have a key?"

Clarey steps back toward the door as Zack approaches. "I, um, I let him in."

Zack stiffens. "He didn't have his own key?"

"No, I mean, he said he forgot his key."

"You wouldn't let me in the building, but you let him in?" Unbelievable.

"That's *why* I let him in. For you."

"Did he show you ID?"

Herb approaches the front and rests his hands on the top of the broom, listening intently. "Zachary, let's not get carried away."

Zack ignores him as his focus burns into Clarey. "Clarey, did he show you any kind of identification before you let him in?"

Clarey's on the verge of tears from the intensity of Zack's questioning. "No, but he had a toolbox."

A sudden rage rips through Zack. "Oh, well if he had a toolbox!"

"Zachary!" Herb shouts.

"I can't win," Clarey says. "Last time, I didn't let you in and I looked like an idiot. This time, I did let someone in, and apparently I still look like an idiot."

Herb looks at Zack pointedly and summons his most insistent, paternal tone. "I'm sure Clarey had a good reason for letting him in. Why don't you let her talk?"

Zack checks himself with a deep breath, then says, "I'm sorry. Can you tell me what happened?"

Clarey's eyes dart between the two men as she gathers her thoughts. "He came up to the door as I was leaving. He said he forgot his key, but could I please let him in because he was under the gun to get it done in time for inspections. I tried to push back. I did. But he begged me to cut him a break. Said he'd been putting it off and was going to be in trouble if it wasn't done."

Zack puffs out a breath of frustration. Sweet Clarey, always a sucker for a sob story. "And you cut him that break."

"I wasn't going to. I'm really trying. To set boundaries or whatever." She juts her chin forward a little, asserting the truth in her words. "But then I thought of you. Of how dumb I felt when I didn't let you in and you were telling the truth all along." He wasn't. He's never told the real truth. Even now, she doesn't know what's really going on. "And of how happy I thought you'd be if all the equipment was working. For when it's raining and stuff."

Zack hangs this head and leans back against the counter rubbing the bridge of his nose. She did it for him. And once again, he's making her feel like crap for something that's all his fault.

Clarey utters a defeated sob. "I thought you'd be happy."

"What a thoughtful gesture. Don't you think, Zachary?"

Zack's fire is extinguished, but not his worry. He looks at Herb and shakes his head. "Anyone could see the gym is unfinished from the street."

"I'm sure it will be fine," Herb says calmly.

Zack winces. Shame and regret rip through his nervous system, replacing the anger that only moments ago made him go full wanker. "I'm sorry about that. I'm sorry about everything, Clarey." He holds her gaze and watches her face soften. "I really am."

"I shouldn't have let him in without verification. I'm sorry."

Zack studies her face. Her green eyes shine as brightly as ever, but her cheeks have paled from their confrontation. "No, I was out of line. I'm sure it's fine." If he can hear the uncertainty in his voice, she likely can too, but he underscores it with a confident nod before shooting a glance out the window to scan the perimeter.

"And even if he is dangerous," Clarey says, "you'll protect me, right?" She's aiming for flirtatious, but her words are laced with a disarming note of sincerity. His rant has unnerved her.

He smiles reassuringly before encircling her in his arms and pulling her tight. His voice is grave when he answers. "Yes. I'll protect you."

Chapter Twenty-One

Lightning Storms and Cinnamon Rolls

When Clarey agreed to let Zack walk her home after she picked up her food, she assumed he'd be waiting at the store, but when she rounds the corner, she spots him sitting on the fountain across the street instead. That fountain, where she first saw him draped like a Greek statue who looked so perfect there he may as well have been spouting water from his mouth. But he looks a lot less relaxed this time, his head on a constant swivel as if on high alert for rogue pigeons or seagulls.

The sky grows dark as she walks toward him. It's only six-thirty and the sun doesn't set until after nine o'clock. She hasn't checked the weather lately – why bother when every day is sunny and glorious this time of year? – but there must be a summer storm rolling in. Fast, judging by the speed of the descending darkness.

When Zack spots her, he moves her direction, though it's opposite of their place. "All set?" he asks when he reaches her. She nods, and he adds, "Good. Let's get home fast." A sweet, pungent aroma of ozone fills the air. He looks up at the increasingly ominous sky and shuffles her rapidly down the street. Not fast enough, however. The warm air changes around them. An unmissable charge surges through every molecule that surrounds them. "Come on!" Zack says, yanking Clarey by the arm.

A single clap of thunder echoes through the sky. The volume alone attests to its proximity, yet surely it can't be that close. Every storm has to roll in from somewhere. That's what Clarey always thought. First a darkening sky, then a quiet, distant rumble, then a sprinkle turned to rain turned, occasionally, into actual thunderstorms. But there are steps. There's a protocol to these things, a proper way to advance through the steps and issue the requisite warning signs, so dingbats too dumb to check the forecast or carry umbrellas can get themselves into safe, dry locations. Not that you should be using an umbrella in a thunderstorm, but the point is still valid. There are steps. And thunder that loud and close is never, ever step one. It doesn't make any sense. But the next clap, which is somehow even louder and apparently directly overhead, suggests the weather gods aren't interested in Clarey's logic.

Zack pulls Clarey into a literal run and dodges under the covered entrance of a nearby building as lightning touches down no more than a yard behind Clarey's last footstep. Her food splats to the ground as her pulse pounds a tempo into her head even louder than the thunder. He grabs her by both arms and ducks to look into her eyes. "Clarey, are you okay?" When she says nothing, he gives her a tiny shake to snap her out of her daze. "Are you okay?"

"Yeah, I..." Outside the overhang is Armageddon. The roar of perpetual thunder shakes the ground as much as the lightning itself as bolt after bolt fills the plaza. The sky has gone black, but blasts into sunlight brightness with a new strike every ten seconds or so. Still dazed, Clarey stares out, eventually catching sight of Mr. G in the shop window across the street, likewise staring out in wonder.

Zack holds his hand up to Mr. G, telling him to stay put. What is happening?

The bank behind them is locked up tight for the night, as are all the other shops and businesses around them. "Clarey, listen. We're going to have to make a run for it," Zack says.

"What? No, we should wait it out."

"We can't," he insists.

"We have to! We can't go out in that. It'll pass eventually. We should stay here."

"Listen to me," he says, shaking his head. "It's not going to pass. Not until we're safe inside. Trust me." Another spear of blinding light rips through the sky and singes the ground directly in front of their overhang. "It's not safe here. Clarey, we have to go."

On the scale of one to catastrophically, suicidally bad ideas, the notion of going out into that chaos breaks the damn scale. There's no possible way they can— Another bolt cracks down on the exact spot where the previous one hit. Then again, running has its appeal.

Zack turns her body and points. "Look, the building's right there. You run diagonally across the street and straight in. Get to the overhang first, then stay close to the building until you reach the door. Go straight in. Don't wait for me."

"What do you mean? You'll be with me, right?"

"I'll be right behind you."

"You're faster than I am."

"You go first," he says. "I want to make sure you're safe."

Clarey stares at the building across the street, one short kitty-corner crossing away. No distance at all. But in this storm, it may as well be the road from Marathon to Athens. It's impossible to make that run. She'll never make it.

Zack closes in behind her, placing his hands gently on her shoulders. He leans in against her ear, and somehow the boom of his quiet voice vibrates past the cacophony of blasts, claps, and cracks of unending thunder. "Don't think so hard. If you stop to think, you're lost. When I tell you, run for all you're worth. Don't look back. No matter what. Just run."

Panic wracks her body as she turns to face him. "Zack, please!"

He clasps her face in his hands and nods encouragingly. "I'll be right behind you."

Clarey looks back to Goldfarb's where Mr. G still stands, transfixed and horrified by the apocalypse outside. But when he locks eyes with her, he sets his jaw and holds up a fist to incite her courage. She's shaking and breathless, but she summons the will to nod back her understanding.

Another bolt sears the ground ten feet away and Zack shouts, "Run! Now!"

With her stomach in her throat, Clarey tears out from the cover at top speed. She's no runner, but sheer terror fuels her feet past their natural limitations. Electricity channels its way to the ground in a blast ahead of her. She zigs to the left to dodge it, only to be met with another to her left, zagging her the other way. She'll never make it. There are too many strikes and she's not fast enough. Everywhere she runs, lightning strikes. Her body stiffens and her pace slows at the realization that it's over. Until Zack's voice behind her screams, "Go!"

Suddenly, a miracle – the path ahead of her is clear. The darkness in front of her is illuminated by the flashes behind her and she takes off running for her life, grateful for the momentary respite that might be her saving grace, however fleeting. She ducks under the lip of the building and then to the overhang at the door. The motion sensors kick the low-level entrance lighting up to full-blast and Clarey collapses against the door, doubled-over and panting. She made it. Somehow. She was dead. She was sure of it. But by some act of God, something drew the lightning away long enough for her to make it.

Despite Zack's instructions, she can't bring herself to run inside without him. But he should be here by now. He was supposed to be right behind her. She presses her hands against the door and climbs her way back to standing, then spins around to find Zack. She expects to see him running up to her any second. Or possibly still waiting across the street under the overhang. But he's in neither place. Clarey screams when she sees him in the middle of the street, rigid and immobilized, pinioned by a devastating bolt of electricity from the sky.

"Zack!"

***

When Zack somehow made his way to the door, Clarey didn't ask questions. She dragged him inside and pulled out her phone to call 911. "No," Zack said, shaking his head, "I'm okay."

"No, you're fucking not. You were struck by lightning."

"Just get me upstairs. Please."

And so she had, because she was too shaken up herself to argue with him. But now that he's here, laid out on her couch, somehow in one piece and seemingly occupying a space somewhere in the vicinity of normal – which in and of itself is very definitely not normal – the questions are bubbling up.

"What just happened? That couldn't have happened, right?" She's ranting. "Did that happen?"

"I think it did, yeah."

Clarey looks outside, where the sky is now completely clear. The sun has returned to gently easing itself toward the horizon, not a cloud in the sky. The only remaining signs of the storm are the black singe marks peppering the street and sidewalk on their block.

She returns to Zack and searches his body for injuries. "Are you sure you're okay?"

"I'm fine, but what about you?"

Clarey takes a few stunned moments to respond. "I'm okay. Shaken, but okay. But I wasn't struck by lightning." He gives her a gentle smile and places a warm hand lightly on her cheek before dropping it back to his lap. "We almost died out there," she says.

"Yeah." He pauses as if to say more, then stops himself. He looks her over closely. "You sure you're alright? No injuries?"

"I'm fine. Someone must have been looking out for us."

"Or someone found us," Zack mumbles to himself.

"Don't you feel so lucky to be alive?" Clarey says. "I do! I feel..." She pauses as she looks Zack over, her manic frenzy of fear and astonishment turning in an instant to unbridled lust. "So lucky." All the adrenaline, tension, and terror coursing through her has amalgamated into a lightning hot passion not just to be alive, but to prove it. And she can think of no better proving ground than Zack.

Clarey zeroes in on Zack's mouth, soaking up every delicious curve of his lips, wondering how those curves would align with her own, and how soon she can find out. When she redirects her laser beam to his eyes, he meets her gaze and holds it. Suddenly, she's breathing hard again, but it's not panic. Without another thought, Clarey lunges for Zack and presses her mouth to his, his full lips opening to meet her. She tastes smoke, desire, and life on his tongue and delves in for more. More life.

He pushes her gently back. "Clarey, you're really shaken up. You might be in shock. We shouldn't do this. Not now."

"Oh, yes, we should," she says. "I want you, Zack. I want to feel alive. Now."

"I can't take advantage of you in this state."

"Then let me take advantage of you." She climbs onto his lap.

"Clarey, please. It wouldn't be right."

Clarey pauses. Despite what he thinks, this isn't shock talking. She's wanted him for ages. Even if it's all over tomorrow and all she has to show for it is a good story she can never tell anyone about the time she fucked a god, she wants him. Badly. But has she misread the signs? Every one of them? Has she been fooling herself all this time? "Don't you want me?" she says. "Because that would be a hell of a cherry on this sundae of a day."

Zack releases a guttural moan of a laugh. "Fuck yeah, I want you." Clarey's heart leaps as her heat rises from just those five words. "I've wanted to devour every inch of you since the moment I laid eyes on you." And as he speaks, his arousal grows beneath her, as if he's only now given himself permission to feel it.

She grinds herself down against him and leans in so her lips are a mere breath from his. "Then devour me."

Zack winces through a moment of obvious self-restraint. "You don't know what you're asking."

"Maybe I want to find out."

Zack raises his hands to Clarey's face and holds her head fast in his gaze. "Are... you... sure?"

Clarey drags her hands out across each of his broad shoulders, traces them down his biceps and then back up to his wrists, which are still locked millimeters from her throat. She wraps her fingers around his wrists, feeling the too hot blood pumping through his veins, and squeezes. "I've never been more sure of anything in my life."

In a flash, he lifts her whole body and flops her down on the couch. He pounces on top of her and thrusts his tongue into her mouth as her hands tear away the scraps of his lightning-shredded shirt. He returns the favor, ripping her own top from her body before pulling down her bra and hungrily attacking her breasts. His mouth greedily clamps onto one nipple, then the other, while his hands explore every curve and dimple of her generous flesh. He shoves her pants down and finds his way to her heat where he discovers she's more than ready.

His lips sealed to hers, he slides his fingers into her and Clarey ascends. He massages her into a frenzy of passion, the lightning returning as she writhes onto another plane of existence. Whatever he's doing, it's working. Every touch is another thunderbolt, electrical currents charging through her in unstoppable waves of pleasure.

The sensation's so intense, she's barely in her body. She reaches for him, to pull herself back to earth. She feels the power of the muscles in his back, and it grounds her for a fleeting moment. But when she opens her eyes to look at him, she sees him literally glowing with the heat of passion. She could swear his eyes flash violet. What the hell is happening to her? Hallucinating through sex is a first, but she's in no shape to fight it.

She closes her eyes again as her climax approaches, she screams, then whites out with the most blinding release she's ever felt. That any woman anywhere has ever felt. She pants heavily, trying to regain her composure. Afraid to open her eyes and find out it was only a dream. As her senses slowly return, she forms her first words. "They'll write books about that orgasm," she gasps before opening her eyes and laughing.

Zack presses his lips to her neck and thrusts himself against her. "I'm not through with you yet," he says with a gentle, but insistent bite. He stands to unbutton his jeans, slides them off, then moves back toward the couch.

"Wait, wait," Clarey pants through her haze. "Do you have anything?"

"Anything? Oh, that. Shit, no."

God damn her clear-thinking brain. "Is Goldfarb's still open?"

"Um...I, uh..." Zack isn't thinking straight. Actually, he doesn't appear to be thinking at all. His not-so-little head appears to be doing the thinking at the moment, but he manages to say, "I'm not sure I want to go back out there quite yet."

"No, wait. There might be one in the books."

"The books?"

"Derek used to keep condoms stashed in my books after we split. In case he got lucky, he didn't want to be caught unprepared."

"I both love him and hate him for that right now." Zack runs over to the bookcase. "So which book?"

"He'd try to be funny. Maybe *The Age of Innocence*?"

Good thing she'd alphabetized the books. Zack scans the shelves, spots the title, and pops it open. "No."

"*Persuasion*?"

He tosses the book aside and repeats the process. "Nothing."

"Shit, I'm sure he's got half a dozen in there somewhere." Clarey rubs her head and thinks. "Oh, I know." She laughs with dismayed certainty and rolls her eyes. "Try *Great Expectations*."

"Bingo!" Zack slips on the condom and climbs back onto the couch on his knees. "Now can we please stop talking about your ex-husband?"

"Who?"

Zack unleashes a wolfish smile as he seizes Clarey's thick thighs and drags her to him, pressing inside. She glides her hands over the sharp angles of his muscular chest she'd admired too often to be anything less than embarrassing. Doubting for a moment that this could be real. That this man could be real. But the hard length now driving into her leaves no doubt.

He pauses and they look into each other's eyes. A delicate moment of connection promises something more than raw, carnal desire. They hold their breath, suspended in their passion. Her fingers trace down his abdomen. He lowers a hand to her sex, caresses her gently, then slides his hand slowly up over her stomach, between her breasts, and to her face. He cups her face and runs his thumb lightly over her lips. He gives a smile as soft as his touch.

Tenderness wells as she whispers breathlessly, "Zack."

Then he clutches her waist and yanks her up onto his lap like she weighs nothing. Already connected, she slides onto him easily and within seconds, they are thrusting for their lives. He lifts her and brings her back down, again and again, while she uses every muscle in her body to hang on, riding the seemingly endless waves of bliss.

"Oh, Zack!" she cries out. "Oh my God!"

"Yes!" he groans into her neck. "Yes!" he repeats in an almost thunderous bellow that vibrates through her body as he clamps his hands hard onto her bare ass.

Clarey collapses against Zack, wrapping her arms around him and hanging her head limply on his shoulder. And as she comes undone for the second time – or is it the third? – she knows two things with absolute certainty. One, this is by far the best sex she's ever had, will ever have, could ever imagine having.

And two, the night has only just begun.

***

Clarey floats blissfully through white clouds flashing even brighter white as she drifts awake. Her head still foggy, the scent of cinnamon greets her even before she opens her eyes. She stretches her arm across the bed and finds it empty, but although she's alone in bed, the sweet spicy aroma assures her she's not alone in the apartment. God, this man really is too good to be true.

Before she can even sit up, Zack appears in the doorway. "I had a feeling you were up," he says with the perfect morning-after grin. He crawls into bed and straight on top of her where he pins her down with a kiss. "Good morning, sleepyhead."

He's heavy and solid and so supremely real lying on top of her. Clarey considers the relative merits of spending the entire day in this precise position and attempts to calculate how long she can hold off a bathroom visit. If he keeps pressing on her bladder like that, not long. Besides, there's that smell to investigate. "Good morning," she replies, making her froggy morning voice as sultry as she can manage. "This is a nice way to wake up in the morning."

He kisses her again. "This is a nice way to wake you up." He rolls slightly to the side and pushes himself up onto one arm while his other hand wanders over her body. "But it's not technically morning. It's twelve-fifteen."

"No!"

"Someone needed her sleep," he says, his hand idly kneading her stomach.

"Well, it was a hell of a night."

"It certainly was." His hand glides up from her stomach to her cheek, which he caresses before kissing her again. "Come on, Red. I made cinnamon rolls."

Like the first time he called her Red, the name blazes through her like a heatwave, but this time it's chased by a giddy lightness that rises like a bright, white-yellow sun in her. She shakes the feeling to stay on topic. "With what? The closest thing I've got to baking stuff is a frying pan and a disposable, cardboard salt shaker."

"Between your half stocked kitchen and mine, I managed," he says as he stands and pulls her naked from the bed. He plants a long kiss on her as he gropes her ass before slapping it and adding, "Now, go put something on that gorgeous ass and meet me in the kitchen."

Chapter Twenty-Two

The Price

Zack slices through the next piece of wood with the kind of care and precision that used to characterize everything he did. Now, as he completes the cut and releases the button on the saw, his attention wanders yet again. He can't seem to get through more than a single slice at a time without his thoughts trailing off to that soft skin. And those gorgeous lips. And those electric curls. And the warm center of her, which is almost all that matters suddenly.

That beautiful girl with the vibrant green eyes and freckles and fire for hair. He would do anything for her. He would climb any mountain, sail any sea, lasso the sun, and smite the moon for her. He would do it all for her without a second thought. He would give it all up for her, if only he didn't have Herb. And that pesky immortality. The knowledge terrifies him.

He forces his way through the last couple slices, then begins the slow, methodical process of gluing the pieces of wood together into the butcher block countertop of his dreams. Or at least, the butcher block of his current design vision, such as it is. It started as a project to keep him busy. Something to help pass the time. But now, with everything that's happened, it's become his saving grace. It's the only thing that's giving him a moment of respite from his constant thoughts of Clarey and all of her glorious Clareyness. He glues each piece quickly into place, then clamps them all together tightly to cure. If only his feelings for Clarey were as easy to cure.

And yet, for all his preoccupation, Zack still has Herb, his literal reason for being here, his last, most important reason for a lifetime of service that will soon come to a bittersweet end. Not today, not tomorrow, but very soon. Okay, it might be twenty years from now, but even that, against a scale of thousands, is basically nothing. The end is coming. But it's not here yet, and Herb remains his first and most pressing priority. Giving Herb every good year he can have remains his sole focus. At least it should be.

Then there's the matter of that lightning storm. He's been thinking about that between Clarey reveries, but it's probably time he did more than think. Ixia is obviously pissed and looking for justice. That could turn ugly very quickly if he's not careful. He's not sure exactly what's coming, or when, but that lightning storm was a proclamation of intent. Which means he probably needs to start digging around before intent turns into action.

***

"That was quite a display last night," Herb says the moment Zack walks into the store. "I assume that was just for you?"

"Afraid so," Zack replies with dismay. "You alright?"

"I'm fine. Although a lightning storm the size of a city block targeting one, single person wasn't something I expected to see in my lifetime."

Zack pulls a soda from a nearby cooler and walks to the front. "To be fair, I think it was targeting the two of us."

"Do you think they were trying to kill you?"

Zack pops open the can and takes a long swig. "Put it on my tab," he says with a nod to Herb, who bats him away. Zack takes another slow draw on his soda, considering the events of the prior night. "Not kill," he finally says. "They don't like to kill humans unless they have to. I think they were trying to scare us. And I haven't always looked like this."

Zack pauses and looks at him, aware he's said something that might surprise even Herb despite all he's seen. Herb looks down and chuckles with a rub at the back of his neck. The news doesn't shock him like it would most people, but even for someone who's spent his whole life with his very own god protection squad, there are still some surprises. "Don't tell me you were a redhead like Clarey."

Zack laughs, thinking back to his periods as a redhead. He hadn't done it often. Redheads tend to stand out, and Zack usually preferred to disappear into the woodwork. But he'd done everything at least once, and red hair was certainly not the most extreme thing he'd done over the years. "I've been like this for a long time, but over the course of thousands of years, I've tried pretty much everything at some point. I've even been more bald than you!"

Herb pats at his remaining hair surrounding his head, avoiding the very naked patch at the top and says, "I'm not bald! Have you seen this gorgeous head of hair I'm sporting? At most, I'm mildly follicly challenged."

"Follicly challenged? Alright, old man," Zack says. The pair laugh like the old, lifelong friends they are, a lifetime of joy, heartbreak, and deep, abiding trust laced through every strained rasp.

This matters. This is why he's here. "In any case, I suspect they didn't know which of us was the god, so they were trying to find out."

"And striking you with lightning told them?"

"No, even a regular person can survive a lightning strike. If they're lucky. No, I think they were hoping I might use my powers, and that would have revealed me."

"But you didn't," Herb says in a slow, measured tone, processing the heft of what this means.

"No," Zack says gravely. If he didn't use his powers, then they still don't know who's the god. And if they still don't know who's the god... Zack leans on the counter and huffs out the worrisome truth. "Which means they're probably not done yet."

***

Zack places the pot of fake marigolds on his balcony and waits. Since he's not allowed to use his active powers, it's his current methodology for calling Xara when he needs her. Most of the time, he's perfectly content to wait until she drops in of her own accord. She's kept him in her rotation over the years and passes by wherever she feels like it, which is plenty often enough for him under normal circumstances.

Xara has been his only link to that other life, the one he reluctantly supposes is his real life, over these thousands of years. She keeps him up to date on the latest "back home" and mocks him for whatever his latest human foible might be. She's relentless in her mockery, preferring to harass him over coddling him every time. But underneath it all, she's been a good friend. She's kept her visits from the higher powers-that-be and remained his one lifeline to a world he'd one day return to. When this is all over. Soon. Very soon.

It's strange to think about that life now. The one without bounds and limits. The one that's so expansive and huge as to be utterly inconceivable to humans. The one where Balder and and Osiris play like children, where Inti shines like the sun, and where Ixia... Well, Ixia does whatever the hell she wants.

It's been nearly three thousand years since he saw any of them, and in a way, it feels like it. His life has been so far removed from all of that for so long that it's sometimes hard to remember it even exists. As if simply walking through each day on this earth, breathing this air, eating this food, wearing these clothes, and carrying the weight of this nearly human existence has reshaped him into something new. Something that could never fit back home after so long. And yet, he'd always assumed he'd go home when it finally ended. What else would he do? After so long, living here among humans felt natural in some ways, but he could never be one of them. Not really. He could never be "just a guy." If it hadn't been for the generation after generation of Herb's family, this would have been a deeply lonely journey. Once Herb is gone, there will be nothing left to keep him here. It would be time to return home, where Xara and many others, maybe even Ixia, would welcome him with open arms.

Or so he thought. But that was before the car accident when Zack instinctively cured Herb without even a flicker of a second thought. If he'd really stopped and thought it through, maybe he would have done as Herb said and let him go. But in the moment, he'd done what the moment demanded and used his active powers to save the old man, his last connection to this world. Well, not his last connection as it turns out. But his connections no longer mattered now, because he had broken the rules. He'd used his active powers and there just might be hell to pay.

Zack jumps at the knock on the door. Xara somehow always manages to surprise him, even when he's expecting her. He opens the door and she marches in, seizing immediate command of the room as if it's her personal kingdom. "Well, you've certainly gotten yourself in a bind now, haven't you?" she says.

Chapter Twenty-Three

Afterglow

When Clarey's sisters pop up onscreen, she nearly cries. They're fiddling around, slapping each other as they fight for space on their shared seat and on camera. "I miss you two so much!" she says before they've even finished settling in.

"We miss you too, spaz," Jessa replies. "This one's impossible."

Hope balks at the dig. "Excuse me, how much rent do you pay again?"

"No one's buying my art right now. What do you want from me?"

"Picking up your endless trail of socks and cereal bowls would be a good start."

Clarey watches them bicker another minute, then finally chimes in. "Should I let you two go?"

"Sorry, honey," Hope coos. "Anyway, I was thinking, we need to find a time to come up and see your new place. Maybe next week?"

"I would love that," Clarey says as if sinking into a puddle of warm fuzzies.

"Alright, we'll figure it out," Hope replies with a glance at a nodding Jessa. Clarey turns to her side to cough out a frog in her throat and Hope's voice immediately raises an octave. "Are you okay?"

"Oh my God! Calm yourself. I'm fine," Clarey says, exasperated. "And I have things to tell you!" She squeals the last bit, unable to contain her excitement.

"How's it going with Thor?" Jessa asks brightly.

"Well, that's an interesting question," Clarey says with delight. "Just hold on a sec. I need some air." Clarey makes for the balcony doors and pushes them open to let in the cool, evening breeze. She glances down and sees none other than that dark-haired woman who Zack swore was just a friend. The gorgeous one with the tall and the thin and the all the things Clarey is not. All the things a guy like Zack would definitely like. As if anyone could be just a friend with a literal goddess like that. And she's walking toward the front door again. Every alarm bell in Clarey's system sounds. She jumps back in front of the camera. "You know what, I have to go! Something came up."

"Wait!" Hope cries.

"Love you, byeeeee," Clarey says as she slams the laptop closed. She paces the room, her thoughts racing twice as fast as her feet. What's he doing with her? Or rather, no, that's not the question because that answer is obvious. Zack might be a god, but he's also a man, and men do think with their dicks a lot. And that Xara is one hundred percent the kind of woman that brings most dicks to attention.

Clarey and Zack never said they'd be exclusive after all. Hell, they never said anything really. They had a lot of sex – oh, so much sex – then they ate cinnamon rolls, fooled around again, and then he went home. There was no talk of exclusivity or even dating. So, strictly speaking, he can do whatever he wants. He can bang Mary one night and pound Paula the next. So they fooled around? So what? One night – or even a night and an afternoon – does not a relationship make. Clarey doesn't care where Zack puts his dick or anything else. His sex life is not remotely her business. If he wants this Xara – and who would blame him? – then fine. He can have her. That's his business and nothing to do with her.

It would probably be just as well. Clarey wants her space anyway. After her previous living situation, what she needs more than anything is alone time. She seems to have forgotten that with this whole, dumb neighborly farce. She should mind her own business, crack open a bottle of wine, open a book, and let him have his fun with his little friend.

So, why is she so tempted to go down there right this very fucking minute?

No, that's a genuinely terrible idea. What's she going to do, walk in on a romantic tryst? Cause a scene? Over what? They had a day of great sex. Terrific! She didn't realize it at the time, but maybe that's exactly what she needed. She got some, and now they can go back to being just friends. Let him wander off to whatever his next sexual misadventure is and leave her out of it, thanks. He's probably exactly like the rest of those impossibly good looking, unattainable men who change lovers as often as they change their shirts.

The whole god thing aside, what does she even know about this guy?

***

Clarey pauses at Zack's door, too terrified to knock. Whatever is going on in there is none of her business. She should go back upstairs before this whole thing takes a turn for the worse. Instead, she knocks.

Voices come through the door. A man and a woman. They're hard to hear, but Clarey leans in, straining to make them out. "What do you see in that little mouse?" the woman says. Is she talking about Clarey? That's it! Clarey pounds on the door.

"Just go," says the man who must be Zack.

"I thought you didn't want me to do that," she says.

Clarey pounds again. "Zack!"

"Scratch, scratch, little mouse," taunts the woman.

"Now," he says.

A brief pause, then Zack calls out, "Right there!" He finally pulls open the door and runs his hand through his hair, brushing it back. He gulps in some air and turns on his smile. "Hi, Clarey."

"Did I catch you at a bad moment?"

"No, never," he says evenly.

She stares at him hard, looking for a crack in his façade, but he holds steady. "Zack, do you have someone here?"

"Here? No, why?"

"I heard voices."

"Oh, that was the TV." He points into the room. "Look, I got a TV! And furniture," he says proudly, waving across his new sofa, chair, and coffee table.

Clarey inspects the room, eager to be appeased, and equally eager to be vindicated in her defensive fury. "The TV's not on."

He tilts his head at her. "I turned it off when you knocked."

"Zack, I know she's here. I saw her." She spits the words with an anger that has her on the edge of tears.

Zack face sags with the apparent effort of it all. "Clarey, she's just a friend. I swear. She came to fill me in. There are things happening where I'm from."

"And she's here? Now."

"She's gone now. I promise," he says with an almost desperate insistence. "Come in. Look around if you want." Clarey stands locked in place, trembling with an excess of righteous indignation, and something much more delicate lying beneath the surface, processing the reality of a world where this woman could be there one moment and simply gone the next. Zack's eyes melt into a tender gaze. "It's good to see you." He folds her gently into his arms and hugs her, then squeezes tighter, lingers longer. "I missed you." Finally, her body relaxes as she sinks into a hug she really shouldn't enjoy this much. When he releases her, he takes her hand and tugs her inside. "Come see the progress I've made."

Instead of another woman, what she does see is the work of a master craftsman in progress. Across the worktable is a slab of butcher block clamped together and drying, and another completed piece already lying atop the island. Set against the forest green cabinets, the shades of dark brown, soft tan, and bright blond woods warm the otherwise industrial space to perfection. It's downright cozy. "You finished the island," she exclaims. "It's spectacular!"

"Not quite. I still need to sand it one more time, then seal it. Want to help?"

Clarey winces. "I don't want to ruin it."

"You won't ruin it. I'll show you." He hands her a piece of purple sandpaper and turns her body to face the island. "Look, 5,000 grit. The surface is very delicate. And with something so delicate and beautiful, it's important to go slow."

"What do I do? Just rub it?"

"Very gently," Zack says, containing his smile. "Here." He steps in close behind Clarey and those pesky air molecules between them burst into motion, sending every hair on her body into high alert. Her breath catches when Zack's own warm breath brushes past her ear as he takes her hand. "With the grain. Like this." His hand resting on hers, his thumb clamped gingerly to her wrist, he slides her hand forward – and with her hand, so goes her body. And his.

Her phone pings with a text, but she ignores it. Together they glide forward. "Then lift…" He eases her hand off the surface, pulls her back, and places her hand down where it started. "And again." Their bodies move in tandem through the back and forth. "Gentle strokes, see."

Clarey quivers from top to bottom. This is… a lot. Only moments ago, she was shaking with anger and now her knees are wobbling from what? Sanding? She's beginning to understand the appeal of DIY. But all of this is a distraction. A very sexy distraction, but even so, her emotions are rubbing her raw. She shouldn't allow herself to be so vulnerable with someone she still doesn't really know, not even a god. With his body curved around her, she says, "Can I ask you a question?"

"Sure," he responds, still leaning over her shoulder. He releases her hand as she rotates her body to face him.

They're face to face now and so deliciously close. She could kiss him. The temptation to lean over and kiss him is almost overwhelming. His full lips like a beacon in the foggy night, summoning her own lips like a moth to a lovely, warm, and almost certainly non-lethal frame. But she wants to know him better. "How did you learn to do all this?"

"I've done some construction work over the years," he says without moving. "And carpentry."

"Construction?" He gives her a heavy-lidded smile, but she's not falling for it. "When you weren't writing code?"

He takes a step back. "Right. Yeah."

"And how did you learn to bake?"

"Just picked it up, I guess. Here and there."

"Hm," she grunts, tight-lipped. Another ping on her phone.

Zack steps away and leans on the island. "Is something wrong?"

"Why don't you ever talk about yourself?"

"I do," he says, moving to pull a beer from the fridge. He holds it out on offer to Clarey, but when she shakes her head, he cracks it open and takes a sip.

"No, you don't. You answer in ambiguities and ellipses. Then you redirect to talk about me." One side of his mouth twitches, flashing a dimple for a split-second. The unmitigated gall of that dimple to show up right when she's trying to stand up for herself.

"I like listening to you."

"And I want to *know* you." Ping, ping, ping. Her phone's blowing up in her pocket.

Zack leans his shoulder against a column and takes another sip. "Aren't we getting to know each other?"

"Tell me one real, concrete thing about yourself." Clarey scans the room grasping for something specific. She spots her paper airplane sitting on his coffee table. Aww. A happy, little sparkler swoops through her chest. Why would he keep it un-less— No, this is not the time. She pushes on. "Tell me how you do that thing with the paper airplanes?"

"You did it too." He tips his head toward the table where the plane sits. A vain attempt to throw her off.

"Only once," she says. "I was aiming down, with gravity on my side. And I got super lucky. You sent yours up. Three times. No, four!"

"Okay." He pauses to consider, then speaks. "I studied aerodynamics for a while."

"Aerodynamics?"

"I was in an aerospace engineering program at the time."

"Right." Her phone pings yet again. She pulls it out and discovers a barrage of messages from Hope announcing she's moments away from calling the police if Clarey doesn't respond to say she's okay. Just what she needs, a full-blown sister panic.

"Aerospace engineers play with paper airplanes. It's really that simple."

"So you're a rocket scientist?"

"Well, I didn't stick with it." When Clarey doesn't respond, he continues. "I've lived a strange mishmash of a life, Clarey. It doesn't even make much sense to me most of the time, so it's really hard to make it make sense to other people. Especially people who don't know what I am. That's why I usually find it easier not to try."

It's true. Little about this guy makes sense. Even considering the godhood of it all. Especially considering the godhood of it all. She has so many questions and so few answers. "I get that. But I want to know you, Zack." She looks at him thoughtfully for a long moment, then adds, "I want you to try."

She stares him down, watching for any hint at obfuscation when he answers. But there's only truth in the warmth of his eyes when he finally offers, "Then I'll try."

Her pocket pings again, and this time, so does her heart. "I better go."

Chapter Twenty-Four

Daring to Be Seen

Zack runs all-out down the street. Runs like someone's chasing him. Runs like someone terrified of getting caught. He speeds past pedestrians in a blur, somehow managing to duck and weave at top speed. He pushes every muscle until the strain and the breathlessness and the euphoria all disappear and there is only Zack and the universe and nothing else. No Clarey. No Herb. No long, inexplicable pasts. No dark, impossible secrets. Just Zack.

When he reaches the park, he finally slows his pace to a jog, then a walk. He walks to the end of the pier and breathes in the lake air, which is blissfully free of puttering boat fumes at the moment. On the beach, swimmers wade in slowly, adjusting to the cold. Taking a dip in that cool drink sounds pretty great in this heat. The temptation lingers, but a fully clothed man jumping into the lake might alarm the families at play. And a naked one would elicit a police response.

Instead, he stares across the lake to the giant houses and tree-lined hillside on the other shore, and to the highest tops of the Seattle skyline beyond. He's thinking of asking Clarey to go to the Seattle sculpture garden, a beautiful place for a walk. But the question remains, how much is he ready to tell her?

***

They nab a parking spot on the street at the top of the hill and gaze out at Elliott Bay. It's another glorious Seattle summer day and the bay gleams in the sun. The park stretches out below them with giant sculptures of every kind punctuating the zigzagging path. The Olympic Mountains rise majestically across the water. This place is a proclamation. It's an unforgivably romantic location for an outing for two. A group excursion, fine. A solo walk, no problem. But strolling side-by-side with someone who makes your head go soft and your dick go hard can only be construed as romantic. It might be a huge fucking mistake, especially when he still has yet another huge fucking secret looming, just waiting to crash the party at some inopportune moment. But if it is a mistake, he can't seem to make himself mind.

In an effort to keep his promise to her, he chooses stories he can safely dole out like passed hours d'oeuvres. A little here, a little there. He talks about his recent travels around the Pacific Northwest. About the mountain town of Coeur d'Alene, Idaho and the breathtaking rocky coastlines of the Oregon Coast. And he tells her where he learned to bake scones – in Cornwall, England – and from whom – an old woman who ran a tea shop. The fact that he learned in the 1940s from a women who has probably been dead for fifty years is where the story gets interesting, but Clarey takes it in stride, or seems to anyway.

A sweet taste of this. A savory amuse bouche of that. It's enough. Because bingeing on a full eight-course meal of Zack's life would be too much. Enough to put anyone in the hospital. But as he shares, little by little, an unexpected lightness at being known sets in. Even these tiny bites. Even with all the missing pieces. This is so much more than he's let anyone see – except Herb, of course – in longer than he can remember. His mask is slowly dropping.

Most never even see him, by design, let alone know him. When they do see him, it's the persona he puts on to suit the occasion, the character they require to play out their own personal dramas. Of lust. Of greed. Of invention. Of survival. He passes in and out of lives taking what he needs and giving others what they need to meet the moment. He takes pleasure or profit and always leaves them better, happier – then he moves on before anyone ever sees beyond their own illusions.

Until Clarey. She sees the real Zack. She may not see the whole picture yet. She may never get the whole picture. But what she does see is the real thing. The original, core Zack. The palimpsest that lies beneath the lies.

And sure, much of that is because he's choosing to show her. Because for once, he's allowing himself to be seen instead of simply fading into the background. But why? It's not only about him this time. It's also because of Clarey. Somehow she looks at him in a way that's hungry, not for food or even for sex, but to know him. She sees him because she *wants* to see him.

Most people are too obsessed with themselves to really see anyone else unless someone self-inserts into their lives. Friends latch on. Lovers magnetize. Children need. They insert themselves. It's the only way to make a real, lasting impression on others. And Zack never inserts himself, so to speak, for longer than a night.

But Clarey is open. Clarey receives. Clarey observes – and absorbs.

"It's my fat girl superpower," she says when Zack comments on how observant she is. "That's the thing, when you're a fat girl, the whole world ignores you. Which means you can spend your whole life watching, unobserved. No one sees me, so I see everyone."

They stroll past a forty-foot high, abstract steel sculpture. It's fire-engine red and stands in sharp relief against the tans of the neighboring buildings, the blue of the cloudless sky, and the white of the Space Needle towering above. "I don't believe no one sees you. You're a beautiful woman. You run a business. And you told me yourself your ex chased you. You're about as invisible as that sculpture."

"Maybe. But I had to learn to assert my place in this world. It didn't come naturally. And for all those invisible years, I watched. That's not a skillset you lose. I put it away sometimes. I get as self-absorbed anyone. But I can still disappear and watch when I want to." She stops walking and turns to look directly at Zack. "Just like you."

Maybe Clarey sees a little too well.

***

Zack exhales a burst of frustration and taps every ounce of his self-restraint to refrain from yelling. "Just tell me what they're saying, Xara."

Xara carries the flowerpot inside and sets it by the door before she glides slowly across his floor and drapes herself onto the couch.

She stretches one impossibly long leg out before crossing it over the other. Everything is a production number with her. She purses her lips and drags out her response, always eager to make Zack sweat. "Well, they won't move on you yet because they're still not sure. But it won't be long."

"But you do think they'll come for me?"

"I can't tell. It's chaos lately. It was all well and good when you were gone. But now that you're back, you've kicked a hornet's nest, and they're none too pleased. Some of them are on your side, but I don't know if it's enough."

"Herb's old. I only need a few more years. That's nothing."

"You're not going to get a few more days at the rate you're going, Elnossys."

"I keep telling you, I'm Zack now. I've been Zack for a long time."

Xara sneers. "You'll never be 'Zack' to me, Elnos."

"Maybe I should go there. Surrender. Get it over with."

"And give up on your little project? Just before the finish line. After *all this time*?" She enunciates the last three words like they're each their own sentence. "Really, Elnos, I never thought you were a quitter."

"I need to talk to Herb."

"And what about your little mouse? Would you leave her?"

"Clarey is why I'd do it. I can't put her in danger again."

Xara rubs her temple with a flourish. "Ugh, this is all so tedious." She puffs out her exasperation before continuing. "Try to restrain yourself from doing anything too stupid. Yet. I'll go back and see what else I can learn. Perhaps the winds might still blow in your favor."

***

Herb opens the door to the darkened cooler. "Bring me those plastic crates from the back, would you?"

Zack walks to the back and returns with a stack of four crates. "How did I let this all get so out of control?"

Herb points to the floor where Zack should drop the crates, then begins moving bottles from the cooler to the first crate. "I think it's about time you let your life get a little messy."

"Well, being struck by lightning's pretty messy."

"That's not what I mean and you know it. I'm glad you let her in. I don't want you to be alone."

Zack watches him shuffling bottles into the top crate. "What are you doing?"

"The cooler's broken. Repair guy comes tomorrow. We need to empty it so we can pull it out."

"You're going to pull all of those out? And then put them all back in tomorrow?"

"It's too heavy to move full."

"Here," Zack says before nudging him aside. He moves the drinks back into the cooler, closes the door, and with a light tug, pulls the full cooler away from the wall until there's plenty of room to access the back side.

"Now why didn't I think of that?" Herb chuckles. "After all these years, I still forget sometimes."

Zack collects the crates again, but pauses on his way to the back room, lost in thought. "She's so sweet, you know?" Herb nods his agreement.

Zack shows no signs of moving, still stuck in his Clarey reverie, so Herb takes two of the crates from his arms and walks them to the back. "She's a special young woman."

Zack follows along with the remaining two then picks up the thread as they return to the front. "What am I going to do?"

"Do you want to be with her?"

"I can't."

Herb reaches under the counter for paper towels and window cleaner. "Stop saying can't. Pretend you can. Pretend you get to choose. What do you want?"

"Clarey."

"Good. Now that's a start." He shoves the cleaning supplies into Zack's hands and points to the front window.

"But I'm putting her in danger. And you, too, now. Regardless of whether I go or not. Which is the opposite of what I'm supposed to be doing."

"Tush! At 78 years old, I'm in no danger at all."

Herb points again, and Zack begins absentmindedly wiping the first window as he speaks. "You could easily get caught in the cross-fire like Clarey. Or something else could happen and I wouldn't be here."

"And? Perhaps you didn't hear this part – or forgot in your even older, and apparently addled brain – but I'm 78. I've lived my life," Herb snips as he climbs onto the stool behind the counter and leans back, resting his weary bones. "Would I like to get older, enjoy a few more years? Certainly. But would it be tragic? Is it tragic for an old man who's lived a good life to die eventually? Of course not. No matter how he goes. Besides, you've been gone a lot over the years, and I've been fine."

"But you were still under my protection. In fact, that accident shouldn't have been possible." Zack furrows his brows, wrestling with an equation that can't be balanced. The agreement was that as long as he remained on this plane, and granted them his protection, they'd be safe. One heir at a time, vulnerable only to self-harm or natural causes in old age. "I can't figure out why it happened."

"Perhaps it's all breaking down. The magic show is ending and all the magic is going away." Herb wiggles his fingers in the air like a magician, then sends them fluttering out like dissipating stardust.

Zack laughs and throws a crumpled bundle of dirty paper towels playfully in Herb's direction. "I've still got more than enough tricks up my sleeve to keep you safe, old man. I just have to stay close."

"Zachary, you've done your job. And like it or not, the business you started is closing up shop. You're going to be unemployed for the first time in how many millennia? Whether it happens now or a few years down the line, it's coming. And as we both know, that's no time at all for you. So what are you going to do next?"

Zack sighs miserably at his paper towels, then turns to the old man. "Well, I've got to tell her what's going on for one thing. She deserves that much."

CHAPTER TWENTY-FIVE

GOING WRONG

THAT AFTERNOON, CLAREY'S MINDING the register when a woman approaches the counter looking sheepish as she drops a massive armload of biscoito de polvilho packets on the countertop. "Comfort food," she says by way of explanation. "My husband grew up in Brazil and he would mainline these if he could. He's been crazy busy with work, so I figured he could use a treat."

Clarey scans the first bag and adjusts the quantity to ten. "I get it, believe me. There are these tiramisu flavored Nippon Chocolates over there that I can't get enough of. And I've never even been to Japan."

"Really?" the woman says, intrigued. She raises a "one minute" finger and runs over to the Asian foods section. A moment later, she returns with a bag. "Just for me. Don't tell." Clarey raises her own finger to her mouth in a promise to keep the secret. And just like that, she's completed her first upsell.

Clarey beams with pride as she wishes the woman a good day, then beams anew when Mr. G walks out from the back. "I upsold a customer!"

"Very good, young lady! You're becoming a pro at this."

Clarey giggles. "I learned from the best, Mr. G."

"Now, Clarey, really, when are you going to call me Herb? Are we not friends?" He'd said that to her once before, but they'd only just met then. So much has happened since then. Mr. G scans the empty shop, then leans in conspiratorially and says, "You and I share something no one else in this world knows. We know the truth about Zachary. That makes us very special friends indeed." He places one of his warm hands on hers. "No?"

It's true. Sharing this knowledge is a bond like no other. To know the real Zack, to be trusted with his identity, is a precious gift she doesn't take for granted. And although she hadn't thought about it, he's absolutely right. To share that knowledge with Mr. G – no, with Herb – is a unique connection unlike any other. "Alright, Herb. You win," she says with laugh.

The bell rings as Zack himself walks in. "Speak of the devil," Herb says. "Your ears must have been burning because we were just talking about you."

Zack smiles "All good, I hope?"

"Always. Always." Herb shuffles towards the back. "Now I'll leave you two to your devices."

"Hey, beautiful," he says with a smile. "How's your day going?"

The sunshine bath of pleasantries with a god isn't something Clarey ever thought she'd feel, let alone get used to. But the cozy way he greets her rumbles her system with a gentle, familiar sense of safety. As if being in Zack's orbit, being one of *his people*, comes with its own warm glow of Belonging. Acceptance. Security. Home. It may be an illusion, but it feels so good, all the same.

Clarey responds with the usual chit chat, and for a moment, everything seems blissfully easy. But the tone shifts when Zack says,

"Listen, Red, I want to talk to you about something. Could we do that tonight?"

She really should go home and get some work done. She still needs to record all her notes from the foodbank's staff session and board session, then combine them and write-up the proposed next steps. She was supposed to have been working on that for the past two days, but well, it hadn't happened. There is a clause in her contract excusing her for failures to deliver due to force majeure, or "acts of God." Did this count? Could she blame Zack for her failure to produce?

"Um, I kind of need to work tonight. I've been putting some stuff off. But I guess I could—"

Before she finishes, he cuts her off. "No, it's okay. Do your work. How about tomorrow? Friday night, you and me?"

"Are you sure?" she asks, bracing herself for something more. For the possibility that whatever Zack wants to say is going to slip out and onto the floor like a giant octopus whose eight arms are suddenly flailing in every direction, hurling boxes of rice noodles and German soda like grenades. Like a giant, ugly monster that is definitely going to fuck up her night. But Zack just smiles.

"Yeah," he says with a definitive nod. And though he seems certain, that tone lingers, the one that forebodes an ugly, smelly, entirely unwelcome danger.

***

After the past few days with Zack, there's only one thing that can possibly make this week better. The four-legged love of Clarey's life is about to waddle in and take her life from fantastic to sublime. While Clarey has, to date, demonstrated a level of patience worthy of Nobel consideration, her endless reserve of kind concern and gracious acceptance has officially run the fuck out. She wants her dog.

In the three, no, nearly four weeks since she moved, she's texted with Zack or Lydia every day to get updates, and spent endless hours scrolling photos and watching her favorite videos of Roxy. Like the one where Roxy latches onto the tug toy and gets dragged on her stomach all the way across the kitchen tile floor. Or the one where Roxy's learning to walk in her new shoes to protect her little paws from the hot pavement. And best of all, the one where she's sleeping in her bed and slowly unfurls from a ball to a stretched-out slug on her back, her snore mounting incrementally from a quiet rumble to a roaring freight train with each expansion of her body. Roxy makes everything better.

Clarey pulls up to the house and is relieved to see both cars in the drive. She had half expected Derek to pull another stunt and be missing once again. The way he repeatedly kept Roxy from her felt almost intentional. But that's silly. Roxy is her girl, and today, Clarey finally gets to take her home.

Clarey smiles at the thought of Roxy rushing out the door and hurling her juggernaut of a body into Clarey's arms. Roxy may be small, but she's mighty and she can definitely catch some air when properly motivated. She knocks and waits. No immediate barking, but Roxy's probably conked out. She gets so worked up during long car rides, she's probably sleeping off the high of the wind blowing back her jowls for the better part of six hours.

Derek opens the door with a quizzical expression. "Clarey?"

"Derek," she replies. "How are you? How was the drive back?"

"Didn't you get my message?"

Mother fffff— "What message?"

"I texted you."

"No, you didn't."

"I did. Look!" He pulls out his phone and scrolls to his texts. "Oh, oops. I never hit Send."

"Oops. Yeah." The annoyance inches through Clarey's body one muscle group at a time, slowly clenching her into one giant fist. "So, what did the text you didn't send say?" Clarey runs through the possible acceptable answers to this question, including *Roxy can't wait to see you,* or... nope, that's pretty much the only acceptable text at this point. What an acceptable text would definitely not include are the words *not here.*

Derek scrunches up his face in that way she used to find irresistible and says, "Roxy's not here."

"I beg your pardon." Under what circumstances is it deemed appropriate to actually unalive your ex-husband? Certainly no jury in the land would convict her for a crime of passion in this scenario. It really is the only logical choice.

"Clarey, it's serious. Roxy got into some chocolate in the back of the car somehow, not long before we got home. We took her straight to the vet. They're keeping her overnight."

***

Clarey breaks the land speed record getting to the vet's office, desperate to see her sweet, mushy-faced girl. She darts into the office and immediately unspools her tale of woe. Her words gush out and end with a fervent plea to see her girl. Finally, the too friendly woman with the tight black bun smiles. She explains that Roxy has made it through the worst and is resting comfortably at the moment, on an IV drip to replace her fluids after extensive vomiting. She's also on a medication to stop tremors and they're going to monitor her overnight, but with any luck, she'll be able to go home tomorrow. Clarey vibrates through the conversation, trembling at the thought of Roxy all alone in there, laid out on an IV and wondering where her mama is after all this time. "Can I please see her? Please."

"I'm sorry. We can't let you in. But we're taking very good care of her, I promise."

Clarey fights back her tears, but fails miserably. The vet tech tilts her head compassionately, but resists comforting the blubbering Clarey with a hug, instead maintaining her distance. "I know it's hard."

"She needs me. And I really need her," Clarey says, wiping snot from her nose.

"Tomorrow," the woman says. "We'll check in tomorrow, okay?"

At this, Clarey straightens and brushes away her tears. "Okay, listen. Roxy is *my dog*. Do you understand?"

"Okay..." The woman nods slowly, visibly nervous where this is headed.

"My ex-husband brought her in today, because she was with him when it happened. And I'm grateful to him for that, although that also means it's his fault. But she's my dog."

"Your dog," the woman agrees uncertainly.

"I adopted her. My name is on the adoption papers and in your records. So when the time comes tomorrow, you call me, okay? Not him. I'll come get her."

"I see. Yes, of course."

"Will you tell everyone?" Clarey leans in with an intense stare. "Only call me."

"Only call you," the receptionist repeats. "Got it."

***

When Gabi pops up on the Zoom screen, her expression mutates instantly from TGIF to WTF. Does Clarey really look that bad? She checks herself in the small corner image, then enlarges it to see better. Yes, she does look that bad. Considerably worse, actually. Her eyes are swollen, bloodshot, and teary, the whites now only a shade less red than her hair. And her nose is catching up.

"Girl... What. Is. Happening?" Gabi says.

"What isn't?" Clarey sobs, before grabbing a tissue and pulling herself back together.

"That's not an answer I can work with."

"I'm sorry," Clarey says, pausing to blow her nose. "I probably should have cancelled."

Gabi nods vigorously. "Oh yeah, the meeting is definitely cancelled. But the conversation is just beginning. Because..." She waves her hands toward the screen in a broad gesture. "This is a whole situation here. What's wrong?"

Where to start? As good as everything is with Zack, none of it matters as long as her sweet puppy girl is in the hospital. It would be bad enough to not have Roxy due to yet another of Derek's schemes, but the fact that Roxy is laid up in the doggy ICU is almost more than she can bear. Clarey flops back in her seat, sagging under the weight of it all. "I don't have the energy to rehash it, honestly."

Gabi nods gravely, takes a slow breath, and blows it out. "Well, here's the good news. On Fridays, five o'clock technically starts at three. Wanna drink?"

CHAPTER TWENTY-SIX

OUT OF THE FRYING PAN

CLAREY BURPS AND GIGGLES as Zack slides open his door. The effects of her Zoom visit with Gabi are very much in evidence as she happily gurgles her hello and stumbles into his apartment. "I'm having a terrible day," she announces with a histrionic flail of her arms that belies her giddiness. Either her manner or her words are a lie, but before Zack has a chance to find out which, Clarey stops short and points. "Who is this?"

"She doesn't even remember me," Xara says, sharp annoyance coating her voice.

"Clarey, do you remember Xara?" Zack says with a gentle prod.

"Of course, I remember you. And your legs. And your hair and, and, and..." Clarey goes cross-eyed a moment, but quickly regains her composure. She turns to Zack. "What is she doing here?"

In response, Xara drops to the sofa and crosses her dazzling, long legs before giving her glorious, lustrous locks a toss. "Yes, Zack, tell her why I'm here."

Without waiting for a response, Clarey says, "If this is a three-some thing, I'm out."

Finally, Zack gets his chance to speak. He steps over to Clarey and takes her hand. "No, of course not. Clarey, I only want you."

Xara's eyes roll prodigiously in his peripheral vision, but he's more interested in Clarey. He watches her eyes fall unfocused, roam the room for a moment, then zoom back in on him. She smiles briefly, the proclamation of his devotion tugging her gently back toward sobriety – until she remembers Xara. "Then why is she here?"

"Clarey, listen, Xara is helping me. I'm in a lot of trouble. With the others. The Ancients. They may come for me soon. Xara's keeping me informed."

"Come for you? What does that mean?"

"A long time ago, I made someone very angry. Ixia. Do you remember? And now I might finally have to pay the price."

"He's been paying the price for nearly three thousand years, but he doesn't like to mention that part. And frankly, the only reason they haven't come yet is because they're still not sure which one of you it is."

Clarey looks blankly between them, apparently attempting to make the impossible possible in her mind. "I don't get it."

"Oh, little mouse, are we going too fast for you?" Xara speaks extra loudly and slowly, like an obnoxious American addressing foreigners by over-enunciating her words. "We can take any form, dear. Look-like-any-one."

"It's been so long since I showed myself, they don't know what I look like anymore. I'm not allowed to use my active powers, but with passive powers, I can still change very slowly over time if I choose. I could be a man or a woman by now. Old or young. Any race. Or I could be you."

"Me?" Clarey says. "You mean they could come for me?"

"They did come for you," Xara points out.

"The lightning," Clarey says, piecing the madness together.

"She's learning so quickly!" Xara mimics a proud mommy voice. "It's like watching a baby toy with its mobile over the crib. She'll be playing with crunchies soon!"

"So they want to kill me?" Clarey's voice trembles with the words. She shuffles to the armchair and drops into it.

Zack shakes his head. "No. Absolutely not."

"We like humans," Xara says before looking Clarey up and down with a slow, assessing eye. "Usually."

"Our kind, they're benevolent toward humans, for the most part."

"You're like cute, little puppy dogs to us." Xara gives a sickening smile. "Or a pet mouse."

Zack takes Clarey's arms gently and leans in to reassure her. "They don't kill humans indiscriminately."

"No, we leave that to all of you," Xara adds, looking directly at Clarey.

"The lightning was just to scare us," Zack continues. "To let us know, to let *me* know they were close. And I think they were hoping I'd reveal myself by using my powers again."

"Again?"

"Remember how I saved Herb? After the accident? That's what started all this. I wasn't supposed to do that. For our kind, that was like sending out an electromagnetic pulse to the entire universe. Unmissable."

"So when they figure out who you are, they'll take you?" Clarey takes all this in with remarkable equanimity. Perhaps after weeks of weathering the slow dribs and drabs of Zack's story, she's simply getting used to his stranger than fiction tales.

"I think so. Yes."

Clarey disappears into herself for a moment, visibly contemplating everything she's heard. Finally, she looks back at Zack. "Is this real?" When Zack simply nods a quiet yes, she adds, "I don't know how to make this make sense."

"Nor should you, dear." Xara hops off the sofa and glides to the door, which she opens. "Now why don't you run along back to your little hole and let the grown-ups talk."

"Xara, that's enough!" Zack shouts. Xara pouts and closes the door. "In fact, I think maybe you should go."

"I beg your pardon?" Xara's face crosses with a hundred emotions at once, not one of which is kind, benevolent, or gracious in nature.

Xara's been a good friend and this is no time to pick a fight, but he needs to talk to Clarey. Zack steels himself, steps gently to Xara, and says in an almost whisper, "I'm grateful for the update, truly. But maybe I should talk with Clarey alone."

Xara studies him a long beat, evaluating the depth of his emotion. Slowly, her face melts from angry offense into impatient indulgence. "Fine, you impossible child. You'd think after thousands of years..."

Just as she lifts her hand to disappear *her way*, Zack stops her. "Door, please."

Xara rolls her eyes again, sighs, and opens the door to leave. As she goes, she calls behind her, "Don't forget to bring the flowerpot in."

"I won't," Zack replies, but Xara is already gone.

He returns his focus to Clarey, but she is somewhere else. She stares blankly, like her brain has gone on holiday and left her head behind for the weekend, and Zack begins to panic. This isn't the Clarey he knows. She's checking out, but she catches up to Xara's last words. "Flowerpot?" she asks in a fleeting moment of presence.

"It's our signal," Zack explains. "I put the pot of marigolds on the balcony when I want her to come by."

Clarey nods, unimpressed at what is probably the least extraordinary piece of information she's learned tonight. Zack watches her slowly process all of it, inching carefully back to something resembling sobriety, or at least sober contemplation of everything she's heard. "My dog's in the hospital," she suddenly says, as if it's a perfectly natural follow-up in the conversation.

"What," Zack says, rushing to her side. He tries to catch Clarey's eyes, but she's still far away, her eyes staring at nothing while her brain runs through a slideshow to which Zack is not privy. He takes her hand and squeezes it, trying to bring her back, but it's like she's in a trance.

Suddenly, she stands and makes her way toward the door. "She ate chocolate," she says as she walks.

Zack catches her and spins her around to face him. "Clarey, talk to me, baby."

Clarey blinks a few times, then looks Zack in the eyes. "I'm fine," she says with a nod. She's back to herself, and still a little tipsy, but she's present and aware again. "I just need some time." Zack feels something inside crumble as she tugs open the door and turns from him. "I'm gonna go now. I'll call you when I..." She trails off as she walks out and makes her way down the hall. She looks back at him as she reaches the fire door for the stairs. "I'll call you," she says again before disappearing and leaving Zack very much alone.

***

The next morning, Zack heads to Goldfarb's to cover for Herb while he runs errands, but Zack isn't alone in the store. As his first customer of the day leaves, another visitor wanders in from the backroom and hops onto the counter. The cat brushes past him and head butts the cash register. "You're not supposed to be in here," Zack says. "You're supposed to stay upstairs."

The cat mews by way of response and sniffs at a gum rack.

"Homer Dickens is a ridiculous name. You know that, don't you?"

Homer offers no reply but a head butt to the gum rack.

"I suppose he thinks it's funny. Some sort of homage. I've told him a hundred times we're not Greek. But I guess you are, *Homer*. Well, half Greek anyway."

Homer stops in front of Zack and reaches out a paw, attempting to bat at Zack's arm for attention. Zack raises his hand to meet the bump of Homer's face, then scratches behind his ear.

"They think I don't like you. But that's not true, is it? I just don't think Herb should be taking you on is all. Plus, you did cause that accident."

Homer meows apologetically and flops on his back, exposing his big, furry tummy and the white tuft at his chest. When Zack grants him the blessing of a tummy rub with the hand Homer will soon attack, the cat turns on his purr machine.

"But where did the Dickens part come from, I wonder?" Zack says, losing himself in the soft belly. "You know, my girlfriend... well, maybe not my girlfriend, but my friend at least. Well, I'm not sure about that either at the moment. Anyway, you know her. Clarey? She loves Dickens. She's got a whole shelf of his books."

Homer Dickens purrs even more loudly as he hops over to Zack's lap. Zack holds his rear while the little creature rests his body against Zack's chest and reaches his face toward Zack's. Zack leans down and kisses the snoot of the stretching kitty.

"You are a soft little thing," he says with a smile. "Quite good animal therapy, I suppose. Speaking of which, Clarey's dog is in the animal hospital, did you hear?"

Homer Dickens does not respond, and instead purrs more gently as his eyes half-close, falling asleep in his new comfy spot in Zack's arms.

"You're right. Don't think about animal hospitals. Better to get some rest. You let me worry about Clarey and her dog." And worry he will. Because no matter what he does, all roads lead to Clarey.

***

Back at his apartment, Xara pops into Zack's bedroom as he's pulling out his swimsuit. He's alerted by the faint glimmer sound of her appearance behind him as he slides the dresser drawer closed. "Xara, what are you doing?"

"Oh, as if I haven't seen that darling, little, well-shaped bottom before."

He shakes his head and slides on his trunks before turning around. "Not the point."

"What?" she says indignantly. "I waited until you were out of the shower."

"How would you know I was in the shower unless you were already here?"

"Fine, I might have popped in." She throws her hands in the air in a dismissive wave. "But I popped right back out when I saw you in the shower. See, I respect your privacy."

"And this is one of the many reasons I asked you to use the door like a normal person."

Xara wanders slowly around the room examining Zack's belongings like museum pieces. "Elnossys, you're so tiresome. Your nudity has no impact on me. You're practically my brother."

He looks in the mirror and runs a comb through his hair. "Practically."

She picks up a book on his bedside table and flips through it. "And if I ever *were* interested again, it certainly wouldn't be in this form," she says, flicking her hand in his direction without looking up.

"Even so, I told you, I don't want active powers used here."

Xara lowers herself to Zack's bed, scoots to the middle, and lies back on the pillow, spreading her arms as if testing the mattress. She pats the surface a couple times and purses her lips as she makes mental notes. "What difference does it make now? They already know you're here." She dramatically shuffles her back and shoulders with a frown. "How do you sleep on this thing?"

Zack ignores the question. "Exactly. And you're making it that much easier to zero in."

Xara snakes off the bed in one, long, fluid movement and crosses to where Zack stands. She grips his face in her hands. "Elnos, relax. I've protected your whereabouts all these years, haven't I? They have no idea I'm in touch with you, so they're not monitoring me. I could come and go riding your cock and they wouldn't notice."

"For the record, I do not consent to that," he says. She gives him a light slap on his cheek and goes to the window where she poses herself against the frame. Zack continues, "So, where do things stand?"

"Things are still coalescing. You're in with a chance, but it's unclear. There are some who simply cannot be bothered to care, one way or another. Even there, this all feels like old news to most of us. I mean, the universe has moved on! Can't we? And others who think it's all close enough and what difference does a few human years make? They're taking your side. But you-know-who won't let it go. And she's as powerful as ever. At least in some circles."

"So they're not coming for me?"

"Not yet anyway."

CHAPTER TWENTY-SEVEN

ROXY MCDOGALOG MCGILL

CLAREY'S HEAD IS BANGING like a pot on the radiator in a speakeasy raid. This is not a normal level of pain. This is the kind of pain typically reserved for amputees just before the snip and severe burn victims regrowing skin one precious, hard-earned cell at a time. This is not a pain that was ever meant to be felt in a suburban loft on an otherwise normal Saturday morning. What exactly did she drink last night? Or maybe the better question is, what didn't she drink last night?

Slowly, the events of the previous day roll back into her brain in waves, along with the nausea and dry mouth. Zack. That woman. Roxy. A full glass of water and two aspirin later, she's beginning to resemble herself again. Did Gabi say something about recommending her to a city contact? She should probably revisit that issue with Gabi. She can use all the help she can get to find clients, but for the life of her, she cannot remember the name or anything else about the person Gabi mentioned. And which city was it? Or was it the county? Damn, she really did tie one on, didn't she?

Despite her hard drinking, her body has awoken before noon, which seems like a mini-miracle under the circumstances. Of course, the fact that she'd passed out by nine o'clock last night might have something to do with it. But the vet's office would have been open for a couple hours. They should have called by now. Why haven't they called yet? She pops a couple extra aspirin, then picks up the phone.

When the vet gets on the phone, he assures her Roxy is doing much better and is ready to go home, which unleashes an embarrassing stream of happy tears. Clarey grabs her keys, stuffs a roll of bags in her pocket, and reviews her preparations. She's stocked up on Roxy's favorite food and her water bowl is out and ready. Her bed is lovingly placed in front of the bookcase, her favorite doggy blanket draped on the sofa, and a basket full of toys next to the door, waiting for Roxy to come make her selection and have at it. All the comforts of home in place and ready to welcome her sweet girl to her new home at last.

On the way to the vet, Clarey imagines her new life with Roxy. Things are looking up. Zack may be being hunted – and yes, well, that's probably something she'll need to deal with in some kind of way – but at least she'll have Roxy. She can't wait to take Roxy for walks around downtown Kirkland, making pit stops at each shop with a dog bowl by the door and detouring to Starbucks for pup cups. But their first stop will have to be the fancy dog boutique on the main drag. After all their time apart, Roxy deserves to be spoiled with a cute outfit or a new toy – or maybe both. Nothing's too good for Roxy, especially after everything's she's been through. And everywhere she goes, folks will ask to pet Clarey's adorable puppy love, and she'll say yes, because Roxy is the sweetest, most affectionate girl in the world and loves to get scritches from strangers.

And on the way home, they'll stop by Goldfarb's to introduce Mr. G, or rather, Herb to the one and only, long-awaited, accept-no-substitutes Roxy McDogalog McGill. Roxy even loves cats because, duh, she's the best dog in the world. Maybe she and Homer Dickens can become friends! Yes, the future is bright.

Of course, in her head, that future includes Zack. It's still so new, though, and so many unknowns around the idea of a life with a god. Maybe it was never a realistic possibility, even without the whole "they'll be coming for me" thing. Still, Clarey couldn't deny that she'd started imagining that life. One where she cooked and he baked and they both shared the news of the day, every day, forever. Not forever in the way that he knew it – the kind of forever that stretched across millennia – but in the normal, everyday, "let's spend our lives together" kind of way. She wanted that with Zack. She wanted simple, happy domesticity with love taps and household chores. Not to mention the sex. Circumstances have thus far prohibited a repeat performance of their first night together, but the memory of it is still more than enough to rock her world. She needs time, just one stinking day, to figure out what all of this insanity means.

And right now, she has Roxy to deal with.

"Hiiii," a chipper blond girl with a long ponytail says in a voice like cotton candy when Clarey enters the office. Clarey explains that she's here for Roxy with the brightest smile she can manage beneath her receding, but still low-level headache. "The bulldog, right?" the girl says in response.

"Right. I'm her mom, and Dr. Krischek said she's ready to go."

"Yeah, she's doing so much better," the young woman coos.

"Oh, I'm so happy to hear that. So, can you bring her out?"

She reaches for her ponytail and wraps it around her fingers. "The thing is, there must have been some confusion because your husband already came to get her."

"My husband?" Fucking Derek. She had texted Derek after she left the vet yesterday and explicitly told him she would pick up Roxy when the time came. He'd replied with a thumbs up emoji that twisted her last nerve into a knot, but under the circumstances, she took it as a win. "But I don't have a husband and I was promised yesterday when I came by that I would be called when Roxy was ready to go."

"And we did. We called this morning and then your husband—"

"Not my husband," Clarey interrupted.

"Then that gentleman came by and got her. I'm sorry if there's been some mix-up. That was the number on the admitting form."

Clarey rubs her face, attempting to erase her face and her frustration with it. "That man was my ex-husband, who brought Roxy in yesterday. But she's legally mine, and your colleague yesterday promised that you would call me today, not him."

"Oh, goshhh," she croons in her tiny, peppy voice. "What a silly mix-up. Sorry about that! But if it's your ex-husband, then great. At least we know she's safe." She offers the reassurance with an alarmingly annoying sparkle. "You can just go get her from him!"

**

Clarey frightens herself with the ferocity of her pounding, but this game has officially gone on too long. She has stolen the referee's whistle and she's ending it now. The absence of Derek's car in the driveway bodes ill, but she raps again anyway. Finally, she digs her key out and jams it in the lock. She flings the door open and calls out, "Roxy!"

No barks or scuttling feet race to meet her, but she charges through the house searching anyway. Maybe Roxy's asleep. Maybe Derek crated her to keep her safe. Maybe Clarey is an absolutely hopeless, delusional doofus who somehow still maintains the dream that people will be honest and good and not screw her over and break her heart again and again. But as she finishes her search of every room in the house, it becomes clear that only the last of these possibilities is, in fact, a reality.

She calls Derek, knowing full well the chances of him picking up are slightly lower than a snowball's chance at being promoted to chief of the fire brigade in hell. But when his voicemail beeps, she finds she can't scream at him. She simply doesn't have it in her. All her fury, all her disappointment, all her heartbreak has tangled her up into such a tight knot of grief that every ounce of her remaining energy must be redirected into simply unraveling enough string to move from her spot in the middle of the room. She makes her way to the door and taps her final reserve to scribble in all caps on the notepad on the entry table, "I WANT MY DOG!!!!!!"

***

Clarey taps into her group thread to her sisters.

Clarey: *Did I overreact?*

Jessa: *absolutely not*

Hope: *Maybe?*

Jessa: *he's a no good lowdown dirty dognapper and you definitely did not overreact*

Hope: *But is he really, though?*

Jessa: *um let me think about that YES*

Hope: *Clarey, don't get me wrong. You deserve to get Roxy back. She's your dog. But let's play devil's advocate.*

Clarey: *Do we have to?*

Hope's aptitude for playing devil's advocate was one of her defining characteristics growing up. She was always saying things like "then again" or "for the sake of argument" or "on the other hand," and Clarey and Jessa would just roll their eyes and walk away. But Clarey needs guidance too much to walk away now. And the annoying thing is, Hope is usually right.

Hope: *The first day, when Lydia took Roxy for a walk, she was trying to help. Isn't that what he said? She didn't know you'd be done so soon.*

Clarey: *In theory.*

Hope: *Then they went hiking. And yes, maybe it was poor judgement to take Roxy, but it wasn't their fault Lydia got injured. And when she did, you said it was okay for Roxy to stay.*

Jessa: *i can't believe you're blaming the victim*

Jessa: *you are not my sister*

Hope: *I'm trying to make the point that this might not be nefarious.*

Clarey: *Then why did they take Roxy on their trip?*

Hope: *They left super early, in a panic, right? They've lived with her as long as you have.*

Jessa: *longer now*

A long pause ensues as Hope's thought bubbles gurgle away. Why do these lapses always make Clarey so nervous? With anyone else, she thinks nothing of it. They're serving a customer, going to the bathroom, reading another text, whatever. Even with Hope, there are a million other things she could be doing. Cooking, yelling at a kid, yelling at Jessa. But somehow, Hope's long pauses never mean she's scrolling cat videos. They always mean she's writing a long-ass message, and those messages usually have a very loving knife hidden somewhere between the lines.

Hope: *It may have been their instinct to pack her in the car with everything else just like you would have done. I can see why they might have wanted an emotional support dog with everything they were going through. And then you said she could stay with them. Again.*

And there's the slash. Yes, Clarey did say Roxy could stay with them. But she hardly needs to be reminded of that right now.

Jessa: *are you even a therapist? you're gaslighting clarey*

Clarey: *You ARE blaming the victim.*

Hope: *No, Derek is a selfish bastard.*

Jessa: *that's the clinical term*

Another long pause. An ominous sign she's preparing to drop a truth bomb.

Hope: *He should have thought to check in with you. And Lydia's just as bad imo. But it's too easy, and not always helpful, to assume motives without talking to someone, and to assign blame without taking any responsibility for the ways we contribute to the problem.*

Clarey: *What did I do???*

This time the pause is followed by a relatively short message, but it packs a mighty wallop nonetheless.

Hope: *Honey, I love you, but did you ask them to bring Roxy back sooner? Or share your feelings in any way?*

Hope: *Or did you passively accept the situation without a fight, and then get mad about it?*

And there's that famous one-two punch.

Jessa: *oh snap! she's got ya there sis*

Sisters are the worst sometimes. Especially when they make perfectly valid points.

Clarey: *I was trying to be nice!*

Hope: *And I love that you are such a kind, caring person. But sweetie, you deserve to get what you want sometimes too. Especially when it matters most to you.*

The absolute audacity to be right about Clarey's very real inadequacies seems awfully rude under the circumstances. Helpfulness is crying with her and calling Derek names and hatching a rescue and revenge plot that involves complicated pulleys and harnesses and maybe a tasteless, odorless poison that will make his dick go limp for seven to ten days. Helpfulness is not assessing the situation with clear-headed reason and actually, you know, helping.

Clarey sighs and types out her response. *Okay, my morale is sufficiently lifted for the moment. I'm gonna go now. xoxo*

A moment later, her phone buzzes with a text. From the lock screen, she reads Derek's message. *Sorry, Clare. Thought Roxy deserved a trip to the park after what she's been through. I'll bring her tomorrow?* Well, that's something anyway. Actually, a pretty enormous something. The return of Roxy the Magnificent will be a game changer.

***

Clarey practically leaps to her intercom when the buzzer goes off. Her voice jumps an octave higher than normal as she speaks into the microphone to the entry below, "Did you bring my dog?"

Derek's voice silks its way through the intercom. "Why do you think I'm here?"

"You have Roxy?"

"Clare, buzz me in already."

Clarey's heart fizzes with joy. "Oh, hi, Roxy sweetheart. Mommy's coming. I'll be right down."

"You're not even going to let me see your place?" Derek huffs back.

If there were a listicle on BuzzFeed entitled 5 Things Clarey Absolutely Doesn't Want in her Condo, Derek would be up there, just below slasher movies and cockroaches. She would have felt differently before all this Roxy stuff. Things had been somewhat tense and certainly awkward, but mostly amiable before she left. But she loved her dog way more than Derek these days, so he had chosen the wrong line to cross. Still, he's bringing Roxy back now. Clarey thinks about what Hope said, about not assuming malicious intent. "Fine, bring her up."

She refills Roxy's water bowl and places it on the floor. She heads for the door, but when she opens it, there stands Derek, entirely unencumbered by the presence of a dog. She immediately takes two steps back. "Where's Roxy?"

He offers a sheepish expression, then pushes the frog out of his throat. "Well, I may have fudged that part a little."

Clarey is not, by nature, a violent person, but Derek really is doing his best to change that. "You lied about bringing Roxy?"

Derek holds up his hands in an infuriating, hapless shrug. "You wouldn't have let me in otherwise."

"Of course, I wouldn't. *You* do not belong here. *Roxy* does. Where is she?"

"She seemed so exhausted after everything yesterday. I was going to bring her, but I could barely get her out of the bed. She probably just needs another day of rest."

Okay, benefit of the doubt officially canceled. No more benefit. Benefit has been slaughtered like the sucker it was and buried in a shallow grave. We're moving on to exclusively dark red, angry, screaming-into-the-void doubt from now on. Still, Clarey is a grown-up and will conduct herself as such. She inhales deeply, then says, "She's my dog."

"And you'll get her, I promise. But I need to talk to you a sec."

"When you bring me my dog."

Clarey moves to slam the door in Derek's face, but he catches it with his hand before it closes. "Come on, Clare." He gives her the sheepish, lopsided shrug of a smile he deployed on all of his psy ops during their relationship. It was usually accompanied by phrases like, "Doesn't barbecue sound better?" or "You don't mind throwing this in the wash for me, do you?" or "Wouldn't you rather go to the beach and enjoy fruity drinks with umbrellas?" And somehow, Clarey always ended up giving the exact opposite answer from the one she wanted to give. Somehow, he always pushed past her defenses, and that smile was usually step one. "You've got to show me around," he says.

"I really don't."

"I came all this way." Clarey stands firm and holds the door, but Derek keeps pushing. "Two minutes. A quick dime tour."

She drops her head in annoyance. "A nickel tour is all you get. And don't so much as breathe on *anything*."

Derek smiles triumphantly and struts in. "Great place! High ceilings. Nice and open. Amazing light." He wanders straight out onto the balcony, as if he owned the place, or was considering a purchase. "Interesting view," he says.

"The view is the main reason I bought it," Clarey responds as she follows him out, but as she joins him on the balcony, she discovers what he was talking about. Not the view of downtown Kirkland or the lake or the Seattle skyline in the distance. No, not those. And this she knows with full certainty because standing shirtless and shining like the sun itself below them to the left is Zack. And he's looking directly at them.

Oh, shit.

"I'll bet," Derek says with a smirk so punchable Clarey's fist forms reflexively as he walks back inside.

"And for the *privacy*," she quips. She glances at Zack again, and unable to read his expression. She gives a quick wave and quickly walks back inside. "So what do you want, Derek?" She nearly shouts it, hoping she's loud enough for Zack to hear. Some small part of her needs him to know this visit isn't of her making.

Derek ignores her question and continues his self-guided tour, wandering around like he's moving in. "It's good you got new things. Our old stuff wouldn't look right in this space anyway. I did you a favor."

"I'll be sure to send you a thank you note."

He struts over to the kitchen island. "Great kitchen!" he says, then gives a little cough.

Clarey trails him, arms folded. "You're breathing on it."

"We sure made some great meals together," he says as he runs his fingertips over the quartz countertop.

"What is this, Derek? Are you flirting with me?"

"Just reminiscing. Relax." He says this as he fingers several paper airplanes on the island. He taps each of them into alignment and raises a quizzical brow at her before scanning the back counter. "And there's the soda maker!"

"This excites you, does it?"

He clears his throat. "Actually, I came to reclaim it."

"Beg pardon?"

"I did buy it."

"You most assuredly did not. I distinctly remember because you wanted to order it over the internet and I insisted it was better to support brick and mortar. But you were itchy to get it overnight, so I promised to get it after work the next day, which I did. So, I bought it."

"Well, we both wanted it. And it was basically shared money then anyway."

"Okay. Since it was all shared money anyway, how about I trade you the soda maker for the big screen TV?"

Derek casts a glance at the wall full of books. "You always were funny, Clare Bear."

"Don't call me that. Fine. I'll settle for my mug." Clarey hasn't forgotten about the way he somehow squirmed out of letting her take her own damn Roxy mug. The one he gave her for her birthday. And while she was willing to put up with that a month ago, it's now just another thorn in her increasingly sore Derek side. "And my dog, obviously."

"Which mug?" he asks, casting his eyes down the hallway. He clears his throat dramatically, then starts walking.

Clarey thinks of Roxy. Imagines her waddling out of the bedroom, her nails noisily clicking down the hallway as she comes running for dinner. God, she would give anything to have Roxy with her now to help her cope with all this madness.

"What's down here?" he asks as he heads toward the bedrooms.

She dashes to the entrance to the hallway and cuts him off. "Nickel tour, Derek."

Derek turns back toward the kitchen. "Look, Lydia wants to make some fancy drink concoction tonight for our six-month anniversary, and money's a little tight since we lost our roommate." And now he's making it her fault. Priceless. "Please?"

"You can buy soda water from the store, you know."

"She says it's more fun to make it 'from scratch.' Besides, you wouldn't want us buying those plastic bottles, would you?"

It's just like Derek to turn Clarey's own values against her. And she hates plastic most of all. Her books are her only significant concession to consumerism, but otherwise, she lives as simply as she can. Admittedly, she lives in a swanky place, but she keeps her windows open rather than running the AC, shops in bulk, uses cloth instead of paper, and buys as little unnecessary "stuff" as possible. In fact, the whole reason she chose downtown Kirkland to buy was so she could reduce her carbon footprint by living a walker's life as much as possible. She would fold herself into knots to keep plastic out of landfills, which Derek knows all too well. Manipulative SOB.

She sighs with exasperation. "Why is 'no' never good enough for you?"

"Damn, you make me sound like a predator." He seems genuinely hurt suddenly.

"I'm not talking about our sex life, Derek," Clarey says. She reluctantly forges forward, sensing this conversation turning a direction she does not want to go. "In the bedroom you were very considerate and respectful. Okay?"

"Thank you."

"Yes, congratulations on meeting the minimum basic standards for human decency," she says. Honestly, he's exhausting. "But I'm talking about literally everything else. You never take no for an answer."

"I do. I *would*. If you ever felt really strongly about something. But we always end up on the same page in the end."

"Yeah, your page."

"Clarey...," he pleads, whipping out the shrugging smile again for good measure. It's one of his greatest weapons in the campaign to drag yet another yes out of her.

"Fine, take it. For now. But I reserve the right to take it back. This is joint custody. Speaking of which, you better bring me my dog."

He unplugs it and drags it off the counter with another cough. "Of course. Scout's honor. Got a box?" She purses her lips and goes to the closet to find one. She carries a flattened box back and places it on the table with packing tape. Instead of setting down the soda maker to assemble the box, he gestures with his full arms. "Do you mind?" She assembles the box and pulls open the flaps for him, then offers a sarcastic presentation bow.

He clears his throat pointedly. "Bubble wrap?"

She fights the urge to tell him where he can stick his bubble wrap and instead returns to the closet to fetch some. After he finishes wrapping it, she gestures to the door. "Okay, time to go." She yanks open the door to a surprised Zack with his hand poised to knock.

Chapter Twenty-Eight

So, This Is Happiness

Zack comes this close to knocking on Clarey's forehead when the door flies open. She's obviously already flustered and his appearance startles her further. She jolts backward like a hidden line has tugged her away from the door. She's visibly upset and simultaneously adorable, and it's all Zack can do not to lift her from the ground and carry her away to some place where none of this matters. But there's still the question of the man standing in the middle of the room smirking.

The moment he saw that dude stroll out onto Clarey's balcony like he owned the place, the armory inside Zack flipped open. Grenades, rocket launchers, and so much TNT, all ready to go off. And hearing Derek's name lit the fuse.

The feeling is uncomfortable and unfamiliar. While Zack knew of jealousy academically, from thousands of books and movies, and had watched jealous melodramas play out countless times in the lives he had overseen for millennia, he'd never experienced it himself. How could he when he'd never allowed himself the most fundamental of human experiences, falling in love? Frankly, he could do without this part. Yet, the sight of another man on Clarey's balcony shot fire through his core. And the fact that it was Derek turned the flame into an inferno.

Zack rushes through a flurry of possible excuses to be standing at Clarey's door at this exact moment, while Derek is still here. He forgot his glasses. No, wait, he doesn't wear glasses. He wanted her to see his new wainscoting. Except then, he'd be calling her to him, plus it's not quite finished. He needs a cup of sugar. From the woman who doesn't bake. Two minutes ago, it was blind rage and intense jealousy that actually sent him flying as he threw on a shirt and came rushing upstairs. But now, as he stands in her door, alternating affectionate gazes at Clarey with staring down her ex, he realizes he doesn't have one good excuse to be here.

Derek sizes up Zack. "Ah, the neighbor. Howdy, neighbor," he says with a decidedly un-neighborly edge.

This guy is a piece of work. And why is he here? There's no sign of Clarey's dog anywhere. At least that would be a good reason. Instead of answering Derek, Zack turns to Clarey. "You okay?"

Derek chimes in, "She's fine. We're both fine. Just old friends catching up. Right, Clare." He adjusts the box in his arms, heads for the door, then pauses. He plants a slow kiss on Clarey's cheek as Clarey sets her jaw. "Nice to see you, Clare Bear."

Zack pushes into the room and stands chest to chest with Derek. Derek's a tall guy, but Zack still has a couple inches on him. Not to mention the god physique. But there's no need to mention that. It speaks for itself. This is a ridiculous show of peacocking. This kind of blustery pissing contest is beneath him, and won't impress Clarey. But in this moment, all he cares about is sending Derek packing.

"Alright, you two, break it up," Clarey says, shaking her head in obvious dismay.

"Making friends in the building, I see," Derek says with a chuckle that hints at a sneer. Then he follows it up with a cough that somehow also sneers. Sneering coughs is elite level assholery. This guy should go pro.

"Goodbye, Derek," she says.

"Thanks, Clare. You're the best." As Derek walks out, he clears his throat again and gives Zack a sly, snide wink.

Clarey follows Derek to the door and clicks it shut behind him, but before she can even turn around, Zack speaks. He can't help himself. "You were really married to that guy?"

Clarey sighs as she turns. It's clear she's had about enough of men and he should tread lightly. "He isn't always like that. You brought out the worst in him."

"He brought out the worst in himself." When Clarey says nothing, but heads for the kitchen, Zack continues. "Are you actually alright?"

"I'm fine," she says with a grimace as she pulls open the fridge. "But I need a drink."

"It's not even noon," he replies, but she's already ahead of him.

She holds up a pitcher. "Iced tea. Want some?" He nods, then waits patiently for her to pour the glasses. When he declines lemon, she seems to think better of it herself and closes the fridge. They settle on the sofa and enjoy a brief respite of tea-drinking quietude before Clarey says, "Okay, tell me about this god-hunting thing."

And there it is. The subject he'd been trying, and failing, to talk to her about for days now. Yet, now that the moment has arrived, he's losing his nerve. All he's wanted since this started was to protect her from harm, and to stay with her. Or failing that, at least to make her ready for what was almost certainly coming, unless they could somehow outsmart the gods. And when has that ever happened? But now, as he sits here next to her on the couch, his thoughts turn to denial and obfuscation. Suddenly, all he wants is to hide the truth from her and pretend that none of this is happening. Pretend that they can be the happy pair of peas in a pod that he wishes they could be. But that's not possible. That was never possible, even before all this.

"I'm sorry I wasn't ready to talk the other night," she says. "Between you and Roxy, I kinda broke for a minute."

"You had a lot to process." He pauses for a beat, allowing her to process her feelings in this moment as well. "And how is Roxy now?"

"She's fine. She's home. Or at least, she's with Derek. So I need to get her from him ASAP. But that's problem next," she says with a heavy sigh. "Right now, I want to talk about you. Tell me what's going on." Zack shuffles through half a dozen different versions of an explanation he's been considering, but Clarey makes it easier for him when she adds, "This all started when you healed Herb?"

"I broke the rules," he says, with an unexpected wave of grief. "It was reckless. But after losing David in such a shocking way, which still feels like yesterday, I couldn't let Herb go. Not like that." Zack feels tears pool in his eyes. Tears for Herb and Mimi and David. For Clarey, and even for himself. For the first time ever, he has something he doesn't want to lose. Someone.

Clarey pushes herself onto her knees and leans over to hug Zack. She wraps her arms around his neck, pulls his head against her shoulder, and holds him. The contact triggers a release in him, of his guilt and grief over putting Clarey through this. And he feels her release as well, perhaps of her anger and frustration over Roxy. She still wants her dog – and she'll get her – but in this moment,

Zack knows that he is all that matters. All of the bad feelings simply draining away until all that is left is each other. They continue to cling as she climbs onto his lap and he looks her in the eyes.

"But that accident shouldn't have happened," he says. "Herb still has my protection while I'm here. Something's changed. I don't know. Maybe Ixia's forcing the issue." Zack seems so depleted as he speaks. As if the sadness and inevitability of what's to come might actually be insurmountable. Even for him. "I think it's endgame."

"Endgame, huh?" she says. "That sounds like a whole lot of terrible."

"For me, anyway."

"Well, at least you won't face it alone."

Zack gives a sad smile and looks away thoughtfully. "I've always been alone. I mean, I've always had the family, but it's kind of like being a single parent. I love them, and I shoulder the responsibility gladly, but I can't share the burden with them. Or anyone. So, yeah. That's the price, I guess. I've always been alone."

Clarey brings a finger to his chin and brings him back to her. "You're not alone anymore." She plants a deep, slow kiss on his lips.

His mouth opens and takes her in for a languorous moment before he whispers, "You really mean that, don't you?"

Clarey smiles softly at him. "Admittedly, I didn't have ancient god smiting on my bingo card for this year. But yeah, I do. I'm with you, Zack." And as he pulls her back to his mouth, he feels his strength returning, in both body and soul. But especially body, judging from the quickly stiffening bulge beneath her. "Feeling better?" she giggles.

He answers by lifting her in his arms as he stands and carrying her straight to the bedroom.

***

Clarey lying in a bed like this is a revelation. Zack's imagined seeing her there so many times. Too many of those times with his hand squeezing his cock, though he had tried very respectfully, and somewhat unsuccessfully to resist such temptations. But now she's actually there with her soft pale skin, her wild, eminently clutchable curls, and a sprinkling of freckles he'd like to lick right off her face or die trying. The emeralds in her eyes sparkle with desire, and more than that, with an affection so deep he dares not name it.

The last time they were together, it had been fast and furious. Time and again, a passion raged through them both that drove them to shared heights and fueled them to be relentless with each other. To her credit, Clarey had proven admirably indefatigable, and they had scaled a mountain together, and then another, and another. It had been frantic and needful and glorious. Her flesh was the answer to every question.

Now as he looks her over, he wants so much more. But this time, he won't rush. He wants every moment to last an eternity that lives forever in her mind like a song. A song she never forgets and never stops singing. Oh, yes, he intends to make her sing.

Zack unbuttons Clarey's jeans and slides them down as she lifts her hips. He doesn't waste the opportunity and kisses her between her legs when she lifts her sex to him. With her jeans gone, he studies the silky, dimpled skin, the ache of those luscious wide hips, and the sexy way the elastic of her panties dips into her hips. Just enough to draw attention to the flesh he needs to worship.

He straddles her and pulls his own shirt off before reaching for hers. He pushes it up, but doesn't remove it yet, instead opting to run his hands slowly over every inch of her stomach, squeezing and molding her softness. His hand grazes over her large breasts and his blood boils up into his cock so hard it becomes tight and uncomfortable in his pants. Reluctantly, he climbs off her and removes his jeans and underwear. He squeezes himself once before pulling off her shirt and repositioning himself on top of her legs while he presses his mouth to her midriff. He kisses her slowly, planting each kiss across her stomach with attention and care.

Then he moves down. Through the cloth, he presses his mouth directly on her sweet spot and tongues at her until the fabric grows wet both from his ministrations and her own response. When she releases a tiny moan, he smiles. There's his girl. He opens his mouth again and this time he runs his tongue directly up her body, short licks all the way up the meridian line to her throat, all combining to form one long, delicious lash of his tongue. Then he blows gently down the still wet line, sending shivers through her.

From her throat, he glides his lips along her delectable collarbone while his fingers find their way into her panties. She moans more loudly this time, then softly calls his name, which sends a surge of pure animalistic hunger through him. He devours her neck and caresses the bumps that erupt on her skin as her gasps roll in and out like waves of the ocean. He's never heard anything more captivating.

He takes her mouth at last and their tongues entwine in a rapturous dance. When he pulls away, he says, "What do you want, Clarey? Tell me what you want."

She breathes slow and heavy and says, "You. I want you."

Zack gives her a ravenous smile. "You have me. I'm yours. And you're mine."

"Yes," she says as he glides his mouth back down and pulls her bra down.

He lifts her magnificent breasts free and kneads them worshipfully before taking a gluttonous mouthful of first one, then the other, her nipples pebbling at his touch. Her nipples, like every part of her, are perfection, as if she's been made specifically to fulfill his wildest desires. He reaches for his erection, raging so hard as to be painful. He strokes it a couple of times to ease the pressure, but he won't take her yet. Not yet.

He pushes her panties off and plants himself between her legs, which he pulls over his shoulders. He dives into her like a deep sea explorer, determined to discover the wonders of every hidden crevice of her very wet depths. Her body reacts instantly and intensely, stiffening to meet his mouth and rocking frantically to chase the release only he can give her. He would gladly taste her forever, but it's only moments before the mounting pressure of all his attentions sends her past the point of no return.

Clarey screams out, "Zack! Oh my god, Zack!" as she comes undone.

Zack smiles to himself, unspeakably happy to hear those words from her lips. Because yes, he is *her* god. All hers.

He climbs back up her body and presses against her, kissing her as softly as a first kiss.

"Zack," she murmurs as she recovers herself.

He holds her face and kisses her again. "Yes, Red?"

"You said you couldn't get sick? Or make others sick?"

He nods tenderly. "That's right." The condoms last time had been a courtesy to make Clarey comfortable. She wanted them and he had simply accommodated her, no questions asked. The fact that he didn't actually need them was incidental. But now it seems she's figuring it out.

She hesitates, clearly nervous to go on. "And... pregnancy?"

A soft smile tips his lips as he processes the two very real questions she's asking with that one word. *Am I safe with you, here and now? And could we have a family someday?* Imagine that. A future with this woman. A bottomless well of tenderness bubbles up in Zack as he answers. "It's possible. But only when we choose it."

"Because you're lucky?"

He looks at her flushed cheeks and chest and runs his hand from her neck to her breast, which he squeezes firmly as he catches her nipple between fingers. "I'm the luckiest man alive." Zack reaches for Clarey's hand and brings it to his mouth. He kisses it first before lightly taking each finger into his mouth, then finishes licking her palm and lowering it to clutch him.

Their lips collide again and her words slip out through her quiet moans, "Fuck me, Zack. I want you to fuck me."

She begins to stroke his already aching erection and he moans. But despite how badly he wants her, he forces himself to say, "No."

She stops stroking. "What?"

"Don't get me wrong. I want to fuck you badly. But tonight isn't about fucking." He reaches down to reactivate her hand, then puts his own fingers to work on her. "What we're going to do tonight..." He pauses to let her gasp through her rising tide. "It won't be fucking. It will be more than that. Because I want more than that from you."

She looks him in the eye, nods, then quivers and moans as he pushes her over the edge once again. And when she opens her eyes at last, she looks at him again and says, "So much more."

And when he sees she truly understands, that the unspoken words have been understood nonetheless, he parts her legs and thrusts into her without another moment of hesitation. Her tight heat and wetness are divinity itself, but the light emanating from her is sublime. Their bodies rock in time until the world disappears and only they exist. He and Clarey. And he is hers. And she is his.

She's his. She's his. She's his.

And he is not alone.

***

When Zack wakes, the first thing he hears is her breath, and it takes his away. She's here. Clarey's still here with him. Or rather, he's with her. For the first time in his life, he doesn't want to leave. Few lovers have even made it to morning in his bed. Most shuffled politely out the door when the festivities ended. Those who did last until morning were quickly guided out with breakfasts or excuses, or in most cases, made their own excuses because they knew exactly what this was.

But with Clarey, there would be no hasty goodbyes or awkward thanks and pecks on the cheek. Because he wants to stay with her forever. And because Clarey also knows exactly what this is. At least, he hopes she does.

He rolls over to look at her and she stirs. He glides his arm around her warmth and shudders at the sensation. "Good morning," he whispers and she smiles. He rolls onto his back and pulls her onto him so her full weight covers him and he can wrap his arms around her. She rests her head on his shoulder to doze and a kind of peace settles over him unlike any he's known. She's his. And maybe it can't last forever in the true sense. Maybe he'll be pulled away against his will by forces beyond even him. Or maybe he'll stay, but their time together will still be too fleeting because, after all, she's only human. But this is worth it all. Whatever pain or loss lies ahead, for this, for her, he'll weather any storm.

He holds Clarey while she sleeps, and while she dreams of sweet mysteries he'll never know, he dreams of a life with her. Of spending his days with her – talking, listening, touching, and feeling things he's never allowed himself to feel. He imagines traveling with her, showing her his favorite places and seeing hers. Meeting her family and growing to love her sisters as much as she does. Watching her grow older and more beautiful with every year. He dreams of simple domesticity with her and of showing her the stars.

Suddenly, it strikes him, the magnificent novelty of this moment. Not just the ineffable joy of holding this woman in his arms, but the monumental sea change of allowing himself to dream. For all his time here, in nearly three millennia, his path has been prescribed, laid out like a well-worn footpath through an endless cornfield. Never any hint of what might lie ahead for him, never a glimmer of possibility beyond the next few clearly defined steps stretching before him. An inescapable trajectory of forward motion, one inevitable step at a time. And while he's never begrudged his charges the time and care he's devoted to them, or the sacrifice he's made for them, the discovery of a dream for himself, for a future, is a revelation.

When at last she drifts into wakefulness, he greets her again, this time with a soft kiss to her forehead. She hums a quiet sigh that vibrates through his chest. "I don't ever want to move," she says.

"Then don't."

Clarey pushes herself onto her forearms and looks at Zack for a long, glorious moment. "My god," she finally says, "you're amazing."

"Your god?" he smiles.

"Pun intended," she chuckles as he pulls her mouth to his.

"So, what do you have to do today?"

Clarey releases a good-natured groan. "I don't even know what day it is, and you expect me to know my schedule?"

"Now you know how I feel most of the time." He reaches for his phone and checks the date. "It's Monday."

"Oh, well, if it's Monday, then I have... nope, nothing. I'm woefully short on clients at the moment, something I need to change soon. But I am supposed to help Herb. And I need to get my dog back."

"How about..." Zack trails his fingers down the middle of her back before landing on her bottom and squeezing. "I go help Herb now while you wake up and get ready. I'll do his deposit for him and bring him a box lunch for later, and then you and I can go get Roxy and do something all together."

"That sounds amazing," she croons. "But I don't want to let Herb down."

"Trust me, Herb adores you. But if there's one thing I know for sure, he would gladly sacrifice your help today for the cause."

Clarey mushes her face into the cutest little scrunch of bafflement. "The cause?"

"Me," he says with a grin. "I'm the cause."

CHAPTER TWENTY-NINE

DAY TRIPPING

CLAREY PREPARES HERSELF FOR a calm, collected, mature, yet firm conversation with Derek. She will give him a chance to explain, and when his explanation once again falls woefully short, she will calmly insist they schedule a time for her to pick up Roxy. She will clear her schedule, cancel any meetings, notify Herb, take her laptop, phone charger, and a book, and prepare to camp out. She will go to the house at the appointed hour, and if Roxy is not there waiting for her, she will let herself in and simply wait. All day and all night if she has to. She will take a toothbrush. Enough of these games.

She takes a slow, deep breath preparing herself. She will remain cool. She channels a peaceful Zen as the phone rings. Then the voicemail picks up. "God dammit, Derek, where is my fucking dog?!" she screams. "You better god damn bring my dog to me by tonight or I will sue your ass for custody! I swear to God I will, Derek! And I'll win too, because you know damn well she's my fucking dog!"

Clarey punches the End button as hard as she possibly can, making a point only her phone will feel. Well, that did not go entirely as planned. Clarey frowns at her phone, then grumbles at it, "He deserves it."

Two hours later, she and Zack pull into the ferry line and switch off the ignition. They should easily make the next boat to Bainbridge Island, but they've still got about fifteen minutes, so they hop out and weave between cars to the waterfront view of the Seattle Wheel and surrounding pier. Zack watches a guy let his dog out of the car for a walk and turns to Clarey. "So, how do you want to get Roxy back?"

Clarey palms her face with frustration. "I left Derek this horrible message and swore if he didn't call me back and give me my dog, I would sue him. But ..." She trails off and Zack squeezes her hand in understanding.

"Well, if you want to sue, I can help with the paperwork."

"You're an attorney too?"

He shrugs. "I practiced law for a while."

"Of course, you did," she laughs. Is there anything this guy hasn't done? "Are you licensed?"

"In a few states," he offers a sheepish grin. "But not Washington. Not yet, anyway."

Clarey shakes her head, a combination of amusement and bewilderment coloring her features. "I don't think I can get used to this."

"Do you want to?"

"God help me, I do."

"Good," he says. Behind them, the gate opens and cars pour off the newly arrived ferry.

Back in the car, he switches on the ignition and waits for their line to start moving. "Tell you what. When we get back, we'll drive straight to the house and get Roxy. How about that?"

"You'd go with me?"

"I'd be happy to. And we'll get her. Count on it." Zack has told her about his luck, or ease as he calls it, how things just tend to go the way he wants them to. Suddenly, she's feeling optimistic.

On the ferry, they leave their car behind for the short trip and find their way to the deck. The wind is less punishing on the aft deck, so they find a spot against a railing and watch the Seattle waterfront drift away. Smith Tower, the Seattle Aquarium, and the Great Wheel dominate their view until their position changes and the Space Needle comes into sight. The sun sparkles blindingly in the waters of Elliott Bay. Clarey glances forward to the tree covered island drawing closer. She leans into Zack's arms, and he kisses her hair. "We're so lucky to live in such a beautiful place," she says.

He kisses her again. "So lucky."

They spend the remainder of the morning wandering hand in hand through the shops of the downtown Bainbridge strip. Zack picks up some new polarized sunglasses for running from the active wear shop, and Clarey fawns over a dozen things at the pet boutique before settling on a little blue dress with white daisies on it that makes her giggle incessantly imagining Roxy in it. "I'm putting it on her the minute I get her home!" They roam through half a dozen more shops perusing high end rugs, home décor, old-fashioned toys, and a small, but mighty record store.

In one of the antique shops, Clarey snaps a photo of an incredible dragon sculpture made of spoons and texts it to her sisters. Within minutes, the onslaught begins. The messages chime in so fast she doesn't even bother trying to keep track of who's saying what. *Where is this? The tag says Bainbridge Island. What are you doing on Bainbridge Island? Are you alone? Is something wrong? Honey, are you okay? Who are you with? Call me!!! No, call us!!!*

Clarey calmly types out a single response to them both. *I'm fine.*

Jessa: *sure about that? you seem weirdly terse*

Hope: *This isn't like you to wander off during the workweek. Are you depressed?*

Jessa: *if you think you're depressed try living with hope*

Hope: *Jessa, this is not the time.*

Jessa: *not the time for what? i was encouraging her to have hope*

Hope's typing bubble gurgles an alarmingly long time. Clarey decides to head it off before whatever Hope is typing appears and ruins her otherwise lovely day.

Clarey: *Everything's fine. I'm with Zack. I'll talk to you both later.*

Hope's bubble stops. Then restarts and pops into a new message within seconds.

Hope: *YOU'RE WITH ZACK???????*

Jessa: *3B!!!!!*

Jessa: *oh this just got good*

Hope: *What happened?*

Jessa: *i swear to god you better call me now or i will kill you into the ground dead*

Jessa: *and i won't tell your boyfriend where you're buried*

Hope: *I wholeheartedly concur.*

Clarey: *Later.*

She follows her last text with a smiley sunglasses emoji, then pockets her phone. Let those two go on as long as they want. She's far too tired to deal with their nonsense. Plum tuckered, in fact. That's what her mom always used to say, and today, it fits because she is legit exhausted. No doubt due to the hours on end making *sweet, sweet love* – which, despite their best efforts, slipped occasionally into wild animal bonking because they couldn't resist – but mostly stayed this side of the sweetest, most tender night of her life. It was beautiful, transcendent, and frankly, exhausting. All that emotional intimacy took its toll apparently, because today she wants nothing more than to curl back up beside Zack and take a nap until tomorrow.

But first, lunch. They bring their food out to a table by the marina and eat while watching the boats rock in the current. Clarey looks around to be sure no one is nearby, then says, "I still don't understand something."

"Only one thing? Impressive."

He grins his gorgeous god teeth at her, all straight and white, and sparkles his glorious god eyes at her, all deep like the ocean blue, and she simultaneously melts and grumbles a little at his perfection. Real people aren't supposed to be this breathtaking. It doesn't seem fair, really. But then she remembers he's all hers now, and suddenly she no longer cares whether it's fair or not. Not even one little bit.

"I don't get why they can't identify you. I mean, maybe they don't know what you look like, but they're gods, right?" He gestures with a finger to his unfairly plump lips reminding her how much she'd like to kiss him – and probably also to remind her to keep her voice down. "Couldn't they spy on you for like two minutes and know who's who?"

"It's not like that. They're not omnipresent. They're not big floating eyes in the sky – or invisible like ghosts. To come here, we have to take a human form, and we do that with care. These aren't the old days when everyone believed in gods like us. We can't pop in and out of someone's house today. We have to be discreet."

Clarey takes a sip of her water and coughs hard. Zack jumps to her side and puts a hand on her back. "You okay?"

She coughs even harder while nodding, then finally settles enough to say with a choked voice, "Went down wrong."

Zack's posture relaxes as he exhales his relief and rubs her back gently as she continues to cough it out. Finally, when she's quiet, he returns to his lunch on the other side of the table.

After a few bites of food in silence, Clarey resumes the conversation. "So, how would they ever find out?"

"Either I expose myself by confessing, or using my powers again now that they're paying attention. Or they find proof. And they have to come here to find that."

"That's what—" A couple strolls toward them, and Clarey cuts herself off. They sit in silence, Clarey coughing nervously, as the couple passes and walks out of earshot. But as she opens her mouth, Zack shakes his head. They're not far enough away yet. Great, apparently they have super hearing. Because that's a thing she she's prepared to deal with. Finally, he gestures for her to go on. "That's what the electrician was doing? Looking for proof?"

Zack nods. "But he wouldn't have found any. I live like anyone else for the most part. So, they would have to overhear us, or Herb, or see me with Xara, to know."

"But the storm?"

Zack sighs under the weight of trying to explain the impossible, then says, "Powers are different. Active powers are like an energy, or a wave, that transcends planes. They crossover from one to the other. That's why they knew when I healed Herb. Active powers are very rarely used here anymore, and I haven't used them in thousands of years. So, when I did what I did, they noticed. They... felt it."

Clarey percolates on the wonder and horror of it all. Of this new, bonkers world that's been revealed to her as if a shroud has lifted. One where everything has changed, though everything looks the same, smells the same, and mostly feels the same. Except when Zack's hands, eyes, or lips are on her and her insides liquefy, then re-congeal into an under-baked, overstimulated puddle of lovesick glop. That's probably not 100% normal, strictly speaking, though she's fully prepared to embrace it as a new normal. If she must. After all, things change and those who fail to adapt get left behind. She will prove her mettle by embracing this new normal with admirable fortitude.

Zack reaches for her hand to pull her back to him, and the liquefaction begins. She coughs again and smiles. He kisses her hand and says, "Want to go see the troll?"

"Yeah," she says. "But after that, let's head back. I'm wiped. You really know how to wear a girl out."

Clarey has been looking forward to seeking out Pia the Peacekeeper. Pia's one of Thomas Dambo's six giant, wooden trolls that magically popped up, or "woke up," around Seattle and the Pacific Northwest one summer not long ago. She was well worth the trip. Nestled in the cozy shade of the woods, eighteen feet high with crossed legs and arms folded in to embrace her visitors, she's sweet and whimsical. And somehow, Pia's magic feels a little more real today.

Clarey snaps a few pictures, then takes turns with Zack posing in Pia's arms, before a passing couple offers to take one of them together. Zack wraps his arm around her shoulder and as much as she loves it, she winces a little. Her shoulders ache with the weight of his arm. She smiles for the camera and they take a couple photos for safety, then step out of Pia's hold. As the couple walks away, she giggles, "What did you do to me last night?"

"Nothing I wouldn't like to repeat very soon." He pulls her into his arms and gazes at her.

She beams back. "That sounds wonderful. But I might need a night to recover. My whole body hurts." The realities of lovemaking with a god might take some getting used to. And stretching. Lots of stretching.

"I'm sorry, baby," Zack says. And his face is creased with worry. "I didn't think we did anything that crazy."

He's so cute. And so sweet. He's positively dreamy and a little part of her crackles with uncertainty about deserving a guy, no, a god like him. But she quickly dashes that part into silence when she presses her lips to his and feels it in her toes. She's feeling warmer by the moment. But also tired. "Let's go home," she whispers.

On the ferry back, they briefly climb to the deck again, but Clarey catches what she thinks is a bug in her mouth and has another coughing fit. They return to the car for the remainder of the short ride, during which Clarey promptly falls asleep.

Chapter Thirty

Sleepy Girl

Zack lets Clarey sleep all the way home, and when she still hasn't woken up by the time he pulls into the garage, he lifts her from the car and carries her up to her place. When he reaches her door, he's obliged to wake her, so he whispers, "Hey, Red, I need your key."

She groggily cracks her eyes and says, "Whaa?"

And she's so cute and so drowsy, it nearly silences him with swelling affection, but he says again, "Where's your door key?"

"Mm, pocket," she slurs.

"Can you get it out for me?" She feels lazily around her body for her key, stumbles on the bump at last, and pulls out her keys. "Can you unlock the door?"

Zack dips down for Clarey who wakes herself enough to fumble with the lock and doorknob. Zack nudges the door open with his foot and walks her toward her bedroom. "You're carrying me," she says with smile of groggy appreciation.

"You were a very sleepy girl."

"Yeah, but you're carrying me," she says again.

This time, Zack gets it. "Yeah, I'm carrying you, Red." Zack remembers the story she told him about the girls at the pool, and how she was never the one the boys would lift into the air. This ravishing, brilliant, kind woman deserves to feel every bit as special and worthy as those girls. "I'd carry you anywhere." He lays her down carefully on her bed. "But for now, you need to sleep."

"I'm sorry I ruined our day," she says as he gently pulls his jacket off her.

"What are you talking about? We had a great day. And an amazing night. And you barely slept. So, rest."

Clarey coughs a little more. "I feel like that bug's still in my throat. Ugh."

Zack fetches her a glass of water, which she gulps gratefully, then lies back. He brushes her hair off her face and says, "You get some sleep. I'm going to go do some research and put some paperwork together to get Roxy."

"Oh, Roxy! We're supposed to get her."

"Tomorrow," he says. He eases her back down and kisses her forehead. "Rest tonight, and tomorrow we'll go get Roxy." He winks and she responds with a hazy smile. "Will you be okay if I go? And take your key for now?" She nods and curls into a ball with a shiver. He pulls the covers over her. "I'll check on you later tonight. And if you wake up and need anything, including me, just call." But before he finishes the sentence, she's already asleep.

***

Zack uses Herb's computer to research the relevant Washington State laws and statutes to determine what legal options Clarey has with regard to getting Roxy back. There's no way they'll need to take it that far. As soon as they show up, hand-in-hand and leash-in-hand, Derek will turn over the dog without hesitation. Because that's what *ease* looks like. But in case they're not home, he'll come prepared with the next step. A little legal jargon, some corresponding paperwork, a letter putting them on notice, all of which can be left behind, and they'll scare the living dog poo out of him. No subpoena required. Either way, Roxy will be coming home to Clarey tomorrow.

He determines the appropriate jurisdiction, fills out some forms, and drafts a threatening letter, then prints them all. As the letter begins to print, however, Homer Dickens decides to help and hops onto the desk to step on the piece of paper emerging from the printer. Crushed under the weight of Homer's assistance, the paper is crunched beyond rescue before it finishes printing.

Zack scoops the cat off the desk. "Come here, you rotten cat." He dangles Homer in one hand while he removes the damaged paper and hits print for a second time. Then he sweeps his free hand under Homer's butt and settles back into his chair. "I don't need your help, thank you," he says, rubbing the spot between Homer's eyes.

The cat replies with a needy meow.

"You're terrible, aren't you?"

Zack scratches under Homer's chin, and Homer proves how terrible he is by purring in response.

"Alright, fine. You're not so terrible." He continues to pet Homer, inciting even more rapturous purrs. "Oh, did I tell you? Clarey's dog is all better and out of the hospital now. I know you'll be happy to hear that."

Homer does not respond, which Zack takes for silent content-ment at the news.

"But we still need to get her home to Clarey. That's what all this is for. Gotta keep my girl happy."

Homer squirms out of Zack's arms and leaps back to the desk where he head butts the monitor.

"You hear that, Homer Dickens? I have a girl." Zack grins happily to himself. The remarkable novelty of having someone for the first time in his life. Someone who makes him laugh, makes him think, and makes him rock hard. Someone who he can trust completely, who knows the real him, and though they've barely scratched the surface, someone who's not afraid to stick around and learn everything. And not just someone. Gorgeous, funny, sexy as hell Clarey. "How about that?"

Unimpressed, Homer splats himself helpfully across the keyboard.

Zack chuckles. Despite all the uncertainty ahead, and the very real risk he now faces for the first time ever to his own survival – ironically when he's finally found his first taste of a real life – he feels unbelievably light. "Lucky for you, I already finished."

Homer looks unconcerned.

***

When Zack returns, it's after eight and she's still sleeping. She must have gotten up at some point because she's shed her jeans and bra, but at the moment, she's out like a light.

He fishes out the groceries he picked up and prepares a Greek salad and some orzo, which he leaves in the fridge for her. He tiptoes into her room and drops a note on the bedside table. He'd give anything to climb into bed next to her, to hold her while she sleeps, but despite everything that's happened, it doesn't seem right to take such liberties uninvited. So, he kisses her forehead lightly and sneaks out again.

The next morning, he pops back in. It's early yet and he debates whether to wake her, but a reminder pops onto her lock screen indicating her next appointment, Goldfarb's at noon. There's no rush. He writes a second note to replace the one from last night.

Missed you last night, but I hope you slept well. I plan to tire you out again tonight if you're up for it. So, I hope you're up for it! I'm going to run a couple errands this morning, but I'll come see you at Goldfarb's when I'm back. Bringing you a surprise.

– Z. xo

He silently tidies her clothes newly strewn around the room, then does the same in her bathroom, which looks like a tornado hit during the night. He'd had the impression before that Clarey was a bit of a neat freak, but the evidence of the last twelve hours suggests otherwise. There's a towel on the floor, another one thrown across the vanity, knocked-over face creams, a toothbrush perched perilously on the edge of the sink, and a spilled bottle of aspirin. The idea that Red could be a closet slob is weirdly endearing, though the mess still seems out of character. Maybe she was sleepwalking. In any case, he leaves the room as tidy as the last time he'd seen it and sneaks out to start a big morning. He's got a dog to rescue.

First, he takes a quick run to clear his head, then showers and heads out to the store. With his ingredients list already assembled – oats, parsley, nonfat dry milk, peanut butter – he makes short work of his shopping trip. He already has the flour, salt, and eggs at home, so he's nearly ready to get home and start baking. Just one last stop.

He calls ahead to the specialty kitchen wares shop in downtown Kirkland to confirm they're open. Half an hour later, he's walking out to his car with one bone shaped cookie cutter and one ceramic dog biscuit canister.

He lovingly measures and mixes the dry ingredients into the bowl, then stirs in the eggs and peanut butter, and finally a bit of water, until the batter is the right crumbly texture. He rolls it out and puts the cookie cutter to use forming dozens of small peanut butter biscuits, which he hopes will be the perfect size for Roxy. It might be a lot of work for a dog he's never met, but if Roxy is happy, Clarey will be happy, and that's all the reason he needs to make the best damn dog biscuits this side of the Rockies. Once they're in the oven, he uses the hour to clean up, wash out the canister so it's ready to be filled, and get himself ready.

When the timer goes off, he pulls out the perfect biscuits and leaves them to cool. When he gets back, he'll transfer them to the canister with a bow and present it as part one of the surprise. But the biscuits are only the opening act, one that despite all Zack's efforts will pale in comparison to the headliner of this show, Roxy herself.

And now it's time to go collect the star.

***

Zack already has Derek and Lydia's address because they put it in GPS yesterday morning when they were planning on the ferry. When he pulls up, there are two cars in the driveway. An encouraging sign. Clarey told him about her failed attempts to go and claim Roxy, only to find the house empty, but they appear to be home now. He'll walk up, knock, say he's there on Clarey's behalf to pick up Roxy, and he and Roxy will leave together.

It's a plan that wouldn't work for everyone, even if Derek does recognize him as the neighbor. And let's face it, after their little chest to chest stand-off, Derek's definitely going to recognize Zack. But that wouldn't be enough to surrender the dog for most people, without at least talking to Clarey, and especially if they don't actually want to give up the dog. But Zack has a way of persuading people, and things naturally fall into place. Ease might not sound like much of a power, but when you're wandering the earth for thousands of years, those invisible currents clearing every path make all the difference.

He hesitates a moment, thinking again about Clarey and whether he's overstepping. She's a full-grown adult, more than capable of taking care of herself and fighting her own battles. Even if she doesn't know it herself. He doesn't doubt her for a moment. But getting Roxy back will make her so over-the-moon, ugly cry, pee herself happy, and that's all he wants. She'll see that. Besides, she'll be too blissed out with her reunion to care about how Roxy is returned.

Zack leaves the paperwork in the car. Since they're home, he won't need it. He grabs the spare leash he took from Clarey's and heads for the door. He knocks three times and within a few seconds, the door glides open. Derek stands in the door, tall and wiry, in his work-from-home uniform of a nice shirt and casual shorts that don't match. "Well, howdy, neighbor," he drawls. Only the snide edge is a bit duller today, his cockiness tempered by weariness perhaps. "This is a surprise. What can I do for you?"

Before Zack can speak, a chunky, little bulldog pushes past Derek to sniff Zack. She's white with brown spots including over both eyes.

She's adorable. Her droopy, little face looks up at him with interest as her whole rear waggles her enthusiasm. Zack kneels to pet her. "You must be Roxy. Hi, girl." Roxy grunts appreciatively. "Your mom misses you so much."

"Yeah, about that," Derek says, "tell Clarey I'm sorry. I meant to call her the other night."

Zack stands. "Well, there's no time like the present to make things right."

"It's just Lydia wasn't feeling well." He hitches a thumb over his shoulder to where Lydia is curled on the couch in front of a quiet TV, coughing gently. "So I was trying to take care of her and lost track of time."

Zack responds, eyes glued to Lydia. "Lydia's been sick?"

"Yeah, but she's on the mend now."

Zack processes what he's seeing against what he's seen from Clarey. The cough, the intense fatigue. And she'd kicked all her covers off, like she was hot. "What about you?" Zack says. "Are you sick?"

Derek coughs again. "Me? Nah. I'm fine."

Of course, a minor cold is just that, most of the time, for most people. But with Clarey's bad lungs, who knows? Zack looks at Derek seriously. "When did this start?"

"It's only been a couple days. No big deal. Lyd wasn't feeling great on Sunday, our anniversary, which is why I wanted the soda maker to cheer her up."

"So, she was already sick when you came over to Clarey's. Which means you were already sick."

"I feel fine, dude," Derek says while attempting to hold in another cough.

He should have recognized the symptoms immediately, but he was blinded by his own happiness. And she'd been so happy too, with all her soft, giggly Clareyness spilling over and filling his heart. How could she be so happy and also be sick? It didn't compute. It was easier to chock it up to bugs and water and screwing all night long. It was so easy to accept those reasons because any alternative explanation was unthinkable. One doesn't find the love of one's life, only to have her fall victim to some stupid virus the next day, right? Right?

"I have to go," Zack says, running for the car. He dials Clarey, but she doesn't pick up. "Red, if you get this, please call me right away. Thanks." He turns on the car and takes off like his life depends on it, except it's not his life he's worried about. He tries her again as he speeds home, but no answer. He's probably worrying for nothing.

But what if she is sick? Lydia caught a cold. Derek barely got a scratchy throat. But Clarey? What if those once sickly lungs of hers have decided to prove their fallibility again and give in? She'd shown all the signs. He'd just been too lovesick to see her very real sickness. Of course, even if she's a little sick, that would be no big deal. A little cold is something he can deal with. People get little colds all the time. Little colds pass. But Clarey's lungs don't like colds. Clarey's lungs have long proven themselves unworthy of her.

Clarey doesn't have Zack's luck on her own. He'd have to give it to her, and there's only one way to do that. But saving Clarey would mean being found, would mean leaving, either by rendition or, best case, by going into hiding. Either way, he'd never get to see her again. And Herb would be left unprotected.

When he gets home, he pounds on Clarey's door. No answer. He pounds again, panic pulsing through his veins like venom. "Clarey!"

he shouts. "Baby, are you there?" He can't let himself in because he left her damn key behind this morning so she'd have it when she went out to Herb's. "Clarey, please! Are you there? Can you open the door for me?"

He contemplates breaking the door down. It would be easy enough. He could take the thing down in one shove. But maybe that's a smidge over the top when he's not even sure she's sick. Breaking and entering, and destroying Clarey's very expensive door, only to find her happily singing in the shower would be fart-in-an-elevator level embarrassing. Not that he ever farts, but he's seen it happen and it's not pretty. He needs to try to keep it together. There might not even be anything wrong. She might be perfectly fine. He'll call again.

He pulls out his phone and finds two recent missed calls from Herb. Of course! She was going to work at Herb's. That's where she'll be. Damn, love really is making him stupid. His head is a complete muddle. This kind of worry is an entirely new sensation, and one that can piss right off, frankly. Sure, he'd worried about his charges and their families over the years, but that was nothing compared to the gut-shredding, brain incinerating fear ripping through him now. Finding Clarey is the best thing that's ever happened to him, but if there's any downside, it might be becoming chronically soup-brained. He'll walk over to Herb's, take her in his arms, kiss her, and all will be right with the world. As long as Clarey's okay, that soup can slosh around until the end of time.

Except, why is Herb calling? Twice. In five minutes. Zack completely forgot he silenced his ringer when he was with Clarey this morning to be sure he didn't wake her. And while he's been staring at this big piece of wood debating whether to chop it down with his bare hand, Herb's been trying to reach him. Rather frantically, it seems. There's a voicemail, but he doesn't bother listening and instead takes off for the shop at top speed.

Zack nearly rips the door off its hinges when he gets to Goldfarb's. "Is Clarey here?"

Herb comes rushing to meet him. "Oh, Zachary, I've been trying to reach you."

"What happened?" Zack asks, bile rising in his throat.

"Clarey came in as usual, but she was so tired. She coughed a little, and then almost immediately said she was afraid she was getting sick and she should go."

"She left?"

Herb nods. "She wasn't here more than a minute, two tops. But she started coughing harder as she walked out and it was shaking her whole body." Even as Herb conveys the detail, Zack's brain is rushing ahead to fears for Clarey's life and his own self-recriminations for not having seen it sooner. He grows more terrified by the moment. "She tried to sit on the bench," Herb continues, "but then she missed and just collapsed."

"Where is she?"

"I called 911. They took her to Evergreen. They just left."

"I have to go," Zack says, turning for the door.

"Yes," Herb says, before fishing a phone out of his pocket. "She dropped this when she fell. Here."

Zack pauses. "Herb, if she's bad..."

"I know, Zachary." He follows Zack to the door and embraces him tightly. A father and son saying goodbye. Each the father and the son. He pulls back to look at Zack. "All my life you've protected me. It's enough. Go."

***

At the hospital, Zack tries to bulldoze his way into the emergency room, but they stop him. Even his charm isn't enough to break through the HIPAA protocols without significantly more effort. They begrudgingly confirm Clarey was brought in, but they won't tell him anymore since he's not family. With a little time, he could persuade them, but he's distracted by Clarey's phone buzzing in his pocket. Her sister Hope is calling.

He slides the button and answers. "Hope, hi."

"Who is this? Is this Zack? Where's Clarey? Have you kidnapped her?"

Zack uses every ounce of strength he has to calm himself enough to calm Hope and explain the situation. Hope screams for Jessa in the next room who quickly arrives and listens in. After a very reasonable few minutes of shared panic and terror, which nearly kill Zack and drain him of every last shred of self-control, he asks Hope to call and get an update. When Hope calls back, she reports they've admitted Clarey, have her on oxygen and anti-virals and she's in and out of consciousness. Most importantly, she got Clarey's room number.

"Did they say anything else?" Zack probes.

"They weren't ready to commit to a prognosis since she just got there, but she's in critical condition."

"So fast?" Jessa says faintly from her spot slightly distant from the phone.

"Listen," Zack says. "Don't you two worry. She's going to be fine."

"You don't know that," Hope says through a snuffle of tears.

"Actually, I do," he says. "Thanks for your help. I'm sorry we didn't get a chance to meet."

Both sisters chime in with "Wait!" and "What does that mean?" as he clicks the button. It's not like him to be rude, but he has somewhere to be.

***

From the room's bathroom, Zack hears machines beep and whir. He'd studied the hospital maps carefully to hone in on Clarey, then focused on the thought of her to locate her exact position. He decided it would be safest to pop into the bathroom in case anyone was around, and now he listens for others in the room. When he's sure the coast is clear, he steps out of the bathroom and sees her. The sight of his red-haired angel lying unconscious with IV drips and an oxygen mask nearly breaks his unbreakable constitution into nothing more than a pile of dusty gravel. But at least she's not intubated. That will make this easier for her.

He slips over to the window by the door and tugs the curtain closed. He'll need to move fast, before medical personnel – or more worryingly, anyone else – arrives to stop him. Now that he's used his powers again, it won't be long before they come for him. He steps to the bedside, sets her phone on the table, and places a hand gently to her cheek. Her skin's so soft it heats his blood, this time not with desire but with simple love. The kind of love that rewrites millennia of history in a single moment. A love that exchanges everything that ever has been for everything that *is* in this very instant, and freezes it there forever. How can she be so beautifully alive and vibrantly perfect, and still loiter so close to the edge of darkness? He can feel her strength waning. He runs a thumb gently over her cheek and her eyes flutter.

She opens them slowly, then blinks as she tries to focus on him through her haze. She gives a muffled moan through her mask, which he recognizes as her attempt to say his name. He leans in close and holds her face. "Shhh, don't try to talk, Red. You're weak. But it's going to be okay. You're going to be okay."

Her breaths start to come faster, distress crossing her face at the realization of what he's saying. "It's okay, Clarey. I promise. But listen, after this, I'll have to go away. You understand?"

She shakes her head, trying to speak through the mask. "No, Zack, no," she gasps weakly.

"Your sisters know you're here. I promised them you'd be okay. You wouldn't want me to let them down, would you?"

Desperation leaks from her eyes with every tear. "No, please," she barely manages to whisper through her virtually non-existent breath. "Stay."

"I can't, baby. But it's alright. It's worth it, I promise." She shakes her head faintly as he says, "*You're* worth it. Look out for Herb for me, okay?"

Clarey nods through her tears and weakly lifts an arm to him. He takes her hand and kisses it before placing it back at her side. He leans close to her face and lifts her oxygen mask away. "Clarey, I love you. Never forget. I'll always love you." And then he presses his lips to hers one last time.

Slowly, the room grows brighter and brighter until all that surrounds them is a pure and unending white light. Zack hasn't healed anyone except Herb in thousands of years, since before everything happened. His protection of the family precluded the need for such things, and since he wasn't permitted to use active powers, he hadn't even thought of using it once in all this time. It was just another part of the Zack he never accessed. Now, within weeks, he's using his gift for the second, and last, time.

It's a gift that never leaves and never goes dormant. It flows through him like blood and now it flows into Clarey, from his heart to hers. His love for her will be his final gift, the one that gives her life not just today, but for all her natural days. Through the energy in his fingertips, he finds the weakness in her lungs and heals it before combing through the rest of her body, infusing every cell with energy and vitality. He floods her with health and longevity and the blessings of a joyful, love-filled life. It's a life he won't be here to see, but it will be beautiful. And it will be what she deserves.

Zack's lips still against her in one final kiss, the white light begins to fade. The healing is complete, and he pulls gently back, knowing that when Clarey opens her eyes, he will be gone.

Chapter Thirty-One

Gone

Clarey's half delirious as Zack fades away. She's not sure what's real and what's not in the fog. Was Zack even here? Did any of that happen? Where even is she? Yet, with each new breath, she draws in lucidity and the fog lifts a little more. With each slow inhalation, the clarity fills her. It wasn't a dream or a delusion. It wasn't a near death hallucination. Zack was here. And now he's gone.

And he's never coming back.

Clarey lies still, immobilized by the tubes in her arm. She's healed. There's not a doubt in her mind. She just has to wait for the doctors to come and declare the miracle. They'll listen to her insides, check their equipment, review her charts, and mull over the impossibility of what's happened. Then they'll start to doubt it was ever as bad as had been noted. They'll convince themselves the notes on her chart must have been wrong and she'd never been that bad to begin with. And then they'll scratch their heads, discharge her, and wheel her out to the street so they can clear the bed for someone who really needs it. And everyone will be jubilant about it. Except Clarey.

Because Zack's gone. He made her heart sing. He made her body sing. And he's gone. He made her believe in impossible things and embrace the unknown. He was somehow as hard as a mountainside to weather all those years, and also as soft as a mountain stream when he let someone in. With a heart that had shut out the entire world to protect himself, yet he loved a single family enough to sacrifice his eternity to protect them. And now he loved her enough to sacrifice everything. And he's gone.

***

By the time her sisters arrive that evening, Clarey is up and eating her hospital Jello. She's fine as she assures them, but the hospital wants to keep her overnight to be sure she remains stable. When they wheel her out of the hospital the next morning, they're in tears of happiness. Once at each other's throats, Hope and Jessa are now arm-in-arm, united by their fear and worry. All has been forgiven. Before piling into the car, they embrace again in a three-way hug of relief, gratitude, and deep, abiding love. And to those, Clarey adds grief at the loss they won't understand. But Hope and Jessa are here and their presence gives her the strength she needs to face the days ahead. They drive her home, and after a quick tour of her place, they ride up to the open air of the rooftop patio to visit.

Her sisters coddle her, fussing over her comfort and offering to run down for a blanket if she needs one. They're terrified of a relapse, but Clarey knows in her gut whatever Zack's done to her, it's permanent. Something will undoubtedly get her one day – nobody lives forever, not even Zack – but it won't be this. She can feel it.

He may be gone, but he's still pulsing through her, radiating an invisible shield that won't be punctured by anything in this world beside time.

She sits silently a long while, trying to figure out how to explain what happened with Zack. The truth about who he is. Or was. She supposes there's no harm in telling now. Now that the Ancients have him, now that he's gone. And yet, her sisters will never believe it. How could they? She barely believes it herself, and she lived it. Perhaps in time, even she could forget the truth of it. Come to think of it as a silly flight of fancy when she was feeling lonely and sick. Perhaps one day, her mind could simply wipe the impossibility clean and patch over it with something more believable. That cute guy who was her neighbor for a little while, who used to joke he was a god or something. Didn't they fool around a couple times?

It seems like a perfectly natural coping mechanism. When reality is too much to handle, the brain concocts alternative realities that are more comfortable, easier to tolerate. Like the doctors at the hospital did. Hope could go on at length about that, no doubt. Except Hope would certainly think the reality was the fantasy, and Clarey couldn't deal with the prospect of being told it wasn't real. Of having to fight her corner just to hold on to the precious truth. So, she says nothing. Because she has no intention of forgetting a single thing.

Instead, she creates an alternative reality for her sisters. One where she decided Zack was cute, but too much trouble to mess with him. They went to Bainbridge because it was something to do, and he happened to be around when she fell ill, and that's it. Eventually she'll say they haven't really seen much of each other and she'll let him gently float away in their minds. It's not much of a story, but they don't need much given their far greater concern about her and her recovery. Lying to them, however, takes nearly all the wind out of her now perfectly healthy lungs. It hurts too much to go on, so she changes the subject. "What do you think of my new place?"

"It's beautiful. I can't believe it took us this long to get up here," Hope says wistfully.

"The roof is top notch," Jessa says as she strolls to the ledge and gazes out to the lake. "It would be a good place to paint with these views."

"Maybe I'll make you a key and you can help yourself," Clarey says. Technically, that's against the rules, but who's going to complain? And if it makes Jessa happy and gets her here to visit more, that's reason enough. Hope and Jessa have been sniping at each other mercilessly lately. Getting Jessa out of the house more can only help. Besides, the universe requires at least one McGill sister to be happy at all times, else the prolonged sadness of all three cause the bad magic. And no one wants to see those days return, as their poor parents can attest. "As long as you swear not to spill any paint."

"That would be amazing!"

"She hasn't painted in months," Hope says.

"Maybe I just needed inspiration. And space. And this is a great space!" Jessa replies. "You could have a real rager here." Jessa begins dancing to an imaginary beat in her head, accompanying herself with her best, very bad effort at beatboxing.

"Nobody wants a rager on a suburban rooftop," Hope says dismissively. "But a cocktail party? That's a yes for me."

Clarey looks around the large space, then out at the breathtaking view of Lake Washington, which she's somehow already started taking for granted. "You're right. This is a great spot for a party." Clarey pulls out her phone. She may well be a wretched lump of

brokenhearted, malfunctioning sad girl for the foreseeable future –
and possibly forever, TBD – but there's no reason everyone should
be as hopeless as she is. "Give me a sec," she says to her sisters before
starting a group text to her favorite client Gabi and her realtor Dana.
Are you two still looking for a wedding venue?

***

When her sisters go, Clarey walks down to Goldfarb's to check on
Herb, but the shop is closed. On the door, a dated note reads:
   Closed due to a death in the family.
   We will reopen tomorrow with new hours from 10 AM to 6 PM.
   We apologize for any inconvenience.
   The words send an unexpected shockwave through Clarey. *A
death in the family.* Yes, of course Zack is family. Of course, Herb is
grieving, too. Herb has never known a world or a life without Zack.
Herb has already lost so much, and now he's lost Zack as well, his
one absolute constant. He must be devastated. And she's the one
who took him away.
   She thinks better of calling him. She's probably the last person
he wants to talk to right now, but maybe in a day or two, when she's
feeling stronger, she'll be ready to face him, tell him how sorry she
is, and beg his forgiveness.

***

The next morning, she calls Derek to arrange Roxy's pick-up. For
once he doesn't dodge her call or deny her access in any way. Clarey

AJ WHITTIER

is clear, direct, and assertive. Roxy is her dog and it's time for her to come home. Derek simply says, "Okay, when do you want to get her?" A triumph at last.

But when Derek tells her that Lydia left him, Clarey's heart sinks. How could Lydia have left him? Weren't they the happiest imaginable couple? He'd been there for Lydia in a way that Clarey now realized he'd never been there for her. He'd nursed her with her sprained ankle and given up everything he loved to rush off to Oregon for weeks to help her care for her father. Clarey couldn't even get him to give up a single afternoon at the ballpark. Wonder of wonders, for all his vexing ways, Lydia had navigated through them and gotten to a version of Derek that was actually there for her. Or so Clarey thought.

"What happened?" Clarey asks with an anvil on her heart.

"I don't know. She was sick, you know. And I was taking care of her, and I thought everything was great. Other than her being sick, I mean." In Clarey's experience, Derek has seldom known absolute perfection from total shit, so Clarey takes his assessment with a grain of salt. Still, if she had to assess from the outside, she would also have said they were great. What could have gone so wrong so fast?

"And then, when she got better, she decided she needed to leave," he continues. "Just like that."

Got better? As the words sink in, Clarey finally realizes with stark clarity that Derek is almost certainly the source of her illness. Because of course he is. Because she was dumb enough to let him in her apartment, and despite her best efforts to be tough with him, he still managed to nearly kill her. Yeah, great. Thanks, Derek. But she's hardly going to pick a fight at the moment, when Lydia has apparently up and walked out on him without so much as a simple explanation. She wants to yell at him and tell him he deserves it. She wants to scream at him that she nearly died because he wanted the goddamn soda maker and was too cheap to buy a new one. And now Zack is gone and it's all his fault. But, oh good grief, is he crying now?

"Hi, sweetheart," Derek says away from phone. "Yes, thank you for the cuddle, sweet girl."

Clarey winces at the sound of Derek talking to Roxy. Her dog, who belongs at home with her. But maybe Derek needs her right now. "Roxy?" she says, as if it's not obvious.

"She's been such a comfort," he replies with a deep, sad breath. He pauses a slow, painful moment, and she recognizes the manipulation for what it is. Still, she feels for him. "Anyway, when do you want to come get her?"

She desperately wants to unleash a furious tirade about all the things he never did for her and all the ways he needs to learn to be better and how she'll be over in half an hour to pick up her girl. Instead, Clarey hears herself saying words she never thought would escape her lips voluntarily. "I can't believe I'm saying this, but you can keep Roxy."

Derek's amazement rings through his voice. "What? Really?"

"Not forever," she hastens to add. "She's still my dog, and I want her back."

"I understand."

"But I'll give you a week. I know you're hurting and I don't want you to be alone through that." Damn it, why does she always do this? Put everyone else before herself? Maybe this is incredibly stupid after all this time, when all she's wanted was to bring Roxy home with her at last. But Derek sounds so pathetic.

It helps that he hasn't *asked* her to make the sacrifice this time, or taken her sacrifice for granted. Or dodged her and hoped she'd just give up. Maybe the very fact that he's finally willing to let Clarey win is why she's suddenly struck with such magnanimity. Because as much as she wants her sweet girl back now more than ever, Clarey decides Derek needs her even more. For now.

"But next week," Clarey adds, "Roxy comes home with me."

"Of course," Derek agrees eagerly. "I swear it, Clare."

***

Gabi and Dana stand on the roof deck with their arms around each other looking across Kirkland to the view of the lake and Seattle on the opposite shore.

"It's an incredible view," Gabi says to Clarey. "This is everything I wanted. Thank you!"

"Well, your fiancée here helped me get this view, after all," Clarey replies. Dana bows her sapphire blue-haired head officiously at the recognition. "And you help me pay for it," she continues, "so this is the least I can do."

"We really appreciate it, Clarey. See, baby, I told you it would work out," Dana says, lightly twisting two of Gabi's braids, one black and one pink, in her fingers.

Gabi giggles, revealing an unexpected soft side Clarey's never seen in their work confabs, even when they got silly. And they've gotten silly a lot. In fact, she should probably knock a couple hours off the foodbank's next invoice. "You were right," Gabi says before turning to Clarey. "She told me not to give up. And she was right."

"Never give up on love," Dana adds. She smiles indulgently at Gabi and they kiss like they're already newlyweds. A pang of comingled sweetness and longing courses through Clarey at the display. "Love always finds a way," Dana goes on. "If you're willing to fight for it."

Fight for it. If only it were that easy. At school and work, sure, Clarey could always fight to prove herself and tick achievements off an ever-growing list. But in her personal life, Clarey's never really known how to fight for anything. At least she's never won. Not her Roxy mug. Not her furniture delivery. Not her dinner selection or her soda maker or even her dog. She'd tried to fight for Roxy, again and again, but despite her efforts, she's still as pathetically dogless as ever, continually defeated by her own weak will and apparent belief that everyone else's needs supersede hers somehow.

And she doesn't have any fight left in her anyway. Certainly not enough to fight for an indisputably lost cause like love when the man she loves has literally been wiped off the face of the earth. And that's best-case scenario. How do you fight for something, or someone, who doesn't even exist anymore?

"How soon can we do it?" Gabi asks, bringing Clarey back to this plane.

Clarey offers a gracious smile as she replies, "Anytime."

"We're going to keep it small, just our closest circle. Maybe twenty to thirty people, including our friend who's officiating," Dana explains. "All we need to do is pull together some food and champagne. We could do it by next weekend."

"Yes! Next weekend!" Gabi says. "I don't want to wait another minute to be married to you."

"Great, just tell me when," Clarey says. "Now, how about I leave you up here to do your planning?" Witnessing Gabi and Dana's flowering love, as touching as it is, stabs Clarey like a very nasty, very pointy stick when her own love has so recently died and turned to desiccated dust. "Y'all can let yourselves out when you're ready. No rush."

"Thanks again, Clarey," Gabi calls out as Clarey heads for the door. Then she turns back to Dana. "I can't believe we found something so perfect."

"Aw, baby, when you gonna learn?" Dana says. "You always gotta believe."

Clarey steps into the elevator reflecting on those words. She smiles, genuinely delighted for Gabi and Dana's happily ever after. They deserve it. Because they never gave up. Because they believed. Because they fought for it. And good for them. Truly. But doesn't Clarey deserve a happy ending?

Never give up. Believe. Fight for it. Hokey, motivational aphorisms are all well and good in inspirational movies. Or in real life when you already have your happy ending. But even if Clarey wanted to, how could she fight? What's she going to do, run down to Thunderbolts-R-Us and pick up a couple lightning swords? And who would she fight anyway? And for what? Zack's already gone. It's impossible.

Then again, isn't Zack the one who taught her to believe in impossible things? Suddenly, something Herb said floods back to her. The only thing that can't be true is the thing you refuse to accept. Or put another way, the only impossible things are the things you refuse to believe.

Clarey walks down the hall to her door, mumbling to herself. "How could I fight? Where would I even begin?" Inside her apartment, she walks straight to her balcony and looks down at Zack's. His table and chairs still sit there like he might come out and kick his feet up again any moment now. Or better yet, step out with a folded piece of paper that he somehow sends sailing directly to Clarey.

If only she could do the same. But she can't, not being a super-powered goddess or Ancient One or whatever. Alas, no one has provided her with the requisite powers to cross over to Godland or Ancientsville, or wherever they're keeping him. If they're keeping him at all and haven't already killed him. That's what Zack expected if they took him. But how will she ever know?

Xara.

The idea pops into her head so suddenly and definitively it feels like it was put there by a muse. Like Leonardo DiCaprio Inceptioned it into her brain or something because all of a sudden, it's so clear Xara is the way. The only way. And it will work.

She walks back inside and quietly says, "Xara?" Nothing happens, so she says it again, a little more forcefully this time. "Xara." Nothing. She raises her voice again. "Xara, please! Can you hear me? I need your help. Please."

This is stupid. Zack specifically said they're not listening in like invisible beings in the sky. They can't just *hear* her. But it's all she's got. So she decides to try one more time. And even with her balcony doors open and the lovebirds right above her on the roof, Clarey takes a deep breath and issues a long, desperate, angry scream into the universe. "Xaraaaaa!"

Once again, nothing happens.

She marches back out to the balcony and stares at the lake. There must be a way. She has to figure it out. This time, when she looks down at Zack's balcony, it hits her. The flowerpot. The marigolds that Zack said he puts out to call Xara. It's not there. But it could be. If she could get in, she could find it and put it out. Of course, now that Zack is gone, Xara might not be checking anymore, but it's worth a shot. If she can get Xara, she has a chance.

Clarey literally runs down to Zack's apartment, hoping against hope that the door won't be locked, but it is. Well, that's going to make things harder. She walks slowly back to her place, contemplating the possibilities. Really, there's only one. And it's insane. It's absolutely freaking bonkers, but she might do it just the same. She walks out to the balcony and looks again. The ledge is more or less wide enough. It's probably a foot and a half wide, which is a lot in some contexts and not much at all in others. It's basically nothing in this context, but she's feeling bold.

She needs to wait until Gabi and Dana leave, and the waiting feels like dragging her body over hot coals. Too hot to feel, but an intense awareness that something very bad is coming. It's only a matter of time before the pain sets in. She needs to get on that ledge before the reality of what she's contemplating kicks in and she loses her courage. When at last she hears the elevator going, she knows they're on their way down to the garage. It's time.

She climbs over her railing and holds on for dear life, staring at the ledge she's about to step onto. She debates the merits of facing the wall versus facing the world and opts for the wall. The less she sees, the better. She says a quiet prayer to whatever god is listening, then steps carefully forward onto the ledge. She flings her body toward the wall and freezes, doing everything in her power not to think about the four-story drop below. Would a four-story fall kill her? Zack's protection might keep her safe from illness, but a fall? Probably not. And in any case, she's doesn't intend to find out.

Slowly, about an inch at a time, she eases her way across the ledge. This isn't a race and the only way to win is to make it to the other side alive. When she foolishly glances over her shoulder, she glimpses the street below and panics. She turns back to the building in a frantic huff, hyperventilating her way into a cold sweat. She's never going to make it. Somewhere between here and Zack's balcony, she's going to slip or misstep. And everyone she's ever loved is going to rush past her eyes in a happy little parade of smiles and waves as she goes plummeting to the earth.

She'll lie bleeding out on the cement below while some random stranger stumbles on her body and calls 911 and they pronounce her dead on arrival. And they'll call her parents, who will call her sisters, and they'll arrange a funeral and all of her old friends and schoolmates will be there. And Derek will probably come. And Lydia, too, even though they're broken up, because hey, they did live together for all those months. But will anyone think to tell Herb? Would he even want to come, or would he still be too angry at her to care? Of course, if she could get to that flowerpot, maybe she could bring Zack back. Too bad she's not going to make it.

Except, when she looks down again, she discovers that while she was busily obsessing over her impending death and who would care enough to attend her funeral, she's made it. Or very close. If she fell now, she'd land on Zack's balcony, and maybe just break a leg or something. That's not so bad! Buoyed by her newfound confidence, she takes a slow, deep breath and drops ever so carefully to her knees. From there, she feels for purchase, grabs onto the ledge the best she can, and dangles her legs toward the balcony. Within seconds, she's plummeted to her knees on the balcony, where she spends the next few seconds kissing the ground and reacclimating herself to a surface intended for human traffic.

When she's ready, she turns to the balcony doors and reaches for the handle, praying for a break, but no such luck. The door is locked. Still, Clarey was prepared for this and is entirely ready with a back-up plan. She picks up a chair from the balcony and bashes through the door in one hard swoop. This is no time for half measures. She reaches through the broken glass, unlocks the door, and walks in. Within one minute, she's found the pot of marigolds. She carries it out and sets it on the railing, as prominently as she can place it.

Clarey's eyes fill with her joy. This is going to work. She might have to be a little patient. She might have to wait. But she believes it. She's not giving up. And she's ready to fight.

Chapter Thirty-Two

Jump

For approximately the one hundredth time in the past twenty-four hours, Zack pops in. This time, it's the back of a café in Paris, the back hallway that leads to the stairs down to the WC that would not pass American standards, but is perfectly fine for locals. Fortunately, no one is there, and when he emerges from the hallway, he leans on the bar and orders "un café, s'il vous plaît" like he's been there all along. He looks through the mirror behind the bar to the people sitting on the street, the ones willing to be seen, wanting to be seen. The ones who experience Paris for all it has to offer. Not the ones just nipping in for a cheap drink and a place to hide for a few minutes.

When the coffee comes, he lays down his credit card and pays immediately. He won't be around long enough for another round. He sips his coffee and wishes it was espresso as he considers his options yet again. He goes through this cycle every fifteen minutes or so, popping somewhere new before the god-catchers catch up with him. It's only a matter of time before they get him, unless he comes up with something good. He spent the first day hopping from spot to spot around the Pacific Northwest, places he'd visited on his most recent travels. He can go anywhere, of course, but more vivid memories make the easiest landing spots. But after three human days, he's long since run out of "recent spots." Now he's moved on to distant memories, and even accidentally hopped back to the same spots a couple times. He can't keep this up much longer.

He's been trying to formulate a plan, but when he has to spend half his time each time picking somewhere to jump next, it doesn't leave him much time to think cogently about how to get himself out of this mess. If that option even exists. For now, hiding is pretty much his only option. But that's getting harder and harder since every time he pops somewhere new with his active powers, he leaves a magnetic trail of breadcrumbs to his latest location for the Ancients. Already, they've popped in right as he popped out several times. And they're as relentless and tireless as he is. Unless he figures something out, it's only a matter of time before they'll lay their hands on him, and then it will be over.

He tried jumping into O'Hare airport once thinking he could catch a flight out. But he realized before he got through the ticket line that he'd never get off the ground before they caught up with him, even in a smaller airport, so he ran out the clock and jumped away. It would have to be something faster. He couldn't get a car fast enough, at least through legal means. That left a bus or train, so he'd jumped into Central Station, which had dozens of trains leaving all the time. But he quickly realized that it was too big. By the time he found a train that was leaving right away and got to that platform, they would have caught up. Or at least, the risk was too great to try it. He needed to find a small bus depot or train station with something leaving immediately. And not just one thing. He needs somewhere where he could get on and get out fast, but also somewhere that has several options so that when his hunters show up, they'll have to guess. Or split up. Either of which will help him.

So that's his plan as the seconds tick down and he gulps the last of his coffee. It would have been nice to actually step outside the café and have seen some of Paris. It's been too long. But at this point, survival is the name of the game, and as much as he loves great architecture, the new Notre-Dame won't mean anything without his old head, which he values quite a bit more. Sightseeing will have to wait.

When the moment comes and his phone beeps, he jumps without a second thought. When he reappears, he's near the back of an Ecuadorean electronics shop. The last time he was here, this was a convenience store, but that was almost fifty years ago. He's lucky the building itself is still here at all. The shopkeeper startles when he sees Zack, but he just assumes he must have missed him walking in. Like they always do. And there could be worse places for him to land since he can pick up a phone charger now, and an international adaptor, and stop relying on the kindness of strangers. He'd charged his phone a little at a time, several times over the past few days thanks to pleasant strangers always happy to help. Because that's what *ease* looks like. But having his own will be a game changer. Once he pays, he gives the shopkeeper his most disarming smile before asking if there's somewhere he can plug in. Sixty seconds later, he's locked in for ten blessed minutes of charging and research.

He watches his clock tick down to his jump. With less than sixty seconds remaining, he pulls the plug from the wall and begins spooling the cord. Then he feels it. The shimmer of molecules that tells him they've arrived. He looks quickly around. They're not inside the shop, but they're close. He should pop away immediately, but something inside him feels the need to tempt fate, so he tiptoes to the door. And there they are directly outside. Two of them, the two who have been following him for days. They rarely catch up with him, but it's happened enough that he knows his luck is running out. They spin quickly in a circle looking for him. He sighs as they catch his eyes through the glass door. Then he smiles, holds up his hand in a wave that's half friendly greeting and half petty taunt, and jumps away. Then the clock restarts.

It takes him several more stops and the corresponding research before he settles on a list of prospective bus stations that fit his plan. Stations that are suitably small to buy and get on a bus within minutes, but big enough to have several buses leaving around the same time. He also reasons that it will need to be in the U.S. He never went home from the hospital with Clarey, so he didn't have a chance to grab his passport. He can pop in and out of any country he wants, but getting a new passport – even a fake one – will take time he doesn't have. Crossing country lines the old-fashioned way won't work. He settles on three cities to try first: Wichita, Kansas, Albuquerque, New Mexico, and Elyria, Ohio.

His plan in place, he makes a stop at a local roadhouse along I-40 in Oklahoma, where he orders a steak sandwich to go. He watches the clock, hoping his food is ready before he's obliged to jump away. This might be his last meal, and he at least wants something substantial to tide him over until... forever? Time will tell. Fortunately, the food arrives just before he has to pop out, so he grabs it and is gone before the door closes behind him.

He pops up into a Singaporean library where he sits in the corner and greedily consumes what could be his final meal. He'd rather it was a fresh deli sandwich with Herb. Or a plate of pasta with Clarey.

Or best of all, wine and good stories with both of them. That's the life he had dared to imagine. One where he got to have loved ones and live a life like everyone else, and actually belong somewhere. That had been the sweet dream only days ago. Even then, he knew it was a fantasy, but somehow it felt like a dream that could one day be real.

But that daydream is now as distant and irrelevant as the restaurant where he got that sandwich fifteen minutes ago. Because now it's time. This might not work. And even if it does, all it does is buy him time to think. But right now, that sounds like a gift beyond measure. He checks his pockets. Phone, charger, wallet. It's time to go.

First, he will jump through six unconnected locations. With any luck, this will buy him extra time and make it harder to trace him on the other end. If it takes them the corresponding time to trace their way through each of the six locales, that will give him an hour and a half, more or less. The odds are greater that they'll catch the scent of the latest transfer and skip the intervening ones, but he wants every advantage he can get, so when his timer beeps, he jumps. A Sydney dentist office. An arctic research station. An Amsterdam hash bar. A mountaintop with bears in Vancouver. A South African marketplace. A Caribbean beach on St. Thomas. Oh, if only he could stay there. But not now. Now, it's time to jump – and ride.

First, he pops into Wichita and walks straight to the line. But there's only one attendant on duty and about ten people in line ahead of him. He'll never make it. So he pops immediately on to the next stop, Albuquerque.

This one looks promising. Two attendants, each with someone at their windows, and only one person ahead of him in the line feeding them both. He should be up to one of them within a minute or two. He waits patiently for the first two minutes, happily content that his turn is coming up. But he starts twitching when the first attendant finishes with his person, and instead of calling the next person in line, he turns to the counter behind him and starts fussing with paperwork. Whatever that paperwork is, it can wait, buddy! Another minute and the second attendant, who is still talking with his customer, calls the roaming, apparently-not-in-the-mood-to-serve-anyone attendant over for help. This is turning ridiculous.

It's been six minutes and they haven't moved at all. They've got two attendants helping one patron and apparently, nobody is going anywhere until they figure out what the problem is. Zack checks his clock. They're up to eight minutes and suddenly this has gone from sure thing to under the wire. He still needs to get to the window, get a ticket, and get to the bus before it pulls out. As the ninth minute ticks over, the first attendant nods his approval to the second attendant, then pats him on the back and returns to his own window. He calls the woman ahead of Zack. Well, that's something. Maybe, if the other guy finally finishes with his person, Zack has a shot at making it. Minute ten clicks and he holds his breath. Finally, the woman at the other attendant's window finishes, thanks him, and leaves. Zack prepares to pounce. There's still time to make it if he's fast. But after fiddling for a moment at his window, the second attendant turns to the first and announces he's off to lunch. He flips his open window to Closed, and Zack is gone.

Elyria, Ohio. His last chance before he has to go back to the drawing board. There would no doubt be other bus stations, but that's time and effort he'd rather not invest. The running is wearing him out and he needs to sit somewhere, if only to give himself time to think clearly. And maybe sleep a little. Technically, sleep isn't a requirement for him. He's as indefatigable as all of his kind, but over the course of thousands of years, he has developed an appreciation for certain facets of this world, including sleep. Yes, after days on end jumping from place to place every fifteen minutes, a nap sounds really good. But for that to happen, this has to work.

He runs to the ticket office and finds three people in line for one attendant after the couple being served. Not great odds, but at this point, he may as well try. The couple at the window finish almost immediately and the woman behind the counter calls the next person up. The two people at the front go together. Good news! That means there's only one person in line ahead of him. So, he waits. Two minutes tick by and Zack's getting nervous. But it looks like the pair are nearly finished when the woman ahead of him pulls out her ringing phone and answers it. She gestures wildly as she answers, excited to talk to whoever is on the other end. As the window clears and the attendant calls for her, the woman looks behind her. When she sees there's only Zack there, she gestures for Zack to go ahead while she takes her call. And Zack is up.

At the window, he confirms upcoming trips to Chicago by way of Ann Arbor, Charleston by way of Philadelphia and Charlotte, and Lexington by way of Columbus. All three are leaving in the next twelve minutes. He buys a ticket for Lexington, pauses, then gets one for each of the other trips as well. It's good to have options, right up until the last moment. The woman looks at him with suspicion, but she gives him all three. He realizes that getting all three will increase the odds of being remembered, but if the Ancients do interrogate her, all she could say is that he had tickets to three different places, which wouldn't help them much. Still, for good measure, the moment before he walks away, he waves a hand toward the woman and quietly says, "Forget." She looks down briefly as he steps away, and when she looks back up, he knows that his transaction is no more than a ghost in her brain.

He looks at the three tickets in his hand, debating which one to take. Chicago has its appeal, but he was just there at the airport, so no. Charleston is lovely, as are several of the stops along the way, but his instincts say to choose somewhere lower profile. So he goes with his gut, the bus to Lexington, but he'll get off in Columbus instead of riding it to the end. He gets to the berth, shows his ticket, and hops on two minutes before departure. When the engine rumbles to life, he holds his breath. Another minute and the bus is pulling away from the station. He looks back until the station is out of sight, and seeing no signs of Ancients in pursuit, he promptly falls asleep.

***

Zack takes the lemon bar from the cashier and goes back to his table. The coffee shop is quiet. He looks around at his co-denizens. A woman on her laptop, typing away. Another woman sitting in a cozy chair facing the window. She hasn't moved in hours, and might be asleep actually. And the two gay men, a couple by the looks of it, leaning in to look at photos on one of their phones. And not one of them remotely interested in Zack. It's bliss. And also lonely.

He's spent two days in Columbus, having finally shaken his Ancient hunters for now. Possibly forever. It's entirely possible that he could start a new life here, or wherever he wants, and live like he's always lived. A quiet, unrecognized life of convenience and pleasant activities forevermore. As long as he never uses his active powers, he could probably manage it. They'd probably give up on him. Consider his power-free exile the same as death and leave him alone. Leave him to lead the same life he's led for thousands of years. Except no Herb, no long line of individuals to protect, no connection. And no Clarey.

He bites into the lemon bar and savors the sweet sourness of it, as the lemon cream, shortbread base, and light powdered sugar dusting meld into one glorious mouthful. He looks up at the light shining through the Pride flag in the window and smiles. The sun is blazing and the sky outside is so blue. This world is beautiful. Yes, it has its problems – oh, so many problems – but at its base, it's a wonderful place to spend a lifetime, no matter how long that lifetime is. He loves it here. But without other people, it's meaningless.

He knows what he has to do.

He gives a wave to the cashier as he walks out, then he walks down the block to the park at the center of the neighborhood. A beautiful, tree-lined oasis surrounded by large Victorian houses on all sides. Victorian Village, they call it. As nice a place as any to enjoy a last walk. He strolls leisurely through the park, enjoying the scattering birds and the sounds of traffic in the distance. He sits on a bench and watches a squirrel creep carefully toward him, then move on to the bush to his left. He looks out at the pond and watches tiny ripples as whatever is swimming below breaches the top and disappears again before it's spotted. Someone's playing tennis on the courts at the far side of the park. He listens to the ball lobbing back and forth in a rhythmic pattern that interrupts itself each time someone misses.

He feels the warm heat of the sun on his face and grins as if to thank it. He thinks of his beautiful Clarey. This has been a good life.

When he's ready, he glitches. It's a sort of fast flicker to change himself, though when the flicker is done, he's still the same Zack sitting on the same bench. Only, now he's a Zack who has called them. The Ancients will be here soon.

Chapter Thirty-Three

Believe

THE FIRST THING CLAREY does when she wakes the next morning is run to her balcony to see if the flowerpot is still there. If it's gone, she'll know the magic's working. Sadly, it's still sitting exactly where she put it yesterday. But if she believes, she believes. And given the alternative – to surrender to the universe-buckling devastation of a loss unlike any she's ever known – she'll stick with believing. She's lit a fuse and it's surely only a matter of time before the keg blows. When it does, she's ready to fight. She won't be giving up this time.

For now, she focuses on getting ready and heading to Goldfarb's where she still owes Herb an apology, and some assistance if he'll accept it. The store is open again and she tugs the door gently, hoping to somehow silence the bell announcing her arrival. Not that she's hiding, but the bell usually heralds joyful things like customers and friends, and Clarey feels conspicuously joyless in her cloak of guilt and regret for what she's taken from Herb. His family, his protection. Not to mention her own loss, which she definitely won't mention because she plans to undo it. At least she's damn well going to try. But until she succeeds, Herb's still all alone in the world, and she's to blame.

She steps into the store with her head hung low, too afraid even to lift her eyes and look for him, but she has to face him, no matter how deep his grief. Instead of the cold shoulder she expects, however, she's immediately swept into a warm hug. Herb squeezes her tight and says tearfully, "Oh, Clarey, dear. I'm so happy to see you." He pulls back and inspects her with a concerned expression. "How are you feeling? All better?"

"Yes." She nods shakily. "Thanks to..."

He hugs her again. "I know."

Of course, this incredibly kind, avuncular old man was never going to be angry with her. That was an absurd fiction she created, woven from her own grief and self-recriminations. But angry or not, she still owes him an apology. "Herb, I'm so sorry. If it weren't for me, Zack would still be here."

"Nonsense. Zachary made his own decisions. And his decision proved that he loved you very much, which is exactly what I wanted for him. To know true love."

"But if I hadn't come along, if we hadn't... gotten involved, you'd still have him. I took away the last of your family. You shouldn't be alone."

"But I'm not alone, am I?" He cups her cheek gently. "Zachary made the right choice. And I will miss him until the day I die, whenever that may be. He was light itself. But I will never fault him for choosing you. You are so dear to me, young lady. Don't you know that?"

Clarey takes his hand and squeezes it. "I don't feel that young anymore."

"You say this to me? You have your whole life ahead of you. You should get to live it. On that, Zachary and I were very much in agreement."

Clarey scans the shop for others, suddenly aware of how this conversation might sound to outsiders. Even if they don't have to protect Zack from the gods anymore, ordinary, everyday humans are more than enough trouble on their own. When she's sure the shop is empty, she says excitedly, "Herb, I'm going to get him back."

"What? How?"

"Trust me. If he's alive, I'm getting him back."

"But that's impossible, surely," he says, a giddy hope bubbling in his voice.

"You, of all people, know nothing is impossible. You and Zack taught me that." As she speaks, she watches Herb's eyes draw away from her and drift outside. "What is it?" she says, glimpsing over her shoulder.

"That woman sitting by the fountain. I haven't seen her in many years, but I know who she is. Here name is—"

"Xara," Clarey says before Herb can. She stares in amazement at the raven-haired vision draped on the fountain's side, much like she once saw Zack. Xara's almost his opposite –feminine, audacious, and dark where he was masculine, discreet, and as Herb said, *light itself*. But equal to his beauty and mystique, she's the yin to his yang. And she's staring directly at them.

"Herb, I think the door just opened. I'll be right back."

Clarey walks slowly across the street, nearly hypnotized by the goddess she has somehow summoned through sheer force of will. It's working. It's actually working. She believed and now Xara is here. "Hello," she says uncertainly.

"About time. I was wondering how long you were going to keep me waiting." Xara sits up from her partially reclining position and crosses her legs with the slow, intentional movements of one who fully expects to be watched.

"Sorry, it wasn't too long, was it?"

"I don't make a habit of waiting on humans at all. So yes, it was, as you say, too long."

"You got my message?"

"Lucky for you, I promised Elnos if anything happened to him, I would check in on the two of you. Don't know what I was thinking! I certainly have better things to do than babysit."

Clarey ignores the slight. If there's one thing she knows how to do after growing up fat, it's ignore bullies. "I need your help."

To Clarey's surprise, Xara doesn't react with the annoyance Clarey was expecting, but rather amusement. "Why would I help you?" she says with a derisive smirk. "You're the one who got Elnos into all of this in the first place." Xara pauses, then adds. "Actually, he got himself into most of it, I suppose. But you certainly did cause a muddle at the end there."

"Fine, don't help me. Help Zack. He needs us."

"I've been helping *Zack* for thousands of years, and he still couldn't stay out of trouble. I think I've done enough."

"Just do this one more thing. Please."

Xara sighs deeply. "As it happens, I can't find him. I've tried, but wherever he is, he's buried deep. I don't know if he's in hiding, if they have him, or if he's already dead. But he's out of my reach."

Clarey drops to the fountain's edge next to Xara and buries her head in her hands. "Oh my God!"

Xara uses the uninvited proximity as her cue to remove herself from the situation and the suddenly sobbing, slobbering mess that is now Clarey. "Yes, by all means, you call your God and leave me out of it. Buh-bye now!"

Clarey looks up. "Wait!" She reminds herself that fighters don't waste time on tears. Or maybe they do, but then they blink away their tears, wipe their snotty noses, and get back in the fight. She stands again to face Xara.

Xara purses her lips. "I'm not known for my patience, little mouse. And even with a literal eternity at my disposal, whatever this is..." She pauses to make a disgusted wax-on gesture toward Clarey before continuing, "Has already gone on too long."

"I don't care if you can't find Zack. I don't want you to find him."

"Oh," Xara says, tilting her head like a curious dog. "Now, this is interesting. Go on."

"Okay, I do want you to find him," Clarey admits. "But I need something else."

Xara studies her a moment, assessing her tone and stance. Clarey stands taller, projecting her warrior within for Xara's benefit. For this to work, she absolutely needs Xara to know she's ready. She's no little mouse. She's the mother fucking king of the jungle and she has not come to play. She eats bullies for breakfast and she's not backing down from this fight.

"Oh, no, this is too good," Xara says, her amusement returning. "You're not asking me to take you..." Clarey nods definitively before Xara can finish. "Well, you are a dark horse, aren't you?" Xara stares grimly at Clarey.

Clarey interrupts her contemplation with a new tack. "You don't like me, I take it."

Xara responds with a mirthless smile. "Caught onto that, did you?"

"Why? You said your kind, the Ancients, like people."

Xara looks across at the store and the old man within trying to ignore them while serving customers. "Elnossys was nearly finished here. He was finally coming home. Then you came along and distracted him. Made him forget who he really is, just when he was finally going to remember."

"So you think I'm bad for Zack?" Clarey says. Xara answers with a listless shrug. "And you care about Zack?" This time, Xara responds by turning to walk away, until Clarey calls out, "But what if I'm the only one who can save him?"

Xara balks at the absurdity. "You? The abominable conceit!"

"Could you?" Clarey slashes back. "You looked for him. Could you save him?" Xara lifts her chin in defiance, but says nothing, so Clarey goes on. "Is anybody else even trying? Does anyone else even care?"

Xara crosses her arms and looks away, a tacit acknowledgement of the truth.

"Take me to them," Clarey pleads. "Take me to the Ancients. You can do it, can't you?" Xara's face is rigid with a barely contained fury, but after a long, tortuous moment of reflection, she nods wordlessly. "Thank you," Clarey says.

"I'm not doing this for you."

"Imagine my surprise," Clarey fires back. Apparently, fighter Clarey is also sassy Clarey, and she's not mad about it. Moments later, she's running back into the shop. "Herb, I have to go now."

"Where?"

"I have no idea." She beams at him, unable to contain her excitement. "But if all goes according to plan, I'm coming back with Zack."

Herb locks the register, then walks to the door. "In that case," he says as he turns the Open sign to Closed, "I'm coming with you.'

"Oh, Herb, I couldn't ask you to do that," Clarey replies. As much as she would love a hand to hold during what is to come, she's taken enough from him.

"You didn't. But if there's a chance to save Zachary, I want to help."

Clarey shakes her head at the old man – who's still strong, sharp, and capable, but undeniably grayed and bent by time – afraid of what she's unleashed. "But it might be dangerous."

His eyes light up as he places his aged hand on hers. "You don't have to talk me into it, young lady. I'm already in. Let's go!"

***

The three of them relocate upstairs to Herb's living room so they're out of sight. Xara pulls the blinds closed and instructs them to close their eyes. "This may feel a little strange, but I suggest you keep your eyes closed until I tell you." Xara exhales a deep breath. "There's going to be hell to pay for this. For me, I mean. You better make it count."

Clarey sways with her closed eyes, feeling strangely unanchored. Her skin is stretched, then pulled, like each part of her is being tugged outward. Then flattened. An intense compression squashes her lungs as every centimeter of her body tingles with tiny pinheads first pressing, then tickling her. The blackness around her deepens until there's no light at all, and then her closed eyes are flooded with a bright, white light that nearly blinds her through her lids. None of it hurts exactly, but every sensation is supremely unnatural. The crushing feeling fades and now her lungs fill with a sweet fog that's so thick, it's almost tangible, yet she doesn't choke. She breathes it in deeply, instinctively, letting it saturate her both inside and out. Then she releases it. When she exhales the last of the fog, she feels normal again.

"You can open your eyes," Xara says.

Clarey finds herself between Xara and Herb standing at a pair of enormous, ornate white doors, at least fifty feet high. No, a hundred feet. No, endless. She looks around her, but sees nothing else. A white nothing. A discernible absence, save for this one impossible set of double doors floating in nothingness. "Is this like heaven's gate or something?"

Xara chuckles maliciously. "Hardly."

"So let's go! Open sesame." Clarey claps her hands twice like an impatient TV genie.

"It doesn't work like that," Xara says. "Did you really think you could just walk in?"

"Actually, I thought you'd zap us in or something," Clarey replies, disappointed.

"Humans don't just get to zap in. Do you think this is an everyday occurrence? People coming and going as they wish?"

Herb chimes in, "What then?"

"You have to make a decision. You have to choose," Xara explains.

"Done," Clarey announces. "Decision made. Let's go!"

Xara rolls her eyes dramatically, then glides a single finger through her divinely silken locks. "You really are the most exasperating woman. You used to be such a delightfully easy pushover. When did you become this?"

"What exactly do I have to do, Xara?"

"Close your eyes—"

"What, again?" Clarey interrupts.

Xara bites her tongue and continues. "And count to three."

Clarey scoffs, but does as instructed.

When Clarey opens her eyes, she's back in the moment of the lightning storm with Zack. It's the exact moment. She's living it again, but with an echo. The same, but different. The pitch black sky has descended, lit only by the constant stream of thunderbolts impaling the ground before them. They huddle under the covering, crouching back against the wall, as far from the danger as possible.

"It's not safe here. Clarey, we have to go," Zack says.

Terror paralyzes Clarey as she watches the apocalypse closing in to claim her. The electricity dancing through the sky stabs the pavement directly in front of her. It's all happening again. And for the first time. But Zack is with her. He's alive and fighting for her.

Zack turns her body and points. "Look, the building's right there. You run diagonally across the street and straight in. Get to the overhang first, then stay close to the building until you reach the door. Go straight in. Don't wait for me."

Clarey hears the words, but the storm forming in her head matches the one outside and obscures their meaning. "What do you mean? You'll be with me, right?"

"I'll be right behind you."

Clarey stares at the building across the street, the storm inside growing, the lightning demanding more from her. She has to make a decision. She has to choose.

"No," she says firmly. "If I run, you'll be struck. I know it."

"And if you don't run, you'll be struck," Zack insists.

Suddenly, her head clears and a determined, resigned smile creeps onto her face. "Then I'll be struck," Clarey says. "I'm not leaving you."

"I can't let anything happen to you, Clarey."

"And I won't let anything happen to you, Zack. We do this together."

Clarey stands tall from her crouch and holds out her hand to Zack. He takes it and pulls her into his arms. The warmth of his embrace shrouds her in certainty. They pull apart, but remain hand-in-hand as they slowly they walk into the storm together. Only steps outside their protective cover, two bolts hit the ground side by side, tearing through both their bodies at once.

Clarey's body seizes in pain, vicious, electrical currents ripping through her flesh and nerves. She's blinded by a light that burns and squeezes her eyes tight to the agony of being riven alive. The pain is excruciating, unbearable, desperate. Her brain is as rigid as her body with the devastation of the electrical current, but she takes it. Every slashing pain slicing through her body reminds her how weak and useless she is, how much easier it would be to give up and let the gods have their way, how much simpler it would be to just go home to lick her wounds. As usual. And still, she holds on. For Zack.

When she opens her eyes, she's back at the doors with Xara and Herb. Her body wretches with the pain still shredding her – and the grief at losing Zack again when only seconds ago he was right there, holding her hand – but slowly, she recovers and crumbles to the ground as she returns to the present.

Herb kneels to comfort her. "Clarey, are you alright?"

Xara wastes not a moment of compassion and simply turns to Herb. "Your turn!"

"No, wait," Clarey says, pulling herself to her feet. "Let me take his turn."

"No, no." Xara waggles a finger as if admonishing a child. "Each person who enters must make the choice."

"You don't have to do this, Herb."

Herb smiles gently at her. "After eight decades, with all the inevitable pain and loss that makes a life, losing my family, my wife, my son... Zachary. What can they do to me now that I cannot bear?" He looks at Xara. "I'm ready."

Xara nods at Herb who closes his eyes, counts to three, then disappears.

"How long will he be gone?" Clarey asks.

"For him, who knows how long it will be? For you, you'll hardly have time to miss him," Xara reassures her. "If he comes back at all, that is."

Chapter Thirty-Four

Darkness

ZACK STANDS IN DARKNESS. Complete, utter darkness. It's the blackest of black, a place where nothing exists except him. It's all he's known for what might be days or might be eternity. It can be hard to tell in a world of nothing. Time does not exist. Light does not exist. Not even a chair. Not even a floor, for while he stands, he stands on nothing, like his body is floating in stasis. It's not even an existence. It's certainly not life.

But he doesn't think it's death either. He's never experienced death, of course, but he's seen enough of it up close to know what it looks like from the human side. Sometimes sad, sometimes resolute, sometimes shocking, sometimes peaceful. But always, there's a moment when the gentle presence of humanity simply leaves, followed by nothing. He always assumed that was death. Simply nothing. Of course, not many of his kind have died, and perhaps death for them is entirely different. But he certainly never thought he'd have his thoughts to keep him company.

Of course, in this blackness, the gift of his thoughts could turn to madness in time. Perhaps that's his punishment, simply to be left alone with his thoughts for the rest of time? Or maybe they're still deciding what to do with him. He has no idea. Will he ever know?

Even as he floats through this eternity of blackness, however, he cannot bring himself to regret a single thing in the past three thousand years. Not a mountain he climbed nor a valley he crossed nor a vista he marveled at. Not the houses he built nor the muffins he baked. Not standing in front of Ixia's blast, nor the one hundred generations of families and friends that filled his life with joy, sadness, chaos, and so much suppressed grief since then. Not Herb, never Herb, and certainly not Clarey. He will never regret a single moment with Clarey, no matter how long this eternity drags out. For now, in a blackness far too dark to see even the things in his mind, he sees it nonetheless. She is the very reason he went through it all. To get to Clarey.

Something like a door opens in the distance. A sharp beam of light. A voice.

CHAPTER THIRTY-FIVE

MAKING THE CASE

WHEN HERB REAPPEARS A moment later, he is hunched and breathless as slow tears wet his cheeks. Clarey places a gentle hand on his back. "I'm here, Herb."

"There, you see," Xara chirps, "hardly any time at all. And now you're in."

As she speaks, the doors before them slowly drag open, the sound of stone scraping stone echoes throughout the non-space. They step into another non-room, but this one is filled with white clouds where there was somehow nothing at all before. And although they see nothing beyond the clouds, the space feels crowded. The energy is crowded. The silence is somehow crowded.

Terrified to raise her voice above a whisper, Clarey whispers to Xara, "Is this what it's like? Where you live?"

Before Xara can answer, a deep, rumbling voice responds. "You cannot conceive of our plane, child. This space was created by you."

"This adorable, little cloud of yours is a collective construct," Xara explains, "made up by you two. A place you can both understand because it comes from your shared imagination."

"It looks like an old eighties movie," Clarey says.

"It looks like a movie David and I used to watch on TV when he was a teenager," Herb says. "Heaven Can Wait."

"Somewhere in Time," Clarey adds with a grin, remembering the end of the old, eternal love story that she and Hope used to watch on repeat in their dreamy, romantic schoolgirl days. A love that lasts forever, no matter what. That's worth fighting for.

"I would have added some color at least," Xara says under her breath.

"Enough," the voice bellows. He sounds like Clarey always imagined Zeus might sound. Probably another manifestation of her subconscious. "Xara, why have you brought these two here?"

"They've come to plead for Elnossys."

"Is that right? That's very noble of you, children." He's paternal too. Like Zeus. "And very brave. But the fate of Elnossys is not up to you. He broke the conditions of his sentence. Now our people must decide his fate."

"He's still alive then?" Clarey asks. Herb clasps her hand hopefully.

"He is quite beyond your reach," the Big Daddy Zeus voice says.

Clarey looks all around, unable to tell where the voice is. "But not beyond yours, right?" She wonders briefly if he's the one who sent all those thunderbolts. But he doesn't seem vindictive, and that lightning definitely felt personal.

"There is nothing in your imagining that is beyond my reach," Big Daddy Zeus says firmly, before softening like an indulgent father. "Now, what is it you've come here to say?"

Oh, shoot, what has she come here to say? Clarey locks up, suddenly frozen in an impenetrable block of fear. She charged in here ready to fight, but it never occurred to her what fighting might look like. This is like one of those nightmares where they thrust you onstage and you don't know a single line, but everybody's watching and waiting for you to make a fool of yourself. Except, in this case, the consequence isn't just public humiliation. It's Zack's very survival.

"I, um...," she stutters, trying to kick start her brain. She tries repeatedly to turn the key, but the engine won't start.

Xara leans in and whispers, "You better say something, little mouse. This is a test and you're failing badly right now."

A test. That's it. This is a test. Maybe not for them, but for Clarey herself. This isn't the play dream, after all. This is the final exam where she forgot to study. But the thing about that dream is that while it might terrify others, Clarey never sweats it. Because Clarey is a star pupil. This is just another pop quiz. No big deal.

She clears her throat. She's still a little shaky and dry, but she can do this. Even if the one grading her is the disembodied voice of Big Daddy Zeus. "I'm here to ask you for leniency for Zack."

"Elnossys," Xara quietly prods.

"Elnossys," Clarey corrects, steadying her voice. She reminds herself of all those capstone presentations in grad school that eventually landed her the valedictorian speech. She can do this. She hasn't prepared any clever remarks this time, but it's time to tap the orator within and improvise. "Elnossys is a good person. Admittedly, I don't know how he stacks up against the rest of your people, but he's the best *person* I've ever known. He's sacrificed his life for thousands of years to look after others rather than return to the comforts of the life he knew with all of you."

"Yes, that was his sentence." Big Daddy Zeus offers this as simple, no-nonsense affirmation, a touch of boredom sneaking out. There's no rancor, but nor is there the affectionate indulgence that warmed his voice moments ago. "Have you simply come to remind us of the facts?"

"Not of the facts, but maybe of his humanity? His kindness. His sacrifice." Clarey hesitates, then says, "I've heard that you like us. Humans, I mean. If that's true, then I have to believe it's the best in us that you appreciate, not the worst. Zack embodies the best of what we are. He chose self-sacrifice because he believed it was the right thing to do."

A woman's voice pours into the space, as smooth and glorious as liquid gold. But there's also a sourness in it. "It was his punishment. For interfering where he did not belong." Hera maybe? Clarey knows they're not actually *those* gods. Or at least they're not *only* those gods. But she has to make sense of all this somehow.

Herb raises his hand to speak. "A punishment that he chose," he says. "Forgive me, but Elnossys, as you call him, has been protecting my family for thousands of years because he didn't think one starving woman should have to pay with her life for taking a smock full of food to feed her dying children."

"That wasn't his decision to make," the woman says. The sky rumbles with a gentle roll of thunder as she speaks. Maybe the Greeks assigned thunder to the wrong person.

"And he paid for it," Herb answers. "He could have walked away and let it happen, but he chose punishment because it was the right thing to do. Doesn't that count for anything after all these years?"

"You presume to know what the right thing to do is?" Maybe-Hera's affront burns through her voice. "Here? Among us?"

Clarey steps in. "Not us. Zack, Elnossys. He's one of you. And *he* decided it was the right thing to do. He stood against injustice and acted with compassion. Yet, even after all this time, you all still won't forgive him?"

The sky rumbles again, more loudly this time, but Big Daddy Zeus remains unperturbed. "We haven't made that decision yet. We are of many minds on the matter."

Clarey shakes her head with a sudden inspiration. "You're angry at him for breaking some arbitrary rule you set, but weren't the terms of your sentence that he was to remain their protector on Earth, with no active powers, for a hundred generations?"

"It was," says the woman.

"And Herb is the one hundredth, right?"

The indulgence in the Zeus voice returns. "What are you getting at, little one?"

"Did you define exactly when his sentence ends? Did you specify that the one hundredth generation, Herb, must die to end Elnossys's sentence?"

"It's implied," sneers Maybe-Hera, her voice dripping with disgust.

"I'm sorry, but I don't think it is. I don't know about here, but where I come from, laws and conditions need to be defined, written down, or at least articulated in some way. Otherwise, they're left to interpretation, and the discretion of judges."

"And how, pray tell, would you interpret it?" The woman's venom seeps through the air as she speaks.

Clarey quivers at the feel of the goddess's voice, which brushes over her skin like a poisoned feather. But Xara steps forward, lays a gentle hand on Clarey's shoulder, and gives a subtle nod of encouragement. Clarey responds with a grateful smile, then pushes forward. "A generation on Earth is considered twenty to thirty years, the time it takes for one generation to reproduce. Well, Herb did that long ago. The one-hundred-and-first generation was born."

Herb nods and wipes an unexpected tear. "His name was David."

"Generations are determined not by deaths, but by births. Which means, by rights, Zack's sentence would have ended then when David was born. How could healing Herb now break the rules if Zack's sentence ended almost fifty years ago?"

"Clever girl," Big Daddy Zeus says.

Thunder cracks through the sky and touches down in the distance as the woman speaks. "This is ridiculous. Elnossys knew his sentence hadn't ended. If he thought his sentence had ended, he would have come back. Why was he still there?"

"Because he loved us!" Herb shouts. "Me. My family. Clarey. He stayed because he loved us."

Another closer strike of lightning shakes Clarey, but Xara steps in with an assist. "It's a compelling argument," she says slyly from the sidelines.

"It's certainly worthy of consideration," Big Daddy Zeus agrees evenly.

A quiet clamor rustles through the air, the first tangible sign that something more, or someone more, is out there. Clarey imagines an invisible British Parliament filled with people in white togas bickering back and forth about Zack's fate. She only prays her argument is persuasive enough to tip the scales.

"Why are you here?" Maybe-Hera asks acidly. "Why would you risk so much, to come here and defy those with power beyond your ken, just for him?"

"Because he's worth fighting for," Clarey says without hesitation. "He's spent an eternity fighting for others. He deserves someone to fight for him for once."

"So that's it?" Big Daddy Zeus asks. "You're simply here out of some cosmic sense of justice?"

"No," Clarey admits, but she can't bring herself to say more.

"She loves him." The woman's voice localizes at last and emerges from the mists. A form follows it, molding itself into a human woman as it comes into full view. The most stunning, most perfect woman Clarey's ever seen with hypnotic eyes as deep as eternity. Her skin shimmers in such a way as to look first pale and peachy, then warm olive, then deep brown. She's mesmerizing.

But she isn't just beautiful. She's fat. Bigger than Clarey. Voluptuous and soft in a way that's irresistible. Her every movement inspires devotion, every curve sings of sex. She glows with the warm heat of pure love and dazzling sensuality. So much so that she could be only one person. Or goddess. Or whatever the right word is. If there's any truth in Greek mythology, any actual parallels to the reality of these Ancients, this woman is not the Hera of the bunch. Her beauty is unmistakable, though the bitterness in her voice has belied her identity until this moment.

Clarey remembers what Zack and Xara told her. They choose their human forms. The goddess of love can look any way she damn well pleases. And this is the form the pinnacle of female beauty has chosen to appear before them. Everything Zack said was true and everything Clarey's ever been convinced by the world to believe about beauty was just plain wrong.

"It's plain as day," the goddess says. "I haven't seen a love shine so brightly in eons. Isn't that so?"

"I'm here for Zack. Elnossys," Clarey says. "Because he deserves it. That's all that matters."

"Now, now. Clarey, is it? This isn't the sort of thing you can hide from me. But I would like to hear you say it, nonetheless."

Clarey drops her head in momentary defeat. The truth is no secret to her, but to say it aloud here, in front of the Ancients, she fears it will sound small and pathetic. Instead of massive and overwhelming like the tsunami of emotion she actually feels. "Yes, I love him."

Xara huffs out an exasperated groan and rolls her eyes. "You had to go and ruin it."

"Enough, Xara," the goddess says. "We don't mock love here. Even if it is terribly misplaced."

Clarey watches a chastised Xara nod in an obsequious bow and back into the mists. "Love," Clarey says. "That's you, isn't it? The goddess of love. The Greeks called you Aphrodite."

The goddess nods. "I have many names, as we all do."

"Please, will you help me? Will you help Elnossys? For the sake of love?"

"You've known him such a short time. A speck of time in the infinite we know. Yet, you fight so hard for him."

"It feels like I've known him forever."

The goddess looks into the hazy distance, reflecting. "Forever, yes. It's a long time. Even for us. Especially for us. To love someone."

A frightening possibility drifts into Clarey's mind. If she's right, this has just gotten so much more complicated than she thought. And it was already a freaking Gordian Knot of a situation to unwind. "Did you love him too?" Clarey asks. Then a new terror strikes and she can't help but blurt out, "*Do* you love him?"

"Here we go," Xara sighs to herself from the mists.

A lightning bolt of violet flashes through the goddess's eyes and then it's gone. She says nothing, but slowly circles Clarey before stepping back and expelling a deep breath of resignation. "And a long time to hold a grudge, I suppose," she says, continuing her prior thought.

With those words, the terrible truth Clarey hadn't entertained until now comes into focus. She's not just Aphrodite. "You're Ixia. You're the reason we're here."

"You are a clever girl."

"Why would you do this to him? Thousands of years of revenge? Over what? A little food? I thought you were the goddess of love. How is that loving?"

"It wasn't the food. What do I care about human food? There were so many temples back then, so many offerings." Ixia says. "And now there are none. And what does any of that matter anymore?"

"You were ready to kill my ancestors over that food," Herb says defiantly.

Ixia shrugs. "I overreacted. I admit it. I behaved like a petulant child."

"But you still punished Zack. Why? Unless..." Clarey briefly debates the wisdom of her next question. Pushing the Ancient One who condemned Zack to thousands of years of exile because she was throwing a hissy fit is perhaps not the smartest thing she's ever done. But this is her only chance. In for a penny, in for a pantheon. "He broke your heart, didn't he?"

"Less a broken heart, more a bruised ego," Ixia says dismissively. "But yes. We were... close back then. And he betrayed me."

"And you'd damn him for thousands of years for that?" Apparently, Hell hath no fury like a goddess scorned.

Ixia doesn't respond, but Big Daddy Zeus booms in. "This has gone on long enough. It's time."

Herb raises a hand. "If I may, perhaps there's a deal to be made."

"What kind of deal?" Ixia asks, intrigued.

"Zachary has spent thousands of years protecting my family. Maybe it's time I returned the favor."

"Do you mean you're prepared to submit to your fate?" Ixia's mouth ticks up in vicious smile.

"My line is at an end anyway," Herb says. "It's over. Please."

Clarey's jaw drops in horror. "Herb!"

He looks at Clarey with the bliss of full acceptance on his face. "He deserves someone to fight for him, right?"

Ixia purses her lips as she considers. "Certainly your death will hurt him more than his own. However, you're still under his protection. And our deals are eternal. Even if I wanted to – and I'm not saying I do – we can never break them."

Xara steps in to clarify. "Elnossys would have to lift his protection, which he would never do."

"Unless...," Ixia says, looking intently around at the nothing that surrounds them.

"Unless?" Big Daddy Zeus responds. The space once again fills with the clatter of voices weaving through each other in waves of harmony and dissonance. It's everywhere and nowhere at once, all around them in an invisible, ever-growing wall of sound. It's not language like Clarey's ever heard, but the commotion has the unmistakable din of discourse. Then, as quickly as it began, it ends.

Ixia nods at Herb. "If you give your explicit consent to surrender your protection."

"Do with me what you will," Herb replies. "Let him go."

"No," Clarey says, grabbing Herb into a hug tight enough to shut out whatever is about to happen. Tears leak down her face, wetting Herb's shoulder.

He hugs her back and whispers, "Shh, it's okay. This is the very least I can do. Promise me you'll be happy. And look out for him, as I know he will look out for you."

"Love?" Big Daddy Zeus echoes through the clouds, demanding a decision.

Ixia stares at the two humans before her. One young and full of life. The other old and near the end. She must see they both love Zack deeply. Enough to fight for him. Enough to sacrifice for him. Far more than she ever loved him. "Send the girl back," she says.

"No, wait!" Clarey screams.

"Done," Zeus booms. Before Clarey can say another word, Xara appears at her side, takes her arm and waves a hand in the air.

"Wait, please! Let him go! Forgive him!" But as she's surrounded in clouds, she realizes that no one hears.

She forgets to close her eyes as her body rips through the dimensions. Stretched, flattened, crushed, tickled, like before, but now her eyes are assaulted as well. An intense sandstorm of interdimensional debris blasts into her eyes, blinding her as the blackness sets in and she knows she's been actually, permanently blinded this time. She squeezes them tight, though it's surely too late, and a millisecond later, the blackness turns to the burning white light. And then everything stops, but she's still screaming, "Please!"

The solid ground beneath her brings Clarey back to the world, but she still can't open her eyes until a small, soft body flops against her and weaves between her legs. Homer Dickens' tiny mew shakes her from the last of her torment. She opens her eyes to Herb's apartment, now empty save Homer. "No, no, no, no, no! Please." She calls out, "Xara! What does this mean? What has she decided?"

Xara materializes before her. "You're more of a fighter than I thought you were."

"You have to take me back," Clarey insists.

Xara shakes her head. "It's too late. It's done. She's decided."

"*What* has she decided?"

"You fought hard for him. If I get a chance, I'll make sure he knows that."

"What has she decided, Xara?"

Xara gives Clarey an inscrutable look and contemplative smile. "One never knows what Ixia will do. She's as capricious as they come. But she liked you. And you may have persuaded some of the others."

"What good does that do me if Zack's not here?"

"You're alive, aren't you?" Homer Dickens jumps onto the table in front of Xara and she reaches for him. "Ooh, you're lovely."

Clarey collapses on the sofa in grief. "But what about Zack?"

"Time will tell," Xara muses. She runs her hand down Homer's long spine and along the length of his tail. "Of course, time is a rather different horizon for us than it is for you. I wouldn't hold your breath."

Clarey contemplates a life without Zack once again. When he first went away, after he saved her, she'd been dragged into a pool of grief so deep she thought she might drown. It was good she'd stayed in the hospital that night because the risk was high she might otherwise forget to breathe. But the pain that left her gasping for breath was too much and she'd quickly shut it down. She'd fallen into a sort of denial and shock that kept her barely buoyed on the surface until she managed to pick herself up and wade through an echo of her life. Talking with her sisters. Checking on Herb. Trying and failing to get Roxy back. Doing a kind turn for Gabi and Dana. All of it an impeccable replica of her life, except for the one essential piece that was missing.

She'd tried so hard not to think about it, and then, when she finally decided to fight, she convinced herself she no longer needed to think about it. Why waste time worrying for nothing? He's coming back. She told herself that again and again. He's coming back. No need to grieve when you know he's coming back. But he didn't come back. And the attempt claimed Herb as well. "It can't end this way," she says through quiet tears. "It can't."

"Trust me. I've seen more endings than you can imagine," Xara says as the cat jumps down. "Every one of them is just another beginning. You'll live. You'll go on. You'll have a happy, little life. One day, this will be no more than a faint memory."

Homer jumps onto Clarey's lap and aggressively nuzzles her cheek. "I really thought, somehow, he'd always be with me. I was so sure."

"Things change. Not always for the best," Xara sighs. And for the first time, she actually sounds sincere. Possibly even compassionate? "But you've played your last card. It's time to accept the game is over."

Clarey stares into space, her hand absent-mindedly caressing the furball on her lap, and murmurs, "Zack..."

"Goodbye, Clarey. I don't think we'll be seeing each other again."

Clarey looks up, suddenly alert and present again. "Wait, you just called me Clarey."

"Did I?" Xara says, an amused smile adorning her exquisite face.

Astonished, Clarey asks, "What happened to little mouse?"

"What indeed?" Xara responds before disappearing.

That's it then. Clarey fought. She believed. She never gave up. Not until the very last play, when the umpire called it. Now the game is over, she lost, and only she and Homer Dickens remain. Clarey packs up Homer's bowls, food, toys, and litter box. She presses her lips to the cat's soft, little head, then ushers him into his carrier. She collects Herb's keys from the table, locks up the apartment, and walks Homer home.

Chapter Thirty-Six

Just Rewards

DESPITE GETTING OUT OF the hospital three days ago, Clarey discovers when she finally checks her phone that it has been blowing up with calls and texts from her worried sisters, and parents as well. She calls her parents to check in, then texts her sisters and reassures them she's fine. Just very tired. They suggest a sister Zoom, but Clarey can't possibly conjure enough good cheer to manage that tonight. She holds them off with promises of tomorrow and turns off her phone because the day's losses have drained every last iota of strength from her body.

She should eat something, but the thought of cooking exhausts her. And ordering in would necessitate interaction with the outside world, which is out of the question. She already ate the last of the orzo salad Zack left for her, so she settles on a bowl of cereal, then drags herself into the bathroom to brush her teeth. With the sun still high in the sky, Clarey pulls the shades and climbs into bed. Homer Dickens joins her and plants himself on her stomach. He stares into her eyes as he makes biscuits on her chest and purrs.

"Thank you, Homer," she says quietly. "What a sweet boy you are." She rubs his head and his sleepy eyes waver between cracked and closed. "I hope you like dogs, honey, because you have a sister and she's coming home soon. I promise."

***

Clarey goes into the shop the next day to look around. She should try to notify someone, though she can't imagine who that would be. Of course, she can't imagine what she would say either. How can she explain Herb's disappearance? If no better ideas come to her, she'll call the police in a couple days to report him missing. Hopefully she can summon enough concern to be convincing, though it seems wrong since she knows exactly where he is. Then again, she can't exactly say Herb decided to stay behind in an ancient god dimension to be executed in a noble, but failed gesture of self-sacrifice to bring an actual god back to life right here in cozy Kirkland, Washington.

No, she probably shouldn't say that.

She walks to the back room and finds everything in perfect, tidy order as always. She pokes her head into the tiny office at the very back and spots a single white envelope sitting in the middle of the otherwise cleared desktop. Handwritten in shaky script on the outside is her name. She drops herself slowly into the seat and stares at the envelope before reaching for it. Her own hands shaking, she slides her finger under the flap and rips it open to find a typed letter inside, dated the same day she was released from the hospital. A well of tears clouds her eyes as she reads.

Dear Clarey,

What a gift you've given me since the day you first walked into my shop. Your kind concern and generosity of spirit have touched me deeply. You've helped me keep the shop running and your company has brought an old man great comfort in my lonely, waning days. In the short time I've known you, you've become like the daughter I never had. Perhaps most importantly, you brought joy and love to my dearest Zachary, who I thought would be my very last tether to this crazy, old world. I am so happy to have another in you, dear girl.

Clarey, I said you'd given me a gift and now I want to give something to you as well. I had planned to leave the store, my apartment, and all my assets (such as they are) to Zachary when I died. I knew he would have no use for them, but I also knew he would dispose of them properly and ensure the proceeds were used for something good and noble. It's simply in his nature. Or it was.

You should know that Zachary spoke of you often, every day. It was clear from the start he was very much in love with you, even as he fought his feelings for all the reasons you now know. Now that Zachary is gone, I'm leaving everything to you, which is what he would want as well. I know this may be a shock, but rest assured, I couldn't be happier to know you will be well taken care of in the future. I have no expectation that you'll keep the store, so please have no reservations on that front. If I can provide you a nest egg to carry you through difficult times and secure your future, please do not hesitate to sell every last jar of clotted cream.

My lawyer's office has instructions to contact you whenever I may pass, be it tomorrow or twenty years from now. But I'll enclose their information here for you as well.

I know you're grieving Zachary now, as am I. We must carry each other through the days ahead. I only hope this news brings you some measure of comfort and the certain knowledge that you are loved.

With love and gratitude,

Herb

At first, reading Herb's words rips Clarey's heart wide open once again, but rereading the letter begins to knit it back together. Herb's extraordinary generosity is one of the many impossibilities Clarey is teaching herself to weave together into a brilliant tapestry of possibilities. She presses the letter to her chest, allowing the love to soak through her skin. The world is so much bigger and more remarkable than she'd realized.

***

The brides look radiant. Gabi's brown skin pops against her white lace gown and her long, dark braids are pulled into an updo with her few pink braids left down to frame her face. Dana sports a tieless white tuxedo with electric blue pocket square to complement her hair. Her pale cheeks are flushed with happiness, a pink that perfectly matches Gabi's braids. Gabi's maid of honor Sarah stands sobbing at her side while Sarah's husband stands proudly by Dana as her best man. This is Gabi's clan, the inspiration for Clarey's stab at friendship turned domestic bliss. Too bad it hadn't turned out as well for Clarey in the end.

A small collection of other close friends and family sit in rented chairs watching the lovers take their vows. The brides and officiant are framed against the backdrop of the lake behind them, the sun in a slow descent now filling the sky with color. Jessa was so eager to get back into her art that she offered to do a pastel portrait of the wedding, an offer Gabi and Dana gratefully accepted. Now Jessa sits at the back sketching frantically while Clarey snaps photos both for the couple and for Jessa's reference. Clarey basks in the closeness of her sister, and to see her passion reignited. Although the space is as open and limitless as the sky itself, it somehow feels filled with love, and so, in turn, does Clarey.

***

Clarey holds the lobby doors open as the wedding party loads out the last of the food, folding chairs, and decorations to an SUV pulled up to the curb. She gives hugs all around and waves them off as they climb in. The car starts up, runs a moment, then pulls away. As it rolls off, a figure emerges from behind it. A tall, blond, unbearably buff, and unfairly beautiful figure glowing in his bright white T-shirt and khakis. Even in the fading light, she can see his bottomless dimples and the sparkle of his blue eyes from here.

Clarey's heart stutters. She rubs her eyes and her jaw trembles. She dares not believe what she sees. He walks slowly toward her, a soft, tentative smile touching his lips, the smile of someone who understands the terror racing through Clarey in this moment. Someone who knows how frightened she is to believe this is real, only to have her heart ripped from her chest yet again.

He reaches her side of the street and stands before her. "Hi, Red," he says softly.

Her lip quivers, and her body follows suit. Her eyes fill as she squeaks out, "Is it really you?"

With a small nod, Zack starts to answer, but before he can get a full word out, Clarey's in his arms. Their bodies collide and cling to each other, the magnetism of their connection supercharged by their separation. Clarey presses her face to him, runs her fingers through his hair, kneads the muscles on his back, doing everything she can reasonably do in public to confirm he's real. He in turn wraps his arms around her waist like a vise before sneaking a hand down to her soft bottom, apparently slightly less concerned about onlookers.

He cups her face and pulls her lips to his. His hand slides behind her neck and they lose themselves in a kiss as infinite as the dimensions they've crossed for each other.

"It's really you," she finally whispers between kisses.

"It's really me," he confirms, still holding her close.

"And you're here to stay?" she asks tearfully.

"As long as you'll have me."

"What if I want you forever?" she says.

He pulls back to look at her, to be sure she really hears what he's about to say. "Unfortunately, forever's not going to work out. But would you like to grow old with me, Clarey McGill?"

Her mouth drops open. "You mean you...?"

Zack smiles his biggest, brightest grin, the one he will save forevermore just for his girl. "I traded in my immortality to come back and be with you."

"But Zack..."

"It was an easy call. Living forever without you would be no life at all."

He kisses her again and Clarey goes all wobbly and gooey inside. If this is her eternity, she'll take it. Walking through life hand-in-hand with this man, god or not, is literally such stuff as dreams are made on. Besides, immortality would have been a bitch to explain to her sisters. She smiles back at him. "So, you're not a god anymore?"

"Well, I kept the good stuff," Zack says with a wink. "That's the nice thing about being a god. Options."

Clarey giggles, then sobers with a bittersweet pang. "You know about Herb?"

Zack nods as grief paints his face. "They let me bring his body back. I've just come from there. We need to call it in. It will look like he died in his sleep." He pauses to catch the breath sorrow squeezes out of him. "Which he did, actually."

"Really?"

"I didn't know about any of it until it was over. But Ixia's better angels won out in the end. Apparently someone," he gives Clarey a pointed squeeze, "persuaded her it was time to let it all go. Almost. She accepted Herb's sacrifice, but she gave him a peaceful end. And then she permitted my release with her blessing."

"And now?" Clarey says.

"And now we just go on living. And loving. Because I plan to love you all of my living days, Red."

Joy flushes through Clarey's system like a shot of pure happiness to the heart. She allows the moment to wash over her, accepting at last that this is real. That it's all been real and Zack is here with her. Forever. She looks up at him, his deep blue eyes fixed on her, and says as their lips press together once again, "I plan to love you a lot longer than that."

When they finally turn to go inside, he wraps his arm around her shoulder and squeezes. "Are you happy, baby?"

"So happy," she smiles. "Though there is one thing that could make me even happier."

***

Clarey and Zack pull up to the old house together. "Ready?" Zack asks as he puts the car into park by the curb.

Clarey swipes through the Instagram photos again. "She's still there. She never left." She swipes again. "I can't believe she never left."

"Want me to go in with you?" Zack says.

"Nah. I got this."

Clarey marches up to the door, knocks, then opens it immediately. "Roxy!" she calls. Seconds later, the tornado of a bulldog spirals into Clarey's arms and knocks her to the floor. Clarey giggles as the mighty little dog grunts and cries and throws her body every which way across her mama's lap, smothering her in kisses. "Hi, my love. Oh, I missed you, too. So much."

When Roxy eventually calms enough to let Clarey catch her breath, she looks up at Lydia, who is standing at the foot of the stairs. "Hi, Lydia."

Lydia gives a heavy-lidded smile. "Hi."

Clarey hooks her leash into Roxy's collar, then stands back up. "Glad to see you're back."

"Back?" Lydia says, slightly dazed by the scene.

Clarey turns to Derek, who's been watching from his perch at the dining room table, where he's bent over a bowl of cereal. And, oh look, Clarey's Roxy mug is sitting next to him. "Hey, Clare," he says. "I was about to call you."

Clarey straightens her back, purses her lips, and walks up to Derek. "Lydia never left, Derek."

Derek scratches his head and tips it toward her. "To be fair, we did have a fight."

"What fight? We didn't fight," Lydia objects from the stairs. "What did we fight about?"

Derek eyes Lydia carefully, apparently attempting to transmit something. "Lydia, babe. We did have a fight the other day. Remember? And then you left. And that's all I think we need to say about it. We don't need to air our dirty laundry in front of Clarey."

Clarey looks at Lydia's baffled face, then back to Derek. "Well, I'm certainly glad you've been able to patch things up."

"Wait, do you mean the milk?" Lydia says.

"The milk?" Clarey says with genuine, perturbed curiosity.

Derek sighs. "Lydia," he says with a quiet frustration and a hint of warning.

"Yeah!" Lydia says. "He finished the milk, which fine, okay. But then he didn't tell me, and I went to make dinner and didn't have the milk I needed. So I had to stop in the middle of everything and go get more!"

"Milk?" Clarey says again. Only this time, her anger shifts into something more akin to amused irritation. This buffoon that has made her so angry all this time isn't worth another minute of thought.

Lydia walks over and pets Roxy, scratching her behind her ears. "You're such a good girl," she says to the frantically tail-wagging dog. "Yeah," she says still staring at the dog, seemingly clueless about the larger drama unfolding around her. "I wouldn't call it a fight. But I was irritated. Oh, I'm gonna miss you so much!"

Clarey turns to Derek. "So, she left you... to go to the store?"

Derek smiles his biggest, shit-eating smile and says, "Look, everyone's happy at home now and that's what's important." He pauses a beat, then shifts tack. "Now, Clare, maybe we could talk about a joint-custody situation." He offers her the most open, affable, non-malicious look he can summon, and Clarey can plainly see every evil machination at work behind it.

She smiles sweetly, wraps Roxy's leash an extra turn around her hand for safety, and looks down at the Roxy mug. Her mug. Clarey picks up the mug from the table, and finding coffee still inside, she pours it into his cereal bowl. "Glad you have more milk." She heads toward the door with the mug in one hand and the leash in the other, Roxy happily trotting behind her.

"Bye, Rox!" Lydia calls cheerfully behind them.

As Clarey reaches the door, she calls out without looking back, "You can keep the soda maker." She marches outside, into the sunshine and a bright future with her dog at her side.

Zack's leaning on the car, grinning at her. "The warrior returns victorious."

"Damn right," she replies. Clarey sets the mug on top of the car and folds her hands around his head, Roxy still tethered to her wrist. Zack scoops her up in a celebratory hug and he snakes her legs around him to hold her aloft. It's something horny teenagers would normally do, not so-called mature grown-ups, one of whom has literally more years behind him than he can count. But Clarey never got to be *that girl* as a teenager, so Zack always makes sure she feels like that girl now. She leans in to kiss him. "And to the victor go the spoils."

"Oh, I'm definitely going to spoil you, Red. I'm gonna spoil you so hard."

"Sweet talker," Clarey giggles. She looks down at Roxy, whose whole rear-end is thumping the car with her over-excited wagging, then back at Zack. "Come on, my loves, let's go home."

CHAPTER THIRTY-SEVEN

AFTER

CLAREY POWERS DOWN HER computer as she wraps up her call. "That sounds fantastic, Harris. I'll put together a project timeline and get it to you by Friday." McGill Consulting's fourth new client in as many weeks. With several projects still ongoing as well. More long nights ahead, perhaps – an occasional necessity with so many balls to juggle – but worth it for her dream.

She gazes down at Roxy, sound asleep across her feet. How is she going to extricate herself from this? "Thank you so much! I'm excited to get started." She hangs up the phone and quietly calls to Roxy, attempting to gently ease her back to wakefulness. "Sweetie, you have to wake up. We've got to go home." Roxy grunts, adjusts herself on Clarey's feet, and returns to snoring.

Clarey looks across the room to Zack's stunning butcher block countertops and spies the dog treats. If only she could reach them, this would be so much easier. She bends down and scratches Roxy's newly exposed tummy. "Come on, girl. I know you're tired," she says, now speaking in regular full voice to the zonked out pup. "We had a big walk today, didn't we? But we've got to get upstairs. Don't you want to see your aunties and cousins?"

Zack's voice booms in through the balcony doors. "Red, you almost done? They'll be here soon."

"Call the dog," she yells back.

"Roxy!" he shouts with his signature call.

Immediately Roxy juts her head up and looks drowsily around. "There's my sleepy girl." Her feet now freed, Clarey hops up and out to the balcony. "Thank you," she says looking up at her hero. "I had canine paralysis."

Zack laughs. "Well, hurry up and get yourself up here. I have a Peach Gin Fizz waiting for you."

"You do know how to keep my sisters happy, don't you?"

"What's a Peach Gin Fizz? And can I have one?" new neighbor Greg says with a laugh from the next balcony over.

Clarey jumps. Even though construction resumed six months ago – and the first neighbors in the building moved in three months ago – she still sometimes forgets it's not just hers and Zack's private playground anymore. Sometimes she misses the quiet, and the free reign. But it's nice to have neighbors too, to feel the building coming to life as she'd imagined it when she first signed the papers a little over a year ago. A community.

Zack leans over to see Greg below him and waves. "How's it going?"

Clarey gives Greg an apologetic smile. "Sorry, family only tonight. But maybe we all go get drinks this weekend? We can invite the new couple in 2A too."

A woman's voice calls through the balcony doors below Greg's. "2A would love to!"

Clarey laughs and promises to let them both know. Inside, she closes her computer and locks up. Having her office in Zack's old place has many advantages. It's a separate space, yet so convenient. It's masterfully finished by a gifted craftsman who just happens to sleep in her bed every night. It's a perfect guest suite for her visiting parents when they come to town. Best of all, it's fully paid for. And when it's time to go home, she doesn't have to pollute the air with her car, or even take a precious spot on the bus. Heck, she doesn't even need to take the elevator.

Upstairs, Clarey opens the door and Roxy immediately takes off to play with Homer who is waiting at the door for her. Somehow Homer always knows when Roxy's coming and never fails to greet her with a loving tackle. Moments later, Zack greets Clarey with a loving tackle of his own. "Hey, beautiful. How was work?"

"Good, yeah. The commute was brutal, but other than that." He stops her silliness with a kiss, then hands her the aforementioned adult beverage. "And how was the store?"

"Great," he says, returning to the stove. "We were slammed today. We might have to hire yet another employee at this rate."

Clarey sneaks up to hug him from behind as he stirs. "You're working so hard at it. I'm proud of you, babe."

Zack leans his cheek back to accept a kiss. "It keeps him close, you know? And I want to honor his legacy."

"And that's why I love you," she says as she reaches for plates to set the table.

"Oh, that's why?"

"Well, that and your enormous..." He stops what he's doing and smirks at her, raising a brow in anticipation. "Compassion for animals. It's one of your best qualities." Zack rolls his eyes and returns to his cooking as Clarey lays out the napkins and silverware. "Thanks for doing so much tonight. I'm sorry my meeting got bumped back so late."

Zack shrugs happily. "You know I like doing it." He swats her ass as she passes by. "But you can thank me later."

Clarey's blood heats as much as it did the first time she saw Zack, but it's followed by a gentle tide of the deepest gratitude. She must have done something really good in a past life to deserve this. She watches Zack assembling a plate of puff pastry hors d'oeuvres that have been resting on the cooling rack. "Speaking of which..."

Zack carries the plate out and sets it on the side table next to the small plates and napkins he's already placed. "Can you grab a pitcher for water, please?" He rushes back to the kitchen to stop the timer and pulls open the oven to check the temperature on the chicken.

"Babe, listen..." Clarey says as she slowly pulls the pitcher from the overhead cabinet. "I've made a decision."

"Yeah, what's that?" He closes the oven and turns to look at her.

She shovels ice into the pitcher, then turns to face him. "I'm ready."

"You will be when that pitcher is full." He smiles warmly as he pulls the pitcher from her hands and begins filling it from the fridge. He's listening, but not really. Not the way she needs him to in this moment. She needs to get his attention.

"Do you still want a little god running around this place?"

This stops Zack cold, then warms him up. "What?" he says, suddenly very interested.

"I'm ready. At least to try."

Zack laughs softly. "Trying with me is one night and a bottle of wine, Red." His eyes are alive with hope and possibility, but he's cautious. "There's no pressure. Not now, not ever. But if you want to... just... be sure."

She looks at this beautiful, sweet, perfect man who walked into her life exactly when she needed him. Who sacrificed thousands of years for others. Who gave everything and took nothing, and now stands here in their kitchen wearing a "Kiss me, I'm the cook" apron and preparing appetizer platters like only a freaking god could. He's perfect. He's everything she ever could have dreamed. Even his floofy blond hair, which will one day turn gray now, because that's what he chose. To grow old with her. She nods with a gentle smile. "I'm ready."

Zack grabs her face and kisses her across the pitcher before it occurs to him to set it out of the way. He sets the water aside and grabs her, holding her as close as he can manage with clothes in the way. "Too late to cancel your sisters?"

The intercom buzzer rings. "Afraid so," she says regretfully.

He catches her hand as she turns and looks at her with a knowing glint in his eyes. "Tonight then?"

Clarey grins in response, her heart beating fast at the prospect. When she pulls away to answer the intercom, Jessa's voice shouts back, "I gotta pee!"

Clarey laughs, hits the entrance buzzer, and opens the door. "And so it begins."